W9-CDG-162

Praise for the Novels of Iris Johansen

"Plenty of action and mystery . . . [does] not disappoint." —*Criminal Element* on *Shattered Mirror*

"Enthralling . . . and completely satisfying."
—*Kirkus Reviews* on *Mind Game*

"The right amount of complexity spiced with danger, thrills, and engrossing characters!"
—*RT Book Reviews* (Top Pick) on *Mind Game*

"A winning combination of thriller elements and love story." —*Booklist* on *Night and Day*

"This first-rate novel of romantic suspense will please Johansen's fans and newcomers alike."
—*Publishers Weekly* (starred review)
on *Hide Away*

"Johansen delivers a no-holds-barred mystery that maintains suspense throughout and boasts a cast of multifaceted characters."
—*Publishers Weekly* on *Shadow Play*

"Gripping . . . Iris Johansen's talent in character development, impeccable plotting, and remarkable depiction is nonpareil."
—*Reader to Reader* on *Your Next Breath*

ALSO BY IRIS JOHANSEN

Mind Game

Look Behind You
(with Roy Johansen)

No Easy Target

Night Watch
(with Roy Johansen)

Night and Day

Hide Away

Shadow Play

The Naked Eye
(with Roy Johansen)

Your Next Breath

Sight Unseen
(with Roy Johansen)

Live to See Tomorrow

Silencing Eve

Hunting Eve

Taking Eve

Sleep No More

Close Your Eyes
(with Roy Johansen)

What Doesn't Kill You

Bonnie

Quinn

Eve

Chasing the Night

Shadow Zone
(with Roy Johansen)

Eight Days to Live

Deadlock

Dark Summer

Quicksand

Silent Thunder
(with Roy Johansen)

Pandora's Daughter

Stalemate

An Unexpected Song

Killer Dreams

On the Run

Countdown

Blind Alley

Firestorm

Fatal Tide

Dead Aim

No One to Trust

Body of Lies

Final Target

The Search

The Killing Game

The Face of Deception

And Then You Die

Long After Midnight

The Ugly Duckling

Lion's Bride

Dark Rider

Midnight Warrior

The Beloved Scoundrel

The Magnificent Rogue

The Tiger Prince

Last Bridge Home

The Golden Barbarian

Reap the Wind

Storm Winds

The Wind Dancer

VENDETTA

IRIS JOHANSEN

St. Martin's Paperbacks

This is a work of fiction. All of the characters, organizations, and events portrayed in this novel are either products of the author's imagination or are used fictitiously.

Published in the United States by St. Martin's Paperbacks, an imprint of St. Martin's Publishing Group

VENDETTA

For information, address St. Martin's Publishing Group, 120 Broadway, New York, NY 10271.

www.stmartins.com

Library of Congress Catalog Card Number: 2018017180

ISBN: 978-1-250-07594-9

Our books may be purchased in bulk for promotional, educational, or business use. Please contact your local bookseller or the Macmillan Corporate and Premium Sales Department at 1-800-221-7945, ext. 5442, or by e-mail at MacmillanSpecialMarkets@macmillan.com.

Printed in the United States of America

St. Martin's Press hardcover edition / October 2018
St. Martin's Paperbacks edition / July 2019

10   9   8   7   6   5   4   3   2   1

CHAPTER

1

WOODSTOCK, MONTANA

Carl Venable, head of the CIA task force on terrorism, was not often out in the field, and even less often in physical danger. But now he was missing. And he was the one man who couldn't be left behind.

And, dammit, there was no way Jude Brandon was going to have that happen.

"They're coming, Brandon!" Nate was skidding down the slope toward him as he came out of the forest. "Just over the ridge. I told you that you couldn't keep searching. Get on the damn helicopter! They'll be here in minutes."

"How many minutes?"

"Fifteen, maybe."

"Did you see Venable?" Brandon asked. "Did you *see* him, Nate?"

"I saw him." Nate jumped into the cockpit of the

helicopter. "We've got to get out of here. Twenty or thirty of Huber's men are heading for that cabin. It's too late. We don't have a chance of retrieving him."

"The *hell* we don't." Brandon was already heading back up the hill. "We've got to get him out of here. He has a damn target on his back. You know what they'll do to him if they get their hands on him. Be ready to take off when I get back."

"It's no *use*, dammit." Brandon could hear Nate cursing behind him.

Screw it. Fifteen minutes could be a long time. Nate should have gotten Venable out when he saw him. It wasn't like him to leave a job undone.

Three minutes later, he was at the cabin.

A minute later, he'd checked out the exterior of the grounds and determined it was clear.

But Venable had not been anywhere in sight, and Nate had said he'd seen him.

Brandon threw open the door, dove in, and rolled to the left.

"You never listen, Brandon," Carl Venable said from across the room. "I've been expecting you."

"Then you should have come when Nate—" He stopped as he saw that the CIA operative was lying on a cot that was as bloody as the front of his white shirt. "Shit." He was on his feet and across the room in two strides. "You're wounded. How bad?"

"Very." Venable's voice was barely above a whisper. "Sorry, Brandon. I know you'd like to rob Huber of this particular victory, but I'm dying. I should be gone in a few minutes."

"Not if I can get you out of here." He was opening Venable's shirt. "I'll just apply pressure and—" He stopped as he looked down at the wound. "Damn."

"Too late," Venable said. "You're good at battlefield wounds. You know it's the truth. Say it, Brandon."

"Okay, it's true." He met Venable's eyes. "But I can get you out of here before Huber shows up and does anything else to you."

"I'll be past worrying about . . . torture before he walks through that door. We both know it."

He wasn't going to deny it. Venable wouldn't appreciate it. "What about your informant? Did Nemesis tell you anything?"

"No time. But I gave him . . . Rachel's name."

He stiffened. "Your *daughter's* name? Are you crazy? Why not mine?"

"A little . . . insurance." Venable tried to smile, but his voice was getting weaker. "Not that I . . . don't trust you. I just trust her more. And it's a way of doubling my chances of getting Rachel out of this alive. Another reason for you to keep Max Huber away from her."

"You don't need insurance. I said I'd do it."

"But you're like me, a driven man. She's had to contend with me all her life, I don't want to leave her to face another struggle alone. Tell her that I kept . . . my promise. This time I'm giving her a choice." He coughed, and a tiny bit of blood appeared at the corner of his mouth. "And I have one final job to do. I have to make sure . . . that Huber thinks he has plenty of time . . . for his next move. That means getting you the hell out of Dodge before . . . he finds out that you're on your way to get her. So on your . . . way, Brandon."

"I don't take orders from you, Venable."

"No, but you'll take this one. Rachel's your only way to score against Huber now. You've fought too long to give up your shot at him. I don't flatter myself you're doing . . . this for me, you're doing it for pure revenge. You're . . . good at that, Brandon. How much time do you have left?"

"Seven minutes."

"Tell me how you'll . . . get out of here?"

"I can't use the helicopter, they're almost on top of us. They'd know that I'd been here. I'll hide the copter in the woods, and Nate and I will walk out, then call for assist when it's safe."

"And then you'll go . . . for Rachel?" Venable was holding his gaze. "Promise me. There won't . . . be much time. He'll know where she is by now."

"I'll go for her." He looked down at him. "She's not my choice. But I'll use her to get what we both want. You shouldn't have gotten yourself shot, Venable."

"I realize it was a major . . . disruption of your plans." His voice was fading. "But you won't have a plan unless you get yourself out of here. Forget that . . . bullshit about not . . . leaving a man behind. I always told you that the Army brainwashed you. That's why . . . I told Nate not to tell you I'd bought it."

"Yet I don't think you would have left me behind." Brandon was already heading for the door. "But I'll get out, and I'll get Huber." He looked back over his shoulder. He didn't want to leave him, dammit. At one time or another Venable had been both ally and enemy to him, but he shouldn't have to die alone. His eyes were closed, and Brandon didn't know if Venable was still alive to hear him. "I've no use for the CIA, they've tended to get in my way. But you were the best and most honest operative I ever ran across, Venable. It's been a privilege."

"How . . . generous. I feel . . . honored that—" His head slumped sideways. Brandon could no longer hear his breath.

Dead.

Brandon could feel the fury tear through him as he shut the door and started at a run toward the hills. He hadn't known Venable that well, but this time they'd been on the same side, fighting the same battle for different reasons. And what he'd known he'd liked and appreciated as much as he'd allowed himself. They were both obsessed, and obsession permitted little else to enter into a relationship. Venable's death only added to the score Brandon had to settle with Max Huber.

And Venable had been his best key to getting Huber, he thought with frustration. He had been so close . . .

But Venable had given him another key. And her name was Rachel Venable. Forget about what might have been and go after the possible.

He took out his phone and dialed Nate. "Venable's dead. You should have told me he'd been shot."

"He told me not to do it. He said if I did, you'd go after him. He was dying, Brandon. I could see it. But you went anyway. I thought you would."

"So did he." Because Venable had wanted one last assurance that Brandon would do what he wanted. "I'm on my way back. Start preparing the helicopter. We're going to hide it in the woods."

"I'm on it. Anything else?"

"Call Monty and tell him to chart a course for Georgetown and make ground preparations. We'll need a team of ten or twelve."

"Georgetown?"

"It's on the coast of Guyana, South America. We're going to Guyana." He cut the connection.

One more call. It was one he didn't want to make. It could mean endless complications, subtle manipulation, and perhaps even duplicity. But he knew it had to be done.

He quickly punched in the private number for Claire Warren.

NALEZ, GUYANA
7:40 P.M.

Just one more drop of the broadleaf palm root . . .

Rachel Venable's eyes narrowed with concentration on the glass vial as she carefully squeezed the yellow liquid into the mixture. Good enough. She'd had to substitute here in the rain forest because the ingredients had to be fresh in order to be at top efficiency.

And top efficiency might not even be good enough, she thought wearily as she put the cap on the vial. She'd already sent Maria Perez's test results to the lab in

Georgetown, and they'd said that nothing could be done. They'd given the little girl perhaps two to three days before she went into a coma. She'd been totally unresponsive to every treatment they'd tried since she'd come down with the virus. It might be another day after that before the virus killed her. The mosquito-borne Taran virus had caused a rare fever that had struck this village in the rain forest with almost always fatal results. There seemed to be no rhyme or reason why some victims were taken and others spared.

"You've been working for twenty-four hours straight, Rachel. Give it up." Dr. Phillip Sanford stood in the doorway of her tent, his gray eyes narrowed on the vial in her hand. "I just received orders from head-quarters. They're pulling us out of Guyana. They said our team has done everything we could do here."

Rachel tensed. She'd been expecting it since they'd sent the last ambulances with the survivors to George-town this afternoon. Their unit of One World Medical was always in demand in war-torn cities or places like this where no one else was willing to serve. They were constantly on the move. "When?"

"Tonight. As soon as we can pack up. They want us in Sudan by tomorrow night."

"No!" She looked down at the vial. "Not that soon. Stall them, Phillip. Give me another twenty-four hours."

"That will be hard to do." He made a face. "Would you care to tell me why?"

"No." She moistened her lips. "Just stall them. It won't be that hard. They think you walk on water. You always manage to bring in mega donations when they trot you out at those fund-raisers."

"But I don't walk on water," he said quietly. "And I do this job because it needs doing. Just as you do, Rachel. Only I'm becoming aware that we approach it from different directions."

"I work just as hard as you do, Phillip."

"Harder. Because after you've spent your time at the operating table trying to heal these people, you're here in your tent playing with all your potions." His gaze ran over the shelves of ingredients above her work-table. "That's been your modus operandi ever since you joined my unit two years ago. You're one hell of a doctor, Rachel." His gaze shifted to her face. "But what else are you?"

"It's all in my résumé." She smiled with an effort. "As you say, I like to play with my potions. I spent years studying with Hu Chang, who taught me a great deal about natural and herbal medicines before I went to medical school. Naturally, I can't use them in my practice, but they keep me interested out here in the jungle." She lifted her chin. "A harmless hobby, Phillip."

"I'm sure you wouldn't allow it to be anything else. You believe in the primary rule. First, do no harm." He was silent. "But I've seen that you occasionally have patients who had miraculous recoveries after we'd given up on them."

"There are always miracles. We've all seen them and been grateful."

"But you have more than your share." He held up

his hand as she started to speak. "I'm not accusing you. We're all in this fight together." He looked at the vial in her hand. "I just want you to know if you need help, I'm here for you."

She inhaled sharply as she saw his expression. During those first years with Hu Chang, whenever she'd looked in the mirror, she'd seen that expression on her own face. The intensity, the eagerness, the potential that if you just reached out, you might make something different and wonderful happen. Of course Phillip would react as she had done. He was a healer of the very best kind, who would do anything for his patients.

But he mustn't do this.

She met his gaze. "You're head of the team. I know I can come to you with problems."

"That's a nice noncommittal answer." He paused. "You held Maria Perez back when we sent the rest of the patients to Georgetown. Why?"

"Her mother, Blanca, wanted to spend her last days with her daughter."

"She could have gone with her."

"She thought Maria would be more comfortable here."

"For the next twenty-four hours?"

"Yes."

"And you won't let me help you?"

"I don't know what you mean." She paused. "But if I did, I hear there's such a thing as plausible deniability." She added quietly, "You're a good man and a wonderful doctor, Phillip. As you said, we approach our profession from different directions. My direction isn't nearly as safe or free from the possibility of guilt or mistakes as yours." She glanced at the rows of potions on the shelves. "Back off. You're not welcome here."

"Have it your way." He grinned at her. "I'll see you at the mess later to have a last cup of coffee. I think it's going to take a longer time than I expected to pack up that mess. I believe it would be a goodwill gesture to deliver the remains of the food to the villagers. And we've left a lot of refuse to clean up around the camp . . ."

"Twenty-four hours?"

"It might take all of that." He turned and headed for the tent opening. "Good luck, Rachel."

"I don't have any idea what you mean." She took the vial and strode out of her tent and across the camp toward the single patient tent left at the edge of the clearing. "I'll see you later, Phillip."

"How's she doing, Rachel?" Nancy Kavitz asked softly as the nurse practitioner came into the tent four hours later. "Such a sweet little kid. Did you know that she's only eight? Even when I gave her shots, she'd try to smile at me." She shook her head. "Until this morning. Is she asleep or has she gone into a coma?"

"No coma . . . yet." Rachel looked back down at the little girl.

Maybe not ever, Maria. You need to stick around and grow up and have kids that are as sweet as you are. You think about it, and maybe somebody up there will hear you. "Though her fever is still high. I was hoping it would come down."

"Why?" Nancy frowned, puzzled. "The fever in the other patients didn't come down before they went into coma state."

"Dammit, that's *why* it has to come down," Rachel said sharply. "Why are you taking it for granted that she doesn't have a chance? They *all* have a chance. We just have to give it to them. She's younger than the others, her body is fighting harder. You don't have a right to—". She stopped and drew a deep breath. Nancy's eyes were wide with distress. Rachel knew that Nancy never really gave up on any of her patients. It was just that with kids like Maria, she couldn't get her hopes up because the pain was so terrible when she lost them. Nancy was in her late thirties, she'd been with the team for ten years longer than Rachel and she didn't deserve an attack from her like this. "Sorry," she said jerkily. "I guess it's been a long two weeks for all of us. Who knew a damn mosquito would cause all this hell?"

"Yeah," Nancy said. "I thought the Zika was bad; and then along came Taran. The government says the spraying is working. They're keeping the infestation localized."

"Too late for Nalez. The village is a ghost town now." She looked back down at the little girl. *Not too late for you, Maria. You keep fighting.*

Her glance shifted to Nancy. "Why did you come? Can I help you?"

"No, I'm supposed to help you." Nancy smiled.

"Phillip said that he told you to join us for coffee in the mess, and you didn't come."

"It was the wrong timing for me."

"Whatever. He said that he didn't think that you'd want him to help you, but I might be able to do it. He thinks you need some sleep since we're not going to be able to pull out of here until sometime tomorrow. I can sit with Maria and give you a break." She paused. "I'll watch her, Rachel. Any change, and I'll come for you. Trust me."

"I do trust you." She got to her feet and arched her back to stretch it. "And I don't really need to check her again until ten tomorrow." She'd given Maria the potion an hour ago and she couldn't give her the last one for at least twelve hours, or it might prove fatal. All that could be done until then was to keep her liquids normal and watch her for any sign of deterioration. "But I'll be back at seven in the morning to relieve you. Thanks, Nancy."

She shrugged. "My job. And if I didn't do it, Phillip would be over here instead. I think he's got a thing for you."

"A thing?" Rachel shook her head. "Not true. He's just got a sense of responsibility for his team."

"Yeah." She grimaced. "As long as his team is a redhead with long legs and big green eyes. He's a man, isn't he? We're always stuck out in these hellish conditions, and it's natural he'd want to jump you."

Rachel chuckled as she remembered Phillip's intense, longing expression as he gazed up at that shelf of potions. "You're wrong, Nancy. That's not what he wants."

She tilted her head. "And that's not what you want either?"

"Right."

"Good." She grinned. "Then you won't mind if I do the jumping? I've always had a crush on him since he took over the team five years ago. I was just a little intimidated by all those letters after his name. But I've decided that no one should wait for what they want. Dedication can only go so far. If I want anything else to make my life worth living, the rest is going to be up to me."

"A sound decision." And Rachel had no idea that Nancy felt that way about Phillip. But then she'd been working eighteen or twenty hours a day, and that didn't lend to noticing much of anything else. "I'll see you at seven."

She watched Nancy sit down in the chair next to Maria's bed.

Sleep well, but not too well. You have to come back to us, little girl.

Ten tomorrow morning.

And then another six hours, and she'd know one way or the other.

She looked up at the night sky. Not that she could see that much of it through the heavy canopy of the trees of the rain forest. But there were stars up there, weren't there? It was important to remember in the darkness there were always stars.

Her phone rang, and she glanced down at the ID. Hu Chang.

She smiled as she pressed the access. Strange that he'd called at this particular moment. He'd always been one of the stars in her darkness and there whenever she needed him. "I tried the broadleaf," she said when she picked up the call. "I don't know if it's going to work, Hu Chang. I used redwood before."

"Neither do I. But I trust in you to choose correctly as you've always done. You have infallible instinct. After that, it's up to the patient." He paused. "But it's weighing heavily on you if you cannot even give me the courtesy of a greeting. Did I not teach you better than that, Rachel? Perhaps you should quit playing around in those jungles and come to me for a refresher course."

"And perhaps you should have told me what to do with Maria instead of just listening to me go over my options," she said tartly. "You persist in telling me that you're the master and I'm only the humble student, yet you don't give me—" She stopped. This would do no good. Hu Chang always did exactly what he wanted to do, and she would not have it any other way. She could almost see him before her in his black tunic, his shoulder-length hair drawn back from that intent face that had always seemed totally ageless to her. Ageless, expressionless, and yet she had felt as if she could sense everything he was thinking since the day he had taken her into his home and his laboratory when she was only fifteen. "I'm sorry, I'm a little on edge. I know I didn't ask for help, I just used you as a sounding board."

"And it was my privilege. I always enjoy seeing how your mind works. And I realize you cannot talk to your learned colleagues about the intricacies of what you do. Such a pity. But then, you knew it was going to be that way. I'm such a magnificent example, am I not?"

Magnificent was not an overstatement where Hu Chang was concerned. She might never know the full story of Hu Chang, but he'd told her once that he had grown up in Manchuria, trained by his apothecary father to be a master poisoner and later became a Doctor of Chinese Medicine. She knew that he had traveled the world, studied many cultures, and lived a life that was solely by his own rules. During the two years she'd stayed with him, she'd accepted those rules because they'd healed her. And God knows she'd needed healing after those months she'd spent in Sazkar Prison. "You warned me. I didn't realize it was going to be this difficult."

"Only because you lack a basic sense of ruthlessness or what some call the killer instinct. But that can be learned."

"I *won't* learn it. Why do you think I'm in the middle of this rain forest in Guyana?"

"It's been safer for you. And allowed you to keep my inimitable teachings unsullied and useful." He paused. "Or at least it was safer. Is everything well with you?"

"No. I don't know if Maria is going to—"

"I'm not speaking about Maria. Is there anything disturbing happening around you?"

"No. The government workers have stopped spraying and pulled out of the area. They think they have the mosquito infestation under control. Though in this rain forest I don't see how they can tell. But I guess the experts know what they're doing."

"Do they? I've always had problems with accepting experts. My skeptical nature. When do you leave Nalez?"

"Tomorrow. I'm only waiting for the last dose for Maria. Phillip wanted to pull out tonight."

"But the good doctor gave in and allowed you to have your chance with her."

She stiffened. "And what's wrong with that? It's a life, Hu Chang."

"And he's a doctor who would embrace any means of saving life . . . even if it came with a price?"

"Yes." She should have known that Hu Chang would have perceived that about Phillip when she had only just realized it. "But doctors like him shouldn't have to make that choice. He's very visible, someone would find out what he'd done, and he'd be destroyed."

"Better that you take the risk?"

"Why not? I'm very low on the totem pole. A dedicated physician with a hobby. Anyway, Phillip will cooperate."

"I'm sure he will. Nothing's wrong with his wish to give you what you want. Don't we all, Rachel? He probably senses that vulnerable quality behind the strong surface and wants to protect you."

"I'm not vulnerable. You *never* found me vulnerable, Hu Chang. You never took excuses, and you made me work all the hours of the day."

"Well, most of them. And perhaps that was my way of ridding you of that vulnerability. Or perhaps it was purely for my own pleasure to see how far I could push you before you broke." He added softly, "And you never broke, Rachel. That's why when you left me, I knew that you were ready to face anything without me."

"Ready, but maybe not willing. It took me a while to get used to all the rules I ran into at the university. I missed you."

"And so you should. I'm totally unique and without peer."

"And so modest." She went back to that odd word he'd used. "Disturbing? Why should you wonder if there was anything disturbing around me?"

"I do not wonder. It was Catherine Ling who called me and asked where you were in Guyana. She's the one who asked me if there was anything disturbing happening in your area."

"Catherine?" That was a complete surprise. She had not seen Catherine Ling for over a year. Catherine was a CIA agent who had been given her orders by Rachel's father, Carl Venable, ever since she'd been recruited as a teenager in Hong Kong. When Rachel was living with Hu Chang, Catherine had moved in and out of her life because she was Hu Chang's closest friend. Somehow during that time, she had also become Rachel's very close friend. "I didn't think she even knew where I was."

"You're her friend. Since you persist in traveling to hot spots with hardly more than a stethoscope for protection, Catherine keeps track of you. She doesn't have that many friends, and she doesn't like the idea of losing one." He paused. "Just because you distanced yourself from her when you broke with your father doesn't mean that she would allow anything to happen to you."

No, both Catherine and Hu Chang had always given her comfort and support during that painful period of separation. She had known they'd always be there for her. "I didn't deliberately distance—It just happened. She works with my father. It was . . . awkward."

"She didn't find it so. She respects Venable. She cares for you. She doesn't take sides."

"And did he tell her to keep an eye on me?"

"You'd have to ask Catherine. I believe she would have done it regardless. Now, may I tell you what she wished me to convey to you?"

"Disturbance. What kind of disturbance that doesn't concern these damn mosquitoes?"

"She said there were rumbles that a revolutionary guerilla militant group had crossed the Venezuela border into Guyana. Not a pleasant group. In Venezuela they've acted with true terrorist behavior, savage attacks on villages, robberies, rapes, killings."

"That's all these poor people need. Then why doesn't she notify the Guyana military?"

"It's only rumbles. They're still in Venezuela as far as anyone knows. The government's not going to pay attention until there's an actual sighting or attack. But

Catherine would like to urge you to be careful and absent yourself with all due speed."

"I'll tell Phillip to call our headquarters in Georgetown and tell them what she said. They'll contact the military and see if they think we have a problem here."

"And if they do?"

"Then Phillip will start packing and get everyone out."

"Except you."

"I'll make my way to the coast later. I don't want to move Maria that far until she's a little stronger. And that means I have to be here tomorrow to administer that final dose after ten in the morning. I'll stay in the village with Maria's mother, Blanca. There are only a few families left in the village anyway. They've all scattered and gone to other villages to get out of the infestation area." She was thinking, trying to find the best solution. "I'll go warn her now that we're going to shift Maria to the village and that she might have to find a place to hide her in the rain forest if it becomes necessary."

"May I point out your team isn't going to appreciate your staying behind."

"Maybe I won't have to do it. No actual intel, it's just rumbles. I have to hang up now, Hu Chang. I need to get moving."

"Because you believe that rumbles sometime become roars. Catherine thought that you would not ignore her warning."

"Catherine realizes that I know bad things happen.

So do you, Hu Chang." She hesitated, then asked the question, "Did the warning come from her or from my father?"

"From Catherine. She's not been in communication with Venable for the last two months." He added quietly, "You know I would not deceive you. I'm aware that you have no trust in him."

"Let's just say that my trust is limited to the given situation. I also know that he can make black seem white if he chooses. He's done it before."

"Have you ever known me to be color-blind?"

"No."

"Neither is Catherine. Trust her."

"I do. I just had to be certain. I'll call and tell you if the Maria formula works." She pressed the disconnect.

She drew a deep breath and looked back up at the sky. She would give herself just a moment, then start to do what had to be done.

Rumbles? Conversations that could be rumors or just gossip that swept through the CIA community. It seemed unlikely to touch her in this place. A poor village in the middle of the rain forest? She heard only the night sounds of that rain forest right now telling her it could be all bullshit. But she knew what evil and pain was out there. All the violence and trickery and greed and death. And wherever that evil and death lived so did her father, Carl Venable. She could imagine him spinning his web of intrigue, plots, and lies. If not this time, then another.

But she was not her father. She would not let herself live in his world.

She took out her phone. First, talk to Phillip Sanford, then go to the village and prepare Maria's mother. It would all work out. She would make sure that it did. Death was always just around the corner, but so was life.

And after all, it might only be rumbles . . .

GEORGETOWN, GUYANA
1:45 A.M.

"Liberation Unity," Nate Scott said to Jude Brandon as he came back from the cockpit of the Apache helicopter. "I think Venable might have gotten it right when he told you that Huber would already be on his way to hunt down his daughter. Liberation is headed by Fidel Morales. It's a small, but vicious terrorist group that has affiliations with Max Huber's Red Star organization. And there was a sighting at a crossing at the northern border two hours ago. No reports of any attacks. They just disappeared into the rain forest heading southwest."

"And Nalez is in the southwest corner of Guyana," Brandon said grimly. "And why ignore all the rich, juicy targets in the north to head for the rain forest where the villages barely manage to survive?"

"And where there's been a medical alert issued," Nate added as he dropped into a seat beside Brandon. "Like I said, Venable might have gotten it right. This may not be Huber's central organization, but he's pulling the strings."

"Right." Huber's Red Star terrorist organization had cells that reached worldwide and used their power to not only cause political disruption and terror but acquire wealth wherever they had the opportunity. That power and wealth made them very attractive to lesser terrorist groups who were more than happy to perform favors. "The minute he located One World Medical, he scouted around until he found a group he could use and sent them across the border on a mission. We're sure Rachel Venable is still in Nalez?"

"According to the report from their headquarters, she was still there yesterday when their team transferred thirty-two patients to the hospital outside Georgetown." He looked down at the report he'd brought from the cockpit. "The entire team is still in Nalez. Dr. Phillip Sanford, Nurse Practitioner Nancy Kavitz, Dr. William Pallis . . ." He looked up. "So do we go and get her?"

"Why else are we here? Venable gave her name to his informant, and she's the only one he's going to contact. We *need* that information. We go into Nalez, scoop her up and get out. Did you get that dossier on her?"

"As up-to-date as I could get on short notice." Nate indicated the folder he was carrying. "Here's the report that Monty got from his contact in Georgetown about her before we took off. It seems fairly complete. But you may be familiar with most of it if Venable told you to—"

"I don't know much of anything," Brandon said flatly. "I didn't want to know. I wanted to deal with

Carl Venable, not his daughter. If Venable couldn't keep himself alive, I don't know how I'm supposed to keep her alive until we get Huber." He took the report and glanced at the first page. The woman's photo jumped out at him. Tall, slim, graceful in tan khakis and white shirt. Red hair just brushing her shoulders, green-gray eyes staring boldly, inquiringly, out of the photo. Not beautiful, but definitely arresting.

"Nice looking," Nate said. "Red hair like her father." He was still reading his report. "Twenty-nine. She had two brothers: James, who was killed in Afghanistan, and her younger brother, Kevin. Her mother and her brother Kevin died when their car was attacked by the Taliban outside Kabul. Venable was stationed there for five years and his wife, Judith, finally insisted on his arranging for the family to have safe quarters in Kabul so they could join him during that last year. Obviously a bad decision. Rachel was also in that car, but she survived and was taken prisoner. She was held hostage for five months while they bargained for her release with Venable, who the State Department had put in charge of negotiations. There was difficulty about prisoner-exchange terms. She was only fifteen at the time." He looked down the report. "She was finally released to an intermediary party who had in-fluence with the Afghanistan government . . . a physi-cian named Hu Chang. But instead of returning to her father, she stayed with Hu Chang for the next two years before she entered medical school." He looked up at him. "Have you ever heard of this Hu Chang?"

"Oh, I've heard quite a bit about him," Brandon

said dryly. "He's fairly notorious in many circles. But nothing in connection with Rachel Venable. Anything else?"

"Brilliance. Dedication. Humanitarian selflessness in her professional life. No money. No important contacts. Why should Huber want to go after her?"

"The same reason he went after Venable. Actually, according to what her father said, he has an even better reason to kill her. That's one of the reasons why Venable made sure I'd go after her." He looked down at the photo again. "Our Rachel Venable is not what she seems . . ."

NALEZ

3:35 A.M.

"Where the *hell* are you?" Phillip Sanford's voice was clipped when Rachel answered his call. "We have to get out of here. Our helicopter should be arriving in another fifteen minutes. I told you an hour ago that I'd gotten that call from Guyana military that there was a report of a village being burned to the ground not fifty miles from here. You said you were on your way back from Blanca's village after settling Maria."

"I lied," she said calmly. "I knew you'd come after me if you thought you had the time. Now you don't have the time. I'll see you in Georgetown in the next day or so." She could hear Phillip cursing. "I'll be hiding out in the rain forest with Maria and her mother.

They know that forest like the back of their hand. I'll be fine with them. When that helicopter comes, get everyone out of here, Phillip."

"We could wait if you tell me you're on your way."

"I'm not on my way. And you're too responsible to wait on one person when you have to take care of the entire team. See you later, Phillip." She hung up and took a deep breath. He was angry, and she'd be lucky if he didn't kick her off the team. If he did, then she'd just have to accept it. Maybe it would be okay, she hadn't deliberately endangered anyone but herself. But discipline was important when you dealt with conditions like the team faced on a regular basis.

But so was a little girl's life.

She turned to Maria's mother, Blanca Perez. "Were you able to arrange to have Maria's stretcher carried into the rain forest? It looks like we're going to have to move fast now."

Blanca nodded. "My uncle and his friend. They'll take us to a cave where I played as a child, then leave us and go east toward Surinam." Her eyes were wide with fear. "It might be bad? Why would anyone want to hurt us? We have nothing."

"I don't know why. Some people are evil and don't want anyone to be happy." She looked down at the stretcher. Maria's cheeks were too flushed. Was her temperature down even a little? "But then you have a treasure like your daughter. It makes up for it, doesn't it?"

"Yes, she's such a good girl." Blanca's eyes were

filled with tears. "And so smart. I was teaching her English before this happened to her. She speaks it almost as well as I do. She's all I have. The angels mustn't take her from me."

"Then you tell them they have a job to do." Rachel turned away. "Get your uncle moving, please. I'll go warn the other villagers to leave, then catch up with you."

CHAPTER

2

Rachel heard the One World helicopter arrive fifteen minutes later and saw the blue lights spearing down toward the hospital clearing in the distance. She stopped on the trail, her gaze lifting to watch it descend. "Right on time," she murmured to Blanca. "That's good. They'll be loaded and out of here in ten minutes, and an hour from now, they'll be landing in Georgetown."

"And safe," Blanca said. "You should be with them."

"No, I shouldn't." Rachel's gaze was still on the helicopter. "I'm exactly where I should be. Maria needs me. My team doesn't have any urgent use for me right—"

The helicopter exploded into a thousand shards of flaming metal!

"No!" Rachel gasped in shock and disbelief.

Rachel watched in horror as the helicopter fell out of the sky like a gigantic burning insect. She heard Blanca sobbing beside her.

Dead. That pilot had to be dead.

What had happened? She wondered dazedly.

And then she heard the gunfire from the direction of the hospital camp, and she knew what happened.

Under attack.

The guerrillas had shot the helicopter gas tank and ignited it.

And now they were firing at the people on the ground.

Her people. Her team.

Phillip and Nancy and Bill. They all had handguns, but would they have time to reach them? It wasn't as if they carried them around with them. Any weapons were probably in their luggage beside them as they waited for the helicopter to descend. She had her own weapon in her knapsack because she'd known she'd be traveling to Georgetown through the rain forest. And what if they were already wounded by that barrage of bullets? She had to *help* them. She grabbed her knapsack from the stretcher. "Blanca, take Maria the rest of the way. I'll be back as soon as I can."

"Don't leave her," Blanca said frantically. "You said you'd stay with her. You promised me."

"I'll come back for her. You've told me how to get to that cave. I swear it. Nothing will stop me." Then she was running back through the rain forest toward the hospital area.

Smoke.

The smell of fuel.

Heat.

She was still at least thirty minutes away, and she could feel that heat.

And the firing was still going on.

Stay in the trees. Don't go running out in the open. Find Phillip or Nancy or Bill and try to help them get away.

Why were the guerrillas still shooting? Maybe that was a good thing. It meant her team was still alive, didn't it?

And then the shooting stopped.

No!

She stopped and listened. She couldn't hear anything but the crackling flames in the distance.

She was still fifteen minutes away. Was that going to be fifteen minutes too long?

Be careful. Be silent. Move as Hu Chang had taught her to move all those years ago.

Still no firing from the direction of that inferno ahead.

Please. Let them be *alive*.

Fifteen minutes later, she'd reached the edge of the hospital clearing. She stood there in the shadows of the trees gazing in horror.

The tents were burning.

The helicopter was burning.

But no one was there. It was as if the guerrillas had struck, destroyed, then faded back into the rain forest as swiftly as they had come. She stood there, staring, because she was realizing that she was wrong. There was someone there.

Just no one alive.

As she moved out of the shadows, she saw Nancy Kavitz's body crumpled beside a tree near the burning helicopter. Her eyes were wide open, staring into nothingness. She'd been shot in the chest.

Rachel moved toward the hospital tent as she saw a glimpse of something just inside the torn canvas.

Bill Pallis had been shot, then sliced with a machete and thrown into the burning tent.

She stared at him, feeling sick. So young and eager. He'd just graduated med school last year and had wanted to save the world.

And Phillip? Where was he? Where was she going to find Phillip Sanford?

She was almost afraid to look around the other tents. She could still see the flames licking around Bill's body. Look. Find Phillip. Maybe he needed help . . .

"Ah, Morales said that you must still be here. No one believed him but me. Turn around very slowly, *chica*. Or I'll put a bullet in that pretty red hair."

She froze. The man was speaking Spanish, and he probably had a gun in his hand.

She slowly turned to face him. Slick black hair, brown-and-green leather jacket, discolored yellow teeth. "You did . . . this?"

"I only took out the helicopter." He was looking at a photo in his hand. "Yes, you're the one he's looking for. They're running all over the forest searching for you, but I get the bonus. Let's go to camp and see Morales."

"No." As far as she could see, he was alone. She had a better chance with him than she would with this Morales and his men. "I don't know any Morales. Let him come to me."

He laughed incredulously. "I could shoot you, bitch. Do what I say."

"You might shoot me anyway. And I don't think I want to know what your friends might do to me at your camp. Morales can come to me." Her hand tightened on her knapsack. It would take only a moment to grab the gun from under the flap, but that might be too long. He had his own gun pointed at her. "I'm not moving."

"Then I'll knock you out and drag you." He was striding toward her. "And maybe I'll take the time to play a little before I share you with—"

She whirled in a roundhouse kick and connected with his chin.

He grunted and staggered backward.

She followed it with a kick that sent his gun flying from his hand. Then another kick to the back of his knees that caused him to start to fall.

Then she took off flying herself.

Head for the trees.

She could hear him cursing behind her. Then the sound of him crashing through the brush . . .

He was so close . . .

She hadn't slowed him down for more than thirty seconds. But sometimes that was enough. He was big, and he had a long stride, but she was light and fast. She was working frantically at the flap of her knapsack. Grab the gun. Duck behind a tree and fire.

She had the gun!

She dropped the knapsack on the ground and sprinted toward the—

Tackled!

She hit the ground *hard*. She hadn't thought he was that close. She struggled to turn over and point the gun.

"Be *still*." His hand was on her neck. She was suddenly disoriented. "Now keep quiet."

She *was* dizzy. The words were English, not Spanish as it had been before.

But now the man was speaking over his shoulder to someone in Spanish as he stood up. "I got her. I was the one who took her down and knocked her out. Now do we share or—" He broke off and leaped forward with lightning speed. His hand knifed down in a karate chop and hit the carotid artery of the man walking toward him.

A man wearing a brown-and-green jacket with slick black hair . . . The man who had tried to take her to Morales. His knees gave way, and he collapsed. Dead?

"Get *up*." The man who had tackled her had turned back and was roughly jerking her to her feet. "We have to get out of here. These woods are crawling with Morales' men. Can you walk?"

English again.

She shook her head to clear it. "Who are you?"

"Brandon. Can you walk?" he repeated as he bent

and retrieved her gun from the ground where she'd dropped it. "I don't have time for questions if you want to live through the night." He handed her the gun. "From what I saw, you do."

She looked down at the gun. She didn't know what was happening, but now she had a way of defending herself. And he had given it to her. So he probably wasn't one of the guerrillas. And she was familiar with the deadly military precision with which he had moved. "I can walk." She touched her neck. It was sore, and she was still dizzy, but some of the disorientation was disappearing. "And you probably know that. You're very good at what you do." She looked back at the smoking inferno in the clearing. "Let's get out of here."

He nodded and turned on his heel. "I'll get you out. You just keep up with me."

And she kept up with him.

She could tell that he expected nothing else. He never looked back as he moved through the rain forest for the next two hours. Twice he made her stop and drew her in another direction as he saw two of Morales' men on the trail ahead. But he did it with hand signals, then continued on the trail.

Dawn was breaking when he finally stopped and let her catch up with him. "Wait." He was on his phone. "I have her. Area secured?" He evidently got the right answer because he hung up and turned toward her. "We're as safe as we can be for the time being. We've had sentries along the trail for the past three miles. The helicopter is just ahead."

Just ahead was close to another mile. And the helicopter was very large, gray, and looked like something from a SEAL operation. Probably an Apache. She stopped, gazing at it. Military, again . . .

"Get on board," Brandon said curtly. "Nate and Monty will be here in a few minutes, and we'll bring in the team and take off."

"Will we? I don't believe I want to get on your helicopter. Not right now. I'm going to rest." She dropped down on the ground beneath a banyan tree. Don't shake. Don't show weakness. He wouldn't understand it. She couldn't remember the last time she had slept, and every step she'd taken since she'd left the hospital clearing had hammered the memory of what she'd seen there deeper into her mind. "I've got to think, and I can't be rushed, Brandon." She looked at him. "It *is* Brandon? You hurled your name at me at a time when I wasn't thinking very straight."

"Jude Brandon." He looked down at her. "And you appeared to be acting, if not thinking, very coherently at the time. I only took you down because I was afraid you'd do something to get in my way."

"And I might have done that." She concentrated on keeping her voice steady. "Since I didn't know who you were, and I'd just seen two of my team, who were also my friends, butchered. Emotion tends to get in the way when that happens."

"Yes, it does. I'm sorry it happened. But you're handling it very well." His gaze was searching her face.

"Unless you're going to have a delayed reaction and fall apart on me soon."

"Possibly. But it won't happen soon. I can hold on until I get through what has to be done."

"What has to be done is getting you out of here. And you *will* be rushed, Rachel. But we can spare a few minutes. I'd built in a little more time because I thought you'd not be this strong."

She didn't feel strong. "Self-preservation is an amazing stimulator. But you probably also know that." She leaned back against the trunk of the tree and looked at him. He was all in black, tall, and muscular, but there was a tough leanness about his entire body. His hips and buttocks tight, his stomach flat. She remembered how powerful his body had been above her in that moment when he'd taken her down. Even when he was in motion, he'd given off an aura of stillness and containment. His face was also lean, with high cheekbones framing deep-set blue eyes. Cold, watchful eyes. "You're Special Forces, aren't you?"

His brows rose. "Am I?"

She nodded. "I think so. You have the look. I grew up seeing men like you drop into my father's office or fade in and out of his life. He found people with your talents very helpful."

"I imagine Venable would."

"You know him? Did he send you to save us?"

"In a manner of speaking."

"That's not good enough. I'm too tired and scared to play games. Why does the CIA think no one should know anything but them? It's as if they're some kind of gods handing out divine providence. Was it Catherine Ling? She was worried about those damn rumbles." She rubbed her eyes. "But whoever sent you screwed up. They should have sent someone who knew what they were doing. You didn't do your job, Brandon."

His lips tightened. "I did my job."

"Bill Pallis is dead. Nancy Kavitz is dead." She struggled to keep her voice even. "I don't know about Phillip Sanford. I didn't see him." She held her breath as she asked, "Did . . . you?"

"No, I was a little preoccupied trying to find you. *You* were my job. Nate may know what happened to him. You can ask him when he gets here. He had orders to get the big picture and smooth the way out."

"The big picture . . ." She closed her eyes. "Yes, I can see every detail of that big picture. It's engraved on my memory. My father is very fond of the big picture. Bill Pallis was only twenty-seven. He doesn't have any picture at all right now."

"Unfortunate. Good men die. Is this where you fall apart on me?"

"No." She opened her eyes. "I just have to know what's happening, so I can decide which way to go. And you're not helping, Brandon. You may not be as callous as you appear, because you probably think that you have to use the spur to keep me going." She met his eyes. "I keep myself going. I always have. So the only thing you have to worry about is casting some light on all this darkness. If you want me to cooperate, you'll do that." She paused. "So let's start with you. Special Forces? What branch?"

He was silent. "Rangers. Several years ago. I'm no longer with the military."

"You're CIA?"

"No way."

"But you're here trying to get me out. Hu Chang?"

He smiled crookedly. "I'm definitely not an errand boy for your old friend." He made an impatient gesture. "Look, we can go into this later. All you need to know is that I came to get you when I heard you might be targeted by Fidel Morales and his Liberation terrorist group. Not in time. We saw the One World helicopter blow up just as we were landing several miles north. By the time we got to the hospital site, it was too late for your team. But you weren't with them, so I told my men not to engage Morales' men and instead hunt you down before Morales found you." His lips twisted. "So you can see that I'm not as secretive as you apparently think."

"Yes you are," she said wearily. "Men like you always have secrets they don't share with anyone. And you always have an agenda that drives you."

"Men like me?" he repeated softly. "I don't believe I like being grouped and thought predictable. But I'll let that slide for now. I just need to get you out of here before I—" He broke off as he saw two men in camouflage fatigues coming out of the trees. "What's the word, Nate?"

The smaller man with dark, curly hair shrugged as he came toward them. "They're still looking for her. Evidently, the price on her head was fairly high. But they're not in this area yet. We should be safe for a little while." He turned toward Rachel. "How are you doing?" He took a thermos out of his backpack and handed it to her. "Coffee. I'm Nate Scott. This is Monty Caplan. Sorry you've had such a rough time, Dr. Venable."

"Rachel." She took a swallow of the coffee. It was hot, black, and felt good going down. "Thank you. I appreciate the concern." She glanced warily at Brandon. "Providing you're not playing Bad Cop–Good Cop with me?"

Nate grinned. "Has he been giving you a hard time? You'll be okay. You don't work for him. Now, I'm just a humble employee. But I'm still allowed to have opinions."

"Sometimes," Monty Caplan said dryly. He turned to Brandon. "When can we leave? Nate has to bring those men out of that rain forest."

"Have them back at the plane in twenty minutes. We leave in thirty."

"I don't think so," Rachel said.

Brandon turned to face her. "But I do," he said. "And you haven't been given a vote, Rachel Venable."

"I have a vote if you don't want me to run back here the minute you land this helicopter," she said fiercely. "And I *will*, no matter whether that's in Georgetown or Washington, DC. Evidently you've been given orders to keep me alive and get me out of here. I don't know if you've been paid or been given a contract by the CIA or someone else. But at some point you're going to have to have my cooperation. So I definitely have a vote, Brandon."

Nate gave a low whistle. "Now you have to admit that's logical, Brandon."

She whirled toward Nate. "And you're the one I want to talk to anyway. You have the big picture." She moistened her lips. "Where does Dr. Phillip Sanford fit into that picture? Did they kill him, too?"

"Not unless they did it in the last thirty minutes."

She let her breath out. "He's alive? Wounded?"

Nate nodded. "Leg. The report said he was hobbling when he was brought into Morales' camp." He added gently, "He has a chance to stay alive even if Morales doesn't think he can trade him for you. He's a bigwig doctor and he might be able to get ransom for him. His Liberation Unity group doesn't get the opportunity to get their hands on a high-profile medic very often."

"A chance? He's *got* to stay alive." But he was alive now, and that was wonderful. She hadn't realized how frightened she had been until this moment. She had probably been too numb with shock to think about it. "And why would this Morales trade Phillip for me? As you said, he's a bigwig. I have to be less than nothing to Morales."

"Not true. You're cash in the hand," Brandon said. "And the reason he hit the One World hospital site." His gaze was searching her face. "Haven't you really made the connection yet? Why would Morales have given photos to all his men so that they could recognize you on sight?"

Dear God, she was making the connection now. But she didn't want to believe it. "I've never heard of Morales or his Liberation Unity," she said jerkily.

"But you've heard of Max Huber and Red Star," he said softly. "And Huber evidently has heard of you. That's why he sent Morales across the border to scoop you up and send you to him. Just what did you do that pissed Huber off, Rachel?"

She didn't answer. After all these years you'd think that question wouldn't bring back the nightmare memory. Yet she could feel the same chill and fear she had known then. No, then there had also been the horror and the anger.

"You're not answering," Brandon said. "Are you still willing to hang around in this rain forest until Morales plucks you like a ripe banana and sends you to Huber?"

"No." She was having trouble steadying her voice. "But I have to be sure that Huber's not paying you to do the same thing." She took another swallow of coffee. "Who sent you?"

He shrugged. "Your father and I had a mutual interest in taking Huber down and scattering his remains into the stratosphere. But as a top CIA guru, he had to be careful of how he did it so that he wouldn't cause ramifications down the line. He told me that he'd been working under Huber's radar for years but then suddenly Huber found out something about him that caught his attention." He met her gaze. "And that 'something' also caused him to focus on you. Would you care to tell me what it was that galvanized Huber to such an extent?"

"No. How do I know you're telling the truth?"

"You don't. But might I point out that you do still have your gun?"

"And you just want to save me from Huber and deliver me to my father?"

He shook his head. "As you suspected, I have my own agenda. I want to keep you alive so that I'll find a way of using you to bring Huber's head to me on the traditional platter." He paused. "And there's no way I'll be taking you to your father. I regret that doesn't enter into my agenda."

"I don't regret it." She tried to think. He could be lying, but there was not a hint of persuasion in his demeanor. Morales and the Huber connection made sense.

Just as it made sense that Huber would eventually find out what she'd done and come after her. She'd been waiting for it to happen.

"Satisfied?" Brandon came toward her and held out his hand to pull her to her feet. "Come on, I'll take you to the helicopter."

She slowly shook her head. "You're not the only one with an agenda, Brandon."

He stiffened. "Money? I have plenty of that. We'll discuss it after we're out of here."

"That's not on *my* agenda." She turned to Nate. "I'm all turned around after that convoluted route Brandon led me. Look at your big picture and tell me how close we are to the Nalez Village?"

"About five miles west. Why?"

She didn't answer. "And how bad did Morales hit the village? Any fatalities?"

He shook his head. "My reports said that it was deserted. They searched it, then they set fire to it."

Violence and destruction, but no murder. How sad to be glad about anything connected to this atrocity. "Are his men still there?"

"No, they've moved on. They're searching the rain forest right now."

"They won't find anyone." She hoped she was telling the truth. But the last of the villagers had left almost an hour before Blanca and Maria had gone. They had a good chance. And Maria had an even better chance, hidden away in that cave in the hills.

If Rachel could get to her in time.

And she *had* to get to her in time.

She turned to Brandon. "The hills start in the rain forest about three miles out of the village. I have to get there right away."

"No," he said flatly. "We're flying out of here in thirty minutes."

"I told you, I'll only come back if I don't take what I want with me." She added fiercely, "What's your plan, Brandon? Knock me on the head like that Morales' ape was trying to do? There are three of you, and you might be able to do it. But you'd probably hurt and piss me off, and you said you wanted to use me. I promise that I won't let that happen if I don't get what I want."

"Yes, you would." He met her eyes. "It will happen."

Power. Intensity. Boldness.

For a moment, she was intimidated. Don't let him see it. She forced herself to hold his gaze. "I have two things I have to do before we leave here. I'll need your help. That's *my* agenda, Brandon. And then you get anything you want from me. No questions. No battles."

He stared at her for a long moment. "Anything?"

"Anything."

Another silence. "You must want this very badly. What did you leave in those hills?"

"Maria Perez, a patient, and her mother. I need to give her a dose of medicine, then we have to get them on your helicopter. We can drop them off at the hospital in Georgetown. I'll need two men to carry her stretcher."

"And fight off any of Morales' men you come across along the way," Brandon said dryly. "That could come at a high price. I might be willing to send in a team to find her, give the medicine, then bring her to the plane. But I'm not going to risk losing you to Morales. Then I'd have nothing to show for giving you the help you need. You'll stay on board the copter and wait."

She shook her head. "I have to be the one to administer the potion. It has very special properties. It has to be *me*."

"No, Rachel."

Her control snapped. "Don't you tell me no. She's eight years old. I promised her mother I'd come back. She's waiting for me. If you want to be sure that I'll come out of this alive, then you come with me. But I'm *going*, Brandon. Blanca and I might be able to handle that stretcher between us, and she knows the rain forest, and we could—"

"Be quiet," he said harshly. "We're wasting time. Nate, how long will it take us to get to those hills?"

"An hour. Maybe less."

He turned to Rachel. "You know exactly where to find her?"

"Yes, I have the directions. You'll do it?"

"I'll do it." He turned back to Nate. "You'll lead the way until we get to the hills." He glanced at Monty. "Send a couple of men to shadow us in case we run into something we can't handle. Pull the other men out and wait for us on the copter." He turned back to Rachel, and said coldly, "I'll see that you get out of those hills alive. You'll get your way. And then I'll get mine."

She nodded as she got to her feet. She'd won the first battle. This wasn't the time to make that second demand. Besides, she didn't know if she had the energy to fight with Brandon. Another hour's walk seemed as difficult as climbing Mt. Everest at the moment. She could only hope that the adrenaline kicked in again soon.

"You can change your mind." Brandon's eyes were narrowed on her face.

"No, I can't. That's another thing that's not on the agenda."

"Then you might as well sit back down for another five minutes." He turned and headed for the helicopter. "I have to go over flight instructions with Nate and Monty before we leave. Monty might have to take off damn quick if anything goes wrong."

Another five minutes to rest.

She gratefully sank down again and leaned back

against the tree. Do what Hu Chang had taught her to do. Close your eyes. Relax. Breathe deep. Sometimes a few minutes could be enough . . .

Another five minutes . . .

Nate glanced over his shoulder at Rachel as he fol- lowed Brandon into the copter. "You didn't tell her about her father?"

Brandon shrugged as he checked Monty's flight plan. "It didn't seem the time. She'd just lost two friends back in that camp. We don't need her to have to face the death of her father right now." His lips twisted. "Though she assured me that she wouldn't fall apart on me until everything had been taken care of."

"Did she?" Nate was still looking at Rachel out the window. "I don't think she will, Brandon. She's very tough."

That wasn't the word he would have used. She was strong, enduring, resilient, stubborn, but tough was too harsh a word for her. In the short time they had been together, he'd been aware of depths that were both frustrating and unassailable. She hadn't shown him her pain, but he could see it was there. "She's going to be very difficult."

"But she won't fall apart," Nate said. "Is that why you pulled us into this copter, to give her five more minutes before you drag her into those hills? I'm not hearing any weighty instructions from you."

"She's dragging *us* into those hills," Brandon said.

"And I won't cut her any slack once we're on the trail. But a little rest now will pay off in the long run. And as I said, she's a difficult woman to handle."

"And she's having a difficult time," Nate said quietly. "I think I like her, Brandon."

"Do you?" Brandon said. "And I think she's a good deal like her father. I've always been wary of Venable . . ."

It took more than an hour to reach the hills and another thirty minutes to negotiate the trail to the cave where Blanca had hidden Maria. They'd had to change directions twice on the way to avoid Morales' men searching through the rain forest.

"They're persistent," Brandon said grimly, as they encountered the second group. "Huber must be paying top dollar to encourage that degree of dedication. You're actually a threat to anyone near you. Your patient would be safer if you'd just come back after they've abandoned searching this area."

"That would be too late." She looked at her watch. "I only have a three-hour window to give her the medicine in order for it to be at top efficiency. The timing has to be just right."

"You're very good with timing," he said as he moved ahead of her again. "You almost took down Morales' man with those lethal kicks. Did Venable teach you kickboxing?"

"No, Hu Chang." They were almost there. She could make it. All she had to do was put one foot in front of the other and follow him. "He knew I had to have a way of feeling I could protect myself after I was released by the Taliban."

"He could have handed you a gun as I did. Kick-boxing can be both personal and active."

"It's too easy to kill with a gun. Violence . . . upsets me. Hu Chang said kickboxing was a great defense but could be almost like dancing." Why was she telling him this? It must be because she was so tired, and it really didn't matter what he thought. "He was right. But then Hu Chang is almost always right."

"About many diverse things I've heard." He stopped his gaze on the hill ahead. "You said a waterfall? There it is."

"Then the cave will be on the other side of the hill." Her pace quickened. "We're almost there. Five, ten minutes, and we'll be able to—"

A bullet whistled by her ear and hit the broadleaf tree a yard away.

"Shit." Brandon knocked her down. "Behind those shrubs!"

She crawled on hands and knees until she reached the cover of the stunted trees and shrubs. She was vaguely aware that Nate was somewhere ahead of her. But where was Brandon?

More shots.

Then Brandon was beside her. But he'd risen to his knees, his gaze searching the brush on the trees to his left. "Two shooters." He turned to Nate. "Get her around that hill to the cave. I'll divert their fire, then take them down as quick as I can. But be ready to move her out. We don't know how many of Morales' men heard those shots." Then he was gone.

"What the hell is he doing?" Rachel whispered.

"What he said." Nate was beside her now. "He has to know location before he goes after them. He's heading for those rocks."

And a moment later, Brandon fired a quick round from the rocks near the waterfall.

And was immediately answered by fire from the trees.

"Come on," Nate muttered. "You heard the man. We're out of here."

She paused. "You're leaving him?"

"Exactly. And so are you." He was crawling ahead of her. "Brandon wouldn't thank me for disobeying orders."

"He might if it meant it kept him from getting his head blown off," she muttered. "I'd think you'd want to—"

"I do," he said roughly. "Now shut up and let me do my job. No one knows better than Brandon how to take care of situations like this. He's an expert. He probably lost track of how many kills he had in Afghanistan. He'll do what he has to do. Move!"

She hesitated only for an instant before she started crawling after him, trying to ignore the shots coming from the trees that were aimed at those rocks. Nate knew Brandon's capabilities, and she did not, she told herself.

Yet it was clear Nate was worried and didn't like leaving Brandon. But then, you were always worried about your friends, weren't you? And she could sense that there was a bond that had nothing to do with the fact that Nate worked for Brandon.

"You'll be okay." Nate didn't look over his shoulder as his pace increased. "He said he'd get you out, and he'll do it. He keeps his word, Rachel."

But he had a reason for getting her out, she thought. Nate might believe he'd keep his promise, but she couldn't be sure of anything except what she had to do to keep her own word. So go ahead and try to ignore that gunfire behind her.

He'll do what he has to do.

That was also her father's mantra.

But people died, and there was pain and suffering connected to that mantra.

But this time, Maria might live because of it.

So accept it, accept the sound of those guns behind her, accept the knowledge of what it meant.

And just concentrate on getting to Maria.

"Now how the hell are we going to find that cave?" Nate was looking up at the side of the hill that appeared to be a solid, thick mass of shrubs and vegetation. "It looks like a jungle up there. You're sure this is the place?"

"It's the place." Rachel was trying to get her breath. "And that's the reason that Blanca chose it. Who'd be tempted to climb up there into a jungle?" She glanced at the trail behind her. "The shooting stopped over twenty minutes ago. Shouldn't Brandon be—" She stopped. Stupid question. How would Nate know what was happening with Jude Brandon and those men? If he wasn't uneasy, why should she be? Concentrate on Maria. "We're here, and that's ninety percent. Now all we have to do is find that cave."

But they didn't have to find the cave. Blanca Perez found them after they'd been climbing for only five minutes.

"I heard the shots." Blanca came running down the slope. "And then I saw you . . ." Tears were running down her cheeks. "I thought you weren't coming, Doctor. I thought you'd left her."

"I told you I'd be back. How is she?"

"I don't know. She woke up several times and smiled at me." She wiped her eyes and started back up the slope. "That's good, isn't it?"

"I hope it is." Rachel was running up the slope behind her. "This is Nate Scott, Blanca, he's going to help us."

Nate nodded. "And right now that help is going to be standing on guard and waiting for Brandon to show." He jerked his head at Rachel. "Take care of business. Brandon wants us out of here."

If Jude Brandon was even still alive.

But Nate didn't seem to doubt him, and she had to do what she'd come to do.

Three minutes later, she'd followed Blanca through a web of shrubs and ducked inside the cave.

Maria was lying on the stretcher, eyes closed.

"Maria," she said softly.

No answer.

Then the little girl's lids lifted and she smiled. "Doctor . . . Rachel . . ."

Almost instant response. Good.

"That's right. I'm glad to see you, Maria." She quickly checked her vitals. Weak, but steady . . .

Fever not gone, but down. Excellent.

Blanca was hovering behind her. "She drank water whenever I gave it to her during the night. We prayed together, and I told her that Saint Gabriel wanted her to stay with me and not go to heaven. She seemed to understand. She's better, yes?"

"I think so." Rachel took out the vial from her knapsack. She hoped so. And she was praying the final potion would make it certain. "Get ready to leave, Blanca. We'll have to go right away." She held Maria's head up and carefully gave her the medicine. "No liquid for fifteen minutes, Blanca." She brushed the hair back from Maria's forehead. "There we go," she whispered. "I've done my part, now you do yours."

"She'd better." Brandon was in the doorway of the cave. "We've all gone to a good deal of trouble for her." He came into the cave and looked down at the child for a long moment. "But I'd say she's worth it."

And Maria was looking up at him. "Saint . . . Gabriel?"

He blinked, then a smile lit his face. "Mistaken identity. But at least you didn't call me Lucifer. And you're nowhere near the gates of heaven. Your doctor wouldn't permit it." He turned away. "Are you done with her?"

"For now." That smile that had so startled Rachel

had vanished. It was the first time she'd seen him smile, and she doubted if she'd see it again anytime soon. She looked back at Maria. "It will be principally observation for the next several hours."

"Then let's get her out of here."

"Nate?"

"Watching the trail. I took down the two shooters, but there is no way we can go back the way we came. We'll go due north, and I'll have Monty bring the copter to us. The hills slope down to a plateau about three miles from here before it becomes rain forest again." He glanced at Maria. "Should you give her something to sedate her?"

"No, that's what we don't want," Rachel said. "She'll be fine. I *know* she'll be fine."

His lips indented at the corners. "Or you'll know the reason why?"

"I'm a doctor. It's my job to find out why and fight to change it." She was looking at the stretcher. "And I might not need Nate. Maria doesn't weigh very much. I could help with carrying the—"

"Forget it." He was already calling Nate on his phone. "I realize you probably think that you can move mountains, but we have to move fast. I want to be at that plateau within the hour."

They were at the plateau in just over that hour, but the helicopter wasn't there.

Rachel stopped short, her gaze shifting frantically

to Maria on the stretcher. The plateau had little vegetation for cover, and they were very vulnerable. No
place to hide Maria and Blanca if it became necessary.

Brandon answered her before she could ask, "The
helicopter will be here in a couple minutes. Don't
worry, Monty always knows what he's doing. I told
him not to take off before we had a chance to get here.
Morales will see it and zero in the minute it takes off."
Even as he spoke, she saw the large gray Apache helicopter lifting in the distance and turning to head for
the plateau.

"When I first saw it, I thought it looked like the military copters I saw in Afghanistan," she murmured.
"Are you sure you're not still in Special Forces?"

"As I said, that was a long time ago. But I didn't
know what I'd need here in Guyana. So I brought
enough manpower to make a difference."

"And you had to have suitable transport for them.
How many men, Brandon?"

"Twelve."

Her gaze flew to his face. "And you wouldn't accept
anyone who wasn't top-notch, would you? Do you usually have your own private army on hand?"

"No, but Nate and Monty know where to go when I
need them. Nate knows everything there is to know
about field operations, and Monty is practically a tech
genius. But this seemed to be one of those times when
I might need a little more firepower."

A small, tight army of highly skilled warriors. Like
the teams that her father had at his command when

needed. "Because you wanted to keep Huber from getting what he wanted. You definitely thought this would happen?"

"A strong possibility." He shook his head. "No, I was ninety-eight percent sure that I'd need those men. I just didn't know exactly who Huber would get to use against them." He glanced at her as the helicopter started to descend. "But I knew if you were here, that there was a chance that all hell would break loose. Venable made that clear."

"Yes, my father is always very clear." Her gaze never left the helicopter. "He weighs every problem and always makes certain that he makes the correct decision for the maximum number of people."

He tilted his head. "Do I detect bitterness?"

"No, I'm sure that clarity has saved lives throughout his career. I was just thinking that your military team was like the ones that my father could call on occasionally."

"But you don't approve?"

"You're wrong. I do approve in this case. It will be a big help." She glanced at him and braced herself. It probably wasn't the time but she couldn't wait any longer. "I told you that my agenda required that I take two things with me when I left here. You didn't ask me what else I wanted besides Maria."

"No, I didn't. I was a bit preoccupied with your patient," he said dryly. "But I had no doubt that you'd collect your pound of flesh. Are you going to break it to me now?"

She nodded. "I want you to drop Maria and Blanca

off in Georgetown." She moistened her lips. "And then I want you to go back and get Phillip Sanford. I won't let Morales kill him."

His lips twisted. "You just want me to skip into Morales' camp and pluck your learned colleague out of his hands?"

"Yes, Nate said no one was better than you at this kind of thing. Can you do it?"

"Probably. Morales certainly won't expect a surprise attack after he sees us leaving in the helicopter." He looked at her and slowly shook his head. "A pound of flesh, indeed, Rachel."

"Phillip's a good man. They might kill him."

"Or try to use him to get you."

"Will you do it?"

He was silent. "It might be to my advantage to get rid of a potential threat. But this particular agenda of yours is above and beyond."

The helicopter was descending, the wind was tearing at her hair, and blowing her shirt against her. "Will you do it?"

"Anything I want?" he repeated softly. "You'll do anything?"

She nodded jerkily. "I told you that before."

"But you've upped the stakes."

"I always knew Phillip had to be part of it."

"You just didn't let me know? Incredible."

She just looked at him.

"I suppose you won't insist on going along this time?"

She drew a relieved breath. He was going to do it.

"No, I have to be with Maria until I'm sure she's out of danger."

"Well that's a plus. But you don't mind me and my men being in danger?"

"I do mind. I *hate* it. But Phillip will be helpless with men like Morales. You know what you're doing."

"Yes I do." The helicopter was on the ground, and the door was opening. He motioned for the man in camouflage who jumped out to help Nate with the stretcher. "And you'll pay me in full for that knowledge, Rachel," he said quietly. "Count on it."

She stood there watching him move toward the helicopter before she could force herself to follow him.

Think about Maria. Think about Phillip.

And handle whatever Brandon had in store for her when they were both safe and well.

CHAPTER

3

GEORGETOWN HOSPITAL
GUYANA

The ambulance pulled up at the emergency-room entrance and Rachel jumped out of the passenger seat. She ran around the vehicle to where the EMTs were unloading Maria's stretcher. Brandon had just parked behind the ambulance and was getting out of the driver's seat and coming toward her.

"You didn't have to follow us," she said. "I can take it from here."

"And you will," Brandon said dryly. "I apparently have something else to do today. I just wanted to deliver you and Maria and make certain that you know that you don't leave the hospital until I get back here."

"I don't intend to leave Maria's side for the next four hours," she said as she watched Blanca hurrying after the stretcher as it was wheeled through the doors.

"You don't leave here until I get back," he repeated.

"I've had Nate call a couple of his contacts here, and there will be someone on guard since I can't spare either him or Monty. I don't believe Huber will know you're here, but you can never tell about the bastard. I'm not going to have you snatched away from me while I go and retrieve this doctor you have at the top of your agenda at the moment."

"I'm not planning on going anywhere. Anything that needs doing will have to be done by phone. I need to call One World headquarters and tell them about Nancy and Bill if they don't know already." Everything had been moving so quickly since she'd seen that helicopter blown out of the night sky that it seemed impossible that everyone in the world wouldn't know what had happened at Nalez. Yet it was only the middle of the afternoon, and in the chaos that always followed terrorist events, nothing might be clear to anyone. "Will you call me when you get Phillip away from them?"

"Probably not. I don't want anyone to know where you are in case Morales is tech savvy enough to trace my calls."

"I don't think he would be. You're very careful."

"I've been stung." He turned to leave. "Good luck with the little girl. She seems to be on the mend . . . except for her exceptional bad judgment pertaining to me."

Before she could reply, he was back in the rental car and driving past the ambulance toward the street.

He hadn't given her the opportunity to wish him good luck, she thought, even though she was the one who had sent him into harm's way. But he probably thought he didn't need luck as long as he had that cool competence evident in every motion.

But she would have liked to have said . . . something.

Maria.

He was dealing with Phillip Sanford, but she still had Maria to worry about. She turned and strode through the emergency-room entrance to see to what room Maria had been assigned.

7:40 P.M.

"The fever's almost gone, Blanca. Temperature close to normal." Rachel turned away from Maria, a brilliant smile lighting her face. "She's not entirely out of the woods. We're running blood tests and checking the exact status of the virus in her—" She broke off as Blanca launched herself into her arms and enveloped her in a tremendous bear hug that took her breath away.

"She's going to get *well*." Blanca's face was glowing as she released Rachel and whirled toward Maria. "You're being careful not to promise me anything— But she's going to get well, isn't she?"

To hell with not raising hopes. "I think the chances are excellent that Maria will be out of this hospital in a week or so."

Blanca's eyes were shining with joy. "I prayed and prayed, and you did it."

"No, *you* did it, remember?" She gently grasped her shoulders. Gratitude could be very dangerous particularly in these first exuberant moments. "I just used the usual medicines recommended by the CDC. You were afraid they weren't working, and without telling me, you gave Maria an herbal medicine passed down through your family by your great-grandmother."

"I'll remember." Blanca went back into her arms. "I promised you. And if someone asks me if I have any more, I give them that little wooden pot with the green stuff you gave me. Right?"

"Right." And the CDC might well ask her. They were desperate for a cure for Taran, and they were not averse to looking at any source to find it. They'd examine and test it exhaustively, and in a year, they might start using it themselves when there was another outbreak. "And that way Maria might help other children. But only if it comes through you, Blanca."

"Crazy . . ." Blanca smiled. "But then, so is a tiny mosquito that can kill my little girl." She stepped back and turned back to Maria. "Will they let me stay with her tonight?"

"Yes, and I'll look in now and then to make sure that she's still doing fine. I'll be in the doctor's lounge down the hall if you need me."

"Thank you." Blanca had already sat back down and was reaching for Maria's hand. "A thousand thanks, Dr. Rachel. God must have sent you . . ."

"I don't know about that, but I'm sure he did send that medicine to Maria if it cured her." She headed for the door. "I'll have a nurse bring you something to eat . . ."

She stopped outside the door and drew a deep breath of relief and gratitude. She'd had no choice but to try that formula when nothing else was working, but it could have been a disaster. She'd tried other variations on yellow fever before, but this was an entirely new virus. But it had done what was needed and dealt with the virus while lowering the fever.

And Maria Perez was on her way back now.

But what about Phillip Sanford?

She was afraid to think about him right now. It was probably too early to expect anything from Jude Brandon. It might be hours before she heard if Brandon had been able to get Phillip away from Morales' men. But there was no way she would not be on edge for every one of those hours.

She had reached the lounge, and she sat down and retrieved her phone. But she had made a promise, and now she needed to keep it.

Hu Chang answered the phone after three rings. "I understand the rumbles turned into something more substantial. Catherine was very concerned when she heard that the One World camp had been targeted. You might have phoned and let me know that you were all right."

"I was a little busy. And I was sure that after everything blew up, Catherine would pull every string until she knew more than I did about what was going on."

"Yes, but there's nothing like firsthand information.

Such as if you'd survived. A small bit of knowledge, but I find it remarkably important in the scheme of things." His tone was silky soft, but that still did not hide the sharpness. "Since one of the pieces of information Catherine gathered was that *you* were being specifically targeted."

She didn't know how Catherine had managed to squeeze that intel out of the chaos, but she could tell that Hu Chang was more than annoyed that she hadn't contacted him. "I'm still alive and at a hospital in Georgetown. But Bill Pallis and Nancy Kavitz are dead, and Phillip Sanford is being held prisoner. As I said, I was busy."

Silence. "I regret to hear that your friends are dead. You're at a hospital? How have you been injured?"

"Not me. I had to come with Maria to have the final tests." She paused. "The potion worked, Hu Chang. She's going to live. I promised I'd let you know."

"I'm glad you regarded something as important enough to call," he said dryly. "Not that I don't agree that's a great victory for the child . . . and for you. You protected yourself?"

"Native medicine passed on by family. Most of the time I wouldn't have had to do that, I'd just send in an anonymous formula and hope someone at the CDC would do something with it. But Taran is high-profile and dangerous right now. I wanted the CDC to take a close look at it." She leaned back wearily in the chair. "Anyway, Maria is safe now. That's the only good thing that's happened in the last twenty-four hours."

"Happy news indeed. And now shall we get back

to tidings not at all happy. Are you going to tell me why you were targeted?"

"Max Huber."

Silence. "Unfortunate. He sent Morales' group after you?"

"That's what I was told by Jude Brandon."

"Brandon?" he murmured. "I've heard of him."

"And he's heard of you," she said. "But I'm more interested in what you know about him."

"Later. Why did Huber send Morales after you?"

"I think that we can both guess why. He wants me dead. I committed the ultimate sin as far as he's concerned. You told me once that he'd find out what I'd done. It was only a matter of time."

"Venable had over four years to find a way to dispense with Huber so that there would be no danger of him finding out you were involved. I was hoping that Venable would be able to protect you."

"Well, Max Huber is still alive, and his organization appears to be flourishing. But somehow he must have found out what I did to him four years ago." She was trying to think how that had occurred. "Four years, Hu Chang. And my father swore that no one knew I was involved. Yet all of a sudden, I'm responsible for the deaths of two of my team who only wished to help people and save lives. They wouldn't have died if Huber hadn't sent Morales after me." She added, "My father would call that collateral damage, but they were good lives wasted, and they were my friends."

"Venable is not as harsh as you make him out to be,"

he said quietly. "He's a hard man, doing a hard job, but he has his moments of softness."

"Which exist only as long as they don't interfere with the greater public good." She said wearily, "But maybe he did try to warn me or get me away from Huber. He sent Jude Brandon, who managed to take me out of Nalez and bring me here to Georgetown. But it's not going to be a free gift. Brandon made that clear."

"Then may I suggest you have your father pay him. You were only an instrument in the Huber matter."

"I wasn't an instrument, I was a fool. And fools have to pay for their mistakes. You taught me that, Hu Chang."

"True. But I find I'm not willing for you to pay for this particular mistake. Nor do I think it's wise to make you have to hide away from that unpleasant barbarian. So I believe I might have to make the effort· to set things right."

"No," she said firmly. "I'll take care of it. You don't step in and try to take charge. I just have to figure out what to do."

"I never try. I always accomplish." He paused. "But I will allow you to go your way for the time being. What do you need from me?"

"Jude Brandon. All I know is that he knows my father, they both hate Max Huber, and he was once in Special Forces."

"He knows why Huber wants you?"

"I don't believe he does. He just knows I might be of value to him. Maybe my father didn't trust him enough to confide in him."

"Quite possible. Your father doesn't trust many people. But he trusted him enough to send him to take you away from Huber. That has some significance."

"I don't want analysis, I want fact and background."

"I'm getting there, Rachel. Our paths crossed, but we did not have any explosive interaction, so I had no reason to delve deep. I know he owns shipyards in Hong Kong and several other cities around the world. The businesses are legitimate, but the money that built them probably was not. His father was well-known as a skilled smuggler and master thief during most of his long career on the high seas. I understand before Brandon came back from the service, his father had purchased the first shipyard and needed his help in keeping it safe from the Chinese triads who were trying to move in on the business. Brandon did the task so splendidly that his reputation attracted my attention. He's very formidable, Rachel."

"I know that. Did he attract my father's attention as well?"

"I have no idea. As I said, he did not get in my way, and I had no reason for close observation. As far as I know, he had no dealings with Huber or any other terrorist that would have aroused Venable's interest. It could be true that they were allies against Huber."

"And that's all you know?"

"At present. Now that I know you're interested, I will endeavor to learn more. In the meantime, Catherine asked me to bring you to her. Even before she knew about Huber, she didn't like what was going on. She said that she's uneasy. She would have gone down there herself, but she was called to a top CIA meeting in San Francisco by Operative Officer in Charge, Claire Warren."

"They think Huber may be planning something?"

"Catherine has no way of knowing until she gets to that meeting. She only knows that Claire Warren is usually in charge of antiterrorist projects and worked with your father on several assignments. She just doesn't want you to be where she can't reach you if she's caught up in something."

"But I appear to be caught up in something as well," Rachel said. But it was good to know that she had Catherine and Hu Chang in the background waiting to help. "I made a deal with Brandon. High stakes. If he comes through for me, I have to come through for him. I made a promise."

"I do not like the sound of that."

"The only thing that would stop me is if he belonged to Max Huber. You said that you didn't think he did."

"I don't think he belongs to anyone but himself, but that does not make anything he does less dangerous. Ask those men in the triads who went up against him in Hong Kong."

"Tell Catherine I'll call her if I need her help. You'll let me know if you find out anything disturbing about Brandon?"

"Yes." He paused. "Catherine is not the only one uneasy, Rachel. You *will* keep in touch with me." He cut the connection.

And that last sentence had been as full of power and dominance as any words he had ever spoken to her, she thought as she hung up. Hu Chang was too clever to insert any element that would make her wary of him. He preferred to play on the love she felt for him and the respect that was always there. It was a sign of his concern that he'd decided to pull out the big guns.

And they'd had the desired effect in that they'd reminded her of both how much she owed him and the strength and power he'd exerted all those years ago to heal her. Though she'd been too defiant and caught up in the hideous nightmare to admit she was broken.

But Hu Chang had known. He knew all about pain and nightmares and how to stop them from happening. She had realized that almost from the moment he had walked into her cell at that Taliban prison in the mountains of Afghanistan . . .

SAZKAR PRISON

LOGAR PROVINCE

AFGHANISTAN

They were coming again.

Rachel tensed as she heard the footsteps coming down the hall.

Two of them. At least two men.

Don't scream. Don't cry.

They liked her to do that.

Don't give them anything that was part of who she was.

They were unlocking the door.

She instinctively cringed back against the wall.

That was wrong. They also liked the fear.

Only one man came into the cell.

He was different. Asian descent. Dark hair pulled back from his face. Black tunic.

He stood there gazing at her, not moving from the doorway. "How do you do, Rachel. My name is Hu Chang. I am not here to hurt you. May I come closer, so I don't have to have the guard outside hear us talking? I find him most unpleasant. I'm sure you do, also."

She stared at him in bewilderment.

"I will take that as permission." He moved toward her.

She stiffened, freezing against the wall.

He instantly stopped. "No? Well, this is close enough." He dropped gracefully to the floor and crossed his legs tailor-fashion. "Let me get the important things that concern you out of the way. I do not belong to the Taliban or any group affiliated with them. I am here to help you get out of here and return to your father. I understand Venable has not been allowed to come and see you, and I'm sure you find that distressing. The Taliban had issues with your father being the one attempting to free you since he was both CIA and had a personal involvement. Therefore, they proved stubborn and difficult. That's why I am here. You will find me very helpful. I was asked by a member of the Afghanistan government to do this since there has been no agreement between the State Department and the Taliban regarding your release. I have a certain influence in both camps." He paused.

"I understand it has been over five months since you were brought here."

She didn't answer. She was too stunned and dazed to fully comprehend what he was saying. Was it a trick? A joke to raise her hopes, then dash them? In the early days, they had done that before they had become angry and more vindictive.

"It's true, Rachel," Hu Chang said quietly. "I will prove it to you over the next weeks because it will probably take that long for me to be able to get you free of these people. But I need to know a few things about your captivity so that I can intercede and make you more comfortable here while I negotiate your release. Will you talk to me?"

She didn't answer.

"You don't trust me? I can see why you would have problems." He was silent, then said gently, "You're only fifteen years old, and your life is suddenly a cruel place. I regret that it happened, but I will not pity you. I can see by looking at you that you would not welcome it. You've realized that the only way to control the pain is to become stronger with every episode that hurts you. I learned the same lesson when I was close to your own age." He smiled. "So until you can trust me, may I suggest that you listen and choose to answer only the questions that you believe won't hurt you if I should be stupid enough to betray you? Does that sound reasonable?"

It did sound reasonable. It could still be a trick, but what if it wasn't? What if there was hope? She swallowed hard. "Yes."

"I will start with something that I know would cause you pain if they used it." His face was without expression. "The ambush."

She felt a ripple of shock. She had not been expecting that.

"You were driving to a village outside Kabul where your mother did charity work with an orphanage. Your car was ambushed by the Taliban, your car disabled by an IED, and then your party attacked. Your mother, your younger brother, and the four soldiers accompanying you were killed. You were not killed because they needed a hostage to bargain for Taliban prisoners being held by your father. Is that correct?"

The words were spoken almost completely without emotion. In a way, she was almost glad that was the case because she was able to keep the memory at a distance since it was as if the experience belonged to someone else. "Yes," she said jerkily. "You must know all that if you are who you say you are. And I don't want to talk about it."

"Nor shall we. I just have one question before we go on to something else."

She glared at him. "Then ask it."

"Did your captors mention your mother's and brother's deaths while you were here?"

She was silent. Bullet-ridden bodies. Her brother Kevin, with no face. "Yes," she said hoarsely. "Pictures. They had pictures . . . of how they looked . . . that they showed me every now and then." The memory was suddenly too close, smothering her. "No more," she said fiercely. "I won't talk about it."

"Not now. But we'll have to talk about it later. But not until you're ready."

"I'll never be ready."

"Yes you will, but perhaps not for a long time." Then he was gazing at her appraisingly. "You're very thin. Do they feed you well?"

She nodded.

"No, tell me."

"Twice a day." She added defiantly, "And it tastes like slop."

His lips indented at the corners. "I don't promise to improve the quality as long as there is quantity. Water?"

"Once a day."

"Accommodations for bathing or showering?"

"No."

"You hesitated there. Would you like to tell me why?"

She didn't speak.

"Very well, let's go on. Have you been subjected to torture while you've been here?"

"Not lately."

"When?"

"The second month I was here. They were angry that they weren't getting the prisoner exchange they wanted from my father."

"What form of torture?"

"The whip. Almost always the whip. They broke my hand once, but they set it right away. Properly applied, a whip doesn't leave marks unless it breaks the skin."

"And that was important?"

"Of course it was important," she said impatiently. "They didn't want any proof of mistreatment. It would have been grounds to break off the talks."

"Are they still doing it?"

"No, not after I learned not to show the pain." She met his eyes. "Not after I learned that was the way to cheat them."

He nodded slowly. "That was very clever of you. But I'm sure there was a substitution." He was silent, his gaze holding her own. "Let us talk about the bathing accommodations again."

"You said I didn't have to talk about anything that—" She suddenly exploded, "But you still want to hear about it? I'll tell you. You can't hurt me. None of you can hurt me." Her eyes were blazing into his own. "At the end of every week that my father refused their terms, the guards were given a night to rape me. But I was so disgusting and dirty that they'd take me down the hall to the shower to make me worthy of their attention. Because if you're careful, rape doesn't leave marks either." She was breathing hard, her heart pounding. "But that didn't matter, none of it mattered. I just had to be sure I didn't let what they did make me the helpless animal they wanted to make me. I didn't let them hurt me. I'll never let that happen." She was shaking. She had to stop. Never show weakness. "Is that what you wanted to know, Hu Chang?"

"It is what I needed to know," he said quietly. "Is there anything else you would like to tell me so that I can ease your time here from now on?"

She shook her head. She wouldn't have been able to answer if she'd tried.

He nodded. "Very well. So here is what will happen in the next weeks. Your food will not be good, but perhaps not slop. You will have unlimited water. There will be no torture, no matter how frustrating I prove to your captors." He paused. "You will be taken to the shower once a day and left there for thirty minutes, then escorted back to your cell. Your guards will have to meet with my approval, and no one will touch you again. Do you believe me?"

She shook her head.

"Then I will clearly have to prove myself to you. It will be no problem. I'm an exceptional human being, as you will soon find out." He rose to his feet with one fluid movement. "Two things you should know about what we're going to be together as we go forward. One, I will never betray you. Two, I expect you to always be everything you can be. I will accept nothing less." He moved toward the door. "And you're wrong, Rachel. You have been hurt, but I didn't tell you I'm also a magnificent physician who can show you the way to heal yourself. Are you not lucky to have me in your life? You'll find my arrival far outbalances all the terrible things that have happened to you in this place." He knocked on the door to indicate to the guard he was ready to leave. "We'll spend many hours together in this cell so that you can learn to appreciate me. I will bring fine books so that your mind can leave these bars behind. According to the report I have

on you, you're quite brilliant and curious. We have that in common, and I've decided that I have need of someone of your strength and endurance in my life." He met her eyes. *"So it's a foregone conclusion that we will be the best of friends, Rachel. Think about that instead of the trials that you were given to make you strong enough to vanquish all the forces that challenge you."* The door was opening. *"Good day. I will see you tomorrow, and we will talk more."* He suddenly chuckled. *"And perhaps I will let you talk without answering questions then. It just seemed wise to impress you with your change of circumstances and my own inimitable character."*

"Wait." She moistened her lips. *"Is it true? You're not lying?"*

He shook his head. *"That would violate the first rule of our friendship. I will never betray you."* He glanced at the guard. *"And you might say farewell to this man. He does not please me. You will have someone else by the end of the day."* He turned and left the cell.

The door swung closed behind him.

She was still shaking, she realized. Was the nightmare almost over? No, she must not get her hopes up. Nightmares couldn't just be banished by one man who walked into this cell and told her everything she wanted to hear. Safety. Comfort. Freedom.

And one more thing, the knowledge that she was right about not being destroyed by these last months. That she could take something away that was far more valuable than what had been done to her.

Together with the knowledge that she was not alone.

"It's a foregone conclusion that we will be the best of friends, Rachel."

Hu Chang had said those words, and in that moment, she had believed him.

Not that she could trust that to be true yet.

But she found herself thinking that perhaps it might be true. He had said he would see her tomorrow.

And maybe she'd know tomorrow if it was true . . .

The best of friends.

Yes, that was what they were today, what they had started to build on that foundation all those years ago, Rachel thought as she stared at the soft green walls of the lounge. He had kept his promise never to betray her. She hoped she had never shown him less than being the very best she could be.

No, that wasn't true. She had been a fool and certainly not her best when she'd made that hideous mistake with Huber four years ago.

But perhaps she could find a way to correct that mistake if Brandon gave her a way to do it.

She was too tired to think about it now. She would try to sit here and wait until Brandon let her know what had happened with Phillip. She leaned her head against the wall next to her and closed her eyes. She would rest just a little while, then go check on Maria again.

Maria who was young and had her whole life in front of her now . . .

*   *   *

"Wake up, Rachel."

It was Brandon, she realized vaguely, and his voice was sharp with displeasure. Well that was no surprise. It was how he'd spoken to her since the moment he'd erupted into her life. Except that moment when he'd looked down at Maria and smiled . . .

"Rachel!"

His hand was on her shoulder.

Her lids flew open, and she looked up at him. It was all zooming toward her out of the fog of sleep. Brandon had come back. He was frowning. That was bad, wasn't it? "Phillip?"

He didn't answer. "It's difficult to have my people guard you when you decide to sleep here in the lounge instead of staying in the room with Maria. Anyone could have given you an injection and whisked you out of the—"

"Phillip?" She grabbed his arm. "Did you get Phillip?"

"Yes." He pulled her to her feet. "He's down in ER being patched up. They should be nearly finished with him. I stayed with him until I was sure there was no internal damage, and then I came after you." His tone was biting. "First, I went to Maria Perez's room, where you should have been, and Blanca said that she hadn't seen you for hours. So I started looking for you."

Hours? She looked at her watch. 1:40 A.M. It *had* been hours. "I just closed my eyes for a moment. I was waiting to hear from you after I knew Maria was going to be— You could have called me."

"He passed out from blood loss in the helicopter on the way here. I needed to make certain I was turning over a negotiable product to you."

"But he's okay?" Her gaze flew to his face. "You're sure?"

"The EMTs in the ambulance had his blood type ready for a transfusion when the copter landed. That appears to have taken care of the problem." His lips twisted. "But I assume you're going to want to go down and see for yourself?"

"Yes." She was already heading for the elevator. "None of your men were hurt?"

His brows rose. "I'm surprised you're inquiring."

"Of course I want to know." Her finger stabbed the elevator button. "I sent those men out there. I was the one responsible. Anyone hurt or killed is my guilt." She glanced at him as she entered the elevator. "I'm not like you or my father and think that because someone is paid to take risks, it's all right to send them out to do it."

"Then you'll be glad to know that you're almost guilt-free." He said as he followed her onto the elevator and pushed the button. "There were a few minor injuries on our side, but nothing that should cause you sleepless nights. However, I can't promise you the same for Morales' men. I didn't stop to get any body counts when we raided the camp and took Sanford. Would you like me to go back and do it? Perhaps you'd like to take a One World team and set up a hospital area to—"

"Oh, shut up. Maybe I did sound . . ." There was no

maybe about it. She'd sounded smug and opinionated and heaven knows what else. It was clear that they didn't think anything alike, but she'd had no right to accuse him of being callous after what he'd just done. "Thank you for saving Phillip. He's worth saving."

He gazed at her speculatively. "Professionally or personally? I've been wondering about where all that passion came from."

She blinked. "You think we were lovers?"

"Perhaps."

"No, we're friends and colleagues." She looked at him. "And I know how prisoners can be treated. Even if they didn't kill him, there could be scars that might not heal."

His eyes narrowed. "Like your scars?"

"No, but then I had Hu Chang." The doors opened, and she moved out of the elevator toward the ER. "Not many people are that lucky. It would be better if he didn't have to go through it. He should be—"

The ER door had swung open, and a nurse was pushing Phillip out in a wheelchair.

"Phillip!" She ran forward and bent down to hug him. "I'm so glad to see you," she whispered. She straightened and looked down at his face. Pale, dark circles beneath his eyes, a bruise on his left cheek. But he was smiling unsteadily at her. "How bad?"

"What you see is what you get." He nodded at his extended right leg. "The bastards weren't gentle, but they didn't do much more than threaten. They were too busy running around trying to find you." He glanced at Brandon and grinned. "And *he* wasn't gentle either when he was jerking me out of there, but I suppose I have to forgive him. How is your arm?"

"Okay," Brandon said. "No thanks to you. What good does it do to have a doctor on board if all he does is pass out on you?"

"My apologies." Phillip turned back to Rachel, and his smile vanished. "Morales wanted you very badly. Why?"

"I'm not certain. Past history. I'm just sorry that you all became involved. I never expected that to happen. You know that Bill and Nancy are dead?"

"I watched it happen. It was so fast . . ." His hand tightened on her own. "I was glad you weren't there, Rachel. I thought any minute, I'd hear that you'd been found."

The nurse took a step forward. "I have orders to take Dr. Sanford to his room," she said pointedly.

"Please. One more moment," Rachel said. "I talked to One World earlier this evening, and they're going to take care of funeral arrangements. I may not be able to go to the services. Tell their families that I'll call them later." She looked at his leg. "You may not be able to go either."

"I'll be there." He made a face. "Though it might help if I had access to a wonderful miracle elixir to make it heal faster. I don't suppose there's any of that around?"

"No, there isn't." She gave him another hug. "A terrific doctor like you should know that miracles are few and far between." She nodded at the nurse as she stepped back. "But before you know it, you'll be back on your feet and One World will be assigning you a new team to go to the Sudan."

"Then I'll request you, Rachel. You'll be first on my list." He was looking back over his shoulder as the nurse wheeled him down the corridor. "Take only temporary assignments until they give me my new team."

"I might be busy for a while. That's why I can't attend those funerals. I have a few things to straighten out."

"Really? Now that arouses my curiosity." He paused. "How is Maria doing?"

"Very well. You might visit her while you're here in the hospital. I'd like you to keep an eye on her."

"My pleasure." He turned around. "I'm a lousy patient. It will be good to keep busy . . ."

She watched him being wheeled toward the elevator before she turned back to Brandon. "You didn't tell me that you're one of the men who was hurt tonight."

"It was only a flesh wound. And after all that emotional, heartfelt speech about guilt and responsibility, I didn't want you to be weeping all over me."

"I would have restrained myself," she said dryly. "You're an exception, Brandon."

He nodded. "Yes, I am. Absolutely." He gazed at her for a moment. "I'm beginning to think that you might be one as well. I gather from the gist of those last words to Sanford that you're not going to try to break your word to me?"

She shook her head. "I said 'anything.' You gave me Maria. You gave me Phillip. I don't care as much about keeping my word to you as I do about keeping it to myself. I'd know if I broke my word, it would damage who I am." She met his eyes. "So tell me what you want me to do. Do you want to use me as bait? That would make sense."

"Yes, wouldn't it? I'll think about it." He took her elbow. "But right now I think I have to get you out of Guyana before Huber finds out where you are and sends in reinforcements. We'll talk about ways and means on the trip."

"I have to go back and say good-bye to Maria and Blanca. Then I have to speak to the resident doctor and tell him that Phillip will be in charge of any future treatment. I'll meet you at the front entrance." She saw his expression and translated it immediately. "Do you think I'm going to run out on you?"

"The thought occurred to me. I told Nate that I thought you were like Venable. Neither Venable nor I would hesitate to slip away if it suited our purpose."

"Then come with me," she said impatiently. "But I'm not my father. I've fought all my life to not be what he is. We don't go by the same rules. The one time I thought we understood each other, he nearly destroyed me. So you'll forgive me if I don't appreciate being compared to him." She turned on her heel and strode away from him toward the elevator. She didn't look back until she was on the elevator and pushing the UP button.

He was still standing where she'd left him and as the door started to close, he slowly nodded.

And what did that mean? That he trusted her? That

he understood? She just didn't know. He was too complicated for her to make any firm judgments. Maybe before this was over, she'd be able to understand him.

Providing they both stayed alive.

CHAPTER

4

What are we doing here?" Rachel was frowning as she got out of the rental car and looked at the dozens of boats moored at the dock of the harbor. "I thought we'd be going to the airport."

He shook his head as he moved toward a sleek, large white cruiser. "Nate's going to take the copter to Miami and await instructions there. By now, Huber will know who attacked Morales' camp and what kind of aircraft. If you're not seen getting on that helicopter, he'll have to scramble to find out how you left here." He lifted her aboard the ship. "He'll make the connection soon enough. He knows I grew up on a boat. But it will give us time enough to get as far as Trinidad, where we can get a jet out for New Orleans or Atlanta." He started the engine. "Sit down. Unless you know enough about boats to help instead of hinder."

She shook her head. "I know how to drive a small speedboat but nothing this big." She sat down and watched him. He knew exactly what he was doing, every movement had purpose and efficiency. They were out of the harbor and on open water in no time.

Moonlight.

Dark water.

She watched Brandon moving, his hands almost sensual, caressing the wheel with complete knowledge, his eyes on the sea ahead of him. The lines of his body were clean and strong, she thought, and there was a rhythm about the way he stood, balancing against the thrust and power of the boat. It was almost sexual, she thought absently. The thought was immediately followed by a clenching in her own body that was as swift as it was surprising.

Where had that come from? Out of the blue certainly. Probably a relief from the physical stress she'd been undergoing for the last twenty-four hours. Sexual desire often followed intense fear and activity. And face it, Brandon was sexually attractive with that lean stillness and—

She was overanalyzing. Hu Chang had told her never to do that. Just accept that it had happened and forget about it. It was all part of the healing.

The boat was throbbing, spraying water as it cleaved the surf.

Fast.

They were going very fast, skimming the waves.

Why did the pace seem so soothing?

"You do this very well," she said. "I knew you must

know a lot about boats, but I didn't know you grew up on them."

He glanced at her. "How did you know I knew anything at all about— Ah, the wonderful savant, Hu Chang. You've been making inquiries?"

"You could have been anyone. I had to find out more. He didn't know much. He said that your father had been a thief and a smuggler and something about some shipyards. He'll know more the next time I talk to him."

"But maybe not what you want to know." He smiled. "I told you I wouldn't keep secrets from you. Though there have been things I decided it would be better to wait to tell you. You have questions. Ask me. You're very sharp, you might be able to tell if I'm lying."

"And I might not." But she would try anyway, she decided suddenly. Because this seemed a completely different Jude Brandon. There was a recklessness about him that intrigued her. It would probably be wise to know this facet if she had to deal with him. "Why did you grow up on a boat? It seems an odd place to raise a child."

"I didn't think so." He shrugged. "Maybe for some kids. I thought it was perfect. There was just my dad and me. My mother decided that she wasn't cut out to be maternal and tossed me to my dad when I was six. I was probably lucky she waited that long, I wasn't easy even at that age. But my dad gave her a hefty child-support check so she put up with me. To her surprise, he took me to raise and didn't leave me at the nearest orphanage, which meant he fed me, clothed me, then let me run wild. When we weren't sailing, we skipped from country to country from Greece to South Africa where my dad had 'business.' As long as I didn't get arrested or put him in a spot where he was forced to face down the local Mafioso, I did what I wanted. Most of which you would have thoroughly disapproved of." He added, "And then when we were back on the boat, he taught me chess, how to count cards, and told me stories about his life that were mostly lies but had great entertainment value."

"Schooling?"

"Computers. Another way to keep me from getting bored. He didn't have any trouble getting me to do lessons. I'm curious . . . and competitive. I had to find ways to be just that little bit better than what I was offered in those courses."

Probably quite a bit better, she thought. She could suddenly see that wild little boy living life to the limit, loving every minute of it. Yet it was a completely different picture than the highly disciplined, lethal man she knew him to be now.

"No more questions?"

"You must have changed . . ."

"Not voluntarily. I would have probably still been out there doing what I did best, which was getting into devilment. But my dad had a sudden crisis of conscience when I was seventeen and decided to take me away from my wicked ways. It shocked both of us. But he said that one brilliantly crooked Brandon in the family was enough and that he didn't intend to spend his old age thinking of ways to break me out of a jail cell in Morocco. He said he wanted me to join the Army so that I'd receive a little of the self-discipline he'd never been tempted to teach me."

"It certainly appears to have been very successful. But I'm surprised that you let him persuade you to do it."

"I would have done anything he wanted me to do," he said quietly. "I fought him, but it was a foregone conclusion. I loved him. He was the only person who had ever cared a damn about me. I wasn't going to throw that away." He smiled faintly. "That doesn't mean that *after* I joined the Army I didn't try to place myself in a position where I could run things. But I was careful not to cross the line until I found my niche."

"Special Forces."

He nodded. "My dad was very pleased, he could see I was changing in spite of myself. But he knew that he had to be ready when I became restless and broke free. That didn't happen until after I'd had a few tours in Afghanistan. It was a challenge . . ." He looked back at the water. "But he was ready when I was. He'd saved enough money to buy a shipyard in Hong Kong, and he sent me the partnership papers. Along with a note saying that there might be a few problems involved."

"Hu Chang mentioned a Chinese triad."

"I'm not surprised he'd heard about that. It earned me a certain amount of notoriety, but it also served to keep the wolves at bay."

And Brandon had already learned how to handle the wolves both in his childhood and the battlefield. "You said your father had been a thief and smuggler all his life. Yet suddenly he decided to go straight and become a legitimate businessman? Why?"

"A perceptive and clever woman like you shouldn't have to ask that question." He glanced back at her. "Or maybe you should, judging by a few cynical comments about Venable you've made here and there. But the answer is easy enough." He added simply, "My father loved me and wanted what he thought best for me. During those years after we started the shipyards, I knew there were times when he wanted to just hop on one of those boats and go back to the old life. Hell, *I* wanted it. But he never took that step. So I didn't, either."

He was right, she had never had that kind of closeness with her father. As a child, she had adored him, but he had seldom been there after she was ten or eleven, and later . . . life had interfered. She had been close to her mother, but she had always been busy raising three children, doing charity work, and dealing with a husband who was moving around the world trying to keep it from blowing up. Yes, her life had been completely different from Brandon's. There had been rules and expectations and the knowledge of what her future would probably bring. All that had changed on that day in the desert outside Kabul. She had learned that any rules and expectations were only what she brought to the table.

And that in the end she was alone.

Until Hu Chang had walked into that cell.

Brandon tilted his head. "You see? I've virtually bared my soul to you. Anything more?"

"I'm sure there is considerably more." She had an idea that she had barely scratched the surface of Jude Brandon. There were so many fathoms of emotions and complications and experiences that had comprised the life he had revealed to her. "But right now I'd like to know why you decided to 'bare' your soul. I find it unusual. What's behind it?"

"A gesture to get your trust?"

She shook her head.

"Actually that was partially true." He put the boat on auto and turned toward her. In the space of seconds his demeanor had changed, and his expression was grim. "The other is that I have an occasional problem with breaking unpleasant news. I discovered that when I had to talk to the parents of my men who had been killed in action. I thought I'd toughened up where that was concerned, but I think I'm going to have trouble dealing with you."

She stiffened. "Are you going somewhere with this?"

"Not very quickly or efficiently. I'm just telling you it helps me to think I'm giving something when I take something away." His lips twisted. "And it's always difficult for me to talk about my life with my dad. Maybe someday it won't be, but that's not yet."

She didn't like where this was going. She moistened her lips. "And what do you think you're taking away from me, Brandon?"

He was silent. Then the next words came quietly.

"Carl Venable died the day before I came to Guyana to get you, Rachel."

Shock. She jerked as if struck.

At first she couldn't speak, she couldn't breathe.

"No!"

"He's dead," Brandon said quietly. "I wouldn't lie to you, Rachel. He was shot in the chest. I watched him die."

She shook her head violently. "It's not true. It didn't happen. It's some kind of mistake." Her voice was shaking. "Or it's some part of your damn agenda. But you don't have tell me that to make me do what you want. I told you that I'd do whatever you—"

"Stop it!" He was suddenly on his knees beside her, his hands grasping her shoulders. "Shit, I didn't know it was going to be this bad." He was shaking her. "But I can't take it. It's not a lie or a mistake. So believe me, dammit."

"But it has to be—" But what if it wasn't? People died, even her father could die. But it shouldn't have happened. Not Carl Venable. She had to tell Brandon that. His blue eyes were blazing, and his face was twisted as if with pain. He should know so that pain could go away. "It can't be true. So how can I believe you?"

His hands were suddenly cupping her cheeks and he stared down into her eyes. "I was *there*. I couldn't stop it. Believe me."

And then she did believe him.

Gone. Emptiness. Nothingness. She felt as if everything inside her was splitting, cracking, twisting. She wanted to scream, but there was only that terrible silence inside her.

And he saw it and suddenly her face was pressed against his chest. "Don't you let it hurt you," he said fiercely. "You're strong. I've seen you go through so damn much. I was hoping you didn't really care for him. But you do, don't you?"

"I don't want it to mean anything," she said dully. "I hoped I was over him, that I could shut out what he was to me. All the pain and the love and the sadness." How strange it was to be held and comforted by this man who was every bit as hard as her father, saying words she had never said to anyone. "But if I feel like this, then it wasn't over. We weren't through with each other. And now we never will be."

"Shh." His hand was on the back of her head. "It can be whatever you want it to be. You can do anything. Didn't you save Maria? Didn't you bulldoze me into going to get Sanford? All in twenty-four hours. You can work anything out."

"This is . . . different. Do you know, I never thought of him dying? He was always too smart, too strong, always a step ahead of everyone." Her voice was muffled. "Ahead of me. Because I wanted so badly to believe in him, to trust him. No matter what he did, I wanted to think that I was important to him, that he'd never want me to be hurt."

"Maybe you were right," he said hoarsely. "He sent me to you."

"And then Bill and Nancy died . . ." She could feel the tears stinging her eyes. She had to stop this. He had said she was strong, but she did not feel strong. She was about to fall apart, and she did not want it to be in front of him. He was a stranger who suddenly was not a stranger. That made her even more vulnerable to him.

She straightened and pushed him away. "I'm sorry," she said unsteadily. "My father and I did have . . . problems. In the past years it's been . . . like a roller coaster. But all I can think of right now is the time when I was a very little girl and he was stationed at Langley. Isn't that silly? I couldn't have been more than six or seven. But he was busy and important and everything was exciting when he was around. Sometimes people would come to visit him at the house, and I could see they also felt it. And there were times when he'd stop what he was doing and he'd smile at me and I'd know—" She had to get away from here before those damn tears started to fall. "I have . . . other things I need to know from you. But I—" She had to stop before she could go on, "But I need some time alone now, please."

He sat back on his heels, his gaze searching her face. "Yes you do. I was told there are rather primitive living quarters belowdecks." He got to his feet and pulled her up. "Take some time. If you want to talk, I promise I won't use it as a weapon."

It would have been an odd thing for anyone else to say but came perfectly natural from Brandon. She found herself grateful, and that also seemed unexpectedly commonplace. Which just showed how far their relationship had come in these hours.

But she was too tired and wounded to decipher the nuances of those changes right now. She kept her head averted as she headed slowly toward the door he'd indicated. The tears were running down her cheeks, and she could barely see. She hoped that area belowdecks was small and cave-like, where she could hide like the animal in pain she felt like right now.

How could she have known that out of all that agony and bitterness, the love would still remain . . .

The first gray light of dawn was just lightening the sky when Rachel came up the steps again.

Brandon's gaze was searching as she came on deck. "Better?"

"Not good. Better." She handed him a cup of coffee. "It's black. I didn't know how you took it. Though if you lived at all those places on the African coast, I figured black was pretty safe." She sat down on the seat and cradled her own cup in her two hands. Hold on tight to the cup, she told herself. It was warm against her skin and would keep him from seeing that she was still trembling in spite of those hours she'd spent away from him. "The coffee I had in Morocco was so strong it almost curled my hair."

"I prefer your hair straight, but black is fine." He sipped the coffee. "We're not that far from Trinidad. Not more than an hour."

She nodded. "I thought that we might be close. That's why I came up." She swallowed hard. "You didn't take me on this cruise to bond with me or tell me my father was dead. Though you did both very well. But I think maybe you might also be aiming at providing the atmosphere that you'd always found comforting to let me know what to expect."

He shook his head. "I don't know what to expect. We'll have to find out. But I thought it would be fair to fill you in on what I know so far."

"Start with my father," she said bluntly. "Start with Venable. You said he was shot in the chest." She had to stop a moment at that image. "Who . . . did it?"

"I think it was one of Max Huber's snipers. I got a call from Venable that said he was in the woods near Huber's compound on the Canadian border. He'd gotten close and was being stalked by one of Huber's sentries. Nate and I were nearby, but not close enough to get to the property in time. He was already dying when we reached the cabin where he'd found shelter after he was shot."

"Max Huber." It was what she had expected. He had always been the nightmare shadow over her father's life. The monster he had obsessed about for years and never been able to touch. "And why did he think he could get near that compound? Surely it was too well guarded for him to target Huber there. Huber has several compounds in Canada and the Northwest, and he moves from one to the other so that no one will know where he is at any given time."

He gazed at her speculatively. "You know a good deal about Huber."

"Not really. Only in a general way. But there were reasons why my father kept me in the loop. Though I never asked him to do it."

He lifted his shoulder in a half shrug. "He wasn't actually targeting Huber. He was supposed to meet an informant there who had told him that Huber was planning a megabig job on the West Coast. He was hinting about maybe a nuclear explosion that would make 9/11 look like a pipe bomb."

"Informant? Do you have a name?"

He shook his head. "And neither did Venable. Code name Nemesis. He hoped to get one during this meeting. Venable wanted to meet him someplace else, but he wouldn't accept any other contact than Venable or any other location."

"A trap?"

"Venable didn't think so. He thought it could be a legitimate chance to get the info we needed."

"But now he's dead," she said dully.

"Because he insisted on going himself. Two weeks ago, we had chatter that Huber had put out a million-dollar contract on Venable. It came out of the blue. Venable was always a threat and problem for Huber and Red Star, but the bastard didn't think it was smart to target someone that important in the CIA. But all of a sudden that philosophy changed." He paused. "I told Venable he was a fool to risk it, that they'd go after him like a pack of wolves for that kind of money. If he waited, there was a chance that Huber might decide the heat he'd take wouldn't be worth it."

"But he paid no attention to you." She looked down into the coffee in her cup. "He knew you were wrong."

"That's what he told me," he said quietly. "He said that Huber would consider risking anything to kill him now that he must know what had happened." He paused again. "That it was a question of vendetta."

She nodded jerkily. "Then he shouldn't have let Huber find out. He should have been more careful. All these years he was safe, then he let his guard slip."

"He said that he hadn't made any mistakes. He didn't know how Huber knew that he was the one." His lips tightened. "Vendetta. Revenge. And you know exactly what happened, don't you? Would you care to share it with me? Venable was very cagey up to the very end. He told me only what he had to tell me to get me to do what he wanted. Perhaps he was trying to protect you." He lifted his cup to her. "But one thing he told me was that if anything happened to him, I should use it to go after Huber. And to get to you right away and protect you because he wasn't the only one that Huber would be targeting."

"No, my father said no one would ever know about me, but I knew that someday I'd have to—" She broke off and said wearily, "Every action has consequences. This is no different." That wasn't true. It was different because those consequences had brought down her father. "But you did what you promised him. You kept me alive. And I owe you for more than that." She raised her cup to her lips. "Share with you? Why not? What do you want to know, Brandon?"

"Vendetta. I believe I know the victim, but I'd like it confirmed."

"Max Huber's father, Conrad Huber," she said curtly. "He was the powerhouse behind Red Star for the last twenty-five years. He had the brains and the influence and drive that kept it going. His son, Max, was just a shadow figure in comparison. No one could touch him. It was like chasing Bin Laden. Every time there was a terrorist episode with maximum fatalities, it was laid at Conrad's door. My father was obsessed with catching him. But Conrad was very smart, and it went on for almost a decade before my father decided that he had to get rid of him. He thought that if Conrad wasn't at the helm of Red Star, there was a good chance that it might fall apart." She added, "So he made it happen. Assassination. But no snipers or drone attacks. He managed to do it in such a way that the death appeared natural, so that it wouldn't cause the organization to go on an immediate terror and killing spree."

"But it didn't work, did it? Max Huber stepped up to the plate and was almost more of a murdering scum than his father."

"No, it didn't work." Her hand tightened on her cup. "But no one suspected Conrad was murdered, so my father had a chance to work on getting rid of his son."

"Until Max learned it was Venable who authorized the hit."

She nodded. "Four years," she said in frustration. "My father had four years to get rid of Max Huber and Red Star. Why would Huber have found out what happened now?"

"An informant? Sloppy evidence surfacing?"

"My father told me that no one knew. And there was nothing sloppy about Conrad Huber's death."

His brows rose. "You say that with great conviction. Would you care to elaborate?"

"No." She met his eyes. "Other than to admit what you must have already figured out. I was the one responsible for assassinating Conrad Huber. Yes, my father was the guiding hand, but in the end, I was the one who did it."

He nodded slowly. "It was the natural conclusion from what you've told me. I've been biting my tongue to keep from asking all the usual questions. Though it's not like me to be that sensitive. But you told me you had trouble with violence. So I'm finding it hard to accept."

"So did I. But it's true, and there's no way I can deny it. So Max Huber will definitely be on the hunt for me. Because on that day in Hong Kong four years ago, I was responsible for killing his monster of a father." She smiled bitterly, "And that's all you're going to get from me on that subject at present. That's all you need to know. It's not a pleasant memory, and I'm already being bombarded with painful memories about my father." Her lips twisted. "Not that Huber hasn't been hunting busily already. I probably won't be able to attend the two funerals for my friends that he's orchestrated." She looked out at the ocean. "Do you know I don't even know what Max Huber looks like? I didn't want to know. Not him, nor his father, nor anyone else connected to that day."

"Well, you *will* know him." His voice was grim as he took out his phone. "I'm texting you his photo right now. The man with him is Adolf Kraus, who was Conrad's chief supervisor and advisor. There's not going to be any more hiding your head in the sand. It's a good way to get it chopped off."

"I realize that. It was just that I wanted to forget it. I didn't want it to be part of who I am. I suppose I thought if I ignored it, I could concentrate on saving lives not taking them. It's what I'd been working toward since I was fifteen." She looked down at the photo. The man who must be Huber was thirtysomething, light blond crew cut, gray eyes, fair skin, and thick lips. He appeared taller than usual and was dressed in a khaki shirt and black jeans. Kraus, the man with him, was in his early fifties, heavyset, dark-haired with a bold hooked nose and gray-streaked brows. "I'll know them both now." She looked up at him. "And judging by the way my photo was being shown around that rain forest, Huber knows *me*. Which means he knows the entire story of his father's death. So how did he find out? When my father swore he hadn't told anyone."

"There are always leaks. Maybe it came from you. Who did you talk to about it?"

"No one. Just Hu Chang."

"There you are. It must have been Hu Chang."

"No," she said fiercely. "He would never have told anyone. Never."

"Perhaps not intentionally."

"Don't be stupid. Hu Chang never does anything without fully intending to do it."

"Then we're back to square one."

"No we're not. Hu Chang would know it would

hurt me, and he would never do that. So stop talking about it."

"Easy." He held up his hand. "No offense. Remember, I don't know your Hu Chang as well as you do. I'm operating on logic and reason, not pure faith. You seem to be more willing to think Venable would talk than Hu Chang."

"Not willing, but your logic would be more accurate if you thought that as well. My father also had his agendas, and they tended to change as his situation changed. He was willing to adjust his needs to accommodate the general good. That's what made him an effective CIA agent." She shrugged. "Hu Chang wouldn't do that. He'd set his course, then find a way to get exactly what he wanted. Though sometimes in a very convoluted fashion."

"Even though Venable promised you he would tell no one?"

She met his eyes. "Even then. How well did you know my father?"

"Not that well. We were allies. We worked together in the past year to take down two of Huber's cells in the Northwest. I spread money and manpower, and Venable had contacts and spy satellites. He knew I'd do anything to destroy Huber's entire organization. I knew the same about him. I thought he was a fine operative and more honest than some I'd run across."

She nodded. "He was totally dedicated. He'd spent thirty years being the perfect CIA operative. He probably died doing his duty to the CIA and to his country." She paused. "And perfect CIA operatives don't always think it necessary to keep their promises if another agenda crops up that would serve their cause more."

"I'd imagine he would think twice if it concerned you."

"And he probably did think twice." She rubbed the back of her neck. She was feeling weary and hollow inside, yet the emotions were still sharp and terribly painful. "And perhaps he didn't find another way to go. But I think we have to find out what happened. Because you said that Huber was planning something very big, and I'm finding I'm curious why at that *very* moment he suddenly found out something that would instantly distract him."

"I wondered that myself, but I've not pulled together a reasonable scenario as yet." He smiled. "But that time you spent curled up on the bunk downstairs evidently proved valuable."

She shook her head. "I'm just letting anything and everything flow out of me. I'm not thinking clearly at all. So tell me what else I should know. Do you have details about this big job Huber is planning?"

He shook his head. "Venable said it was supposed to be a major disaster to take place in San Francisco. He had a date and a city. He was supposed to get the rest of the details from the informant he met at the compound."

"San Francisco . . . I have a friend, Catherine Ling, who has contacts in San Francisco. I'd think my father would have asked her to talk to them. She took her orders from him." She was thinking, remembering.

"And Hu Chang told me tonight that she was on her way to a meeting in San Francisco with Operative Claire Warren."

He was silent. "Claire Warren?"

"I've never met her. But she's high-echelon CIA and worked some antiterrorist cases with my father. Catherine says that she's very sharp."

"Then maybe Venable felt comfortable telling her about Conrad Huber."

"Perhaps. Or maybe she would know the same informant he was using to find out what's going to happen in San Francisco." She finished her coffee and put the cup in the holder on the stand beside her chair. "Either way, I think we should go to San Francisco and see how she's involved."

"Do you?" He smiled. "From profound dejection, you appear to have bounced back with amazing strength and determination. Am I allowed to have a say in this?"

"Yes. I haven't forgotten what I promised you. But I have problems being passive." She shook her head in wonder. "Particularly now. I'm . . . confused. For years I've worked at not being like my father, to not let violence rule my life. But this shouldn't . . . have happened to him. None of it. It's all wrong. And Huber shouldn't be allowed to get away with it." She drew a deep breath. "I'm shaken and I'm unbearably sad but there's so much more . . ." She stopped, trying to see clarity in all the hurt and anger and bewilderment. "You'll have to accept that until I'm able to get my head together, you can't expect me to be either meek or passive."

"Oh, I've already noticed passivity isn't your strong suit."

"But if you tell me how you want to use me, I'll let you do it." Her lips curved in the ghost of a smile. "And I don't think I'd mind at all. You can see I'm having a good deal of trouble with what you told me about my father's death. I'd like to do anything that would keep me busy enough to forget it for just a little while. So if you think of a way to stake me out as a sacrificial goat, I'll be there."

"Would you?" He slowly shook his head. "I think we'll wait a little and use it as a wild card. You don't remind me at all of a sacrificial goat. We might have to go in another direction." He turned around and took the controls off auto. "In the meantime, I'll set up a safe house in San Francisco, and we'll see what we can come up with in the way of killing Huber and saving the Golden Gate Bridge."

"I forgot about the Golden Gate Bridge." She smiled sadly. "I suppose that's an actual possibility?"

"I wasn't serious, it's a little obvious, but I wouldn't put it past Huber after he took down that dam in Indonesia." He checked his watch. "We'll be in Trinidad in another thirty minutes. Why don't you go downstairs and get a little more rest?"

She shook her head. "I can rest on the jet to San Francisco. I'll go down and clean up, then see if I can get in touch with Catherine."

"No, don't do that. I don't want anyone to know we're coming until I get you in that safe house."

"Catherine is my friend." She made an impatient gesture when he just stared impassively at her. "All right, this time. But if you can't be reasonable, this might get very old in no time, Brandon."

She turned and started for the door.

"Rachel."

She looked back at him.

"You said I handled telling you about Venable's death very well," he said quietly. "That was a lie. I was clumsy as hell. I probably made it worse than it would have been coming from someone else." His lips twisted. "Maybe I should have had Nate tell you. But I didn't think that it would affect you this strongly. The report I had said that you hadn't lived with your father since you were fifteen and your mother was killed. I thought that meant you were estranged and it might not—"

"I don't want to talk about my father right now." He was bringing up too many memories, and she had to shut him down. She had been fighting to keep those memories at bay since she had fled down those steps hours before. It was as if every word, every thought, brought her father closer when he'd never be close again. "You did as well as you could. You don't know me or what my father and I were together. Our relationship wasn't . . . the usual . . . things happened." But she could see that he was genuinely troubled, and she tried to explain. "And some of those things hurt me and made me push him away. But I always loved him, and

I think he loved me. We always wanted it to work. It was just . . . complicated." She smiled unsteadily. "And I'd never think you'd react this way, Brandon."

"Neither would I." He looked her in the eyes. "It comes as a complete surprise to me. I can't seem to let it go."

"Then just don't *talk* about it, dammit." She slammed the door behind her and ran down the steps. The tears had come again, and she ran into the bathroom and splashed water in her face. She needed to be busy, but she had nothing to do but sit in this tiny space and wait until they got into Trinidad harbor.

Or go back on deck and face Brandon after she'd lost control and run down here. She wasn't ready for that either. His one sentence had triggered a very deep response.

You hadn't lived with your father since you were fifteen and your mother was killed. I thought that meant you were estranged.

Estranged. Yes, that was a word that could describe what had been between them since that last day at the prison.

Don't think about that day.

Don't think about her father or how he'd looked at her.

Because now that hurt would be as fresh and raw as that moment when she had been sitting in her cell waiting for her father to come down the hall.

Block it.

Don't think about it.

But it was too late . . .

SAZKAR PRISON

LOGAR PROVINCE

AFGHANISTAN, 14 YEARS AGO

"You can change your mind, Rachel," Hu Chang said gently. "Venable is a good man. He says he wants you back."

She shook her head. "Not unless you've changed your mind," she whispered. "Only if you don't want me. Then I'll have to find another place."

"How can I say that I don't want you? You're an extraordinary student, and a master always needs someone to whom he can pass on his brilliance." He smiled. "And I told you we would be the best of friends. I've found my hours spent with you in this cell not at all unpleasant during these last months."

And she had found salvation in those hours, she thought. He had sparked her imagination, made her smile, and taught her to block out the darkness. He had asked her no other questions, but he had listened when the dam had finally broken and she had started to ask questions of herself and the reason why this could have happened to her. Now she was starting the slow process of coming back and could feel the strength returning. Yet when he had told her that the prisoner-trade agreement had finally been settled and she was going to be free, she had not felt at all strong.

Because she had known that this hour might be coming.

And now it was here, and she was sitting in this cell with an unlocked door and all guards gone.

She could walk out of here at any time.

"I can't go back to him, Hu Chang," she whispered.

"Then talk to him. Let him talk to you," Hu Chang said. "I've done as you wished and told him that it will be my pleasure to have you in my home. But if you are going to be the best you can be in taking this action, you must face it and face him."

The best she could be. It was the rule that he had taught her to believe in. She nodded jerkily. "I know that."

He inclined his head. "Then I will send him to you. He's in the hall. I'll be waiting outside for your decision." The next moment he was gone.

She sat there, tense, waiting for the door to open.

And then it did swing open, and her father came into the room. Dark suit, big and burly, graying red hair, and an expression as tense and pained as her own must be.

"Rachel!" He came toward her, then stopped before he reached her. His gaze was fixed with shock on her face. "God, you've changed."

"Have I? I guess that's natural. But Hu Chang says I'm better than I was. And I'll get better and better and nothing will—" She was talking too fast. She stopped, and said, "You don't have to worry about me. Hu Chang will make sure that I'm all right."

"I don't want him to have to do that." His gaze was still on her face. "And I want to be the one to worry about you. But I didn't mean to make you think I didn't—you're beautiful. It's just that you're not my little girl any longer."

"No, I'm not."

He drew a deep breath. "I want you to come home with me."

She tried to smile. "But you were hardly ever at home. Most of the time, you were out of the country. Now that Mom's gone, I'd just be in the way."

"We could work it out."

She shook her head.

"Rachel, I didn't know." His hands were clenching into fists as his sides. "I had an informant in this prison who sent out messages that you were being treated decently. I had no idea what was happening until Hu Chang told me after he took over the negotiations."

"I guess your informant wasn't what you'd call a reliable asset." She met his eyes. "It was five months, Daddy."

"I know that. But I had to negotiate. I had no problem with the first four prisoners. But there were two terrorists they were bargaining for you that were terribly dangerous to release. They were affiliated with other terrorist organizations and had access to explosives supplied by them. They could cause major loss of life with one bomb. I had to make a choice." His voice broke, and he had to stop for a moment. "I swear to God I thought you were safe and being treated decently."

"And you made the choice," she said. "And Hu Chang says that you only had to release one of those prisoners when he was finished with the final negotiations. That must have relieved you. I'm sure you've

made arrangements to make sure he's no future threat?"

"I did," he said bitterly. "That prisoner cost me a price that cut too deep. I'm not going to let Hassan Ibn Bahir cause any other chaos to the rest of the world." His lips were tight with pain as he stared at her. "I lost your mother and your brother. I don't want to lose you, Rachel. Come with me. Believe me, I didn't know."

"I can't do it," she said unevenly. She'd hoped he would just let her go away, but she was going to have to say the words she didn't want to say. "I believe that you had this informant. I believe he said all the right words to make you sure you were doing the right thing about keeping the negotiations going. I even believe you probably believed there was no mistreatment that would have given you reason to cancel the talks because they'd broken their word." She stared him in the eye. "But if you'd been in this prison instead of me, I wouldn't have taken some 'informant's' word about what they were doing to you. I would have found a way to see for myself. You're so smart, you have so many contacts, it shouldn't have been that hard for you." She moistened her lips. "I've thought a lot about that since I've been capable of thinking at all. You're CIA, and you live in a world of violence and cruelty. Yes, you're the good guy, and you try to prevent it, but you had to know the threat was here. But I can also see that you didn't want to believe it because of all the people who might die if you did." She had to get the rest of it out quickly, "And you did the right thing, the patriotic thing, the thing that would save the most lives. So how can I condemn you?" She shook her head. "I can't do it. But I also can't forget that every time I was beaten or raped, I was told that it was your fault it was happening. I can't stand to face that memory every single day." She said shakily, "So I won't be going home with you, Daddy."

"Dear God." He was silent. His face had turned white. "Do you hate me?"

"No. I don't know how I feel right now. I think . . . I still love you. I just can't look at you right now without remembering. And I don't want to ever live in the violent world you do. All my life I've watched you dealing with dirt and scum. There has to be something better, and I'll find it." She tried to shrug. "It might take a while. Hu Chang says it's going to take me time to heal. Maybe he's right."

"Of course he's right. I just want to be there to help." His face was twisted with agony. "And, God, I hope you're wrong about me. I hope I wasn't careless of you because it meant so much, because everything was so very personal to me this time." He closed his eyes. "But it doesn't matter what the reason. I let it happen." His eyes were moist when his lids lifted. "I'll give you that time," he said hoarsely. "I won't give up, Rachel."

"Mom used to say that you never gave up." Her lips were trembling, and she just wanted this to be over. "That's why you're so good at your job."

"How long, Rachel?"

She helplessly shook her head.

"You don't know. How could you?" He nodded and

took a deep breath. "That's okay. I'll make it happen." He turned to go. "You're my daughter. You were always more like me than either of the boys. I won't let you go. If you or Hu Chang need me, let me know."

She watched him walk out of the room. She felt a terrible emptiness and sadness and bewilderment. She knew she could not have done anything else, but she suddenly wanted him back again.

But she couldn't have him back. She had to move forward. She started toward the door. She had to leave what had happened to her here and begin to see what was out there in the world.

Hu Chang was waiting.

CHAPTER

5

PRESENT DAY

*D*ammit, stop crying, **she told herself.**

Life was life, and she and her father had made decisions that had caused them both pain. None of that could be changed now. She couldn't keep breaking down when she had to function. Brandon had just unloaded an entire scenario with which she'd have to deal. And then he'd tied her hands and left her alone with only him to help her handle it all.

Or maybe not.

She'd made a promise not to call Catherine Ling yet. She'd not said anything about Hu Chang.

She quickly dialed Hu Chang.

"I only have a few minutes to talk," she said shakily when he picked up. "And I'm not being very coherent at the moment. But I knew you should know as soon as possible." She paused, then said, "My father is dead, Hu Chang."

Silence. "I find that both sad and unbelievable. Venable has been . . . unconquerable all the many years I've known him. How do you know this?"

"Brandon told me he saw him die. He was shot by one of Huber's men."

"You believe Brandon?"

"I believe him. I didn't want to believe him. But, yes, he was telling me the truth."

"And I trust your judgment." Silence. "You must be in a great deal of pain. I feel your sorrow, and it is mine."

"I didn't think I'd feel like this," she whispered. "He hurt me, Hu Chang."

"Yes, but not with intent. He always loved you. It was just that destiny placed the two of you in a position where you were bound to conflict considering who you are."

"Screw destiny. I want my life back. I want *his* life back."

"What do you wish me to say to that?"

"I don't know. I'm not thinking clearly. I just wanted to talk to you. You were his friend. You took his part when he wanted me to come back to him."

"How could I do anything else? I was stealing someone very precious from him. It was not important that you were also very precious to me." He paused. "But I think you must call Catherine now. She must not know yet, or she would have told me. She's known your father almost as long as I have. She was only fourteen when he hired her as an agent in Hong Kong. He changed her life."

"Yes, she told me. I wasn't sure whether she became my friend because of you or my father."

"Neither. It was because you are who you are. Now call her."

"I can't. I promised Brandon I wouldn't. I told him it was ridiculous. He wants to set up a safe house in San Francisco for me and didn't want anyone to know we were going to—"

"Safe house? It appears that there is more going on than you're telling me. What is it?"

"I have no idea yet. Something's supposed to happen in San Francisco. It has to be Huber because my father was supposed to meet with an informant, Nemesis, who told him something was on Huber's radar in that city."

"So you're going to step into the lion's mouth where he's planning his next 9/11? Not clever, Rachel."

"Dear God, I hope it's not that bad. But it might be, Hu Chang. Why else would Claire Warren set up that meeting in San Francisco?"

"I believe I'd better pursue an answer to that question. I'm not at all pleased that Catherine was brought into that city without being given warning."

"Then give her warning," Rachel said bluntly. "I made a promise, but you didn't. Call her."

"I shall," Hu Chang said. "Just as you intended me to do when you phoned me."

"I admit I wanted that to happen. But that wasn't the only reason." She paused. "I needed to hear your voice."

"And now you've heard it and know that I feel as you feel. When do you leave for San Francisco?"

"Probably in the next few hours. As soon as we can get out of Trinidad. Tell Catherine I'll contact her as soon as I get there."

"I imagine she will be quite busy until that time," he said dryly. "She will not be pleased about any of this. Not only has she lost a great friend, but it seems strange that his death has not been reported by Langley. You said two days?"

"More than that now."

"And Brandon is certain of his death."

"I told you. He didn't want to tell me. He said he saw it."

"Then there's some reason why they don't want it revealed. Curious . . ."

"Not really. The CIA always has agendas they keep hidden. *Need to know* is their byword."

"You've certainly been privy to the effects of that philosophy. Well, I guarantee that Catherine will know in short order. And I'm just as happy that Brandon is keeping you isolated so that you won't bump into Huber while he's trying to cause destruction and havoc. Now I must call Catherine, so I bid you good-bye." He hung up.

And Catherine would be just as upset as Hu Chang had been, Rachel thought. Catherine genuinely cared about Venable, he had been part of her life since she'd been a child collecting information on the streets of Hong Kong. Of half-American heritage mixed with Russian and Korean, she had been beautiful and exotic even then, and she had made the decision to ignore the obvious path and use her mind and ingenuity instead. Over the years, she had grown in strength and knowledge until she was one of the most respected agents in the CIA. She balanced raising her son, Luke, with her profession and did a superb job with both of them. There was no one Rachel trusted more, and she knew Venable had felt the same way.

Past tense. Even that small thing hurt when applied to her father.

And it would hurt Catherine, also. Rachel had wanted to share the pain and sorrow with the two people who had cared so much about him. Now, she wondered if she should have waited and given Catherine a few more hours before the shock and pain attacked.

No, Catherine would not have thanked her. She always faced problems head-on and confronted sorrow with equal courage. Besides, this problem looming on the horizon could literally be earth-shattering. She did not have the right to hesitate for kindness' sake. She could only share whatever burden was to come.

And leave Catherine to handle the loss of Venable on her own.

HYATT HOTEL
SAN FRANCISCO

"Dead?" Catherine whispered. Her hand tightened on her phone. "It's not true, Hu Chang. It can't be true."

"I felt the same way when Rachel told me," Hu Chang said. "He seemed unconquerable, yet all men have to cross that final threshold. But Venable reminded me of the North Star that was always there for us."

"You sent me to him that day in Hong Kong. You said I would be safe with him. I thought it strange because I knew what the CIA was and did on occasion."

"One must always take a man for what he is. Venable had a sense of honor that was unusual in any profession. I knew you were strong enough to make your way in his world, and he would let you learn at your own pace."

And he had done that, Catherine thought. Venable had thrown her into danger any number of times but had never been reckless with her life. "I could trust him."

"Which is rare in the world you both lived in." He added, "And why death should not have come to him by the hands of men who care nothing for trust and honor."

"It was Huber?"

"So Jude Brandon told Rachel. I cannot be certain. I'm sure you will verify this. However, I find it curious that you did not know of his death. I realize that you weren't in constant communication with Venable, but the CIA does not let one of their premier operatives be killed without being aware of it." He paused. "And they do not set up a meeting in a city across the country from Langley immediately after Venable found it could be threatened. I do not like that you are there, Catherine. You told me that Claire Warren set up that meeting. What do you know about her?"

"Not as much as I will after I hang up," Catherine said grimly. "I know she has a sterling reputation as a case officer, she's smart as a whip, and she goes strictly by the book, which I sometimes have trouble doing. Venable had a few problems with her for the same reason, but he respected her. He said she was in line to become the next Deputy Director at Langley. If she knew Venable was dead, then I can't see her not telling me. But sometimes people who go by the book have it written by someone else higher up." She drew a shaky breath. "Since she's only two floors down from me at this hotel, I think I'll go and ask her."

"Excellent. And Rachel asks that no one knows that she will be arriving in San Francisco shortly. Brandon seems to be rather adamant on the subject. But since so far he's kept her alive, I believe we should go along with her on this."

"I don't want her in San Francisco at all," Catherine said flatly. "Not if Huber is after her. What the hell can Brandon be thinking?"

"You will probably be able to ask him yourself soon," he said. "But you will not be able to keep her from doing as he asks. She said she owed him a debt, and you're aware of what that means."

Yes, Catherine knew very well, she thought in frustration. "Being the best she can be. Sometimes those philosophies of yours can be very irritating. They can certainly get in the way."

"I agree, but she was halfway there anyway. I did not force her." He paused. "Any more than I forced you, Catherine. Honor and striving for good in oneself is natural and right. Particularly in certain individuals. You've never objected when I exposed your son to that philosophy."

"No, I didn't." Because Luke was everything to her, and his life had been dark and complicated. Now she wanted nothing but good, bright paths for him. But that didn't necessarily mean Hu Chang's association with her son was free of complications. "Never mind, I'll try to persuade Rachel to leave here the minute she contacts me. But I don't know how long I'm going to have to be here now. I sent Luke down to Eve Duncan's lake cottage in Atlanta to be with her family while I was gone. Will you stop by and make sure that he's no trouble and happy?"

"Catherine, you know Luke loves being with Eve and Joe down at the lake. He will be fine. However, I will do as you wish. I can always take a flight out of Atlanta if I so choose."

"Flight?"

"To San Francisco. Rachel now belongs to me even more than she did before. She's starting out on a dangerous path that's going to take her down to places she won't want to go. *You* belong to me. Where else should I be?"

"Anywhere but here in San Francisco." She paused. "I know that you feel you have to be here with her, but it's not true. Not at this time. It might bring her more pain than comfort. There were occasions when she chose you instead of her father. Having you here would bring it all back to her."

Silence. "I will think about it."

"Trust me," she urged. "I won't let anything happen to her."

He wasn't answering. She held her breath.

"You will keep me informed?"

"Would I dare do anything else?"

"No. You'd dare almost anything, but I believe you'd hesitate to disobey me." Another long silence. "Be very careful, Catherine. I will not lose you. I would behave in a totally irrational and violent manner if this Max Huber tried to take you from me." He cut the connection.

Catherine hadn't been sure she'd be able to persuade him. Once he made up his mind, there was no moving him. But he was also the wisest man she had ever met, and he would realize how complicated his role had been in the relationship between Rachel and Venable. Perhaps he knew by taking a step back he would avoid more worry, more frustration for her.

And more sadness.

Venable dead . . .

She could feel the tears sting her eyes for the old friend who had also been her mentor.

She swallowed hard.

Give herself a moment to get a grip on herself. This was not the time for tears. She had learned through the years that you didn't allow yourself to mourn while there was a job to be done. Venable had taught her that lesson when four agents had been killed outside Lima on her second mission.

Find who did it.

Retrieve the information.

Dispose of the perpetrators.

On your way back to home base, grieve for fallen comrades.

And now Venable was the fallen comrade.

And it was not time to grieve.

She went to the bathroom, washed her face, and drank a glass of water.

Then she squared her shoulders, left her room, and took the elevator down to the fourth floor.

She knocked on the door.

No answer.

She knocked again.

The door swung open, and Claire Warren stood there. She was still in the silk blouse and expertly tailored black trousers she'd worn when she'd met Catherine in the lobby. She was chic, vibrant, more fascinating than attractive. She was in her mid forties, with glossy dark hair in a sleek chignon, smooth alabaster skin, and magnificent hazel eyes that were now staring coldly at Catherine. "You didn't call me, Catherine. That was not courteous. I'm very busy. Perhaps we can get together later to—"

"I need to talk to you now." She brushed past her into the room. "If you tell me what I need to know, then I'll get out of here, and you can go back to what you were doing that was so important."

"That's my choice," Claire Warren said crisply.

"You aren't invited, and I find your attitude rude and insubordinate. I've heard that you've always been a trifle—"

"Precipitous?" Catherine whirled to face her. "More than a trifle, particularly where my friends are concerned. I have no desire to be rude, but I don't give a damn about being insubordinate. I want to know why I wasn't informed that Carl Venable had been killed."

Claire went still, but her face was without expression. "It wasn't your business to know."

"The hell it wasn't. I'm hardly a security risk, and he was my good friend. It happened more than two days ago. Why were you keeping it a secret?"

"Don't be overdramatic. I didn't even know if it was true for twenty-four hours. Brandon had let us know after he left the cabin, but when we sent our people there, Venable's body had disappeared. The next day, we found him at the bottom of a canyon where he'd been thrown."

"I feel like being overdramatic." And she was sick at the idea of Venable's body having been thrown away like some kind of garbage. "And that was only twenty-four hours. Why wasn't anyone told after that time?"

"It was a decision made at the highest level. We didn't want Max Huber to know that we were aware of Venable's death. It left our options open about what to do with Rachel Venable."

"What?" Catherine was staring at her in disbelief. "Options?"

"Do you think we wouldn't know that she was a target as well as Venable? No one was more responsible to the Company than Carl Venable. Of course he'd let us know that Rachel could be in danger when he realized that Huber was coming after him full force." Her lips tightened. "He wouldn't confide why that was true, but when Brandon told us that Venable was dead, we had to take it into consideration. We knew Huber was planning something here in San Francisco, and we were busy looking at every way to stop it."

"And Rachel might prove a distraction to Huber? If he felt safe about having time to scoop her up, you'd have more time to find out what he was planning. So you took your time finding Venable's body."

"Shocked? Don't be naïve. I'm sure Venable was thinking in the same vein until he drew his last breath. Besides, Brandon was on his way down to Guyana to run interference with Venable's daughter. Venable told me he was very good. I had no doubt he could handle the problem temporarily."

"Until you could clear the decks to examine your 'options.'" She shook her head. "If Venable told you that Huber was after Rachel, he meant you to protect her, not find a way to use her. He spent years working for the CIA. I think he deserved to have you do that."

"I did protect her. I gave her to Brandon," she said coolly. "It was my decision, and I don't regret it. I don't have time to regret any action I take at this point. We're on the verge of a national catastrophe, and I will use any means I can to prevent it." She stared her in the eye. "And I did not bring you or the other agents here to question my judgment. You're here in San Francisco for one thing, and that's to prevent Huber from doing megadamage. You'll do anything and everything to find and disarm any device Huber's managed to smuggle into the city. Do you understand?"

"I understand. And there's no question I'll do what I have to do." Catherine took a step closer. "But I also understand that you knew what my attitude was going to be about Venable and Rachel. It would have been easier for you to ask for another operative. But you didn't do it because you knew I'd work harder, try harder than anyone else. Because I wouldn't let the bastard who killed my friend destroy this city. And you thought perhaps because Rachel is also my friend, that I might be able to manipulate her if it became necessary. Because you knew she was on her way here, didn't you?"

"Did I?" she asked mockingly.

"Yes, because Brandon is as obsessed as Venable was, and he'd want to be here if Huber was set to take action. Or maybe you even told him to bring her here? That was why you were pleased Brandon was going after Rachel. It gave you the opportunity to pull your strings."

"Very perceptive." Her brows rose. "And Clever. Venable always told me how clever you were."

"And he told me that on many levels he admired you." She added deliberately, "I don't believe this would have been one of those levels." She turned to leave. "I'll do everything I can to obey any of your orders pertaining to finding what Red Star is planning to do here. But you'll leave Rachel Venable alone and not involve her in any of your games. If you do, you'll have me to contend with. You can put me on report, try to have me dismissed, take away my operative officer's credentials, and set me to scrubbing floors at Langley. But I won't let it happen."

"Really?" There was no expression on that smooth face. "You persist in indulging in melodrama. You don't want to go against me, Catherine. I'll do whatever it takes to get the job done. Just as Venable would do." The tiniest smile lifted the corners of her lips. "Just as you would do."

"There are limits." She headed for the door. "And you'll find me loyal within those limits." She looked over her shoulder. "Don't go beyond them."

She closed the door behind her. She stood there and drew a deep breath. There was every chance that she'd deep-sixed her career with the CIA. Claire Warren was clearly a powerhouse and not averse to using that power. She had not been able to read all the facets of the woman, but she could see ruthlessness and that sharp brilliance that Venable had so admired. There was probably no question that she and Catherine would collide before this was over.

Well, what if they did? Just because she had been a CIA operative since her teens did not mean that she couldn't do something else. She would probably see more of Luke if she had another job.

So she would not worry about Claire Warren. She would take the situation as she found it and go forward. She would do as Hu Chang had taught her all those years ago. It might frustrate and drive her slightly mad, but there was no better advice.

Just do the very best she could and let the chips fall where they might.

And be wary of the Claire Warrens of the world.

EAGLES REST
CANADA

"Morales didn't get Venable's daughter for us," Adolf Kraus said as he hung up his phone and strode across the concrete tiles to where Huber was sitting watching the new fighter being tested in the fight ring. The kid wasn't going to last, he thought absently, as he saw the fair-haired young boy weaving on his feet. The boy was slim and fit, but he was being beaten by two of Max Huber's strongest pugilists. He'd be dead before midnight. "The fool is making excuses about running into interference from Brandon. We know Brandon's helicopter left Georgetown for Miami several hours ago. She might be aboard. We'll be at Miami Airport when it lands."

"Son of a *bitch*." Huber's eyes were blazing. "Don't I have enough problems without you bungling a simple retrieval? You told me Morales and his men would have no problem."

Kraus had known this would be coming, but it still annoyed him. "We didn't realize that Brandon would move so quickly. We didn't even know that he knew about the woman."

"You should have known. He and Venable have been hand and glove for the past year." He got to his feet and moved over toward the portrait on the far wall. "Just as you should have known that bitch murdered my father." His eyes were glistening as he looked up at Conrad Huber's portrait. His admiring gaze going over the strong features, the powerful shoulders and body encased in Conrad's favorite taupe-and-gray militia uniform. "Just look at him, he was as strong as a bull. As strong as all the Hubers have been through the generations. You should have realized that there was nothing weak about his heart. He was a true lion."

"Do you think I'm not aware of that?" Kraus said sharply. "I spent twenty years serving your father, working for the cause, showing the world what men could do if they had the courage to be bold enough. Your father and I knew how to make all those politicians and world leaders bow down to us. He might have been a lion, but together we were kings." He had said too much, but the situation was grating on his nerves. Sometimes pretending to kowtow to this weak, vicious boy, who was nothing like Conrad, was unbearable. He tried to hold on to his temper. "I ordered all the right tests. They all came back negative. What was I supposed to do?"

"Dig deeper. Once you were told what to look for, you had no trouble checking for her damn poison."

"But I had to be told where to look," he snapped. "And it took me four years to get that information. It's not as if I pulled it out of a hat. I told you it was given to me as a gift."

"And, in turn, you gave it to me as a gift," Huber said coldly. "For all the good it did me. I had enough to do making the arrangements for our grand celebration in San Francisco. All I asked you to do was to see that I had Rachel Venable to complete it."

"It will still happen. I had to go through that fool Morales, or we would have already had her. Once we have our own people after her, it will be easier."

"You don't even know where she is right now."

"She's with Brandon, and he wants you enough to take any chance to get you. There are boundless opportunities in that scenario." He looked at the face of the man in the portrait. And his old comrade would have seen every one of those opportunities and exploited them, he thought. It had been hellishly difficult pushing and leading Max Huber down the path his father would have wanted him to go. Kraus had been the one who had held on to the power he and Conrad had forged and made certain Red Star wasn't taken down. But now he wasn't certain how long he could continue without disposing of this little bastard. He had been useful as a figurehead, but his arrogance was proving infuriating. "We'll find the best one and move."

"It has to be by the twenty-fifth," Huber said. "All my plans are for the twenty-fifth."

And the prick was so consumed by his "statements" and grandiose plans that he couldn't adjust them if something better came along. Conrad would never have been that foolish. But Kraus could go along with him and bring his plans to a glorious climax. Then make his decision when he'd make his own move. "You'll have her by the twenty-fifth."

Huber smiled without mirth. "Promises."

Kraus was getting too angry. Change the subject. Lead Max away from that path. His gaze went to the young boy, who was now trying to stay on his feet, then to the hungry expressions on Max Huber's militia favorites gathered outside the ring. "You don't usually pick them that young. How old is he?"

"Fourteen. Old enough for the test." He was instantly distracted, and his expression was almost as intent and hungry as his men's as he watched the boy struggling as the two fighters pummeled him mercilessly. "But he's failing to please me. We have tradition and the heritage of clean, strong Aryan bloodlines. Even you can see that he's a weakling."

"I yield to your judgment. You have much more experience in this than I do."

"Yes, I do." Max's head lifted as the boy stumbled and fell to the mat. "There. See. He's *down*." He turned and strode toward the ring. "He's failed me." Then he was inside the ring and gazing down at the boy. "You've wasted my time." He told him softly, "That's not permitted."

"Please . . ." The boy could barely speak. "Don't . . ."

"And you're a coward, not worthy of me." He pulled back his leg and kicked him in the ribs with his steel-toed boot. Again. Again. Again.

The boy screamed!

Kraus thought the distraction was firmly in place and turned to leave. Max Huber would continue to kick the boy until he was dead or he possibly lost interest in the sport. At that time, he would turn the boy over to his militia guards, who were waiting their turn.

But Max paused and looked over his shoulder at Kraus. "It might help if you tell me the name of that 'giver of gifts' so that I can contact him and talk him into letting me know where I can find her."

Kraus shook his head. "It's rather difficult. Though naturally as head of Red Star you're the only one he considers important. Which is as it should be. Perhaps you intimidate him. If I'm contacted, I'll let you know."

"I expect you to do your duty in every way. I hope that you don't disappoint me again, Kraus." He turned back to the boy and kicked the boy in the stomach. "You can be replaced."

"I realize that," Kraus said humbly. "But I trust you'll remember that old friends are the best friends. We've been together a long time." He turned away, headed for the door, and added blandly, "You know I only wish to serve you as I did your father. It will always be my privilege."

HYATT HOTEL

Catherine's cell phone was ringing when she woke at six the next morning. No ID. At least it wasn't Claire again, she thought wryly. She'd had more than enough of her since their vitriolic interchange last night. But it could be Rachel if Brandon had given her a burner phone, so she'd better answer it. "Catherine Ling."

"You sound a little annoyed, and I haven't even had the opportunity to make you that way."

Cameron!

She couldn't speak for a moment. She could hardly get her breath. It had been a long time since she had heard from him, months and months. At times she had thought she might never hear from him again. "You're not the only who can annoy me, Cameron." She had to steady her voice. "Though you're definitely the frontrunner. Isn't it splendid that I haven't had to worry about that lately?"

"Is it? You crush me. But then you've always been able to devastate me with that tongue . . . in more ways than one."

She had a memory of her tongue on his body, his hands threaded through her hair as he looked down at her.

Heat seared through her. Other memories of Richard Cameron were cascading through her, and she was starting to shake.

The first time she had seen Cameron in that firelit study in Tibet. Standing before a fireplace in jeans and a close-fitting black shirt, his body outlined by the flames. Power. Grace. Electricity. Sexuality. Brilliant blue eyes gazing at her with humor and curiosity. Everything about him beautifully lithe and masculine . . .

Stop feeling. Stop remembering. Cameron would know, and she would be at an immediate disadvantage. Go on the attack. "No one can crush you, Cameron. You're unbreakable. I found that out a long time ago. A *very* long time. Why are you calling me now?"

"Ouch. That stung. And completely unfair by the

way. I wanted to take you with me. You wouldn't come. I thought I'd give you time to change your mind. I was being patient."

"Bullshit. We both know that there was no way that I was going to change my mind. We're so different, we might as well have come from different planets."

"But we managed to integrate magnificently," he said softly. "And someday you might decide that's enough reason to come to me. Until then, I'll have to be content with the fact that you haven't seen fit to go after me with guns blazing. As a CIA operative, that must have been a significant sacrifice."

"Not really," she said curtly. "I couldn't have proven any of it anyway. You're too clever. You don't leave any loose ends. A scientist disappears, a Tibetan war lord is assassinated, plans for a technical invention that could change the future suddenly can't be found, an acclaimed teacher leaves her post in Beijing, disappears into the mist and isn't heard from again. It goes on and on."

"Then there must be a reason," he said quietly. "Except for an occasional military encounter, there doesn't appear to be any force being used. Life is just shifting to accommodate change."

"And yet you have military teams in all sectors of the world who 'assist' in those changes."

"But so does the CIA, and the armies in every country. Venable has sent you on missions to that end many times. We both know it's sometimes necessary."

"And it's necessary that you're stealing brains and

talent and the best and brightest from all walks of life? You set them up with new identities in the back of beyond and tell them they're preparing to save the world after the bad guys destroy it."

"It must be very attractive to them if they believe me," he said gently. "Sort of like the knights of the round table?"

"Or Shangri-La. Neither concept will work in this world." Though she couldn't deny that idealism was one of the principal attractions that drew his followers to Cameron. "But you also lure them with money and opportunity and the chance to break new ground. Irresistible, Cameron."

"No force. Their choice. Always volunteers."

"Of course not, they have *you*. They don't need force. You're possibly the most persuasive man in the world."

He chuckled. "You think so? Yet I couldn't persuade you to come with me."

"You know what I mean." And she had come so close that night. She hadn't even realized how close until the next night when she had lain in bed aching . . . and remembering . . . "That was . . . different."

The difference between pure erotic obsession and the telepathic talent that had made him known as the Guardian. He had told her once that he worked for an international organization with worldwide membership. When they had been looking for someone to set up their private little haven to survive any catastrophe, they found Richard Cameron. A man who possessed mind-control abilities that were even more astonishing than his military skills. "No one really has a chance with you if you decide that they have the qualifications you need. Your superpack chose well when they brought you into the fold. You step on the scene, and you control it."

"I have to remind you that your CIA also has a similar program, Catherine. So do most governments. I understand they've had some success."

"Not like you," she said flatly. "Not only mind reading but the ability to go in and actually mold the will if you choose."

Silence. "No, not like me. Maybe someday. And, if your government did succeed, they'd be the ones to have the power to use those people or destroy them. I was given choices. Which is why I never use the control option unless absolutely necessary."

"Because your superpack has the money and power to afford you as the Guardian of their grand dream of a perfect society. They know they couldn't choose anyone who would come near to you."

"It *is* a grand dream, Catherine," he said quietly. "And sometime we're going to need a new dream when the hatemongers decide to blow up the one we have now."

"Then you should be out there fighting to keep them from doing it instead of building your own glorious Shangri-La," she said fiercely.

"As you're fighting? Really? How's it coming along with Huber on one border and ISIS across the pond?" He didn't let her answer, but immediately said, "That wasn't fair. I didn't call you to rehash our differences of opinions and philosophies. I should have known that your first instinct would be to attack. I know how you feel. You're very vocal on the subject."

"Yes, I am." He, on the other hand, never really discussed who and what he was unless she demanded it. She just knew he was the warrior, the Guardian, the designated crown prince who would someday control the project he now protected so zealously. "Because I get so frustrated that I can't get you to understand that our government could use all those brilliant minds you're so carefully nurturing."

"Until they choose to break them." He added quickly before she could reply, "Hush, now. I thought this might be a bad time but I had to call you anyway. Forget about who and what I am. I just talked to Hu Chang. He told me about Venable. I knew you'd be upset. I wanted you to know that I'm with you, that I'm thinking about you."

The mockery had vanished, and she couldn't doubt his sincerity. Her anger and defensiveness ebbed away. She was touched in spite of herself. "That's very kind. You didn't really know him, did you?"

"True. My main agenda with Venable was always to avoid making contact with him. That way I'd avoid scrutiny from the CIA, and that was always a plus. I usually prefer to be the invisible man." He paused. "But you told me that he'd helped you as a child in Hong Kong. That meant that he was my friend whether I liked it or not."

"He was a good man," she said unsteadily. "My life would have been different if he hadn't been there."

"That's the best epithet you can give a friend. Is there anything I can do for you . . . or him?"

"No, I'm handling it."

"I know you are. Hu Chang says that you're doing more than that. Venable's daughter?"

"She doesn't need you either. She's very strong."

"So I've heard. She's extraordinary . . ."

She stiffened. "Have you been watching her, Cameron?"

"Perhaps. I knew she was your friend, and that aroused my interest. She was worth watching. Doctor, expert apothecary, innovative, original thinker . . . survivor. As I said, she's extraordinary."

"And you look only for the extraordinary when you're trying to recruit talent for your damn new world. Back *off*. She's got the life she wants and needs here. I don't want you near her. And I don't want to hear she's disappeared into the mist someday."

He chuckled. "No mist. It was just a thought. You're very protective. I understand that concept." He paused. "I'm having a few protective instincts of my own rearing their heads. Hu Chang didn't call me, I called him. Because I had a report from my agents of something very ugly going down in San Francisco. And who is usually called in to sterilize that ugliness when it occurs in the CIA realm? So I decided to check in with Hu Chang and see where my Catherine was spending her time these days."

"I'm not your Catherine."

"It's a matter of semantics and viewpoint. I immediately felt very possessive when Hu Chang told me you were in San Francisco." His voice was suddenly dead serious. "Get out of there, Catherine."

"That's not going to happen. My job is here right now."

"Because rumors are flying about Max Huber. It's no rumor. Get out of there. You can trust my information."

She knew she could. She was aware of the enormous depth of Cameron's contacts. If Catherine had any doubts that Red Star was bluffing about their threat, they would have vanished. "I can't do it. Even if wasn't my duty, Rachel Venable is here, and I won't leave her alone."

Cameron muttered a curse. "Maybe I should rethink the mist. If Venable's daughter wasn't there, I might have a better shot at getting you out."

"No you wouldn't."

Silence. "No I wouldn't," he agreed. "I only wish Venable was there with you. Will you at least call and let me know if you run across anything I'd consider unacceptable? I don't like what I'm hearing."

"Neither do I." She added brusquely, "So I'll just have to take care of it. That's how people in the real world handle problems. They don't run away. They don't disappear into the mist and wait for Armageddon. They stay and fight. Thanks for calling and giving me your condolences, Cameron." She hung up.

No one hung up on Richard Cameron. Not because he was arrogant or vindictive. It was that silent power hovering over him, waiting to move forward out of the shadows. Or maybe it was the charisma that made everyone want to please him. She didn't know, and she didn't want to analyze it. She just knew she had done it because she couldn't bear talking to him any longer. Their relationship had been too hot and tempestuous, and she was still feeling the emotional earthquake he always brought into her life.

It was almost laughable that only last night she had been so irritated and frustrated about Claire Warren. Having Cameron coming on the scene could be so much more disruptive and traumatic. It was just like him to ignore her for months, then just pop back into her life and attempt to take control. And that could mean a struggle far greater than she'd face with Claire.

But she didn't even know that Cameron was in a position to interfere with anything she did. He'd been gone all these months and had probably been bouncing from country to country, wielding power, infiltrating universities and prisons, hijacking whatever target he chose as being worth his interest. Who was to say where his priorities lay?

And Rachel had clearly been worth his interest, she thought with exasperation. She had warned him off, and she thought that would be sufficient. However, no one could tell what Cameron would do next. It was best to always be on guard.

Tell Rachel there might be another player on the scene?

No, she had too much to worry about now without fretting about a threat that might not materialize.

Just keep watch on him herself as she was doing with Claire Warren. Do her job as she had been trained, recognize that Cameron could be either an enemy or an ally depending on what he deemed best at any given time. Or perhaps that he would fade back into the shadows and not be involved at all. That last would probably be the best choice of the three for all concerned.

Yes, that should be the game plan.

And, dear God, try to forget that jolt of pure lust that had gone through her when she had first heard Cameron's voice today.

SAN FRANCISCO AIRPORT

"You told Catherine Ling you were coming to San Francisco, didn't you?" Brandon asked Rachel quietly as they started down the jetway at their arrival gate. "What am I to expect when we get outside the terminal?"

Her gaze flew to his face. He had not made any comment nor asked one question during the connecting flight they'd taken out of Trinidad. "I didn't call Catherine."

"No, you wouldn't do that since you'd told me you wouldn't. I've begun to know you, Rachel. But you would see nothing wrong in phoning Hu Chang and leaving the decision up to him. You have infinite faith in your friend." He grimaced. "And you certainly have no faith in me. Not that I blame you."

"I have faith that you would not hurt me intentionally. If there had been a danger of that, my father would not have sent you to me. He must have even thought you could save me." Her lips twisted. "And he certainly must have thought that you'd be smart enough to use me to stop Huber from blowing up this city. Yes, I have faith in you, Brandon."

"Great." He muttered a curse. "What the hell? I don't even know why it makes a difference to me. You don't seem to have had much more faith in Venable than you do in me."

"I have the faith that my father was a great patriot."

"But not such a great father?"

She could feel the tears begin to sting. "When I was a little girl, he was wonderful to me. Later, I didn't see much of him. But I'm not talking about him anymore. He was what he was. He had priorities. We all have priorities." She looked away from him. "How did we get on that subject? You wanted to know what you should expect because I told Hu Chang I was coming here? Nothing. Neither he nor Catherine would interfere with your arrangements for me. They want me safe. They care about me. Anything I tell either one in confidence remains in confidence. That's why I thought it ridiculous you should try to shut them out." As they reached the gate area, she whirled on him. "There will be no one following us, but I don't guarantee that they won't find me. Hu Chang knows this city. He had a laboratory here when I first came to live with him. He has another house near Catherine in Louisville, but he liked the availability of the plants in the redwood forest. He thought it would be easier for me."

His gaze narrowed on her face. "Plants?"

She shook her head. "You really don't know much about Hu Chang, do you?"

"It appears not as much as I need to know." He took her elbow and nudged her toward the escalator. "But I'd already promised myself I'd rectify that omission. I believe I'd better up the priority on that immediately. Now, since you assure me that we'll be free of surveillance, we'll get out of here and get you to that safe house."

"You'll trust my judgment?" she asked skeptically. "You weren't ready to listen to me before."

"I'm not accustomed to trusting many people. Particularly in situations like this. But it seems I have no choice in the matter. You will clearly do as you like if you find it meets with your rather unique sense of honor. I'm something of a cynic, and I haven't been exposed to the concept of honor very often." His lips twisted. "And honor can be interpreted is so many ways, according to the person expressing it. But I find myself wanting to believe I can work with yours." He shrugged. "At any rate, we'll make the attempt. Okay?"

It should have made her more wary of him to realize that he had been watching, analyzing, and had still been willing to take the chance of a possible threat. He was getting to know her far too well.

But she had known when this began that he also could be a threat, and this was only a part of it. Yes, there was wariness, but she was beginning to feel a frisson of excitement and challenge as well. It was strange it should come in the midst of this time of emotional trauma. She gazed at him and nodded slowly. "I think I can deal with that, Brandon." She looked away from him. "Now where is this safe house you're going to take me to?"

BEACH HAVEN

"The sea?" Rachel looked out the window of the Toyota rental car at the blue expanse of the Pacific Ocean, then to the gray stone house on the cliff. "The boat out of Georgetown and now a house on the beach. Am I detecting a pattern here?"

"Perhaps." He drove up the driveway and parked. "It's called Beach Haven, and you'll find it comfortable. I told Nate I wanted something out of the city with multiple ways to exit. There's a private helicopter pad down there on the beach where a helicopter can land, the ocean is an obvious exit." He smiled as he got out of the car. "And, of course, Nate knows my preferences."

"And that you grew up on a boat."

He nodded. "I usually choose a sea view wherever I am." He opened her passenger door. "Predictable. It might become dangerously predictable at some time."

"But you do it because it reminds you of the years with your father?"

"Maybe. Though, as I told you, those memories could be bittersweet."

She looked up at him. "But you didn't tell me why."

He smiled crookedly. "Perhaps I thought you'd

guess. Three years ago, my dad was blown up in his sailboat in Venice. Courtesy of Max Huber."

She stiffened in shock. Maybe she should have guessed, but she had been so involved with her own tragedy that it had obscured everything else. "Why?"

"Huber sent word ordering my father to find a way to get his men into a gallery in Brussels, so that he could steal a few masterpieces, then stage one of his famous disasters. He probably thought it was an entirely reasonable demand since my father had a reputation for having slipped into some of the most high-security museums in Europe at one time or another. But my dad wasn't about to get involved with a terrorist like Huber. He sent back a message to Huber that he was no longer in that business. The next day, his boat blew up as he took it out to sea." His lips tightened. "I couldn't find enough body parts to bury him."

And that was why he'd said that it might get easier to talk about his past someday, but that time wasn't now. His expression was controlled and so was his tone, but she could feel the pain. He had told her that it helped him to give something when he took something away. This had been something very personal for him, even more personal than she had thought. He had known he was taking her father away, so he'd replayed his own pain. It was a strange and remarkable gift. "I'm sorry you had to go through that," she said haltingly. "You were very kind to me. It probably brought back—"

"Yes, it did," he said curtly. "And your reaction nearly tore me apart. Now let's forget it."

She didn't know if she could forget it. Somehow, the pain they had both felt and how he had dealt with it was having a profound effect on the way she was seeing him.

"I mean it," he said roughly. "I can see you softening like you did when you were bending over that little kid. That's not what I'll ever want from you."

He was right. She was softening, trying to understand him, and it was probably crazy to think he'd need either. She drew a deep breath and tried to get back on track. She returned her gaze to the ocean. "But you said that Huber might know that you have this particular predictability." She got out of the car. "Or maybe you didn't want to make it difficult for him to locate us."

"You keep persisting in believing that I'm staking you out." His lips tightened. "I don't deny that time might come, but it's not now. And I've no intention of letting Huber have you even if it comes to that. Nate makes sure that any rental can't be traced. And you're safe here." He turned and headed for the front door. "And you might find the sea has a therapeutic effect. I always did."

"Because it was home to you." She followed him to the front door and watched him enter the combination on the automatic lock. "Different people have different ways to cope."

"And what's your way to cope? Where do you go?"

She didn't answer. There was an unexpected intensity in the question that made her uneasy. He was probing, trying to go beneath those layers that protected her.

"The mountains? The woods?" His voice was soft, persuasive. "I've told you mine. Where's your place to cope? Where's your place to heal?

"Why do you want to know?"

"I'm not sure, but I do. I'm finding that I want to know all kinds of things about who you are, how you think. Maybe because you're avoiding telling me about it." He smiled mockingly. "And you did promise me 'anything,' Rachel."

"Then is this some kind of a test? If so, you've chosen something of totally no importance."

"Then why not answer me? Where do you go? Scuba diving on the reefs?"

He wasn't going to give up, and she might as well tell him, then dismiss it.

She shrugged. "I go to work in Hu Chang's lab for a while. Or in my own lab if it's closer to where I am at the time. Satisfied?"

"No, but fascinated." He threw open the front door. "It sounds like hard work. I wouldn't think that would be in the least soothing or healing. Why?"

"It keeps my mind working. It takes me away. I can create solutions instead of feeling helpless about any given situation."

"Now I can see how that would have an appeal for you." He frowned, his gaze narrowed on her face. "And now that I think about it, one of the things I heard about Hu Chang was that he was a brilliant apothecary and developer of homeopathic medicine."

"He's a genius," she said simply. "In many ways."

"I'm sure that goes without saying as far as you're concerned." He paused. "Hu Chang's lab. That's your lab of choice. Why?"

"Why not? He has almost every kind of natural ingredient and herb you could think of having. From the mountains of Tibet to Mongolia, to the fjords of Norway."

"And that's the only reason?"

"I guess everyone feels more comfortable in the place where they were taught. I spent hours every day for two years drinking in everything Hu Chang would teach me." Hours of healing, hours of becoming born anew, hours of finding resolution and understanding when she had thought it could never happen. "It's natural I would feel a sense of coming home."

He tilted his head. "And that was right after you came to live with him after you left Afghanistan?"

He was studying her again, and that question was verging on exploring places she didn't want to go. "That's right." She strode into the foyer and looked around the high-ceilinged living room with its huge stone fireplace and comfortable, cushioned furniture. "This is very nice. I like the fireplace. My team and I have been working principally in the tropics lately. I haven't used a fireplace since I was at Catherine's house in Louisville two Christmases ago."

"And I assume this is a signal to indicate you're closing me out and that any in-depth discussions are over," he murmured. "Actually, I feel I gained more than I lost this time." He turned and locked the front door.

"Nate said that there are three bedrooms, a library, a kitchen, and a nice veranda. He's also arranged to have basic wardrobes and some groceries delivered. Why don't you go choose a bedroom while I go to the kitchen and see what I can do in the way of throwing together a meal?" He moved down the hall. "And after dinner we can have wine on the veranda and watch the sunset. The wine might help you to relax." His lips quirked. "Sorry that I didn't know it was necessary to furnish you with a fully equipped lab to release tension."

He was gone.

And she moved toward a door across the living room in search of the bedroom wing. He had come another step closer, and it was on sensitive ground that was intensely personal to her.

And she had not had to let him take that step, she realized. She had told herself it was easier and not important, but was it that she'd wanted to share the intimacy of that part of her life in exchange for what Brandon had given her that night on the boat? Or maybe it was simply sex and nothing deeper. There was no doubt that she was sexually drawn to him. Though she had not let herself think about it since those first moments on the boat after they had left Georgetown. After that, she had been lost, torn apart, completely devastated, when he'd told her about her father. But Hu Chang had taught her to know herself, particularly when it came to any of the damage that had been done to her in the past. And those small lapses that had been occurring since then were more revealing than she liked to admit. If she was vulnerable to

Brandon in any way, then she had to face it so that she could come to terms and make decisions.

But not right now. She would give herself time to rest and have a few hours to think about what was happening around her and to her. God knows she hadn't really had that opportunity since Brandon had erupted into her life.

It had all been about little Maria and Phillip and her promise to Brandon. And then it had been her father emerging from the shadows where she'd left him because she couldn't bear to have him beside her. But he was now closer to her than he'd ever been when he was alive.

It was all too painful and bewildering, and there was no way that it could stay that way.

Yes, give herself time; and then face both the pain and the questions . . .

"That dinner was pretty terrific for just throwing it together." Rachel's gaze shifted from the scarlet-streaked sky of the setting sun to Brandon's face. "Where did you learn to cook?"

"The computer. I told you, my schooling was all Apple-oriented. Do you know how many cooking shows you can access on the computer?" He grimaced. "Plus when I was onshore, I often had jobs at restaurants and casinos. My dad insisted I bring something of value back besides what I won shooting craps in the alleys behind the kitchens."

"I'd say that chicken Parmesan recipe tonight definitely had value." She made a face. "It's not one of my skills. Hu Chang said he'd rather swallow one of my poisons than something I cooked from scratch. And my father was a very good cook and agreed with him. I kept forgetting ingredients. And I let things burn."

"It sounds like a case of serious disinterest." He poured wine into her goblet. "Attention and alertness is required. Without them, most dishes turn out as disasters."

"But yours evidently didn't." She smiled. "So you must have had more discipline than your father thought you had."

"No, I was just as wild as he thought me. He knew exactly where I was heading." He took a sip of wine and his gaze shifted to the sunset. "Poisons?" he repeated softly. "Swallow one of your poisons, Rachel?"

She had wondered if he'd pick up on those words. It was really a foregone conclusion since Brandon never appeared to miss anything. It was like him not to mention them immediately, but go back to them later. But she'd known as soon as she'd said them that he'd ask her about them. "Yes." She smiled. "Do you think you've discovered one of my dreaded secrets? I'm no Lucrezia Borgia, Brandon." She held up her hand. "No poison ring."

He took her hand and ran his index finger over each finger. "No ring. But I've always liked your fingers. They seemed very capable, yet graceful and full of life . . ."

Her hand was tingling beneath his touch. She pulled her hand quickly away. "Definitely capable. I'd be a lousy surgeon if they weren't. I might not be as good as Phillip, but One World wouldn't have hired me if I didn't have qualifications in something other than internal medicine. Anyway, I became very good at poisons by the time I'd been with Hu Chang for a year. By the time I was ready to enter medical school, I was almost as good as he was. Though he would never admit it."

"A trifle unusual. Is there some reason why you studied how to make poisons with Hu Chang when you were being taught homeopathic medicines?"

"Hu Chang thought it was important. It was very good training. He'd grown up as the son of an apothecary who specialized in the creation and sale of undetectable poisons to governments and persons who paid highly for his services. Hu Chang learned that combining ingredients for poisons that had to be undetectable was much more difficult, subtle, and required more knowledge of results and effects on the body than any other possible blending. If I could do that well, it would help me in any other medicine I tried to create." She shrugged. "I found he was right, so I learned everything he could teach me. I learned to create new poisons, and derivatives of old, and I used the techniques I learned doing it to apply to my other work."

"Such as the medicine you were willing to trek through the rain forest to give to Maria?"

"I don't know what you mean." She gazed at him blandly. "I heard she was taking some brew her grandmother passed down to her mother, Blanca."

He chuckled. "You're not shy at talking about poisons, but you won't admit to creating a medicine to save a child?"

She was silent. "It would be totally irresponsible to use anything experimental when a life could be in the balance. It could only be excused if there was no possible hope. Even then, it's questionable. It takes years to get a medicine approved, then it sometimes isn't made because an illness doesn't affect enough people to make it profitable. It's smart that they're careful, but people sometimes die."

"And decisions have to be made in a life-or-death situation?"

"Blanca made her decision for Maria." She smiled. "She gave her an old family recipe." She stared him in the eye. "You should understand, you're obviously into recipes, Brandon. And why shouldn't I be willing to talk about poisons? They were a big part of my life with Hu Chang."

"That's what I've been thinking. And perhaps not only your life with Hu Chang." He paused. "*Undetectable* was the key word, wasn't it?"

And he had known from the moment she had first mentioned poison how important that comment had been and where it was leading. He'd gathered all the information together and come up with answers. She could back off, even lie, but she suddenly knew she wasn't going to do it.

"*Undetectable* is always the key word with a poison," she said recklessly. "But it's almost impossible to create an undetectable poison with all the high-tech tests these days. Hu Chang said it was much easier in his father's day."

"How fortunate. How close did you come, Rachel?"

"I took the blue ribbon." She got to her feet. "Or so my father told me. Is that what you wanted to know? Well, there it is. Now I think I'll bid you good night."

"Wait." He stood up and faced her. "Before you run off to your room and tell yourself how I've grilled you into letting me guess how you killed Conrad Huber, I have a word or two. Since Conrad Huber's death was only recently found to be a murder, I suspected it had to be a poison. And you're much too clever to have let that poison bit just slip out. You wanted me to question you. You wanted to tell me about it. So tell me."

She froze. "It's not as if I have some reason to be that convoluted. And I'm usually very honest with myself, so why would I make an excuse to blame you?"

"That's why you have me confused. I've found you remarkably clear-sighted in our short acquaintance. Maybe you felt the need to share, but it could be that you panicked at the last minute and had to back off." His lips tightened. "And the only other thing I can think it might be is that you wanted to cause some conflict between us. You picked a subject that's probably one of the most sensitive, painful events in your past, then set me up to interrogate you about it. A perfect excuse to push me away."

She moistened her lips. "I wouldn't need an excuse to push you away. We barely know each other."

"But we've come a long way down the path, haven't we?" He met her eyes. "And I believe I want to see where it goes from here. So I'm not going to let you hold me at a distance. Yes, we have a job to do, and we'll do it. Huber's going down. But there's no telling what else is going to happen along the way." He reached out and touched the hair at her temple. "Think about it. Expect it."

She pulled her gaze away and took a step back. Her heart was beating fast, and she could feel the heat in her cheeks. Just the lightest touch, and she'd had this response. Maybe he was right, and instinct had made her try to drive him away in the most certain way for her to keep him at bay. Or maybe it was something else entirely different.

"I'll do what you want me to do to get Huber," she said unevenly. "Other than that, don't expect anything of me, Brandon. And I certainly won't expect anything of you."

She turned and walked into the house.

She didn't know what had happened out there tonight, but she'd had little or no control of it. She needed to have a sense of control, she thought desperately. Her father's death and the memories that assaulted her because of it were very strong. And Brandon's arrival in the wake of it and his effect on her had also unsettled her. The last thing she needed was to do something stupid like fall into his bed because all her emotional responses were exaggerated right now. So do something to show herself she was still functioning as usual.

She stopped just inside the door of the house and reached for her phone.

She dialed quickly, and when the call was picked up, she said quickly, "Catherine, Rachel. I'm here in San Francisco. Do you want me to meet you somewhere or come here to me?"

CHAPTER

6

Forty-five minutes had passed.

It was time.

Rachel left her room and moved out onto the veranda. Brandon was still there, sitting watching the surf. But there was something different . . . His every muscle was taut, ready.

It was what she had expected . . . and feared. What would you expect from the ultimate warrior Nate had told her about?

"Get back inside, Rachel." He didn't look at her. "Now!"

"No." She came toward him. "It's okay. Relax. No threat. It's only Catherine. She said she'd come on foot from a few miles down the road. Do you know where she is?"

His tension ebbed a little. "Near that dune forty

yards down the hill. I was about to go and greet her."
He got to his feet. "After I took her down."

"That's why I came out to make certain that you
didn't do that." She moved across to the edge of the
veranda and motioned to Catherine. "I thought you'd
act first and ask questions later."

"You phoned her?"

"I told her I'd call her." She watched Catherine move
like a graceful shadow toward the veranda. "I did what
I promised."

"You might have let me know," he said dryly. "Or
were you afraid of arguments?"

"Why would I be afraid? We're after the same thing
and so is Catherine. I don't have to consult with you
unless I choose, Brandon. I agreed to do anything I
could do to take down Huber. That doesn't include
slave labor."

"Wrong. It includes anything that makes it more
likely that I can kill the son of a bitch. That means a
coordinated assault, not random acts that could get you
killed." He turned to Catherine Ling, who had just
reached the steps to the veranda. "Hello, Ms. Ling, I
don't like you here. Houseguests aren't on my list of
desired personnel at the moment."

"Catherine." She took the steps two at a time.
"Sorry, Brandon. Rachel offered to meet me somewhere, but I didn't like the idea of her exposing herself in case either one of us had been made. I could lose
anyone following me and control the situation if I came
here instead."

"You think you might be followed?"

"Later, Brandon." She turned toward Rachel. "This is more important right now." She took Rachel in her arms and hugged her. She said softly, "I grieve with you, my friend. Venable was many things to me, but he was always someone I could turn to in need. Just as you are, Rachel. There's no way we can make this right, but maybe we can do something to make it better."

Rachel was blinking back the tears. "I'm glad you're here, Catherine."

"Why did you think you might be followed?" Brandon repeated.

"Leave her alone." Rachel turned and slipped her arm around Catherine's waist and led her toward the French doors. "I made coffee before I came out here to rescue her from you. Come inside, and I'll let you interrogate her."

"If I choose," Catherine murmured. "Did you really think I'd need rescuing?"

"I thought I'd avoid the possibility," Rachel said. "He'd already seen you when I came out, Catherine."

Catherine shook her head. "Not possible."

"No, quite possible," he said. "Though you're very good." He followed them into the house. "And I agree we shouldn't be out there in the open now that you're an unknown element in the equation." He closed the veranda doors. "Now, I'll go to the kitchen and bring out that coffee. You two can bond until I get back. Which will be in about three minutes. After that, I want answers." He strode down the hall and out of sight.

Catherine's thoughtful gaze followed him until he disappeared. "I can see why Venable asked him to go after you. I never worked with Brandon when he and Venable were taking down that cell last year, but I know your father trusted him to get the job done." Her gaze shifted to Rachel. "I've only run across two or three men in my career who gave out that particular vibe."

"Vibe?"

She motioned impatiently. "Power. Sheer power. You know what I'm talking about. He's . . . not usual."

"That he's not," Rachel said dryly. "Yes, I know what you're talking about. So did Morales and his men in that jungle in Guyana."

"But what's your judgment? Can you trust him?"

"I think I can. Do you mean would he run right over me if it meant getting Huber? He's driven, but I don't believe he'd go that far. He told me he wouldn't. You don't have to worry about that."

"Yes, I do. But I just have to know how close I have to watch him." Her gaze shifted to Rachel. "Because he's watching you very closely, indeed. That could be good or not so good. This is a very dicey situation. More than I first thought."

"You're not responsible for keeping an eye on Brandon," Rachel said quietly. "You have your own job to do. Leave Brandon to me."

"Yes, by all means, leave me to Rachel." Brandon was coming down the hall carrying a tray with a carafe and cups and saucers. He added, "And leave

Rachel to me, Catherine. It will be much more efficient all around." He put the tray on the coffee table in front of the fireplace. "Now why did you think that there was a possibility of you being followed?"

"Because I don't know what's going on," Catherine said bluntly as she poured herself a cup of coffee and one for Rachel. "And I don't like being in the dark." She looked at Rachel. "And Claire Warren is very interested in you and how she might manipulate you to take down Huber. She wouldn't give a damn about protecting you if it meant that she'd have a chance to get rid of him."

"Which only means she's an operative of the caliber of my father," Rachel said quietly. "He'd weigh all options as he should. There's nothing wrong with wanting to save the world."

"Absolutely not, but there's something wrong with sacrificing lives unnecessarily because it's convenient to do so," Catherine said bluntly. "And not searching for ways to get to the same destination without handing you over to Huber if it comes to a deal."

"You believe she's heading that way?" Brandon asked.

"I believe she's ruthless and will stop this attack on the city at any cost," Catherine said. "She made that very clear. She delayed announcing Venable's death so that she could get all her ducks in a row. You're one of those ducks, Rachel." She stared coolly at Brandon. "And Claire Warren said that she sent you down to Guyana to herd her into position."

"What?" Rachel's eyes flew to Brandon's face. "When I was talking about her, you never mentioned you knew her."

"It wasn't relevant at the time. It might have just gotten in the way. And my relationship with Claire Warren would not give her the authority to order me to do anything." He met her eyes. "I called and told her that Venable was dead and that I was going after you. I thought someone at the CIA should know what was happening, considering what Huber was planning for San Francisco. I did *not* ask permission. Claire and I have had problems in the past, so that wouldn't happen." His lips twisted. "And I do not consider you a duck any more than I do a goat."

"Goat?" Catherine echoed. "Did I miss something?"

"Goats, tigers, ducks," Rachel said impatiently. "I'm tired of comparisons. And it all goes back to whether I'm going to trust Brandon." She paused. "And I suppose I do." She added fiercely, "Though I don't like it that you just *happened* to not mention you knew Claire Warren."

"Objection noted," he said. "However, I don't see how you can expect me to be totally open when you're hardly forthcoming yourself." He turned back to Catherine. "Since when would a CIA officer order that one of her operatives be followed when on assignment?"

Catherine shrugged. "I could be overreacting. But she specifically requested me for her team, and she knew that I was friends with both Venable and Rachel. It seemed to be a little too convenient." She made a face. "And I had a little spat with her, and she was cold as ice. I decided I wasn't going to risk her getting her hands on Rachel and trying to use her. That was why I decided I needed to come here." She stared him in the eye. "And I had to make sure that, in a pinch, you wouldn't use her either. Or I'd have to take her away from you."

"That might be interesting," he murmured.

She smiled. "Yes, it would. Pity that Rachel's decided that you're marginally trustworthy and that I trust her judgment." She lifted her coffee to her lips. "So we work together. But Claire Warren was very clear about Rachel's being an asset that we couldn't ignore. She was certain that Huber would do anything to get his hands on her. She wouldn't tell me why." She looked at Rachel. "Are you going to tell me?"

"I was responsible for the death of Huber's father."

Catherine gave a low whistle. "That would do it."

"And one other thing that I might throw into the mix," Brandon said quietly. "I don't know if Huber is aware of it yet, but Venable gave his informant, Nemesis, from Huber's camp, Rachel's name as the person to contact with any information if he was taken out."

"What?" Rachel stared at him, stunned. "And when were you going to tell me that?"

"Not until it was necessary." He shrugged. "But you're insisting on total frankness, and I can't risk your walking away from me."

Catherine was shaking her head. "And if Huber does know, he'd want to take Rachel out just to keep her quiet." She added skeptically, "You're quite sure you're right about trusting Brandon, Rachel?"

"Dammit, I thought Venable would give Nemesis *my* name," Brandon said. "But he didn't trust me enough. You're the only one he trusted, Rachel. He said to tell you that he was sorry to do it, but it was time for you to make the choice. That he'd promised it to you."

"And put her squarely in the crosshairs," Catherine said.

Not for the first time Rachel thought dazedly. Choices . . . "I suppose that's true. But he wouldn't think—he'd only think about what was the right thing to do. He was dying, Catherine."

"I know," Catherine said. "But he could have given him my name if he didn't trust Brandon. You're a doctor. You wouldn't know how to handle any of this."

"I guess he thought I'd learn." She looked at Brandon. "How is this Nemesis supposed to contact me?"

Brandon shrugged. "Venable said he communicated by computer with him until he set up that last meeting. Venable probably gave him your email address."

"It would have been nice if you'd told me to check it," she said sarcastically. "I've been a little too busy to go online lately."

"I would have gotten around to it soon. I wanted to let you get your breath."

"I don't believe Max Huber or Nemesis would be equally considerate."

"I had a little time. At least a week or so. Venable said that nothing was going to happen until the twenty-fifth. He said that date was locked in place."

"The twenty-fifth of September," Rachel said slowly. "Yes, that would make sense."

"Why?" Catherine asked.

"It was the twenty-fifth of September four years ago when Conrad Huber was killed. His son evidently wants to make a statement." She moistened her lips. "Vendetta. Not only to kill the two people responsible for killing his father but to cripple an entire city in his honor." She shuddered. "And who knows how many fatalities would be laid on the altar."

Brandon nodded grimly. "Max Huber is exceptionally good at statements. The count would be high. He'd want to go over 9/11 for bragging rights."

Bragging rights. Rachel felt sick at the thought. "No wonder he wants to get his hands on me so quickly. I'd be the centerpiece of his celebration, wouldn't I?"

"If he had his way." His lips tightened. "But he won't, Rachel."

"If you say so." She was shaking. Her mind was spinning. She needed to get out of here so that she could make sense of what she had been told.

"*It's time to make a choice.*"

Brandon said that was the message her father had sent her. But she couldn't think, much less make choices, right now.

"It's going to be okay," Catherine said gently. "I'm here for you, Rachel. I know this all seems overwhelming. But this is what I do. This is what Venable did. I'll get you through this." She cast a glance at Brandon. "I might even let him help."

"Many thanks," he said dryly. "I don't believe you have a choice."

Choice again, Rachel thought. That word that Venable had used. The word that was taking her breath away and knotting her stomach.

"Well, the two of you can argue it out," she said jerkily as she put her cup down on the coffee table. She gave Catherine a quick hug and turned away. "Yes, okay, I'm shaken and confused by all this. I need some time. I'll call you tomorrow morning. It seems the world's not going to crash before then. Thanks for coming to the rescue."

"I haven't tried to rescue you from anyone but Brandon so far," Catherine said. "You haven't seen anything yet." She put her cup down. "I'll keep a close eye on all intel and get back to you if there's anything interesting. And I'll do a little probing to see if I can find out another name for Nemesis. That's a bit melodramatic for me. It reminds me of Deep Throat."

"Venable said the same thing when he first told me about him," Brandon said.

"Venable and I always thought a good deal alike." She added to Rachel, "Except about putting you in the crosshairs. He should have given Nemesis my name to contact."

"But he didn't." Rachel was heading for the door. "Good night, Catherine." She glanced at Brandon. "And I'm having trouble with you for not telling me everything. It smacks of manipulation. But then every interaction between us since the moment I met you has been manipulative. I'm going to have to think about that."

"By all means." He was smiling crookedly. "But remember that at least two of those initial interactions have involved manipulations by you. Good night, Rachel."

He was right. Maria Perez, then Philip's rescue. But she was not about to go into either right now. She just needed to get away and think about this Nemesis, whom her father had handed to her as a terrible gift.

And September 25 and all the thousands of deaths Huber was determined to lay at her door in commemoration of that day four years ago.

But three hours later, Rachel was still tossing and turning in bed. Nothing was clear, and everything was a jumble of her father's words and all that he had been to her. Catherine had not understood Venable's actions, but she had not had that problem. He had warned her this time might come, but she had not thought that he would not be here with her when it did. That he would never be with her again.

Time for choices.

I don't want to lose you, too.

But he *had* lost her, and she had lost him in the most final way possible. She had thought that she had lost him before that shot that had taken his life, but he had proved her wrong. He had still been with her, like a shadow, like a memory that was engraved on everything she had done during those years without him.

I don't want to lose you, too . . .

NEW YORK CITY
FIVE YEARS AGO

But the loss had seemed inevitable.

And it had first begun both for Venable and her during those years when she had studied with Hu Chang and gone on to the university and medical school. Her father had lived his life, and she had lived hers. Occasionally, she had received a gift or phone call from him, but he had never tried to reunite with her.

And she had never tried to reach out to him, either. Not until today, when she called him and asked him to come to her apartment for lunch. It was the week after she graduated from med school, and she had been filled with enthusiasm and eagerness and the hope for new beginnings. She had been nervous, filled with misgivings, yet there had been that hope . . .

The doorbell rang.

She stood there and took a deep breath. This might be a mistake. Venable had not been the one to make the move. Perhaps he didn't really want to see her.

Stop making excuses not to open the door. She had thought about this for months, a new life was nothing without resolving what had been left behind. And there was that hope that had never gone away . . .

And she thought she saw the same hope in her father's expression when she opened the door.

He looked the same as he had that last day at the prison in Afghanistan. Maybe his hair was a little more gray than red, perhaps there were a few more lines in his face. "Hello." *He smiled.* "You look beautiful. Shouldn't I be taking you out to lunch? I hear you graduated with honors, Dr. Venable. I was very proud when Hu Chang told me."

"I sent you an invitation."

"I didn't want to intrude. It was a special day for you." *He paused.* "And I didn't believe I was part of your life any longer. I figured you didn't need me there."

"That's not what you said that last day."

"That was before I realized how well you were doing without me. Hu Chang was healing you as I never could." *His lips twisted.* "I was supposed to step in and be the cause of your having a fresh set of nightmares? That's the last thing that I wanted, Rachel. Hu Chang kept me updated about you." *He met her eyes.* "And I hoped one day that I might get a call from you inviting me to lunch or dinner. Or just to sit down and talk. I'll take anything I'm given."

"Then I'd better invite you in instead of letting you stand out in the hall." *She smiled unsteadily.* "Though you'd probably prefer to take me out to lunch. Hu Chang says I'm the world's worst cook. I tried to solve the problem today by fixing frozen lasagna casserole that won't totally be a disaster." *She stepped aside.* "So step into my brand-new parlor whose only real advantage is that it's close to the hospital where I'm doing my residency. But thank heavens it also has a microwave oven to keep me from starving."

He went past her and looked around the apartment. "It's warm and colorful, and it looks like you." He glanced at the long table and shelves with multiple vials and bottles against the wall across the room. "That's your lab? Very neat. Though I didn't expect you to have a lab here."

"Why not? It's more convenient than arranging time at one of the labs at the hospital. And I keep all the poisons secured in that cabinet when I'm not using them. I love to experiment. You might say it's a passion."

"Hu Chang told me that you were a remarkable student."

"He's a remarkable teacher." She braced herself. "I'm feeling awkward. I knew it would be like this. But I couldn't avoid it any longer. I thought it would be worth it . . . to both of us."

"Just being here is worth it to me," he said quietly. "And I'm not feeling awkward, I'm feeling grateful. Perhaps you'd feel less awkward if you talked it out. You always did when you were a little girl."

And he had always understood that about her. He had understood so many of her traits and dreams. "That's very smart of you. You were always so clever . . ." She gestured to a chair. "Want a cup of coffee? I have an automatic coffeemaker, and even I have trouble ruining coffee."

"Later." He dropped down into the chair. "Talk to me, Rachel."

She didn't speak for a moment. "I wasn't . . . fair to you. I think I knew it at the time. But I couldn't get past . . . It's just that you're so smart. I've always thought you could do anything. I couldn't understand why you couldn't save me from . . . that."

"I should have been able to do it," he said hoarsely. "You were right to blame me."

She shook her head. "I was too young to realize that you weren't superman and that you'd always do whatever you could. It took a long time for me to think clearly enough to sort it all out." She grimaced. "And you and I don't think alike. You run toward all the blood and gore and try to battle it. My instinct is to come later and try to heal the wounds. You said I was more like you than my brothers. But I don't think that's true."

"I believe you'll find it is." He reached out and took her hand. "I watched you growing up, and you never turned your back on a battle. You may be a healer, but there's always a time to make a choice. If the battle is worth it to you, then you'd go running toward it, too." His hand tightened on hers. "I think perhaps what happened to you caused you to run the other way. God knows I was glad that you were burying your head in your books and studies. You've gone through enough violence to last your entire life."

"And so have you. Why don't you step away from it?"

"Because someone has to stop it, and I'm good at it. That's where my instinct lies, Rachel." He looked down at her hand, and said haltingly, "Do you remember I told you that I hoped that you weren't right about my accepting the report I had on you too readily? I had nightmares about that." He added harshly, "Because I didn't want to give up those two prisoners. I'd found a link between them and another terrorist organization that was pulling the strings of that Taliban group. I didn't want to give them up before I traced that link."

"I . . . see."

"No, you don't," he said roughly. "I can feel you drawing back from me. It's not what you think. Those two prisoners trained outside Dusseldorf, Germany, with the Red Star terrorist organization. I've had a good deal of interaction with Conrad Huber of Red Star. I get in their way. They punish people who get in their way." His eyes lifted to meet her own, and they were glittering with moisture. "Or the families of people who get in their way. I thought there was a good chance that they might have orchestrated that ambush that killed your mother and brother . . . and stuck you in that hellhole of a prison."

She gazed at him in shock. "And did they?"

"I still don't know. I had to return one prisoner to get you released," he said jerkily. "He disappeared into the hills and hasn't been seen since. The other one conveniently escaped prison, at about the same time we'd heard that there was a Red Star presence in Kabul, before I could question him. I still haven't been *able to track him down. His name is Karim Ali Telvar and the last I heard, he'd left Afghanistan and was working for Conrad Huber in Shanghai."*

"You didn't tell me all this," she whispered.

"I had no proof. I still have no proof. I wasn't about to give you excuses after what you'd gone through. Regardless, I'm still to blame. But I believe I'm close, Rachel. I have a good lead. I swear that once I'm sure that Red Star is responsible, I won't let those bastards live no matter what the cost." His tone was grimly absolute. "I promise you that nothing will stop me."

"You should have told me."

"I was afraid that you were right, that I'd made a terrible mistake because I wanted to keep my hands on that son of a bitch. I didn't think I did, I prayed it wasn't true, but I couldn't be certain."

"It would have helped me to know about . . ." But would it really, she wondered. It had been a time of pain and horror and bitterness. She thought that she would have been able to temper that with understanding, but she had been so young. "How do I know?" She drew a shaky breath. "But what I do know is that I called you before I knew any of this. And I did that because I wanted a fresh start, it was important to me. It's still important." She met his eyes. "Could we have that, please?"

He nodded. "Oh, yes, we can have that." An eager smile lit his face. "I'll be around so much that you'll get bored with me. We have a lot of time to make up."

She tried to laugh, but it came out a little husky.

"Yeah, sure. That won't happen. My hours are completely crazy, and you're busy saving the world. I'll be satisfied with seeing you occasionally." She smiled. "But I like the thought. Maybe we could invite Hu Chang next time. He scorns my culinary abilities, but he actually cooks very well."

"So do I." He got to his feet. "And we'll invite Hu Chang, but I like the idea of being alone with you and able to make myself at home here. Hu Chang seems to dominate any room, and I like to occasionally do a little dominating myself." He headed for the coffeemaker on the kitchen counter. "I need to catch up." He smiled at her over his shoulder. "Okay with you?"

Warmth, affection, understanding. They were all in that smile. She felt as if she were being wrapped, stroked, cuddled as she had been when he'd held her as a child. She hadn't realized how lonely she'd been for that smile in these last years.

Lonely for him.

She smiled and slowly nodded. "Okay with me."

EIGHTEEN MONTHS LATER

Carl Venable.

Rachel glanced at the ID on her phone and made a face. She hoped he wasn't canceling again for tomorrow night. Her father had already broken two dinner dates in the last week because he'd had missions out of the country. Not that she had any reason to complain since she'd canceled on him the week before.

As she'd first told him, they both lived busy lives. But it didn't keep her from feeling disappointment when it happened. She always so looked forward to seeing him. He'd become such an integral part of her life during these last months that she felt empty and hollow without him. She accessed the call. "Okay, where are you going this time?"

"I'm just back." He paused. "I need to talk to you, Rachel. Could I come over tonight?"

"Instead of tomorrow? Yes, I just got off duty. I should be home in about thirty minutes. Is everything all right?"

"No. Yes. Not what anyone would term perfect. I'm on my way to your place now. I'll probably be there before you are." He ended the call.

She slowly hung up. She didn't like this.

She felt chilled and uneasy. Her father was usually cool and totally in control. He hadn't sounded either on the phone. Anything that could disturb him to that extent couldn't be good.

The door was unlocked when she got to the apartment. She had given Venable a key a few months after that first afternoon because it had seemed more convenient when they were trying to spend more time together "to catch up" as her father had termed it. She opened the door to see him across the apartment at the bar in the kitchen. She was used to seeing him there as he made coffee or cooked or poured a glass of wine for both of them. It was a casual and warming sight that she now valued.

But he did not look casual at the moment.

Her pulse leaped as she stood there in the doorway. "What's happening?"

"Sit down and have a glass of wine." He handed her a glass of her favorite red. "You may need it." His lips twisted. "Or you might want to throw it at me. I'll accept either response."

She lifted the wine to her lips. "Why would I want to throw it at you?"

"Because I've done something that you could think unforgivable. I hope not, but it may take some time to—" He met her eyes. "I didn't want to do it. It's the last thing that I wanted to involve you in. But I couldn't see any other foolproof way."

"Foolproof?" She was staring at him in bewilderment. "What are you talking about?"

"I found Karim Ali Telvar." His lips tightened grimly. "I told you I thought I was close. A month ago, I located him in Shanghai." He paused. "And I made him talk."

"And?"

"It was Red Star, special orders from Conrad Huber that coordinated the attack on your mother's car through his Taliban affiliates. It was aimed at me, but you were the ones who paid the price. God I'm sorry, Rachel."

It was shocking to know that her father had been right about that attack. She felt almost numb. "How could you know we'd be targeted? You had guards to protect us. It was so unexpected and vicious . . ."

"Vicious. Yes, that's the word," he said bitterly. "Kill the innocent, rape a young girl, murder a boy *who had his whole life to live. I've been living with that ugliness since that night they told me what had happened in Kabul."* He looked at her. *"And that's not all. I've been living with the deaths Conrad Huber has been causing all over the world for decades. We can't seem to stop him. Every attempt meets with massive reprisals. But I had to stop him. It's my job and my duty as a human being."*

"What are you saying?"

"I'm saying if Conrad Huber dies, we have a chance of the entire organization falling apart. He's the powerhouse in the organization. His son, Max, pales in comparison. But we can't have Max and Conrad's advisor, Kraus, blowing up another office building to revenge his murder." He paused. *"His death had to look absolutely natural. No way to detect that he had anything but a massive heart attack brought on by purely natural means. There was no way that it wouldn't be thoroughly investigated."* His glance moved slowly to her lab on the other side of the room. *"I looked into every means we had at our disposal at Langley, but nothing was totally foolproof. It had to be absolutely perfect. So I began to look outside."*

She inhaled sharply because at last she could see where this was going. *"My God, you want me to let you use one of the poisons I created."*

"No." His gaze shifted back to her face. *"I want to tell you I've already done it."*

She went still. *"What?"*

"Hu Chang told me years ago that you were almost as good as he was, and there's no one better than Hu

Chang. I knew he'd refuse to give me what I needed, so I had to find another way."

She gazed at him, dazed. "Me?"

Silence. "Yes. Two weeks ago I came here and substituted a bottle from your cabinet where you keep your poisons. I had it tested and it was every bit as effective as I thought it would be." He paused. "I received word thirty minutes before I called you tonight that the poison had been administered and Conrad Huber had collapsed in his home in Hong Kong with a massive heart attack."

Shock. She couldn't breathe, she could only stare at him.

This had to be a nightmare.

"I . . . killed him?"

"No!" He was across the room, his hands grasping her shoulders. "I killed him. You had nothing to do with it. You have absolutely no guilt. That's why I made sure that you didn't know."

"But I . . . created that poison. I let you in my home where you could take it, where you could give it to Huber."

"I was afraid of this." His face was pale, twisted with pain. "Conrad and Max Huber are monsters. They killed your mother and your brother. They've killed hundreds of people since then. Three weeks ago, I heard they were planning on launching another terrorist attack on a cruise ship. Do you know how many deaths that would cause? It had to stop, Rachel." His voice vibrated with agony. "You were on duty that night, and I came here and sat in the dark and looked at those bottles in the cabinet. It was as if all the years, all the killing Huber had done, had led to that one moment. It seemed as if fate had brought me to the one person who had the right to avenge all those deaths. You, Rachel." His lips twisted bitterly. "Yet I knew how you'd feel. I knew what it was going to do to what we had together."

"How . . . could you? You made . . . me a murderer. And you gave me no choice." Her voice was shaking. "I think that might hurt the most. You gave me no choice."

"It was the best way to keep you safe. I promise you that no one will ever know you were involved. I made certain that this wouldn't touch you any more than it had to. The blood was all on my hands."

"Was it?" She stared at the red wine in her goblet. Blood red. Would she ever be able to drink or even look at wine without remembering this conversation? "Then why do I feel . . . touched? You've told me about monsters, and I believe you. You've told me about the death of the mother and brother I love, and I'm hurting and angry for them. You say you wanted to protect me, but you only make me feel more helpless. It was the greatest sin I could ever commit, and I committed it blindly." The tears were suddenly pouring down her cheeks. "Blindly. How could you do that to me? You gave me no choice."

"I thought I was doing what I had to do in the most humane way possible." He added bitterly, "I should have known I'd screw that up. If there's any way of hurting you, I always seem to find it. It could be I lied to myself. Maybe I was afraid of asking you for your help even in fighting these monsters who had hurt us so terribly. You told me once that I ran toward the bad guys to battle and that your job was to come later and heal." He released her shoulders and straightened. "But sometimes you have to go after them, Rachel. It's the only right thing to do. Even if it makes you lose everything else you want." His gaze was searching her face. "You're not going to want to see me again?"

Yes, she wanted to see him. The idea of losing him again was agonizing even in this moment of bitterness and bewilderment. "I . . . don't think I can. Everything's changed . . . You shouldn't have used me. You gave me no choice."

"No, I didn't. It will never happen again." His eyes were fixed on her face. "From now on you'll always have a choice where I'm concerned. Always yes or no." He turned away and headed for the door. "And right now, it appears to be no, and good-bye." He added thickly, "I love you, Rachel. I'll miss you. Thank you for these months. They've meant everything to me. Remember that when you're remembering what I did today."

The door closed behind him.

PRESENT DAY

You'll always have a choice where I'm concerned . . .

Venable's words kept repeating over and over in Rachel's mind as she sat staring blindly out the French doors. It was like a mantra trying to pound through the pain and the bewilderment to the truth of what she and her father were to each other.

But sometimes you have to go after them.

It's the only right thing to do.

It will always be yes or no.

Rachel got up, moved the few yards to the French doors, and went out on the veranda. The moon was no longer hidden by clouds and was shimmering on the surf below her. She stood there, feeling the breeze on her cheeks and legs bared by the sleep shirt, breathing in the salt air.

But where was the feeling of peace and tranquility Brandon must feel, she thought wryly. It was just a big ocean in a bigger world that she had to face with more questions and dilemmas.

And she'd had enough of both.

She walked down the steps to the beach and dropped down on the sand. She drew up her knees and linked her arms around them. She felt like rocking back and forth as she had when she was a child and things had gone wrong for her. But she was not a child, and the things that had gone wrong would be much harder to fix.

"Is it helping?"

She turned to see Brandon standing on the veranda behind her. She had not heard him and was once more aware of the stillness that was such a part of him. "Not much," she said unevenly. "I didn't think it would. But I don't believe my lab would offer any comfort either right now. It would bring back some very disturbing memories." She turned her back on him again. "And I don't believe I should be looking for comfort anyway. Why are you here? I'm fine, and I'm not going to run away. Go back to bed."

"The hell I will." His voice had a leashed ferocity that startled her.

"Suit yourself." She steadied her voice. "Then you won't mind if I ignore you. I think you've told me all you needed to tell me now. Unless you have some other surprise to spring on me."

"No, I think that last message from Venable was enough to knock you down and cause you sufficient trauma for the time being," he said roughly. "Catherine was right, he had no right to put you in the crosshairs. He shouldn't have done it."

"He didn't really. You heard my father's message. I have a choice. He promised he'd give me a choice, and he did it."

"Promised?"

She was silent. Why was she even hesitating, she thought wearily. He knew so much already about her and her father. Why not this? "He didn't give me a choice about the poison. He thought it was the right thing to do, but he didn't ask, he took. He said he'd never do that again."

"My God." She heard movement behind her, and he was suddenly kneeling on the sand in front of her. "Damn, that must have hurt you . . ."

She nodded jerkily. "He did it for all the right reasons. To save lives, to revenge hundreds of deaths including our own family. And it hurt him, too. He knew he'd lose me again." She swallowed. "And he did, you know. It sent me into a tailspin, and the next year, I signed up for One World. I believed in the cause, but now I'm wondering if I was also running away from what I'd done."

"Bullshit, you didn't *know*."

"Because he wanted to protect me. But it also kept me from facing what I would have done if he'd come to me and asked. I've been thinking a lot about that tonight. What would I have said? And was I afraid that it would have been yes? If that was true, then that would have made me a complete coward to condemn him." She paused. "And very cruel to let him face it alone."

"There's nothing cruel about you. Stop thinking like that." His light eyes were glittering in his taut face. "Not everyone is like Venable . . . or me."

"But he said I was like him. He told me there was always a moment that you couldn't just wait to heal the wounds. He said that you had to go after the bad guys and stop them." She gazed out at the dark surf. "But I didn't stop them from killing my father. I wasn't there to help him. I was in a dozen other countries healing and making the pain go away. I didn't make his pain go away, did I?"

"Do you want to beat yourself up? Go ahead, but it doesn't make sense. Remember, I couldn't stop Venable from getting killed that day, either. I was too late, Rachel."

"But you weren't his daughter. You're not family. I told him once that if he was in trouble, I wouldn't ever believe what others told me, that I'd go find out for myself. I lied, I wasn't there for him." She was saying words that hurt her, but they came from somewhere deep within. She suddenly realized that this was where she'd been heading earlier in the evening, then backed away in panic. The hidden thoughts and beliefs of years were coming together even as she spoke. "And killing Conrad Huber didn't work, so he had to go after his son, Max, to stop the butchery. I didn't help him then, either. And when Max found out that my father and I were to blame for Conrad's death, I wasn't there to try to figure out how it had happened, what we could do. And he wouldn't come to me for the same reason as before, to protect and keep the guilt away from me."

"You're building Venable up to be some kind of hero." Brandon's gaze was narrowed on her face. "I don't like this. I've seen how you respond when you—"

"He's no hero. He's made mistakes. But he always tried to do the right thing, and sometimes that translates to being a hero. I believe you realize that, don't you?"

Silence. "Yeah, sometimes. Where is this going?"

"Where he wanted it to go." Her gaze shifted back to his face. Suddenly everything was crystal clear, like a pattern laid out before her. "He told me it was time to make a choice. That's what I'm going to do." She slowly got to her feet and looked down at him. "No, that's what I've *done*." Her voice was suddenly vibrating with passion. "I'm going to go stop the bad guys and worry about healing wounds later. I'm going to find Max Huber and punish him for killing my father.

I'm not going to hide and wait for someone to come and try to kill me. I'm not going to hope this Nemesis will do what my father told him to do. I'm going to go find him." She smiled crookedly. "And if I choose, I'll be the one to set myself up as bait and not wait for you." She turned and started back toward the veranda. "So hold on tight, Brandon. It might be a wild ride."

She could feel his gaze on her back until she reached the French doors.

As she opened the door, she heard him give a low whistle. "Holy shit . . ."

CHAPTER

7

She stood there on the other side of the door, trying to get her breath. Fine, bold words, but how was she going to translate them into action? Worry about that later, it had to be done, so she'd think and plan and find a way. She'd made a decision, and she'd do what she had to do.

She pushed away from the door, crossed the room, and slipped into bed. Relax. Clear her mind. Try to let the answers come to her instead of frantically searching for them. It was not as if she wouldn't have help. She had Hu Chang and Catherine, and Brandon would be there when she needed him. He had made her a priority because he needed her to bring Huber to him.

But there were moments when she'd be on her own. Her principal value might be as a target. That would place her in the most vulnerable of positions. In the end, she couldn't really count on anyone but herself. She couldn't depend on luck or the kindness or self-interest of the people surrounding her. She had to be ready for those times that almost certainly would come.

And she wasn't ready. She was a healer, not a warrior. It was all very well for her father to tell her that someday she'd have to choose to go after the bad guys because there was nothing else to do. It was another thing to find a way to do it. It was like Hu Chang telling her how to make a poison or medicine without giving her a list of ingredients.

But Hu Chang might very well do that if he wanted to challenge her, she thought suddenly. He always liked to make her think and come up with her own answers. Was that what her father was doing?

Not likely. He had been dying and probably had just been forced to throw her headlong into the situation because, as usual, he was trying to do his job and keep disaster at bay. But maybe somehow he'd known she'd never do what she had to do in the same way he'd do it. He had come to know her very well in those last months when they had been friends as well as father and daughter.

She could feel the tears stinging, and she blinked them back.

No more tears, Daddy. And I can't second-guess you. But I promise I'll get the job done my way.

She closed her eyes. Okay, I can't think about you right now. It hurts too much. I need to know what

questions to ask and decide where I need to go from
here . . .

4:40 A.M.

Rachel hesitated, then knocked firmly on Brandon's door. "It's me. I'm coming in. I'd appreciate it if
you didn't do anything lethal." She threw open the
door. "I'm not up to that nonsense at the moment."

"Then you should pick your time and place more
carefully," he said dryly from the darkness of the bed
across the room. "You're lucky I heard you coming
down the hall and recognized your step."

"I don't feel lucky at the moment." She came into
the room and dropped down in a chair against the wall.
"And how did you recognize my step?"

"It's lithe, strong, a certain rhythm, you carry your
weight close to the balls of your feet. We were together
in the rain forest for a long time." He leaned over and
turned on the bedside lamp. "What do you want, Rachel? I don't believe it's anything near what I'd like it
to be."

"No." She firmly kept her gaze off his body and on
his face. He was naked, and his body was lean and
tough and masculine beneath the sheet that only covered his hips. "I couldn't sleep, and I had no intention
of letting you. You can go back to sleep after I finish
with you."

His lips turned up at the corners. "I'd be delighted
to have you finish me." He held up his hand as she

opened her lips. "True, but you're not in the mood, and so you'll think me out of line. But what can you expect when you barge in here in that scrap of a nightshirt?" He sat up in bed. "But by all means, state your business, so I can concentrate on that instead of the very obvious." He met her eyes. "I wasn't sleeping very well myself after your explosion on the veranda. I was going over all kinds of scenarios I could use to keep you under control and not have to watch Huber kill you."

"You're not going to keep me under control," she said. "But you can work with me if you'll cooperate instead of trying to dominate the situation. I need answers, and you seem to be able to supply them."

"I told you that I'd told you all I know. You persist in thinking I'm keeping secrets from you."

"I believe you told me all you know about my father's death and this Nemesis. But you worked with him for two years, so you probably know almost as much as he did about Max Huber."

"You said Venable told you quite a bit himself."

"Only about things that would keep me apprised about whether or not Huber had discovered anything about his father's death. Other than that, I didn't want to know anything about Red Star."

He nodded. "Understood. That's how I felt about you. I didn't want to deal with you. Now it appears that neither of us has a choice. Ask your questions, Rachel."

"Do you have any idea which compound Huber is using in Canada right now?"

"There are several possibles. We don't know all the

locations Red Star uses. You were right, he tends to move from place to place. Every time we thought we'd zeroed in, Huber disappeared from the area and moved on. That's why we couldn't touch him. The one outside Calgary seemed the most likely. Venable had satellite surveillance, and it showed movement in that area recently. That's where Venable was supposed to meet with Nemesis. But it proved to have been a false trail. I sent men to check it out after Venable's death, and the compound was deserted."

"So we don't really know," she said, frustrated. "We'll be acting blind."

He nodded. "Just as we have for the past years. And he might not even be in Canada. He might want to be hands-on for his grand celebration here in San Francisco."

"Is that your guess?"

"No, I believe he'll have Kraus set up everything here and stay in palatial comfort until the last moment. Then he'll fly in to accept all the drama and glory. Huber Junior is very fond of being thought a chip off the old block. That's why he was so upset about your killing his father. He took it as a personal affront."

"I wonder how the relatives of all the people Conrad Huber murdered felt about it," she said bitterly. It was obvious Brandon did have a grasp on how Huber thought and felt. Why not? He admitted it had been an obsession of years' standing. But she was intrigued in what he'd said about Kraus. "He'd trust Adolf Kraus to take care of arranging for his great event? I don't remember my father talking about Kraus. It was always about the Hubers."

"He'd trust him," Brandon said flatly. "Max Huber grew up in Adolf Kraus's shadow. Kraus was his father's right-hand man and advisor. If Conrad wanted a hotel blown or a premier assassinated, he was right there for him. They'd been best friends since they were in their teens and met when they'd both joined a neo-Nazi group in Berlin. Both of them were fanatics about selective breeding and their Aryan heritage. They would have been right at home in Hitler's hierarchy. When Conrad left the party and created Red Star, Kraus helped make it work for him."

"And Kraus is just as loyal to Max Huber?"

"Presumably." He paused. "I've wondered that myself. Max Huber doesn't have the same dedication to the Aryan state as his father and Kraus. He believes he's one of the master race but has no problem using the Taliban groups when it suits him. He even convinced Conrad to do it on a limited basis before his death. Kraus would hate giving up the philosophies of a lifetime. He stays in the background, but there's no question that he might be the power behind the throne. Max Huber calls the shots, but Kraus might control the weapons."

"Could we use him? Threats? Bribery?"

"Perhaps. It depends on how he feels about Max Huber and if he's as much of an egomaniac as Conrad was. I'm looking into it."

She was silent. "Can I contact him?"

"*We* might be able to do it. You don't do anything by yourself. Monty's managed to locate a Silicon Valley genius who's found a way to hack into Max Huber's telecommunications. It's only another step to find the link to Kraus." He added grimly, "But we hack them, and we also open ourselves for them to find you. Goodbye safe house."

"We could find a way. I told you I wasn't going to hide out if it's time to go after Huber."

"And I could see that this was exactly what you meant," he said grimly. "No, Rachel."

"We'll have to consider it." She got to her feet. "It might be a bit aggressive, but that might work for us. Otherwise, I'll have to wait for Huber or Kraus to contact me. And they will, Brandon, my phone shouldn't be that hard for them to hack."

"I'm going to furnish you with a burner phone."

She shook her head. "No, don't do that, I want them to be able to reach out to me. Though it would help if they couldn't get a trace." She grimaced. "Because they'd probably just try to come and get me. I'd be that tethered goat we talked about. I'd prefer to be in control of the situation at that point." She headed for the door. "But I have a few things to prepare before that happens. So I figure we probably have a day or so to come to an understanding."

"What things to prepare?"

"I'm not like you and Catherine," she said simply. "You were right about my not having the background for dealing with all this. I've got to try to remedy that as much as possible."

"And how are you going to do that in the next day or so?"

"I won't, but I can make a start. I'm not my father, and I'm not like you or anyone but myself. I'll have to make that work for me." She looked back over her shoulder. He was lying there, angry, naked, sleek, and totally sexual, and the sight of him was arousing all kinds of primitive emotions.

Ignore it.

"Find me a way to reach Kraus, and we'll see if he's the way we should go." She opened the door. "Good night, Brandon."

"Stay."

She went still. His voice was soft and rough at the same time and infinitely seductive. She looked back at him. She inhaled sharply as she saw his expression. Intensity. Desire. Heat. It struck her like a bolt of electricity. She moistened her lips. "No way."

"You'd like it." He met her eyes. "I promise."

She knew that she would. Her body was readying just looking at him. "But I couldn't trust you not to use it against me. You like control entirely too much."

"Dammit, I wouldn't—"

But she had closed the door and was moving quickly down the hall. Close him out the way she had shut that door, she told herself. Her reaction to him was too strong. Sex was natural and a part of life, and Hu Chang and Catherine had taught her that she must not cheat herself because of what had happened in that prison. It had taken her a long time, but she had won that battle. She enjoyed sex, but she had never before felt this fever of intensity. It made her wary. She could feel the heat, the tension, the tautness of her breasts. One moment, a few words, and she had been very close.

But she had stepped away from him, and it would be okay now.

Maybe. Her heart was beating so hard . . .

Concentrate on what was important.

She closed her bedroom door and went over to the small cherry desk against the far wall. She had placed her computer on it earlier and now flipped open the top.

She sat down and brought up her email page.

Blank except for the messages from One World.

She didn't read them. Later.

She sat looking at the screen for a long moment. There had to be a way to communicate with Nemesis. He was taking far too long reaching out to her. Perhaps he didn't even know her father was dead. Langley had not told Catherine. But she had no address. She had to wait for him.

Or maybe not. He must have been constantly in touch with her father because of the wariness and lack of trust between them. It would be reasonable that he would monitor Venable's computer.

Give it a shot.

Then she sent a text to her father's computer.

NEMESIS
MY FATHER IS DEAD.
I'M WAITING.

* * *

Move swiftly, Rachel thought, as she circled Cath-erine. Catherine was always lightning fast herself and so precise that unless you caught her off guard, you ended up hitting the deck.

"Come on," Catherine murmured. "Come and get me. Do it again. You're too cautious."

"Because you're so damn good," Rachel said. "I'm not stupid, Catherine. I don't want any broken ribs when you—" She suddenly feinted to the left, and her toe came around to hit Catherine in the midsection.

Catherine immediately dove to the ground and swung her legs in a scissor move to Rachel's hips. But Rachel had expected it and was no longer there. She moved forward, but Catherine kicked the back of her knee, and her leg buckled.

But the moment she hit the tiles of the veranda she bounced up, and her right leg moved in a roundhouse kick that only clipped Catherine. She was already moving in for the counter.

"I hate to disturb you ladies." Brandon was at the French doors, leaning on the doorjamb. "Since I've been enjoying watching you try to kill each other. It was very entertaining, but you've had a delivery, Rachel. I was wondering where you wanted me to put it." His voice was not pleased. "And why the hell you risked placing an order. It wasn't COD. Which means credit card and very traceable indeed."

Rachel was trying to get her breath. "I needed it." She grabbed her hand towel from the back of the rattan chair and tossed Catherine's to her. "And it won't be traced to me." She wiped her face and neck. "I would have told you, but I didn't think they'd get it to me until later today."

He looked at her, then at Catherine. "And you were busy, you said you had preparations to make. Hello, Catherine. I didn't know you were paying us a visit today."

"I didn't either," Catherine said. "Rachel called and said she needed me." She grinned. "She did, but not as much as she thought. She was a little rusty, but when you're as good as she is, it comes back fast."

"Yeah, with a few kicks to jar it into me," Rachel said dryly. "You'd have broken my ribs if we hadn't been wearing padding."

"Likewise." She wiped her forehead. "Are we done for the day?"

"No, I need at least another two hours. And maybe another four tomorrow if you can make it. It won't be enough, but it will have to do. I have to iron out all the kinks." She smiled. "You know how I hate to feel helpless."

"Yes," Catherine said quietly. "But you know I'll be here for you."

Rachel nodded. "Always."

"Very touching," Brandon said as he straightened away from the door. "It's good that you trust someone, Rachel."

There was a distinct edge to his tone, and Rachel's gaze flew to his face. No expression, but she could sense the leashed tension. Hell, she was feeling the

same tension after this morning. Confront it. She refused to walk around on eggs while she was with him.
"Do you have a problem, Brandon?"

Silence. "A small one. I find it upsets me to see you
being kicked and beaten. Even when you regard it as
a favor." He met her eyes. "And you didn't tell me
where you wanted me to put your package."

She finally managed to pull her gaze away. "In my
bedroom. I'll deal with it later."

"As you command." His lips twisted. "Actually, I
usually approve of bedrooms as a destination. I'll let
you get back to your workout. Enjoy."

The next minute, he was gone.

"Whew," Catherine said softly. "You didn't tell me
you were sleeping with him. Recent development?"

She should have known Catherine would have
caught all the nuances of those few moments. "No."
She took her bottle of water from the table and opened
it. "I'm not sleeping with him." She took a swallow of
water. "That would be a mistake."

"Mistake or not. He wants it to happen. And I don't
know many women who would say no to him." She
took a swallow of her own water. "Particularly when
there's that much electricity crackling around between
the two of you." She added quietly, "Your attitude worries me a bit. I thought you were handling what happened to you really well. Do you want to talk about it
again?"

"No." She grinned. "Therapy according to Catherine Ling? I'm handling what happened in that prison
just fine. Do the nightmares come? Yes, but then I'm

the one who chases the bad guys away. And when I can't, I just wake up. I know that no one can hurt me but myself. You taught me that, Catherine."

"You already knew it, I just let you see that you weren't alone. Rape is probably the hardest thing a woman can deal with if she can't talk to someone who's been through it." She took another drink of water. "That's why Hu Chang asked me to talk to you. I faced it on the streets of Hong Kong when I was even younger than you were." She shrugged. "But in a way, I was luckier than you. You told me that there were four guards involved in your assault one night every week during those last two months. I had only one man who used me as his toy and tried to break my spirit. I could zero in and concentrate only on him."

Rachel shook her head. "The violation is the same. Why were you luckier?"

"I found a way to kill him," Catherine said simply. "And that put a period to that time in my life. You never had that release." She smiled. "At least you didn't realize you did."

Rachel frowned. "What do you mean?"

"I imagine if you went back to Afghanistan, you'd find out that those guards at Sazkar Prison all had untimely demises in the next couple years after your release."

"What are you saying?"

"Hu Chang wasn't pleased. He always makes his displeasure known. He cares about you. He would take his time, but he would get the job done."

Rachel slowly shook her head. "He never mentioned those guards after we left Afghanistan."

She shook her head. "Hu Chang is very wise, but sometimes he didn't read me as well as he thought he did either. Rape is hard for a man to understand. He probably thought that guilt might be worse for you than any satisfaction that justice had been served." She added softly, "You might be a good deal gentler natured than I am, but I believe you have no objection to seeing those bastards punished."

Those terrible nights surrounded by them in the shower. The laughter, the brutality, the helplessness.

"No," Rachel said jerkily. "Hu Chang read me wrong, too."

"I thought so. In which case, now when you have another nightmare it should go poof and disappear," Catherine said. "And if you choose to go to bed with Brandon that might—"

"No, I told you, that would be a mistake," she interrupted. "Letting Brandon too close would be—I can't do it. He likes to be in control. He'd be like my father. I'd never be able to trust what he'd do next. You don't understand."

"Yes, I do. More than you know." Catherine's lips twisted. "I've been there. Let's drop it; you can make your own decisions. I just wanted to make certain that it didn't have anything to do with what happened in that damn prison."

She nodded. "It's all present, not past."

"Not entirely. But it's not the stuff of nightmares." Catherine put her bottle on the table. "Ready?"

"Absolutely." Rachel took one last drink and capped the bottle. "Let's get to it."

She leaped forward toward Catherine with a kick to the chin.

"That smells good. Rachel told me that you were a great cook. What are you making?"

Brandon glanced up from cutting the tomatoes to see Catherine standing in the doorway of the kitchen. Her tee shirt was wet with perspiration and so was her face, but it only made her look more vibrant and alive. "Just a salad and roast. Care to stay for dinner?"

She shook her head regretfully. "I need to get back to the hotel. I don't want Claire Warren to get curious about any long disappearances on my part." She strolled into the kitchen. "Rachel just hit the shower so I thought I'd take a minute to speak to you when she wasn't around."

"Indeed? Secrets?" He continued to cut the tomato. "Rachel informs me that she doesn't like secrets. I'd think you'd know that, Catherine."

"Oh, I do." She took a slice of celery from the cutting board and nibbled it. "She's had too many thrust at her. And a good portion of them at an age where she'd have trouble dealing with them. It's a wonder that she managed to survive."

"But she assured me that's all due to Hu Chang," he said coolly. "And, of course, her friend, Catherine."

"And you don't like being closed out," Catherine

said bluntly. "You like being number one in charge. You like getting your own way, and you have to be in control. Rachel recognized that immediately. That's why she's backing away from you. It took her a long time to get her confidence back, and she's not going to let it be taken away."

"I've never noticed she lacked confidence. On the contrary, she's very strong." He frowned. "And I don't believe this is any of your business."

"The hell it's not." She met his eyes. "She's my friend, and I won't have her hurt. She feels something for you. It might be pure sex or something more. Either way, she's probably out of her league with you. From what Venable told me, I'd bet you're a master manipulator. I can see you trying everything from seduction to playing on her feelings to get what you want. True?"

"Perhaps."

"No perhaps," she said flatly. "Don't do it."

He was silent, staring at her impassively.

"This is just what I expected," she said. "I could see how much you wanted her this afternoon. But I thought I'd try to deal with you myself first."

"First?"

"Before I turned Hu Chang loose on you."

"Oh, is that going to happen?"

"Yes, we both have a considerable emotional investment in Rachel. Neither of us will let her be hurt again if we can help it." She added steadily, "And we can help it. Because you might be selfish and horny as hell, but you're not a complete son of a bitch."

"Thank you," he said dryly. "I repeat, not your business, Catherine. By all means, call your Hu Chang. I'd look forward to making contact with him."

"Only for the first few minutes. And I'm not going to call him. I want you to do that." She paused. "And I want you to tell him that Catherine asked him to let you know about Sazkar Prison."

He was silent. "That's all?"

"That's enough. If it's not, I'll take it from there." She nodded at his phone lying on the counter beside him. "Phone him now. Consider it a challenge. I can tell you're a man who thrives on challenges." She turned and headed for the door. "Good-bye, Brandon. I'll be in touch as soon as I hear anything about Huber."

Brandon watched her walk out of the room. He felt angry and frustrated and definitely wary. He'd never wanted a woman as much as he did Rachel Venable, and he felt annoyingly like a teenage kid who was having to confront irate, suspicious parents when he wanted to take his date to the prom. Not that there was anything even mildly near that innocent in his intentions. He'd been planning a purely erotic agenda since this morning.

And he could make that agenda a reality. She was fully adult, no teenager, and her responses would be fantastic. He just had to focus his attention and use persuasion, then—

And he wouldn't make that call to Hu Chang. Why should he? He knew all he wanted to know about Rachel Venable. He knew he wanted her. He knew he could have her. That was all that was important.

Look upon it as a challenge.

But Rachel had always been a challenge from the first moment he'd seen her in that rain forest. She seldom did what he expected, and she managed to touch him when he should be angry.

And he was lying to himself, he had been asking questions, probing the person who was Rachel Venable also since that first moment.

Because he wanted to go to bed with her?

Of course that was the reason, the only acceptable reason why he'd let personalities get in the way of the hunt for Huber.

And if Catherine Ling thought his calling Hu Chang would stop him from getting what he wanted, he should definitely not do it. It would hopelessly confuse the situation.

Sazkar Prison.

Damn it to hell!

He snatched up his phone and dialed his directory for Hu Chang's number.

Rachel checked her email just before she left her room to go to dinner.

No answer from Nemesis.

Maybe there would never be an answer. Perhaps he'd been caught and killed. Or it could be that he'd only been a trap to get rid of her father.

Stop second- and third-guessing. There was still time to wait before she looked down any other paths. Keep checking. Keep preparing in every way she could.

Which meant she'd have to open that package on the floor beside the door when she got back to her room after dinner. She'd considered skipping dinner and opening it after her shower, but then Brandon might think she was avoiding him.

And that would be a victory for him, she thought as she made her way toward the veranda. They had to work together, they had common goals. This sexual explosion that had suddenly erupted between them was a disturbance that had to be smothered. She had to keep their relationship balanced and not show him weakness. It was going to be difficult because that hot, melting weakness was there, and he knew it.

And she knew he would exploit it.

So get through dinner and escape back to—

Not escape. What was she thinking? Don't run away, handle him.

But he was not in the kitchen, and she could see that the table on the veranda had been set. He was standing with his back to her at the stone wall, gazing out at the sunset with a glass of wine in his hand. The sun was touching his dark hair with russet light, and he was wearing dark jeans and shirt that made his body appear leaner and stronger.

She braced herself and opened the French doors.

Evidently, he heard her because though he didn't turn around he said, "I was just going to call you. I was afraid that you'd decide to hide out, and you need to eat."

"Hide out?" She came out on the veranda. "I don't hide, Brandon."

"Not generally. I thought I might be the exception. I stand corrected. Sit down and eat your salad." Brandon turned to face her. She stiffened as she saw his expression. Or perhaps the lack of expression. None of the intensity and coaxing seduction of this morning. Only the stillness with which she was so familiar and that she'd always found so intriguing. His pale blue eyes appeared darker in this light, but they, too, were cool and still. He was the same . . . yet different, and that difference was making her uneasy.

"It would take more of an exception than you to keep me from dinner tonight," she said lightly. "I've worked up an appetite."

"I could see that you would." He seated her and went around to drop into the chair across from her. "You look in pretty good shape for all those hours with Catherine. No limps, no stiffness."

"There's a little stiffness. I'll feel it more tomorrow." She glanced at the glass of wine in his hand and the lack of place setting as she picked up her fork. "You're not eating?"

"Perhaps later. I felt the need to have something stronger, but wine will have to do. I wanted a clear head."

"Well, I won't need wine to relax me this evening." She took a bite of salad. "I should sleep well tonight."

"I imagine you will." He leaned back in his chair, watching her eat. "Since Catherine was careful to make certain that I not interfere with it."

She stopped in midbite. "Catherine? What are you talking about?"

"She stopped for a chat with me before she left today. She's very protective of you." He paused for a sip of wine. "She wanted to make sure that I not behave carelessly or in what she perceived would be my usual barbaric fashion. I take it you discussed me?"

"Not really. Just a few sentences." She looked away from him as she took another bite. "But, yes, she is protective. However, I didn't know she'd talk to you. I thought we'd agreed I could take care of myself." She forced herself to look at him. "And I'd already made the decision that you'd be a mistake. I told you that, Brandon."

"But I hadn't made that decision," he said silkily. "And it must have been clear to Catherine because she pulled out the big guns. She had me call Hu Chang."

"Hu Chang?" she repeated warily. "Why?"

"Two words. Sazkar Prison."

"What?" Her eyes widened in shock. "Shit." Catherine, must have been more worried than Rachel had thought. She wanted to *shake* her. "I don't know why she'd do that. It was a long time ago and no business to anyone but me. I'm sorry that you were dragged into it." She tried to smile, but she knew it didn't quite come off. "I assure you that Catherine doesn't generally break confidences and try to influence people by—" She pushed back her chair. She couldn't sit across from him while he was gazing at her with that still watchfulness and realize that he *knew* what a victim she'd been all those years ago. "Forget about anything either of them said. Pretend it didn't happen. None of what went on at that prison has anything to do with you. I *hate* this."

"I can see you do," he said grimly. "I knew you would, and I was debating whether to even tell you. I don't believe Hu Chang thought I would."

"But you did, didn't you?" She was suddenly on her feet. "Why?"

"Because I'm not going to let Catherine or Hu Chang dictate what we're going to be together." His lips twisted. "But there are all kinds of problems on the horizon. The only way I can see getting what I want is to be absolutely honest with you. So that's what I'll do." He gestured to her chair. "Sit back down and finish your salad."

"I don't think I'm hungry anymore."

"You will be after we get through this. All that exercise this afternoon burned up a lot of calories. Don't run away."

She stiffened. "That's the second time you mentioned something like that. I *don't* run away."

"So I've noticed." He gestured again. "So sit down."

She slowly dropped down on her chair. "I'm sitting. But I'm not going to stay long. I don't want to discuss this. But I feel as if I owe you something for having to go through—" She broke off and drew a breath. "Talk."

"I intend to do that. First, you don't owe me anything, and it was perfectly natural for your friends to try to protect you from me." He smiled crookedly. "I have a tendency to return to my wild days and forget all about discipline where sex is concerned. And I don't believe I'd have any discipline at all when it comes to you. I was certainly not planning on it. Catherine could see that in me." He grimaced. "Hell, so could you. I suppose that call to Hu Chang was supposed to arouse my conscience and make me pity you. But I don't seem to have—"

"*Pity* me?" Her eyes were suddenly blazing at him. "Don't you dare say that. Don't you dare think it. I didn't need pity then, and I don't need it now. I'm not crippled. I didn't let them hurt me. They only made me stronger."

"I can see that." He held up his hand. "If you'll stop attacking and let me finish? I was going to say I don't seem to have a conscience where you're concerned. At least it's not getting in the way of me wanting to jump you and spend the next month in bed with you. Maybe longer . . . The only thing Hu Chang's little story did was make me want to kill the bastards who hurt you. But Hu Chang said I wasn't going to get that pleasure. And it also made me realize that there might be a few stumbling blocks along the way." He paused. "You mentioned control. That might be one, and I'll have to watch it if I'm to get you where I want you. But control isn't always a bad thing if I put it at your disposal and you can handle me, can't you? You can handle anything. I would never do anything to hurt you. I'd only give you pleasure and take my own. Of course, you should know I do believe in extreme overindulgence." He tilted his head. "Are you beginning to feel more comfortable now?"

Incredibly, she *was* feeling more comfortable. He

had been almost brutally honest, but she much preferred it to the sexuality and seduction that had gone before. "Let's see, shall we go down the list? No pity. You're still going to try to get me into bed. You obviously paid practically no attention to Catherine. Nothing much has changed, has it?"

"You forgot I wanted to spread death and mayhem on that prison. And that now I realize I might have to go slower and be more careful. Not because what happened to you had changed or weakened you." He was holding her eyes, and his voice lowered to softness. "But because it made you stronger, and you learned from it. I think I can let you set the pace. Waiting doesn't suit me at all, but I can live with it. Can you?"

She couldn't look away from him. He had come away from that talk with Hu Chang with an understanding of her that was unexpected . . . and strangely warming. He knew all her most intimate and terrible secrets and still believed and wanted her. Not that she should be surprised, she told herself. She was worth it, dammit.

She finally jerked her gaze away. "This isn't about us, Brandon. We're still where we were in Nalez. Nothing's changed."

"Yes, it has." He lifted his glass to his lips. "But I'll let you slip that by in the interest of maintaining the hunt and my decision to try to go slower. But just because I'm tamping down the aggression doesn't mean that nature won't replace it. I firmly believe in the power of nature. We feel it every time we're in the same room. Finish your salad, Rachel." He got to his feet. "I'll go get the main course. Then you'll tell me what's in that package that was delivered today."

She watched him disappear into the house. She loved to watch the springiness of his stride, the contained stillness that was totally fascinating, the way he moved.

The power of nature . . .

In the last few moments, he had switched from bold frankness and intimacy to lightness and their common goal. She felt relief . . . and disappointment. She was behaving without reason, but that was normal with Brandon. Particularly facing what she'd gone through with him today.

But that was over.

For now.

She picked up her fork and started to finish her salad.

CHAPTER

8

"Where am I supposed to be carrying this?" Brandon said as he hoisted the box on his shoulder. "And why did you tell me to put it in your bedroom if I was going to have to move it?"

"Complaints, complaints," she murmured. "I didn't want to deal with it then. And I knew you were probably going to be cooking later and might have objections."

"Objections?" he asked warily.

"The most reasonable place is the kitchen. It has a water source and plenty of counter space." She headed down the hall toward the kitchen. "But I thought you might—"

"Have objections," he finished for her. "And I'm beginning to have an idea why you didn't want to discuss your package at the dinner table."

"I was hungry. And that was a delicious roast." She entered the kitchen and looked around the room. "Yes, this will do fine. There's not even much cleanup to worry about. You took care of most of the dishes before you served dinner."

"I grew up on a boat, remember? You don't leave anything sitting around or you get overwhelmed." He set the box on the bar. "Now tell me what's in the box."

"Just a number of common natural ingredients." She met his eyes. "And a few that are considered fairly rare."

"And fairly deadly?"

She shook her head. "Exceptionally deadly."

"Such as?"

"Most of them you wouldn't recognize. Actually, the plant and animal world is full of unexpected poisons. For instance, did you know almost every part of a pretty daffodil is poison?"

"I can't say that I did. So you're making a daffodil cocktail?"

"No, that was just an example. I didn't order anything to do with daffodils. What would you recognize?" She thought for a moment. "I think I ordered some tetrodotoxin from the puffer fish. You've probably heard it mentioned on forensic shows. It's twelve hundred times more deadly than cyanide, and there's no antidote. The directors like to stress all the dramatic, lethal properties. It's good theater."

"Oh, yes, I've heard of puffer fish. When I was in the service, I recall we were warned against eating it in any foreign port. Would you care to tell me why you're going to need it?"

"No. I may *not* need it." She smiled. "But I didn't think you'd like to have it sharing space with your salad ingredients."

"Good call," he said dryly. He was silent, gazing at the box. "I take it that you're going to do some concocting yourself."

She nodded. "Preparations," she said quietly. "I'm a healer, not a warrior. I don't know much about guns or knives. But I won't ever be helpless again. So I have to make do with the talents I have."

"Like kickboxing and creating potent brews."

She nodded. "The first is marginal when I'm against someone as good as Catherine. But Hu Chang says there's practically no one with the skill I have at the other." She smiled bitterly. "I believe I've proven that, haven't I?"

"Yes, you have." His mouth tightened. "But I don't like the idea of your using that particular skill. Huber will be on the lookout for it."

"He won't find it."

"Why are you so sure?"

"Hu Chang taught me that the key word is always undetectable. The next necessity is unexpected."

"But you said that creating the poisons was only a way of learning how to invent other medicines."

"And it was my purpose." She began to carefully unpack the bottles and bags of dry goods. "But Hu Chang never teaches a part of any skill, it has to be the complete package."

"I got that impression from talking to him. I wasn't sure if he was threatening or informing during most of our conversation. I don't believe he would have told me anything about that prison if Catherine hadn't made the demand."

"Of course he wouldn't. He promised me once he would never betray me. This came very close. But he and Catherine have been together for a long time, and he trusts her. He knew she must have a reason." She took the empty box and put it against the far wall. "Even though she was completely mistaken."

"Perhaps not completely." He gazed at the collection of bottles on the bar. "But their relationship interests me. Did he teach her the art of poison, too?"

"Only the basics. She wasn't that interested. But she respects it, and she's very wary about it as far as her son, Luke, is concerned. Luke loves Hu Chang, and all this fascinates him. He likes nothing better than to spend hours in his lab."

"Most kids like chemical experiments. It can be harmless. How old is he?"

"Twelve. And he knows it's not harmless. Catherine used one of the poisons to kill the man who had kidnapped Luke as a small child."

"Perhaps he's like you and doesn't embrace the dark side."

"Perhaps. But his life during those years of captivity didn't tend to sweetness and light." She shrugged. "But he's smart and has a good heart, and Catherine will work it out."

"With some help from her friends."

"That goes without saying. That's what friends are for." Rachel looked at the dishwasher. "I can give you forty-five minutes to wash those dishes, but then I want you to clean out the cabinets and put everything out on the veranda for the night. After I finish, I'll scrub up and put everything back myself."

"Very cautious."

"First lesson. If you don't want to kill, you don't take a chance on anyone else. Carelessness can kill just as easily as a deliberate act."

"I'm not a careless man, Rachel. I'd think you'd know that by now. Let me help."

She shook her head. "First lesson. And I'd have to be particularly careful with you because I have a tendency to trust you. As you said, I've seen that you're not careless. I'd let my guard down."

His lips twisted. "Heaven forbid." He nodded his head. "I'll get the kitchen spic-and-span and everything cleared. How long is this going to take?"

"Most of the night."

"Am I allowed to watch?"

She shook her head. "I have to concentrate. I might not remember some of these ingredients or I may decide to substitute. Although they should be adequate. I called and had them sent from Hu Chang's lab outside the city. That's why I know they couldn't be traced. All of Hu Chang's assistants are superdiscreet."

"Why did I not guess that was a given?" He made an impatient gesture. "So get out of here and give me room to move. Go outside and get some fresh air. I doubt if you're going to do anything but work all night." He added mockingly, "Your lab will be at your disposal on time as ordered."

He was upset. He didn't like being tossed out, and she hadn't been very diplomatic. "It's the way it has to be, Brandon."

"No, it's the way you've been trained it has to be. But I'm accepting it. Just as I accepted the training I received in Special Forces until I could bend the rules to suit myself."

"And take control?"

He inclined his head. "But there has to be a certain amount of trust involved in those around you before you can think about control. You don't have it, so I have to work on that first. Venable told me that he hadn't given you reason to trust him." He smiled faintly. "And that brings up the question, if trust is present, is it really control?" He turned toward the cabinets. "But neither of us wants to answer that at present. So go get that breath of air while I prepare your den."

She hesitated, watching him, before she turned and went outside. It was fully dark now, and she stood there, listening to the surf. She wanted to trust Brandon. The last few hours had been . . . good. She had not wanted the meal to end. He was intelligent, warm, and dryly amusing, and the stories he had at his disposal must have been as entertaining as the ones his father had told him when he was a boy. And she'd bet Brandon's stories were probably true.

But trust was rare in her world. She trusted Hu Chang and Catherine. Her father had never given her reason for total trust, as he had told Brandon.

And how much she had wanted to trust her father, to feel that he loved her as much as she loved him. He had said the words, but did they mean the same thing to him as they did to her?

She might never know.

People felt things differently. She had already accepted that in her father. Why had Brandon's words triggered that memory? Because she also wanted to be able to trust him? Because for some reason it was important to her?

Good God, all she needed was to have Brandon become emotionally essential. Far worse than needing him sexually. So much easier to be irretrievably hurt.

Not irretrievably. She would survive and go on. What was she thinking?

And it might not happen. Now that she was aware of the danger of caring about him, she would be as wary as she was of those poison ingredients on the bar.

Those ingredients . . .

Concentrate on her task for tonight. Go over the possibilities mentally and make the decisions. Stop thinking about anything other than preparing another protective barrier against Huber.

The puffer fish?

Deadly, but it might take too long to take effect.

Maybe go in another direction . . .

4:35 A.M.

"That's it. You've been working all night." Brandon was standing in the doorway of the kitchen, watching her scrub the tile floor. "I believe I can be trusted to scrub that floor." He strode forward. "Unless you coated it with some exotic poison. I wouldn't put it past you." He pulled her to her feet. "Tell me now, or I'll throw you out of here."

"No, it's just a precaution in case I dropped something and didn't notice."

"And did you do that?"

"No, but that's why it's called a precaution. You shouldn't be touching me. I've washed, but I haven't showered yet."

"More of Hu Chang's rules? I'll take the chance. I trust you." He looked at the row of small vials on the counter. "All these hours to produce that?"

She yawned. "Hu Chang would say that each one is worth a fortune to the right purchaser. You have no appreciation."

"I appreciate the fact that you're almost collapsing. Your eyes are red, and the circles are black. I'm not fond of that color combination. You should have stopped hours ago."

"I couldn't. You never stop in the middle. You can spoil everything."

"Well, now you're done. Get out of here while I finish cleaning. Do you want me to pack those vials up for you?"

"No, I'll do it." She took a small plastic container

and put the vials in it. She was so tired, her hand was shaking, but this was her responsibility. "I haven't made the choice yet. And I haven't decided how to do the presentation . . ."

"Presentation," he repeated. "Never mind. We'll go into it later. Just tell me if there's anything that I should be careful about before I kick you out?"

"Everything."

"So says your teacher, Hu Chang. What do you say?"

"No, I was supremely careful. I didn't miss anything. It's cleaner and more sterile than when you left it last night."

"Now that hurts. I did a damn good job for the time you gave me." He turned her around and gave her a gentle push. "Go to bed. You'll probably have Catherine knocking on your door in a couple hours wanting to beat up on you again. You should at least have some sleep so that you can stay on your feet."

"In kickboxing, staying on your feet isn't always a good idea. You need to be more mobile than—"

"And you need to get some rest so that you make sense. Go take your shower and spare us the micro possibility that you've made a mistake. I'll handle everything here."

"Control again."

"Bullshit. You know better. Partners, Rachel. Say it."

She looked back over her shoulder. He was standing there staring at her, demanding, impatient, but there was a kindness . . .

He smiled. "Say it."

She wasn't sure it was true, but it would be nice if it was. Nice to not be alone. Nice to reach out and have someone there . . .

She turned away, and said what he wanted her to say, "Partners . . ."

Fifteen minutes later she had showered and washed her hair and was heading for bed.

Brandon was right, she had only a short time before Catherine would be here, and she needed rest. Those hours in the kitchen last night had been draining. They'd required not only intense concentration but an emotional commitment. She was dealing with death instead of life, and she always felt it weighing on her.

Admit it, the memory of the guilt she'd felt when she'd found out how her father had used one of her poisons was also still weighing heavily. She might have accepted that she had to stop Huber any way she could, but the philosophy of a lifetime wasn't easy to banish.

It would be fine, she told herself. It might take time, but she would become accustomed to the thought that she had to—

The message light was blinking on her computer.

She stopped short in the middle of the room, staring at it.

It might be Phillip or One World or some company wanting her to buy software.

Or it might be Nemesis.

She moved slowly toward the desk.

Why wasn't she more eager and excited? This was what she had been waiting for, wasn't it?

Because if it was Nemesis, it would mean everything would begin, and she might not be ready.

Screw it. She'd make herself ready.

She flipped open the computer and pressed the access.

Nemesis!

You're the daughter? Venable is really dead?

She sat down and typed:

I'm Rachel Venable. Yes, my father is dead. You didn't know? I find that hard to believe when Huber killed him. If you worked for him, you must have known.

The answer came swiftly and rudely.

Why should I care what you believe? You're the one who wants something from me. Who else can tell you Huber's target in San Francisco? And who says that I work for Huber? I told Venable I had information about Huber, not that I was in his pocket.

That didn't make sense.

But my father was shot because he went to meet you near Huber's compound. Why would you be there?

It was convenient for me.

It was a trap.

**Think what you like. Venable said you'd nego-
tiate with me if he wasn't around to do it. Is it
true? If it isn't, I can sell the information somewhere else. It's not as if there aren't thousands
standing in line who'd want to save this fair cty.
I only went to Venable because I knew he'd
have the influence at Langley to get me the
money quick. I need to get this deal done and
catch the next flight out before Red Star finds
out what i'm doing. Yes or no?**

Rachel tried to stall so that she could think.

Are you here in San Francisco?

Yes or no?

She couldn't let him hang up.

Yes. How much?

Twenty million.

That sounded exorbitant to her.

Too much.

Cheap. I'd charge more if I didn't need to get out

of here. I don't like it that Venable was killed.
It makes my position less than secure. I'll send
you my bank ID, and you'll deposit one million
by tomorrow noon after you receive my first
verified piece of information. We'll negotiate
the final payment after you're suitably overwhelmed by how valuable my association with
you will prove to be.

She felt a chill. She didn't like this.

Noon tomorrow? Why not now?

Because it's not up to me, it's up to Huber. It's
all up to Huber, haven't you found that out yet?
You will, Rachel. Venable did, didn't he? [A
pause.] I'll be in touch tomorrow after Huber
gives the world a taste of what he has in store
for them on the 25th. It was supposed to be a
little surprise preview, but I know he wouldn't
mind me letting you know. It would amuse
him to see you scramble to stop him. But don't
get too close. He really has problems with you.
I need to have someone left alive to authorize
that money transfer.

She was shaking. It was horribly clear what he
meant.

Preview? Where? You're lying. Nothing was
supposed to happen until next week.

Yet you believe me, don't you? Huber likes his surprises. A little teaser to show everyone how helpless they are against him. Don't panic, it's not one of his more spectacular demonstrations. You're right, that comes later. Did I mention that Huber wants to shape the California Coast to suit himself? How arrogant can you get?

She was desperately trying to fight through the shock and get something of value from him.

If it's just a teaser, tell me when and where. I'll get you payment. Don't let it happen.

The answer came immediately.

But then you might not be impressed enough to do anything I wish to make the bigger threat go away. No, you have to see it, Rachel. I look forward to doing business with you.

The message had ended.

Rachel was shaking as she stared at the screen. She wasn't sure she knew what had happened. She had negotiated for $20 million she didn't have. She had made contact with a man who was quite possibly as bad as Huber. He had been totally callous about having a part in getting her father shot. And she was scared to death that something terrible was going to take place tomorrow that she wasn't going to be able to stop.

She took a deep breath and read over the text. It was

just as cold and faintly mocking as she'd thought when she'd first read it. As well as there being a definite element of threat to the message. Preview? It was those last few lines that were frightening her, and she wasn't going to try to decipher them alone.

She jumped to her feet and was out of her bedroom and running down the hall toward the kitchen.

Brandon was still there and looked at her quizzically as she came into the room. "Checking up on me? I assure you that I didn't do anything that wasn't strictly sterile and hygienic. You have to learn to—"

"Come with me." She took his hand and pulled him from the room.

"May I ask where we're going?"

"My bedroom. You wanted to be partners. Now's your chance."

"Provocative. But I don't believe you mean what I want you to mean." He was looking at her face with narrowed eyes. "What's upset you?"

"You'll see." She opened her bedroom door and pushed him inside. "The computer. Nemesis. Did I screw everything up? Am I right about what I think is going to happen? Or was he bluffing. And what can we do to stop it?"

"Nemesis." He was over to the desk in seconds and sitting down at the computer. "Why didn't you call me when he came online?"

"I didn't think about it. He was just there. Read it."

He was already reading the text. "You tried to bargain with him?"

"I didn't know what else to do. I thought he'd expect

it. I'm not accustomed to dealing with terrorists, dammit."

"And that's why you should have called me." His lips tightened as he finished reading the text and looked up at her. "Though he is right, his price is cheap considering what he has to sell. It's clear he thinks that Huber might be suspicious."

"And he said he didn't work for Huber, but he was at that compound."

"Which might be true or false."

"But if it was true, why would it be convenient for him to be there?"

"I have no idea. We'll have to find out. I'm still leaning toward him working for Huber."

"And I'm leaning toward him trying to trap my father." She gazed down at the computer. "Huber is going to do something tomorrow, isn't he, Brandon? I thought we had time, but he's going to make his move."

He nodded. "That's what it sounds like, but it won't be the big one. I think Nemesis was telling the truth there. Otherwise, he wouldn't make it his opening gambit. He'd go for the big bucks."

"It will probably be bad enough." She crossed her arms across her chest to stop her shivering. "How can we find out how to stop it?"

"First, we have to find Nemesis. I'll go into your computer and try to trace his message."

"Can you do that?"

"Probably not, but it's possible. I had Monty put a bug device into your hard drive while we were on the helicopter taking Maria to the hospital. Chances are Nemesis is too savvy not to have that covered but there's a slight possibility."

"Why doesn't that surprise me?" Rachel asked dryly. "Like Nemesis, you were too savvy not to make sure that you'd get everything I had to give."

"Yes, I was. I couldn't be certain that you'd be willing to go along with me." He added grimly, "That was before we agreed to work together. Don't start backing away. I'm being honest with you. I could have taken the computer and pretended that I was having it gone over by some high-tech Silicon Valley guru. But I said I wouldn't lie to you."

And he hadn't lied, but he hadn't told her about that bug before he had to do it.

He nodded as if he'd read her thoughts. "We're very fragilely balanced, Rachel. I wasn't going to do anything to rock the boat."

She waved her hand dismissingly. "I guess I should have expected it. It's exactly how my father would have handled the situation. It's very familiar." Her lips twisted. "Need to know all the way."

He muttered a curse. "I'm not Venable, Rachel, and I don't appreciate your comparing me to him. He told me before he died that he had regrets about the way he treated you. Let me make mistakes of my own and not have to shoulder Venable's."

She shrugged. "I only remarked on the similarity. You both have a military mind-set, you're both warriors. It's hard to accept for me." But she had to accept it if she was going to deal with Huber and now Nemesis, who also seemed a threat. She made a dismissing gesture. "But I'll get used to it. Our psychological differences are the least of my worries. All that's important is what's going to happen. I don't want anyone killed. How can we stop it?"

"I'll see if I can locate Nemesis's IP address. If I can't do it myself, I'll call in Monty. Like I told you, he's close to genius with anything to do with computers or high-tech stuff. You call Catherine Ling and tell her we need her to come here right away. We need to know if there's been any chatter about a possible target in the next few days." He looked back over his shoulder. "I don't suppose I can talk you into an hour's nap before we go into full throttle?"

She gazed him in disbelief.

"I didn't think so." He headed for the door. "Dry your hair and get dressed. Then grab some toast and a cup of black coffee to keep awake. Call me when Catherine gets here."

She stared after him and reached up to touch her still-sodden hair. She'd forgotten all about it when she'd come out of the bathroom and seen that message light on the computer. Not that it made any difference. Or maybe it did, Brandon might have realized that she would feel and function better if she wasn't looking and feeling like a Holocaust survivor. At the moment, she was ready to take any advice that would make her feel more in control and moving forward.

She placed the call to Catherine and headed for the bathroom to dry her hair and get dressed.

EAGLES REST

CANADA

Yes!

It was about time.

Kraus pressed the disconnect on his phone and turned and strode into Huber's library.

"I've just heard from my contact," he said as he dropped down in the leather visitor's chair in front of Huber's desk. "Rachel Venable is in San Francisco."

"Where? How do you know?" Huber asked eagerly. "You said I'd have her before this. You should never have let Morales lose her. When can I get my hands on her?"

"One question at a time." Kraus held up his hand. He should have known that Huber would expect the world if he gave him even a hint of information. "I haven't gotten a precise location as yet. My contact is still working on that. But he assures me that she is in San Francisco. He's managed to hack into her computer and monitor a text she just received. He says she's definitely in that city and that she's looking for you. She appears to be a bit bitter about your killing her father."

Huber cursed. "What about what the bitch did to my father? Then let her find me. I'm waiting for her. When can you take her, Kraus?"

"Unfortunately, it's not that easy. It seems there has to be a monetary compensation. He's willing to hand her over to us, but he wants us to give him enough money so that he can lose himself where the CIA can never find him."

"And how much is that?"

"Thirty million. But I can negotiate."

"Pay it. I don't want any slipups. You can get it back later." He smiled sardonically. "The CIA might not be able to find him, but I have faith in you, Kraus."

"When it suits you," Kraus said sarcastically. "But you should have faith, I've never failed you. I promised I'd find her for you, and soon I'll give her to you, gift-wrapped."

"I don't like the word *soon*. I want her now. I want to see her suffer before she dies." He frowned. "You should let me do the negotiating with your contact. I told you that before."

"I seem to be managing fairly well. And he only wants to talk to me. He's probably afraid of you." He stood up. "I'll tell him that he'll get his price, and you want the woman as soon as possible." He headed for the door. "I guarantee you'll have her to play with long before it's time to do the final kill."

Huber still looked discontented. "It's all too . . . remote. I don't feel like being patient. I don't want to wait. I want her to know what's in store for her."

"Surprise ambush is always the best plan."

"Not when I want it another way," Huber said pettishly. "I want to talk to her. Set it up so that I can do that without her tracing the call. You can do that, can't you?"

"With difficulty, now that she might be aware we think she's a threat. My way would be better." He added persuasively, "Just let me handle it. I've already got a plan in the works that will bring her to you on her knees."

Huber frowned. "This wonderful contact of yours? Thirty million isn't at all humble, Kraus."

"No, another backup that will please you even more."

"Nothing would please me more than to tell that bitch what I'm going to do to her."

And the prick was stuck in a groove and wouldn't be moved. Okay, give him what he wanted and make the adjustment that would suit himself. "Then, of course, I'll give you what you want. Don't I always?"

"When?"

"Soon. I promise you." He glanced back over his shoulder. "You're not planning on being in San Francisco tomorrow? I'll have to arrange special protection if you are."

"No." He shook his head regretfully. "It's tempting, I'd like to see it close-up. But it's only a minor event, and I trust that you've made it memorable. I believe I'll wait until the twenty-fifth to make my appearance. That's the grand occasion that will make everyone realize that no one can touch me. Is everything going forward as planned for that?"

He nodded. "As *you* planned. Lawrence Fasrain was never my choice. I don't trust those mongrels. I believe them all to be a little mad. But I've done as you've asked me to do. He'll be ready by next week. Between the drugs we've furnished and those last three weeks of religious instructions the Imam has given him, he's been honed to a fine edge. He can't wait for his chance to go to Paradise. You'll probably be pleased." He opened the door. "But if you're interested in watching the excitement generated by your surprise play tomorrow, tune in to CNN at noon. They should have the best coverage."

"Wait."

He glanced back at Huber. "Yes?"

"I want his name," he said impatiently. "You're being entirely too secretive about this damn contact. You must know more than you're telling me. There must be a way you can contact him."

"He calls me. I've tried to trace the calls, but I've come up with zilch. He said he'd call tonight for a yes or no to his proposal. Maybe I can get more information then."

"See that you do."

"As for his name . . . that would make it entirely too easy for me to track him." He turned to leave. "He calls himself Nemesis."

"Nemesis," Catherine repeated. "It sounds like he's no better than Huber." She glanced at Brandon. "And you weren't able to trace his IP address?"

Brandon shook his head. "It bounced off half a dozen satellites in Europe and the Middle East. It's tremendously well crafted. I have Monty working on it, but even if he cracks it, there's a chance it might be too late." He paused. "We might need all the luck we can get. And chatter. What have you heard about a possible incident occurring in the next few days?"

"Nothing." She glanced at Rachel. "As soon as you told me about that damn email, I tried to gather every bit of info I could from our sources here on the West Coast. Nothing definitive. In high-risk situations, there are always alerts because everyone is on guard, but I can't see a threat to any specific place or person."

"But there *has* to be a threat," Rachel said. "And I don't want to find out when the threat becomes reality."

"Do you think I do?" Catherine's eyes shifted to Brandon. "You're certain that Venable thought that Nemesis was the real McCoy?"

"He got himself shot trying to get information from him. You can't have much more faith than that," Brandon said dryly. "He was very closemouthed about Nemesis. But whether Nemesis is as crooked as Huber or not, Venable thought his information was valid and could tip the scales."

"And Venable must have been ready to set up a funds transfer before he was killed," Catherine said. "That amount of money isn't exorbitant for the company to pay in circumstances like this, but they would have had to trust the operative who was dispensing it. Only someone as powerful as Venable would have that kind of clout." She paused. "But it's not likely he'd be able to do it alone."

"Claire Warren?" Brandon asked.

"Maybe. She does have clout. And who the hell knows what she's doing at any given time."

"Who, indeed?" he murmured.

"Then would she know more than we do about Nemesis?" Rachel asked. "Could she help us reach him and make him talk?"

"I doubt if she can if he was Venable's asset." She added grimly, "But I think we're going to have to try to find out. It's too dangerous not to do it. Not only might she have information we need, but she can bring in all the technical skill of the Company to try to trace him. No insult to your Monty, but he's in Neanderthal category compared to our tech center."

"You'd be surprised. Monty would definitely consider that an insult." He grimaced. "Though I agree that Venable got some amazing results using them on occasion. But with Claire, there's always a trade-off. I was hoping we wouldn't have to deal with her."

"But this could be an emergency," Rachel said. "She's CIA, like my father. Surely she wouldn't play games with so much at stake."

"She likes games," Catherine said dryly. "How do you think she climbed so high in the CIA? And we have nothing concrete to give her. Nemesis's email was incredibly lacking in details, and he didn't even say outright that he was talking about a terrorist event to-morrow. She could believe it or not. If she chooses to believe it, then her duty would involve going after the terrorists full-scale. That would mean bringing in the FBI and Homeland Security, which becomes very complicated and a big headache. At that point, she's going to want something for sticking her neck out and taking the risk."

"My father wouldn't," Rachel said. "He'd take the chance because it was the right thing to do."

"Yes, he would," Catherine said quietly. "But then he was a patriot. There aren't that many around. Claire Warren will do her job, but you can bet she's going to bargain to get all she can that will help her climb the ladder."

"And you believe you know what the bargaining point is going to be," Brandon said slowly.

"And so do you," Catherine said. "She's going to want Rachel."

"No way," he said flatly.

"I agree," Catherine said. "But we've got to be prepared for it. She knows Huber wants her, and she'll assume she can use her." She smiled crookedly. "She's well versed in the art of using people. Of course, she doesn't know our Rachel. She thinks she's a do-gooder who was probably manipulated by Venable. She might have a few surprises coming."

"Those surprises could ignite a number of uncomfortable actions on Claire's part. I'd prefer that Rachel not have to face them."

"Are you quite through talking about me as if I weren't here?" Rachel asked in exasperation. "It's my decision if I judge it worth it. Can Claire Warren be of value?"

"There's a chance she might be," Brandon said.

"Is there anyone else who will give us a better chance?"

He was silent. "Not that I can confirm positively at this time."

She looked at Catherine.

Catherine shook her head.

"Then we go to see Claire Warren," Rachel said. "Right away. Will you call her and see if she's available to see us?"

"Oh, she'll be available if she knows you're coming," Catherine said wryly. "She'll consider you a lamb I'm leading to the slaughter. She might even write me a letter of commendation."

"You're going to do this?" Brandon asked Rachel.

"Yes. I've got to see what she's got to offer. She's CIA. I can't believe she won't try to help when she realizes what it could mean," Rachel said. "There's not much time. Less than twenty-four hours."

Brandon turned back to Catherine. "Then we meet with Claire at one of the sidewalk cafes in the Mission District. Alone. No hotel. Crowds of people all around."

"I'll take care of it. Though it's not likely that Claire will try to—"

"I'm not taking chances," he said. "I don't like the idea of Rachel's being used." He smiled mockingly. "Though she will tell you that I have a tendency in that direction myself. But I've always been a selfish bastard. I don't like to share."

"Whatever," Catherine said. "My job will be to make sure neither of you causes Rachel problems." She got to her feet and took out her phone. "And now I'll go tell her the lamb is ready to be presented to her." She strolled out onto the veranda as she punched the number. "And warn her that presentation is all she's going to take away from the meeting."

Rachel watched her pace across the veranda as she talked to Claire. "It might not be that easy to resolve if Claire's anything like my father," she murmured. "He seldom took no for an answer."

"She's nothing like Venable," Brandon said. "The only thing they had in common was that they both have a bulldog perseverance. Claire is very political, and her efforts are usually aimed in that direction. She often takes a step beyond to get what she wants. Venable kept his efforts within bounds because his ambitions weren't focused on his career but on the current mission."

"You know them both very well." Her gaze was narrowed on his face. "You've told me about the relationship with my father. But not about Claire Warren."

He shrugged. "I admit I explored that possibility. I thought at one time she might be more valuable to me than Venable. Ambition can be hard and ruthless and jump-start everything in its path. I wanted to move faster."

"But you changed your mind?"

"We played games with each other for a few weeks, then I decided that she was taking too much of my time trying to manipulate me. It was easier and more efficient dealing with Venable."

"Games?"

"We slept together," he said bluntly. "I told you that she has no problem going the step beyond. She thought that would seal the deal."

She felt a ripple of shock. "And I'm certain you had no problem. Catherine said that she's attractive."

"No problem at all. I told you, with us it was a game." He added quietly, "I'm trying to be honest with you. I realize that you might not be able to look upon sex in that light considering what you went through."

"No, I can't." She moistened her lips. "It took me a long time, but I've gotten to the point where I accept sex as joy, but I couldn't regard it as a competitive game." She shrugged. "But there are all kinds of people in the world. I guess you can, Brandon. It's not my business."

"If it wasn't, I wouldn't be mentioning it. Everything we do together from now on has to do with us. Since Claire Warren is a factor, then you have the right to know everything I know about her." His lips twisted. "Even though I didn't want to tell you. I was afraid you'd take it like this. You just had to be aware that I *know* Claire and that you should pay attention to me if I tell you we have to walk away from that table this afternoon. And if I tell you to *run* away from that table, you do it."

She nodded. "Of course I will. I don't believe your relationship with her would make you abandon me. I just had a little trouble understanding the nuances."

"There were no nuances. It was just a game where sex was just another— Never mind. Just try to forget it." He got to his feet. "I've got a call to make to Monty. Let me know when Catherine has the meeting set up."

She watched him walk away. He had been exasperated with her although she thought she had been reasonable and honest. She had not let the shock she felt overcome her ability to think it through and realize that everyone had different views on sex. Hu Chang and Catherine both had stressed that during those talks she'd had with them over the years. She was probably less sophisticated than any woman Brandon knew, but she couldn't help that. She could only be what she was, and he would have to accept it.

Or not. What difference did it make anyway? Particularly when so much else might be at stake in that meeting with Claire Warren.

It made a difference because she had felt an instant rejection when she had thought of him with Claire Warren.

Which was not sensible when he had been perfectly honest with her when he didn't have to be. And, in spite of what he'd said, it was none of her business.

Do what Brandon had told her to do.

Just forget about it.

But she had an idea that wasn't going to be easy . . .

CHAPTER

9

Leonardo's Restaurant in the Mission District was modern, sleek with glass windows that looked out on the outdoor veranda and the dozens of colorful umbrellas shading the tables.

"Just as you decreed, Catherine," Brandon murmured, as the three of them strolled down the street from the parking lot toward the restaurant. "Perhaps. I don't see Claire yet."

"I do. She's at that corner table away from the others," Catherine said. "And she's probably paid the waiter to keep other guests at a distance when we arrive." She nodded to the far corner, where a chic, slim brunette was sitting under an orange umbrella. "And this is where I make my exit."

"You're leaving?" Rachel asked, surprised. "I thought you'd be here with us."

"You don't need me to run interference. I've told Claire what we need, and she said she'd never heard of Nemesis." She shrugged. "It might be true. You'll have to judge for yourself. Brandon can step in and help if you run into trouble." She smiled. "But you won't, Rachel. You can hold your own with anyone. Where we might have a problem is if she decided not to obey my instructions about keeping the meeting private. I'm going to cruise around and make certain that she didn't bring reinforcements in case she decided that you should be taken into 'protective' custody." She glanced at Brandon. "Then I'll go back to the car in the parking lot and wait for you. If you need a fast getaway, call me. I'll be out front within a couple minutes."

He nodded. "I've noticed you know Claire very well."

"Well enough to be careful." She cast a worried glance at Rachel. "I would rather have set up this meeting later in the day. You're still exhausted. You don't need to deal with Claire right now."

"I'm fine. Stop worrying. You said yourself I could handle her. Second thoughts?"

"Nah, forget it. Just overprotective." She lifted her hand, then faded back into the crowds behind them on the street.

"She thinks it might be a trap?" Rachel asked as Brandon took her elbow and nudged her toward the veranda. "How can she work with her if there was even that possibility?"

"Because Claire's smart and powerful, and most of

the time, there might not be a conflict. Why are you here? Today, the risk is worth getting what we want. Claire might be able to give it to us. Tomorrow, that might not be true." He was smiling back at Claire Warren as she smiled at both of them. "It's part of the game, Rachel. And Catherine plays it superbly when she chooses. Right now, she's handicapped because she feels very protective of you. She'll go for the jugular if pushed."

They had reached the table, and his smile never left his face as he nodded at Claire Warren. "Hello, Claire. Thank you for meeting with us."

Her smile deepened, and she was suddenly more than interesting but almost beautiful. "I've always found our encounters fascinating, Brandon. But you're not the reason I came today."

"No, your focus is on the daughter of your old friend." He gestured to Rachel. "Rachel Venable, Claire Warren. Claire worked with your father on a number of projects over the years."

"Yes, I know." Rachel met Claire Warren's eyes. "And I'm sure he'd want you to help with this one. That's why I'm here."

"So I understand from Catherine." Claire's expression softened, and she was suddenly on her feet and coming around the table. "I'm so sorry for your loss." She gave Rachel a warm embrace, then stepped back. "And I'm sorry we've all lost a patriot and great man in Carl Venable. Venable and I were very close. He saved my life at least twice when we were working together." She gestured to the chair across the table as she went back to her own chair. "Sit down. May I call you Rachel? I'm Claire. We need to talk. Catherine's told me that my old friend has shifted a terrible burden on your shoulders. Let me help you with it."

Rachel hesitated; the affectionate greeting had caught her off guard. "I want you to help me." She dropped down on the chair that Brandon was holding for her. "That's why I'm here. I need you to find out what Nemesis meant when he said that I should ask Huber about what's going to happen tomorrow. Catherine said so far there had not been any chatter about a potential threat happening in the next forty-eight hours. But you can reach out, talk to different agencies?"

"And I will, but I'll have to do it quietly and discreetly. You don't understand the interagency conflicts I have to deal with on a daily basis. The CIA doesn't even have authority within U.S. borders. That's FBI jurisdiction. And Homeland Security is always giving me a hassle. We're only permitted to be part of the team here because Huber is an international figure and resides outside the U.S."

"I know all that." Rachel tried to keep the impatience out of her tone. "You're treating me as if I hadn't grown up living with my father. But I also know that we might be facing a disaster tomorrow. My father would recognize that and bend the rules. If you knew him as well as you say, then you'd agree that would be the only sensible act to him. It should be the only rational act to you, too."

"Of course the public good is always the most

important thing to consider." She sighed. "Unfortunately, Venable and I often had disagreements about his rashness in taking action before we could verify information." She paused, then said gently, "There's no proof other than that wild text you received, Rachel." Her brows rose. "Nemesis? Why wouldn't Venable bring me into dealing with him if he was of any importance?"

"I'm sure he had his reasons," Rachel said. "You might know better than me." She glanced at Brandon. "He trusted Brandon enough to tell him about Nemesis. It was Brandon who told me that my father told Nemesis to contact me."

"Really?" She smiled at Brandon. "How curious. Then you have to trust that the message was truly sent to you from Venable and not from Brandon himself?"

"Brilliant, Claire," Brandon murmured. "Now she has to decide if I'm the bad guy."

"I'm only pointing out that it's a strange message to entrust to a stranger of your dubious background. Particularly when he could share it with a coworker of my status." She turned back to Rachel. "Brandon is very clever, but I never knew whether he'd managed to con your father. Venable was always vulnerable to people he cared about. You'll have to decide that for yourself."

Rachel stared at her. "You're suggesting that Brandon is working with Nemesis or perhaps with Huber and conned my father into believing he was his friend?"

"It's possible," Claire said. "I have to look at all sides of a question in a situation like this. It's part of my duties with the agency." She reached out and covered Rachel's hand with her own. She added softly, "Including the fact that he was the last person to see Venable alive. You have to remember that, Rachel."

"Magnificent, Claire," Brandon said. "Now you've added murder to my dubious background?"

"She's the daughter of my friend." She looked into Rachel's eyes, and urged, "I can't have her victimized, Brandon. Believe me, Rachel, I'll do everything I can for you. Just put yourself in my hands."

"Yes, that's all you have to do." Brandon leaned back in his chair. "She's made an interesting case. Now all you have to do is decide if it's strong enough for you."

"No defense, Brandon?" Claire asked.

"I've had time to offer my defenses since the day I met her. Some of them have been pretty weak, but in the end, she has to decide if they're strong enough."

"And you can be so very persuasive, can't you?" she asked silkily. "No one knows that better than me."

"I never tried very hard with you, Claire. I didn't consider it worth my time." He looked back at Rachel. "Weigh what she's saying carefully. It does have a certain logic. But in the end, the bottom line is whether you trust me. Knowing our precarious relationship, you'll not feel guilty about telling me if you don't."

"No, I won't."

"And I know you'll make the right decision," Claire said. "Your father thought a great deal of your intelligence. We often discussed it."

"Did you?" She gazed at her for a long moment. Every word appeared to have the ring of truth, her expression was sympathetic and sincere.

She was lying.

She glanced at Brandon. "You're right, she's totally brilliant. It's too bad that I don't think I can trust her to help us." She turned back to Claire. "You lied to me. My father and I haven't been on good terms for quite a while. You might say our relationship was almost painful. He would never have had those warm, casual discussions about how clever I was."

"No?" Claire recovered quickly. "But it doesn't mean the rest of what I said isn't true. As Brandon said, it has logic."

Rachel nodded. "It could go either way. But it's like a poison with all the correct ingredients. Sometimes if you leave out the shaking or stirring, the deadly ingredients sink to the bottom and the liquid becomes ineffective."

Brandon chuckled. "Interesting comparison and typically you. And I hope it's Claire who left out the shaking and stirring."

"It doesn't matter. It just wasn't there for me." She shrugged. "So I guess I do trust you."

"You're making a mistake," Claire said. "And it might have terrible consequences. What we do know is that for some reason, you're important to Huber. You need to let me protect you and find a way to make this threat go away."

"Or not protect you, considering the circumstances at the time," Brandon said. "You don't like the game concept, Rachel. You certainly wouldn't like being a pawn."

"Stop this," she said through set teeth. She leaned forward and glared at Claire. "I don't want to talk about how you're going to protect me and save the world. I want to know how you can stop what's going to happen tomorrow. Will you do it?"

"I told you that I would try," she said. "We don't know if this Nemesis is even a valid threat. It would help if I could tell everyone you're an asset under my protection."

"I'm *not* your asset." She added desperately, going down a new path, "Look, he also said Huber said something about the major disaster he was planning for next week would have something to do with changing the California coastline. If I give you my computer, maybe you could try to trace the address so we can find out more from him. And if that doesn't work, my father sometimes got authority to use satellite surveillance to scan areas to find suspicious activity. We might be able to discover what Huber is doing along the coast. Couldn't you do that, too?"

"It's possible. But probably not in the time you've given me. It usually takes at least four days to get that authority even if it's a proven threat. And I can't really argue Nemesis is a valid source and worth the money it would cost to implement the use of a satellite. Give me the computer, and I'll see what I can do about the trace for this Nemesis. But as Catherine and Brandon told you, it's probably a slim chance." She said curtly, "I'll do what I can with what you've given me. When you decide to come to me and cooperate fully, we'll have another discussion."

Rachel couldn't believe what she was hearing. "People might *die*."

"It won't be my fault. I'm doing my duty as I see it. I'm sorry you're being this stubborn. So like Venable . . ."

"Now *that* was the truth." Rachel's voice was shaking with anger. "I'm finding I'm more like my father than I dreamed. Stubbornness can be good. Lying, on the other hand, is never good." She got to her feet. "And the way you're seeing your duty could be criminal. Change your mind. Do what my father would do."

"Sit down," Claire ordered. "Let's talk about it. You can't win with me, Rachel. I don't want to cause you undue distress, but get in my way, and I'll have to take action."

"You're incredible," Rachel said in disbelief. "Screw you."

She turned and walked out of the restaurant.

"Would you mind waiting?" Brandon said as he caught up with her. "I was busy enjoying the show, but I really prefer not to tag at your heels. It lacks dignity."

"I wasn't enjoying the show," she said, not looking at him. "She's an arrogant bitch. I wanted to strangle her."

"That became obvious. I thought she might have you in the beginning." He shook his head. "No, I have more faith in you than that. But you have to admit she's good."

She nodded jerkily. "She moved from strength to

strength. But all she could think about was getting her own way. She wasn't thinking about what might happen. Will she do anything?"

"Yes, it would be her job if she didn't move on any potential threat. Will she go the extra yard? Not likely. You didn't give her enough material to make her Wonder Woman saving the day. Now, if she'd had you as a potential wild card, she would have had a chance at more power and glory for her efforts."

"That shouldn't matter. Everyone should go the extra yard when there's a threat."

"That's idealism striking again. Nice concept for an exceptionally nice person. But not realistic in this arena."

"I didn't feel like a nice person back there. I wanted to slug her."

"Which also makes you an exceptionally human person." He looked at her. "You did everything you could to get her to move on Nemesis as soon as possible. Everything except wrap yourself in shiny gold tissue paper and let her use you as she saw fit. I appreciate the fact that I didn't have to step in and stop you from making the final sacrifice."

"I'm usually more patient. But I could see that she—" She looked at him. "You were stupid to go to bed with her. She's completely self-absorbed."

"Not stupid. It was an experiment that failed. And one that evidently raised very vengeful feelings within our Claire."

"She tried to convince me you were a murderer. A woman scorned?"

"I was polite, not rude, when I parted ways with her."

She shook her head. "Stupid."

"Have it your own way. You seem to appreciate stupidity a little more than games." He smiled. "I'll take it, Rachel."

"I just like the idea of her being scorned. I don't want her to win anything."

"Then hopefully she won't," he said quietly. "Unless we need to use her as she wants to use you. You'd do it then."

"Yes, I would." She drew a deep breath. "If she won't help us, what are we going to do, Brandon?"

"I have a few plans that we might tap. I would have brought them up before, but you were so determined to see if Claire could help. It was natural that you'd trust the CIA since that was your father's vocation for all those years." He shrugged. "And it might have been more promising as a way to go if you'd been able to persuade her. But I didn't have much faith that was in the cards. Now we have no choice but to—"

"What plans?" she interrupted.

"Presently. We have something to take care of first." They had reached the parking lot, and he waved to Catherine to get out of the car. "A preventative effort . . ."

"No progress?" Catherine asked as she studied Rachel's expression as she came toward them. "At least you didn't have to send up an S.O.S. I wasn't sure what her reaction would be when she faced you, Rachel."

"Multifaceted," Rachel said dryly. "But definitely

not encouraging. She was more interested in me than what Nemesis might do. She might make a token gesture, but Brandon says that we're pretty much on our own." She grimaced. "And I suppose he should be able to judge. He knows her well enough to read her reactions."

"Really?" Catherine's brows lifted. "I didn't know they were that . . . close." She gazed at Brandon speculatively. "Interesting."

"You might stop trying to decipher her statement and help me." Brandon nodded at Rachel. "The first thing Claire did was to get up from the table and come around to give Rachel a warm hug. It was done with affection and smiles and sympathy. Which could have been part of her ploy to pull Rachel into her camp." He paused. "Or it could have been something else."

"Yes, it could," Catherine murmured. "Did you check it out?"

"I thought I'd leave it to you." He smiled. "I might enjoy it too much." He took a step away from Rachel. "And I'm being very careful right now."

"That's wise." Catherine took a step closer to Rachel. "Stand very still and raise your arms, okay? I'll be thorough, but this shouldn't take long."

Rachel slowly raised her arms. "You believe she might have planted some kind of bug on me?"

"Entirely possible," Catherine said, as her hands ran over Rachel's body, concentrating on her back, jacket, and upper hips. "Almost standard operating procedure if an operative doesn't have the opportunity for surveillance. And I searched the area thoroughly, and Claire didn't have any operatives in the restaurant or surrounding shops. She knew I'd be wary and checking." She was going over the folds of the sleeves. "Claire is very savvy, and it would take her no time to do the plant." She went still, her fingers probing. "Here it is." She carefully removed a tiny device that was almost microscopic in size. "GPS. She slid it in the seam of your jacket." Catherine looked at Brandon. "Misdirection or destroy it?"

"Destroy it," he said.

She dropped the GPS on the ground and crushed it beneath the heel of her boot. "Then we'd better get out of here before Claire scrambles to get a team to track us." She was heading toward the car. "I'll drive. Back to the house?"

"For the time being," Brandon said as he nudged Rachel to the car. "But we might be moving out soon. Monty and Nate are heading this way from Miami, and I'm hoping Monty will be able to track the Nemesis IP address." He glanced at Rachel. "And, though I realize it's not as urgent as this potential attack tomorrow, when I checked with him this morning, he said he might be able to hijack the signal of a South African satellite and use it to do the job you asked Claire to do."

"He can do that?" Rachel asked, stunned.

"He can do it." He opened the car door for her. "He's done it before for me. That's why I smiled when Catherine compared Monty to a tech Neanderthal. It was usually when Venable was having trouble cutting through the government red tape to get permission to use one of the U.S. satellites to track Huber's cells. Of course, Venable preferred I didn't do it unless it was an emergency. Hijacking satellites causes such nasty international incidents."

"But he let you do it."

"He merely looked the other way. As you told Claire, he knew how to bend the rules."

"And Claire said that it could take up to four days to get permission to use a satellite. Possibly longer since there was no proof that either Nemesis or his threat was reliable." She asked Catherine, who was now backing out of the parking place. "Is that true?"

"It depends on the circumstances and how much clout you have." Catherine met her eyes in the rearview mirror. "And how much the operative wants it. But she had a valid argument, and she used it." She smiled. "And she made you mad as hell."

"In more ways than one."

"I gathered that." She glanced at Brandon. "How certain are you that Monty can hijack that satellite before the twenty-fifth? I have to know whether I have to go back to Claire Warren and try to convince her to change her mind."

"I have a better chance than you do to make it happen." He added, "And I'd better stop talking about a strictly illegal activity to you. I hear the CIA's lie detectors are very sophisticated these days."

"Yes they are, but I'd have no problem with them. I have a friend who made sure that I could pass any test."

"My, what a very suspicious talent for a CIA operative. Who is this friend? Hu Chang?"

"No, someone else. I do have friends other than Hu Chang, Brandon."

"Yes, me," Rachel said. "Who has absolutely no influence or knowledge in that area. Leave her alone, Brandon. It's her business."

"Just curious." Brandon leaned back in the seat. "You have such fascinating friends, Rachel."

"I don't have one who can hijack a satellite," she said dryly.

"But then you haven't been operating on the dark side. You've been concentrating on being an angel of mercy. It's somewhat stunted your growth." He smiled. "Although I'm sure that you can catch up if you study hard. Even your father had reservations that kept him from reaching his full potential."

"I don't want to be on the dark side if it has anything to do with Claire Warren," she said coldly.

He gave a mock shiver. "There's dark, and then there's dark. Mine is shot through with interesting highlights and variations. Claire wouldn't be able to adjust to it. But you could learn to live there."

"I don't think so."

"I do." He made a motion. "But we won't talk about it right now. You're so exhausted, you look as if you're fading away. Just lean back and relax until we get back to the house. We've closed the page on Claire Warren for the time being. She can't hurt you."

"But that doesn't mean that what she doesn't do might hurt other people," she said wearily. "I wanted to find a way to stop it . . ."

"And we might, we still have a chance."

"Maybe she's right, it could be that Nemesis is a phony, some kind of confidence man."

"That's true. Do you believe that?"

"No, but then I want to believe that Huber can't win all the time," she whispered.

"That's what Venable wanted to believe."

"And what do you want to believe?"

He pulled her head down to rest against his shoulder. "That he won't be able to win anything but six feet of earth and a gravestone when I get through with him."

She thought about sitting upright again, but it didn't seem worth the effort. She was tired and discouraged and the path ahead seemed too long and hard. "Nothing like going all the way."

"It's the only way I know." He added, "Now stop talking and rest. If you can't rest, think about what you want to say to Nemesis next time he contacts you."

That also seemed hard, but she'd try to do it . . .

She was being carried . . .

Brandon . . .

She recognized his scent, the way he moved.

But he shouldn't be carrying her.

She forced her lids to open. "No . . ."

"That's a word you like entirely too much." He smiled down at her. "Try, yes, thank you. It won't hurt you at all." He negotiated her bedroom door and carried her toward the bed. "There's no reason why you can't say it. You spent all night working on those fiendish poisons that you appear to do so well. You're so exhausted, even Catherine approves of your taking a short nap. She's off to smooth Claire down and try to dig information out of everyone surrounding her."

"She's gone?"

"And trusting you to my evil clutches. Imagine that." He laid her on the bed and stared down at her. "I have work to do setting up a lab in the library. Monty and Nate should be here by dark, and I want it ready for them. You're not needed. You'd get in my way. You'll be much more valuable with a clear head and fully functional." He turned toward the door. "But if you disagree, then do what you wish. Just stay out of my way."

The next moment, he had closed the door.

He had given her a choice, she thought drowsily. Choices were important. Her father had finally realized that, and it was why she was here with Brandon. But Brandon realized how important that was to her, so had he manipulated her or really given her the decision?

It didn't matter right now. His argument seemed reasonable, and she was too exhausted to analyze it. There would be time for that when she woke . . .

9:35 P.M.

The room was totally dark, she realized, when she opened her eyes. Her gaze flew to the French doors across the room. She could see the crescent sliver of the moon on the horizon.

Damn.

Her gaze flew to the clock on the nightstand. After 9 P.M. She didn't know exactly what time she had fallen asleep, but it had been hours ago.

And Brandon had not tried to wake her. He'd probably thought she would get in his way, she thought as she threw the blanket aside and jumped out of bed. The alternate was that he was trying to protect her, and that annoyed her even more. Her meeting with Claire Warren had made her feel helpless, and she didn't need Brandon patting her on the head and sending her off to bed.

She was in the shower two minutes later and was dressed and out of her bedroom fifteen minutes after that. No one was in the living room, but she heard whistling in the kitchen and followed it down the hall.

Nate Scott looked up from the bacon simmering in a frying pan on the burner to smile at her. "Hi, you look great. It must suit you taking on the Madame De-Farge of the CIA. Brandon said that it wasn't Claire who put you down, but working all night here in the kitchen. What were you doing? Brewing up more life-saving medicines like you did for little Maria?"

"Something like that." At least Brandon had protected her privacy on that score, even from his friend. "Madame DeFarge . . . Oh, yes, she was the spectator who sat and knitted while all the victims were guillotined." She made a face. "I definitely see the resemblance. We did not get along." She went to the refrigerator and got out a can of orange juice. "Though I understand Brandon did at one time."

"I wouldn't know about that," he said blandly. "Brandon is a pretty private person. I'm making a BLT. Would you like one? You slept a long time. It could be breakfast for you."

"Not that long." But the bacon did smell good. "Yes, please, thank you." She deliberately said the words Brandon had told her she should be saying. Why not? Maybe he was right, and she was struggling in battles that weren't worth the effort. She sat down at the kitchen table. "Where are Brandon and Monty?"

"In the library, where Brandon's set up a makeshift lab for Monty. They're trying everything they can to isolate that IP address."

She made a face. "Then I assume Monty's temporarily given up the idea of hijacking that satellite?"

Nate looked at her in surprise. "No, he checked that out before we got ready to leave this morning. Brandon said it wasn't as important as finding Nemesis right now, so he put it on hold. No problem."

Her eyes widened. "What? No problem hijacking a satellite in less than a week?"

"Not as long as Brandon gave him fair warning," he said cheerfully. "That's why he made sure Monty knew it was coming up. It's never good to spring it on him because Monty has to be given as much time as possible. And Brandon always does what's needed."

"That sounds familiar. You mean what he decides

is needed," she said. "I wonder what he would have done if Claire Warren had come through for us about the IP address and the satellite."

"Made adjustments." He handed her the plate with her BLT. "That's what he was trained to do in the Special Forces." He sat down opposite her at the table. "And I guess growing up traveling around the world with his father. Make a plan, then make a backup plan. It works for him." He bit into his sandwich. "And most of the time, it works for everyone around him." He tilted his head. "Are you pissed off at him because he didn't tell you all this?"

She thought about it. "No." She picked up her BLT. "I would have been if he hadn't tried my way first. I'm slowly learning how he thinks. In his rather convoluted way of looking at things, he didn't betray my trust if he didn't actually lie to me. He just prepared the way for getting what he wanted."

"Exactly." He beamed. "Adjustments."

She was eating slowly. "And if I ever find out that he 'adjusted' me out of something I think I wanted to happen, I'll go after him with both barrels."

Nate chuckled. "Good for you. But I don't believe he'd do that to you. He's being very careful not to offend you."

"I didn't notice. You're obviously seeing something I'm not." She finished her sandwich and changed the subject. "So how is Monty managing to hijack a satellite in a matter of several days? Isn't all kinds of technical wizardry necessary to do that?"

He nodded. "But it depends on the satellite and its

defenses. This one is seven years old, small, commercial, and not equipped with the complex firewalls developed in recent years." He smiled. "But Monty still had a hell of a hard time getting control of it when Brandon told him to do it two years ago. It took him more than a month to finally break through."

She frowned. "Why did he do it then?"

"Something to do with work Brandon was doing with Venable. Brandon got in, got his information, and got out without the South Africans knowing what he was doing. But Monty knew he'd probably want him to do it again, so he left a back door in the program so he wouldn't have to start from scratch."

"So several days instead of several weeks?"

Nate nodded as he finished his sandwich and pushed his plate away. "Or even a few days. He still has to be careful, but he'll slide in slick as greased lightning. It will take a while for him to mask the repositioning, but then they'll start to scan the coastline to see if they can detect anything suspicious."

"We don't even know what we'd be looking for," she said gloomily. And why was she worrying about this now anyway? she thought impatiently. One disaster at a time, and the one that Nemesis had thrown at her was terrifying enough. For some reason, the fact that he had told her about it seemed to make the responsibility peculiarly her own. "Brandon is right. It doesn't matter at the moment. Are they making progress on Nemesis's IP address?"

"You'll have to ask them." He was looking down at his sandwich. "Monty said it was going to be a big headache. But he's terrific at what he does. He might be able to—"

"Might?" She froze, stunned. "Don't use that word. Anyone who could do what you say Monty can do with a damn satellite should be able to find that IP address in no time."

"It's not the same thing," Nate said gently. "Hacking can be one of the most complicated talents on the planet. There can be virtually hundreds, thousands of codes and almost as many protective firewalls."

"You're saying he might not be able to do it," she said slowly.

"I'm saying I've seen Monty have to spend days breaking through a single firewall," Nate said. "He has hours, not days, Rachel."

"But someone should be able to do it." That sounded stupid and pitiful, she realized. Of course someone should be able to break a code that could save lives. That didn't mean it was going to happen. "Is there anything I can do? There's got to be *something*."

"We'll probably have to sit this one out. Unless you're better than I am at this stuff." Nate shrugged. "Brandon's an expert, and Monty's a damn genius. I'd be in there with them if I thought I could help."

"Sit it out?" She couldn't stand the thought. "Maybe go back to bed and forget about it? I'm no genius, but I have to try." She got to her feet. "And I won't know unless I go ask if there's anything that—"

Her phone rang, and she glanced down at the ID.

Unknown caller.

She tensed and hesitated. Nemesis? She'd received

an email before, but that didn't mean it might not be him. She punched the access. "Hello."

"I hear you've come to see me to pay your last respects, bitch." The voice was masculine and the words a vicious snarl. "Or so you think. That's more than you did for my father. No good-bye, just one of your damn poisons, and an hour later, he was dead."

She froze. She couldn't breathe. "Who is this?"

"But I killed your scum of a father, and I'll kill you, too. Are you listening, cunt? You're going to wish you'd never been born."

And then she knew who it was.

"Huber," she whispered. "It's Max Huber, isn't it?"

She saw Nate stiffen, his eyes widening. He whirled and ran out of the kitchen. He was probably going after Brandon she realized vaguely.

"You sound as weak as I thought you'd be," Huber said scornfully. "Just a cowardly woman doing her father's bidding."

"I'm not weak, I'm just surprised." There was something she should be doing. The recording button, press the recording button. Her hand was shaking as she did it. "And my father wasn't weak either. It was probably a freak accident that caused you to be able to take him down. He was brave and smart and on his way to making you and Red Star history."

"Liar."

"I'm not lying." She moistened her lips. "Where are you? Hiding out in a hole somewhere? You wouldn't have to be burrowing down if my father hadn't worked

for years to keep you and your maniac of a father grov-
eling in the dirt."

She could hear him cursing. "I'm not hiding. I'm
just getting ready to show the world that a man as great
as Conrad Huber can't be destroyed by vermin like
you. You'll see, bitch. You'll all see."

"Is that why you're calling me? You can't touch me,
so you're trying to tell me how big and bad you are? If
you were really a threat, you wouldn't be afraid of
naming your target. But you'd rather skulk around and
hope that you can get lucky, then—"

"Shut up!" His voice was low and seething with
rage. "I can't touch you? You'll see if I can touch you.
You've never been *anything* to either my father or
me. You were just someone I could use." His tone was
suddenly dripping with malice. "And we did use you,
Rachel Venable. Your father found out that the attack
on his family in Afghanistan was planned by us,
didn't he? But he didn't realize until too late that we'd
bribed his informant in the prison to tell him how
special those guards were treating you." His voice was
low and spitting ugliness. "I was being groomed by
my father to take over Red Star at the time, and I can
remember sitting in his study and laughing with him
about it. I even made a few suggestions of my own
about what those guards should do to you."

"Did you?" She was having trouble holding on to
her control. He had chosen a weapon that was agonizing, and shock after shock was searing through her.
She couldn't let him see that hurt. "It doesn't surprise

me. It doesn't take much to target a fifteen-year-old girl. It probably only showed your father's men how weak and ineffectual you were. No wonder there are all kinds of rumors about how much better Conrad was than you'll ever be."

"There are no rumors! Everyone knows that I'm—"

"Everyone knows that you're a fool."

Brandon ran into the room with Nate at his heels and skidded to a stop. His gaze was fixed on her face.

She shook her head at him. What could he do? She had to handle this herself. Huber was pouring malice like a scalding acid with every word, and she could only either answer in kind or let him believe that she was helpless before him.

"You didn't hurt me at Sazkar Prison," she said. "Adversity just makes everyone stronger. You wouldn't know about that because I hear Conrad always pampered you. Does his old buddy, Kraus, pamper you, too?" Stab deep, don't let him think that he'd taken anything from her during that time. Don't let him guess he was hurting her now. "That must be why you're still an immature asshole."

"No one pampers me, you stupid bitch. Particularly not Kraus. I'm the one who runs Red Star. Everyone obeys my orders, as they should."

"And then laughs behind your back."

Brandon closed his eyes for an instant before instinctively taking a half step forward as if to protect her.

"That just goes to show how ignorant you are. You'll find out that no one dares to laugh at me." He hissed. "You won't laugh when I give you to my men and let them do exactly what I want them to do. I'm not going to worry about no marks of abuse this time. I'll let them cut you up. They'll beat you to a pulp. Rape will be the least of it."

"I'm tired of listening to you bragging. Yes, you hurt me before, but you didn't win."

"Yes, I did," he said maliciously. "When I killed Venable."

"And because you did, now you have me to deal with, Huber."

"You're nothing," he hissed. "You're a weak woman only fit to wait on me. Venable just used you to—"

"Or did I use him?" Strike him to the heart. "The poison was mine, I created it. I had reason to want revenge. So I took it. *I* killed Conrad Huber. What a fool you are. You might have killed my father, but you destroyed the wrong person. Because you're stupid, and you wouldn't believe a woman was capable of doing what had to be done to rid this world of scum. Well, now you do know, so what are you going to do about it?"

He was cursing again. "I'll remind you of that question when I have you with me, Rachel Venable. It will be soon, very soon." His voice was shaking, and she knew she had driven him as far as she could. "So think about it every minute until we're together."

His disconnect was almost a crash.

It was over.

She stood there. The call had been so full of ugliness and terror and memories of that other terror that she could barely pull herself together.

"Okay?" Brandon asked.

"No, but I will be." She swallowed. "He . . . wanted to hurt me. That's why he called. I . . . couldn't let him do it."

"From what I heard, he didn't have a chance," Nate said dryly.

"I . . . hope not. I can't think of any other reason he would have called. He was so . . . vicious. I couldn't give him that satisfaction. Half the time, I wasn't sure exactly what I was saying. I was just acting on instinct."

"And you have great instincts," Brandon said gently. "You were a powerhouse. What can I do to help you now?"

He was being wary, treating her as if she was very fragile. She wasn't fragile, but she was grateful that he wasn't going too fast in this moment when she was still recovering. "Nothing. I just need a little time to myself. I'll go out on the veranda and get some air, then I'll be fine. I'll see you in a few minutes." She thrust her phone blindly at him as she passed him. "I pressed record. I don't believe there's anything there that you can use, but you can listen and see for yourself. He was all about pain and ugliness and . . ." She was out the door and breathing in the cool night air.

Just stand here and take deep, steady breaths. Do what Hu Chang had taught her and let all pain and ugliness flow out of her.

She was strong. Nothing could hurt her if she didn't permit it. Not today. Not tomorrow. Certainly not yesterday. The past was gone, and she would take only what she wished from that time.

She could almost hear Hu Chang saying those words. The pain was easing, and she could begin to think again. A few more minutes and she would be what she should be.

She was strong . . .

CHAPTER

10

I brought you a cup of tea." Brandon was stand-ing behind her in the kitchen doorway. "I know you said you wanted to be alone, but it's been almost an hour, and I decided to check in with you before I went back to work with Monty."

"Thanks." She crossed the veranda and took the cup from him. "But you didn't need to baby me. I was just coming back inside. Time kind of got away from me."

"No, I don't need to baby you." His lips were tight. "You can take care of yourself. Huber was trying to tear you apart, and you managed to hold your own."

"Better than that," she took a sip of tea. "If I'd only held my own, I would have lost. I didn't lose, Brandon. I couldn't let him win anything more from me." She smiled with an effort. "But it was very, very hard."

"Tell me about it," he said grimly. "Listening to that

son of a bitch almost tore me apart. I can imagine what
it did to you."

"I'm fine now. It's all gone."

"Not for me."

"Then maybe you'd better spend a little time with
my friend, Hu Chang." She took another sip of tea.
"You didn't hear anything in the conversation that we
could use against Huber?"

"No, as you said, it was all about viciousness and
pain. I notice you did attempt to taunt him into giving
us a location for his disaster scenario. I knew that
would be a lost cause." He watched her lift the cup to
her lips again. "But you're right, you came out on top.
You met attack with attack. Even to telling him that
you were the instigator of Conrad's assassination. You
do realize it's going to make him more determined
than ever to get hold of you."

She shrugged. "He was already there. I couldn't let
him believe by killing my father that he'd beaten the
man who'd taken away the only person Huber appeared
to love. He was so smug about it all. I had to take that
away from him."

"Well, you succeeded. Now we've just got to make
sure that he doesn't get his hands on you."

"Or make sure he does," she said thoughtfully. "He
wants it so desperately that it could pave the way to a
big mistake. I knew he wanted me, I just didn't realize
it was to that extent."

"No," Brandon said firmly. "We've discussed this
before. It's off the table now that we know what a nut-
case Huber is about you."

She shook her head. "Nothing's off the table. One thing we did learn about Huber tonight is that he's immature, an egotist, and that you were right about Kraus possibly running things behind the scenes. He responded very violently to my comment about Kraus. Some conflict there . . ." She finished her tea. "I'll think about it and see what else occurs to me. But not now, you've got to go and help Monty." She swallowed. "I'm praying that you'll be able to get what we need. Nate scared me before." She looked at him. "I think you meant him to do that. You didn't want to raise my hopes." She smiled without mirth. "You didn't have to do it. I guarantee, my hopes weren't soaring."

"I wanted to be honest with you."

"I know."

"We're doing the best we can. We sent Claire Warren what she'd need to have her tech group check. Monty persuaded Sam Zackoff, one of his old buddies from MIT, to dive in and help. He's one of the most brilliant hackers in the world and does nothing else."

"But you were still covering your ass because there's no way it's anything but a long shot?"

He was silent. "You've been through too much. The last thing I wanted was to disappoint you."

She nodded. "Then don't treat me the way Huber was doing on the phone tonight. I'm not weak. I'm not helpless. I can handle anything he throws at me. And if we lose this battle, I'll also handle that." She forced a smile as she went into the kitchen and put her cup on the counter. "I was surprised Monty didn't run after you when Nate sounded the alarm about my call from Huber. You three are usually joined at the hip."

He shook his head. "Only when necessary. Monty stayed behind to plug into some high-tech monitor and make certain that your phone line wasn't compromised and broadcasting a trace."

"I should have known. It wasn't?"

Brandon shook his head. "But he wasn't able to trace Huber's call, either."

"I never thought he would. Of course, I wasn't thinking of much of anything while I was dealing with Huber. Except surviving. Surviving was very big on my agenda." She headed for the door to the hall. "You said you had to get back to Monty. Stop wasting time on me, Brandon." She glanced at him. "Unless there's some way I can help. Is there?"

He shook his head.

"Nate didn't think so. If you change your mind, call me. I'll be in my room."

He hesitated. "You'll be okay?"

"Brandon."

He held up his hands. "Sorry. I just didn't like the idea of your being alone and remembering all that shit Huber—"

"I won't remember it. I'll close it out. Call me if you need me." She went past him down the hall.

A few minutes later, she'd closed the door of her bedroom behind her.

She stood there a moment, letting the darkness of the room soothe her, take away all the frustration and pain.

Huber. Close him out.

Claire. Close her out.

Nemesis. She could *not* close him out.

She turned on the light and went over to her desk. She took out the computer Brandon had given her to replace the one with which they were working.

She sat down and flipped open the laptop. She typed in her email account number.

No mail.

What had she expected? Nemesis had told her no contact before noon the next day.

She expected nothing, she desperately wanted everything. She had been reasonable and practical and had let Brandon push her out of the picture, where she had no real place. She was no expert, she could not track Nemesis.

All she could do was make herself available to him.

And hope that element of malicious mockery she had sensed in him would cause him to step forward so that he would talk to her again. She had been so on edge at that first encounter that she hadn't been able to do anything but be defensive. But in retrospect, a few things about Nemesis had become clear to her. He was arrogant, money-hungry, mocking, and probably completely callous. But he was also afraid of both Huber and the consequences of what he was trying to do to Red Star. He had been so wary of Huber and his own deal with her father that he was taking less money so that he could escape as soon as possible. Nerves. There might be something she could use in that weakness . . .

At any rate, she was sure that he'd still be monitoring her messages. He'd been too verbose, and he'd enjoyed the domination he'd exerted over her. He wouldn't want to give up that power. And the anxiety that he'd revealed wouldn't allow him not to keep an eye on her to make certain nothing had changed. She started to type.

Nemesis.
I need to talk to you. It doesn't have to be this way. Whatever your demands, I'll see that they're met. By keeping silent, you're making yourself an accessory to what happens today. You can still get your big payoff for giving us Huber. Just tell me what's going to happen.

She leaned back after she sent the message.
She waited.
No reply.
She steeled herself against the inevitable disappointment. She could imagine him sitting there, smiling, as he caught the nuances of desperation in what she'd written. But if he'd read it at all, it was a minor triumph. She'd made contact when he'd arrogantly cut off all contact.

And every instinct told her that he'd read it.

And he'd keep on reading her messages. It didn't matter if it was to gratify his ego or to make certain she wasn't saying something of actual importance. She didn't care as long as it kept him busy tonight, and wove a thread of connection between them. He might feel annoyance and impatience before this night was over. She hoped he did. Because she wasn't going to sleep tonight.

And neither was Nemesis.

She started a new message.

Nemesis.
I need to talk to you.
Why are you afraid?
We can work together.
Did you know Huber called me a few hours ago?
We can talk about it.

She sent the message.

She waited.

No answer. He hadn't found the bit about Huber tempting enough? Or maybe he had to think about it. Don't worry, I'll give you time.

It's going to be a long night.

She waited for another five minutes. Then she began the third message.

Nemesis.
I need to talk to you. How can we trust you when you do something that throws you into Huber's camp? You need to defend yourself so that I can justify the money to the CIA. Can't you see that?

Message sent.

No answer.

She waited ten minutes and started again.

Nemesis.
You can see that I'm not giving up. All I'd need
is a hint about where Huber is going to strike
today. It would make the CIA much more likely
to negotiate. My father isn't there to pull strings,
but I'm trying to be here for you.

No answer.
She typed.

Nemesis.
I need to talk to you.

Again.
And again.
And again.

BEACH HAVEN
7:05 A.M.

Do you think all this pleading is going to get
you anything with me? What do you think you're
doing besides annoying me?

Rachel inhaled sharply as the text appeared suddenly on the screen in front of her. She had almost
given up. She was blurred and exhausted and had
started wondering if this was a total lost cause.

It might still be a lost cause, but not total. She'd

made him answer her. She took a deep breath. Her fingers were shaking as she typed back.

> I didn't consider it pleading, I thought I was reasoning with you. And, if you were annoyed, it might be more with yourself than me.

> Bullshit.

> I don't think so. You had to realize that my arguments were sound. You're either a terrorist or you're not. The minute you tried to intimidate us by dangling another disaster as you did today, you became a terrorist. That means you're solidly in Huber's camp as far as homeland, CIA, and FBI are concerned. You can't just take your money and run. We'll run after you. [She paused.] But not if you show us that you tried to help prevent it. If your fine plans fall through, that might save you from a death sentence.

Silence.

> So you said in those forty-two texts you sent me tonight. Forty-two! Ridiculous.

> But you read them. You know that what I said is true. Negotiate all you please. Make us pay. They tell me that's how this works. But you need to protect yourself, and the only way is to help protect those victims Huber's trying to murder

**today. What do you care? You're only using the
information to prove that you're reliable. You'll
still prove it if you let us save them before Huber actually takes them out. [She paused.] Give
me a place. Give me a name.**

Silence.

She wanted to jump in and attack again. No, she had
pounded him all night. Wait. She had laid out her arguments time after time. The fact that he had not answered was almost immaterial. His stubbornness had
only assured that he'd given her no arguments. But her
words had been before him on his computer screen,
sinking in every time he glanced at it.

I don't have a name.

Her heart sank with disappointment. He was re-
fusing?

His next words came immediately.

**And you will pay. That's exactly how this works.
[Another pause.] But it will do no harm to take
out a little insurance. It's true that I've no desire
to be thought to be one of Huber's puppets.
That could prove dangerous. The CIA under-
stands money, they're touchy about terrorists.**

Even though he might have been one in the past?

But you said you have no name to give me.

I have a place. Huber has a passion for sending hotels to the depths of hell. Have you noticed? Six hotels in the last eight years. The one in Rome was my personal favorite. That hotel was the size of the Colosseum, and the ruins actually looked like it. My information says that he wants another one to add to his résumé.

Which hotel?

Am I bad? A slight problem. It's one of the hotels on San Kabara island, but I didn't investigate which one since it wasn't my prime concern. I'm sure you'll be able to find out since I've given you the principal location. You can't expect me to do all your work.

San Kabara Island. Rachel vaguely remembered seeing TV commercials about the island north of the city that was described as a lush new tourist destination that was offering lavish hotels and casinos, sports meccas, and magnificent views. She'd paid no attention to them, she thought in a panic. How many hotels were on the island? She couldn't remember. Five hours left . . .

You've got to know which hotel. Are you playing me?

Would I do that? I'm counting on you to save me if I stumble and fall. I honestly don't know

which hotel. I've done my part, it's up to you to do the rest, Rachel. You should feel good that you convinced me to be a superhero. I'm feeling so much better about myself. I'll get with you later to discuss our primary arrangement. I'll allow you a little more time since you might be busy with San Kabara.

The next moment, he was no longer there.

And Rachel was jumping to her feet and grabbing her laptop.

San Kabara!

Then she was out of the bedroom and running toward Brandon's library.

"San Kabara," she said when she burst into the room. "It's going to happen on San Kabara Island, Brandon. It will be a hotel. That's all I could find out." She looked at Monty. "Tell me that you've found his IP address, so I can call him back."

He shook his head. "Nemesis? No such luck." He stiffened. "Back? You've talked to him again?"

"Not what you could call conversation. I did most of the emailing until the very end. And then he might have been lying to make a fool of me. He was mocking as hell." She threw herself into a chair. "But I don't think so. He's not stupid. San Kabara didn't matter to him, so he was willing to give me a little on the chance that he might need a safety net at some point." She tossed her laptop to Brandon. "You can skim it until you come to the last pages. That's the only important thing to us." She closed her eyes. "I hope it's important.

He might have played me." Her lids flew open. "But I think we have to go with it, don't we?"

"Shh." Brandon was already scanning the message. "My God, what have you been doing, Rachel?"

"The only thing I could do. I couldn't help you, so I thought I'd try to reach out to him. I knew it would be a long shot. But judging from his remarks and attitude, I thought there would be a good chance he'd be monitoring me. I had all night to see if I could make him listen to me."

"Evidently you did . . ." Monty said. He'd come around to read over Brandon's shoulder. "No one could say you aren't persistent, Rachel."

"It paid off . . . maybe. I think it's worth a chance." She fell silent, waiting for them to finish.

"Hell, yes," Brandon said as he glanced up from the screen. "Monty, you look up everything you can find on San Kabara Island. I'll call Claire Warren and see how fast we can put something in motion." He reached for his phone. "I don't think she can refuse to explore the possibility of an attack since Nemesis furnished her with a specific target. Langley would roast her alive if she screwed up."

"He didn't," Rachel said. "Not specific." She jerked upright in the chair, galvanized by Brandon's acceptance of the hope that she'd been trying to keep alive. "But maybe enough." She got to her feet and was dialing as she headed for the door. "And I've got to call Catherine." She hadn't talked to her since yesterday afternoon, she realized. Everything had been so crazy, she hadn't even told her about the call from Huber.

Catherine was not going to be pleased. But perhaps the information Rachel had managed to get from Nemesis regarding San Kabara might distract her.

It did distract Catherine, but not enough for her not to say grimly when Rachel had finished, "Unacceptable. You ever leave me out of the loop again, you're going to hear from me. I can't help you if you don't let me know what's happening. I don't care how upset you were."

"Warning noted," Rachel said. "And deserved."

"You bet it is." Catherine was silent. "You think that he was telling the truth?"

"I believe that there's a good chance . . . if I read him right. He wants to have it all ways." She added, "But there's also a chance he's playing me. I just don't think it's a good idea to risk it. As I said, Brandon is calling Claire right now, so he doesn't either. There's less than five hours left, Catherine."

"I know that. San Kabara. A hotel," she repeated thoughtfully. "By not telling you the name of the hotel, he might be trying to save his ass with Huber."

"Or he might not know it; he said it wasn't of value to him." She turned as Monty came out of the bedroom with laptop in hand. "Wait a minute. Monty just came in, he's been looking up San Kabara." And his expression was not encouraging. Her hand tightened on the phone. "Got it, Monty?"

He handed her the laptop. "Or it's got us," he said curtly. "Look at the number of hotels on San Kabara. Brandon said to tell you to get Catherine nudging Claire Warren to get Homeland out to that island and begin evacuation. She was giving him double-talk and stalling." He turned and headed down the hall. "I've got to get Nate to arrange for a speedboat at the marina. Brandon said he wanted to leave the house in five minutes." He disappeared around the corner.

"Did you hear any of that?" Rachel asked Catherine as she balanced the computer Monty had thrust at her. "Brandon asked you to make Claire begin evacuation and—"

"I heard it," Catherine said shortly. "I didn't hear why."

Neither had Rachel, but she was trying to read the page Monty had pulled up on his computer. San Kabara was a jewel of an island, it had a full-service marina and all the sport and casino facilities anyone could wish. The photos showed a magnificent white beach dotted with colorful umbrellas only a short distance from the marina. Wonderful exotic hotels stretched beyond the pounding surf and curved toward the south end of the island. A lush green rolling ridge bordered and formed a background for the hotels. A winding path planted with a hibiscus tree border led up the cliff to a few more hotels.

All those hotels . . . Rachel's gaze was frantically racing over the text, weeding out the hyperbole that publicity had issued about the island. Then she came to the sentence that had sent Monty scrambling.

"Oh, shit," she breathed.

"What is it?" Catherine asked.

"Nineteen luxury hotels," she read to her. "And most of them are on wait-list status during this season."

"And it's an island," Catherine said. "It could be an evacuation nightmare if we don't have an exact target. I've got to go, Rachel. Claire can't ignore this, and she's going to need every one of the team to help Homeland. We've got to get to San Kabara." She hung up.

Rachel's heart was beating fast as she thrust her phone back in her pocket. Nineteen hotels. Four hours before one of them could be destroyed. How many people could die if those hotels weren't evacuated on time? The numbers and possibilities were overwhelming. Except she couldn't be overwhelmed. She wouldn't curl up and let Huber have it all his own way.

Five minutes.

Brandon had told Monty they'd be leaving the house in five minutes for the marina. Not that she was probably included in their plans. As she'd told Brandon, he and his men were joined at the hip by the experiences of years. She might have given them the clue to lead them to Huber's disaster scenario, but that didn't mean that she'd be invited to help stop it.

Too bad.

She turned and made a stop in the kitchen before she headed for the front door.

Two minutes later, she had reached the car where Brandon sat in the driver's seat. Nate was in the passenger seat, but Monty had not yet arrived.

"No, Rachel," Brandon said. "You've no business on that island. We'll take care of it."

"Business? No one has more business there than I do." She opened the rear door and put her black-leather medical bag on the floor before she got in the car.

"None of us knows what we're going to face when we get there. But I do know it probably won't be good. I spend my life facing disaster situations of one kind or another. I might not be able to stop this one, but I'm better qualified than you to face what comes later." She met his eyes in the rearview mirror. "So shut up, Brandon, I'm going."

"Evidently you are," he said curtly. "I don't have time to throw you out or argue with you." As Monty got in the backseat beside Rachel, Brandon backed out of the driveway. "It will take us at least forty minutes to get to the island from the marina, and by that time, if Claire's done her job, Homeland will be in the process of locking it down. That may not be good. All we need is to have to cut through their red tape."

SAN KABARA ISLAND

Brandon was right, Rachel noticed, as she jumped out of the speedboat onto the pier. Even in this short time, there were two Coast Guard ships already at the pier, plus multiple police and civilian boats. Even as she watched, two helicopters were landing about a mile down the beach in front of the Andorra Hotel, which towered at least twenty stories above the crashing surf. Hotel personnel were shepherding bewildered guests out of the other hotels along the strip to the beach. Two police officers were putting up a yellow crime-scene-tape barricade to keep anyone boarding any of the boats at the pier.

"Wait here," Brandon said curtly as he made his way toward the police officers. "I need to know where the command center is going to be—"

Then she didn't hear anything else as she saw Catherine get off that second helicopter. She ducked under the tape and started running down the beach toward her.

"Rachel!" Brandon was right behind her. "Stay close, dammit. I don't need to be chasing after you."

"No, you don't." She said over her shoulder, "Go look for someone suspicious or something. Can't you see they need help to get those people out of the hotels? I'm going to ask Catherine to put me to work."

Brandon muttered a curse. "We don't even know what the threat is going to be. We assume that it will be a blast because that's Huber's modus operandi, but we can't be certain. We need to go with the bomb squad into all the hotels and see if we can find anything."

"Then go do it. I don't know anything about bombs, but I know about people. Those guests streaming out of those hotels look like lost sheep. Some of them may have decided to stay put instead of wandering around on the beach. That can't happen." She put on a spurt of speed as she saw Catherine coming toward her. "Get away from me, Brandon. I didn't come here to have you hovering over me." She'd almost reached Catherine, and she called to her, "Tell me what to do. Where's Claire?"

"The other helicopter," Catherine shouted over the sound of the rotors. "She wanted to show up with Matt

Delvan, who's heading the Homeland investigation."
She looked beyond Rachel's shoulder. "Where's Brandon going?"

Rachel glanced at Brandon, who had done an about-face and was heading toward a police command center that was now being set up near the pier. "I have no idea. Probably something world-shaking. That's his business. My business is to save as many of these people as I can." She glanced at her watch. A chill went through her. A little less than three hours. "Can you give me an ID or something so that I won't get arrested for interfering with Company business?"

"Better than that." Catherine took off her CIA windbreaker and handed it to Rachel. "But I don't believe you're going to have problems. Everything is going to be in frantic mode from now on. No one's going to ask too many questions if you appear to be rescuing, not killing, someone. Phone me if you get into trouble. I'll take care of it."

"You always do." She slipped on the windbreaker. "But then we'll both be in trouble. What should I do first?"

"Start at the Andorra and work your way down the beach toward the path that goes up the cliff. The Andorra Hotel is the largest on the island, and the bomb squad has already checked it out. But we can't be too careful." She nodded at the hotel. "Knock on doors. Get a master key E card from security and throw open all the doors you can. If any are on security chains and your E card doesn't work, make a note and have someone go up and cut them. Make sure

everyone knows there's a threat. We called manage-
ment and told them to set off the fire alarms because
we thought that would be the quickest way to alert the
guests. But when you're dealing with this many people
in a tourist area, you can never be sure that someone's
not drunk or ill or whatever." Catherine was looking
up at the glittering glass windows of the Andorra. "We
think that Huber would probably choose the largest,
most prestigious hotel because it would garner him the
most attention. We've narrowed it down to five possible hotels in that category. The Andorra, Sea Surf,
Gold Haven, Neptune's Castle, and The Vineyard."
She gestured to the luxurious skyscrapers dotting the
beach. "We're sending bomb-detecting crews to all
five, and they're going through them from top to bottom."

Rachel slowly shook her head as her gaze traveled
up to the top of the Andorra. "That's a very high top,
Catherine. Less than three hours now. Can they guarantee that they'd find it even if you're right?"

"No guarantees," Catherine said. "That's why we're
knocking on doors and making sure that everyone is
out." She was looking at the dozen hotels in the curve
of the beach at the far end of the island, then to the
small hotels nestled on the cliff overlooking the sea.
"We can only do what we can. We had to pick and
choose and hope they can get a few more bomb units
to us ASAP." She was still frowning at those small hotels. "Look, I'm going to take a couple operatives
down to that end of the beach and make certain the
evacuation is going well there. Those smaller hotels

may not be priority, but they deserve our attention. You stay here and help out at the Andorra, then go to Neptune's Castle." She was already moving away. "But Claire wants everyone out of those hotels by ten thirty regardless of what they find. Good move. How can we be sure that Nemesis was accurate about Huber's time frame when he didn't even know which hotel is targeted?"

"Or told us that he didn't," Rachel said. "But changing the evacuation limit means we only have an hour and thirty minutes left."

"Providing that there's even going to be an attack on this island," Claire said shortly. She had come up behind them and was frowning at Rachel. "I'm forced to treat this as a credible threat, but this is a very expensive operation, and my reputation is on the line. I hope you realize that I'm not going to be pleased if this turns out to be a puff of smoke."

"And I'll be very pleased," Rachel said quietly. "I hope I'm wrong. I hope Nemesis lied to me. Excuse me, I've got to go knock on doors. Don't you have a bomb or something to find? I hear Huber's very fond of explosives." Rachel heard Catherine smother a chuckle as she turned and ran into the hotel.

The lobby was in turmoil. Hotel personnel, police, military, and panicky guests were everywhere.

The evacuation had clearly not gone as planned, she thought as she saw the guests streaming down the exit stairs. The elevators had stopped and locked when the fire alarm had gone off, a common safety measure.

She fought to get to a police officer who seemed to

be in charge, then gave up. She shouted at him over the crowd. "How many floors have been checked?"

He recognized the CIA jacket. He tossed her an emergency master key. "Fifteen through twelve," he shouted back.

She turned and ran for the staircase. She had to fight the downward flow of panicky guests to get up the stairs. By the time she reached the eleventh floor, she was bruised and breathless. But once she was away from the staircase, the corridors were almost empty. She ran through the eleventh floor, knocking on doors, throwing them open, shouting.

No reply.

The same for the tenth and ninth floor.

On the seventh floor, a heavyset man in Room 701 opened the door. Weaving back and forth, drunk, and belligerent. It took her almost five minutes to get him to the staircase and put him in the care of one of the policemen on the landing.

No reply on the sixth floor.

On the fifth floor, she found little Dory. She was a big-eyed little girl of about five or six who reminded Rachel of Maria. She was wandering around the halls with her *Frozen* Elsa doll clutched in her arms. Rachel knelt beside her. "Hello, I'm Rachel. What's your name? And where's your mama?"

Tears were running down her cheeks. "My name is Dory," she whispered. "I think Mama went to the pool. I can't find her."

"Then let me help. I'll take you down to find your mama." She took her hand and led her to the stairwell.

But she had to take her down to the next floor before she could turn her over to a policewoman. Then she ran back up the steps and did a tour of the floor to see if the child's mother was not at the pool but in one of the rooms.

No reply to her shouts.

No reply from any of the rooms on the fourth floor.

No reply on the third floor.

When she reached the second floor, she saw two National Guard soldiers going down the halls and knocking on doors.

Time to go next door to Neptune's Castle to see if she could help there.

She fought her way through the lobby and out onto the beach.

Her phone was ringing. Brandon. It had been ringing all the time she was in the Andorra, but she hadn't taken time to answer it.

"Where are you?" Brandon asked as soon as she answered.

"The beach. I just left the Andorra."

"Stay where you are. I'll be there in five minutes."

"I'm going to Neptune's Castle."

"Did you hear me?" His voice cracked like a whip. "Stay where you are. I've just come from Neptune's Castle. I was with the bomb squad team that was searching the hotels. Don't move until I get to you."

"There's no time to wait around. It's almost ten, and Catherine said—"

"We found an explosive rigged to explode in the basement of Neptune's Castle."

"You *found* it?" Relief was flooding through her. "Were they able to disarm it?"

"Yes. No real problem. Which made it one hell of a big problem."

She frowned. "That doesn't make sense. What do you mean?"

"Stay where you are, and I'll tell you. I'm almost there. Don't you dare take off again."

She could see him now coming from the direction of the pier, pushing through the crowds on the beach.

Then he was beside her. "Come on." He grabbed her arm and drew her away from the Andorra. "I don't want you anywhere near these hotels. Hell, I want you off this island."

"What are you talking about? You said you'd found the explosives and disarmed them." She grimaced. "Claire will be ecstatic. She'll claim she saved the day."

"It was too easy," he said curtly. "The captain of the bomb squad said the same thing. Those explosives were easy to find and only a little difficult to disarm. Huber has experts who set his explosives. I saw their work firsthand when he had my father's sailboat blown up."

"I remember." She frowned, trying to understand what he was telling her. "Then it wasn't Huber?"

"Oh, it was Huber," he said bitterly. "It was Huber with a message. He wanted us to be able to disarm that explosive so that we'd be able to take it apart and see what he'd sent us."

"Sent?"

He reached into his pocket and took out a small, glossy photo. "Surprise."

She stiffened.

Not surprise, shock.

It was a photo of herself, her hair tousled, her eyes wide with fear, a bruise on her cheek. There was stone building in the background with an arched doorway.

"It's me." She moistened her lips. "Or it was me. I've never seen that photo."

"No, it was probably sent as a souvenir to Huber from the Taliban." His lips were tight. "He must have enjoyed it. It was taken at Sazkar Prison, wasn't it? It had to be, you look so damn young and scared."

"Fifteen." She swallowed. "And I was scared. It must have been taken during those first months before I learned that was a victory for them. I don't believe I looked like that later. I hope I didn't."

"Don't look like that." He was cursing. "Of course, you didn't let them see a damn thing. You were always stronger than they were. They didn't take one single thing from you."

She drew a deep breath. "I know that, it just took a little while to learn it." Her lips were trembling. "And I don't like that Huber had this photo. Can we burn it?"

"No, it's mine. I'm going to hold it in front of him while I tear his heart out."

She felt a ripple of shock at the sheer savagery of his tone. "That doesn't seem fair." She smiled unsteadily. "Maybe we should flip a coin. I have such fine plans for him." She drew a deep breath. "And maybe we should concentrate on why this photo suddenly appeared here instead of on the memories it's triggering. It doesn't make sense." She reached a shaky hand to her temple. "None of it. Why this photo?" She was looking at the picture more closely. "He wanted to make sure I'd recognize it and remind me of what I'd gone through." She looked up at him. She whispered, "Did he know I was coming? How long has it been here? Was it Nemesis? Was this all a trap?"

"Possible." Brandon took the photo from her. "Nemesis could be a paid assassin or just so clumsy that he let Huber find out he was an informant. He might have sold you out."

"But why leave this photo?"

"Whether he knew you'd be here or just knew the police would find it later, he wanted to let you know he still had you in his sights," he said flatly.

"I don't see how he could have left it today," she said. "San Kabara is teeming with police, FBI, Homeland Security, and CIA, and it would have been difficult not to be seen or even to get off the island. It was already in lockdown, any suspicious action would have stirred up a hornet's nest." She was trying to work her way through his thinking process. "No, I don't believe it was a direct threat. I think that it was aimed at making me feel as helpless as I did when the Taliban had me at Sazkar. He mentioned that when he called me last night, and I could tell the bastard enjoyed it. He wanted to show me that nothing had changed since I was fifteen. He was still the master." She was going step by step, working it out as she did one of her potions. "But he wouldn't give up blowing up that hotel just to mock me and cause me a few nightmares. It had to be something else. I couldn't be that important to him."

"Oh you're important. He wouldn't have showcased you so spectacularly with that bomb if you weren't. But he might not be willing to give up his demonstration." His lips twisted. "I'd bet he wanted you to see it. That's why I told that captain of the bomb squad to keep on going through the hotels to make sure that they don't run across another device."

She went still. "Dear God, of course that's what he'd do. Give us a little time to let our guard down, then hit out." Her gaze flew to his face. "What hotels?"

"They were at the Sea Surf when I came here after you. They might have moved to the Vineyard by now."

"The top five hotels . . ." And the Neptune had been in the top five also. Huber had given them exactly what they had expected with that explosive. And now they were busily looking in the same direction. "But what if he isn't interested in destroying the best and most splendid," she asked suddenly. "What if he's looking for something else this time?"

His eyes narrowed on her face. "Where are you going with this?"

She was terrified at where her mind was going. "He passed up on the Neptune. He used it as a tool to show me how helpless I am. And Nemesis said something the first time he contacted me . . ." Her gaze slowly lifted to the cliff and the three small hotels that looked out over the Pacific. "He said Huber was arrogant and wanted to change the coast of California. This is an island off the coast. Maybe he'd want to change it, too. Look how those hotels are balanced on that cliff . . ."

And Catherine had told her she was going up to those hotels when she'd sent Rachel into the Andorra.

"*No!*"

She started running up the beach toward the path that led to the cliff. "Call that bomb squad and tell them go check those hotels on the cliff first, Brandon. A powerful enough explosion would send that cliff into the sea . . ." She was calling Catherine as she reached the path.

Answer me, Catherine.

Get out of there! Please get out of there.

No answer.

She punched in the number again as she started running up the path.

No answer.

She was halfway up the cliff and could see the men, women, and children milling around the lush grounds of the three hotels that Catherine had been trying to evacuate.

But she didn't see Catherine.

It might be fine. She could be wrong.

She started to dial her again.

Please, make me wrong, she prayed.

She could see two little children playing tag near the wall that bordered the cliff.

So close to that cliff . . .

No!

Catherine, dammit, answer your phone!

I need you to—

The entire mountain blew!

Darkness when there had been sunshine.

Pain.

A roaring, shaking, screams.

She had been hurled to the ground, Rachel realized dazedly. Her shoulder had struck one of the hibiscus trees beside the path. What had happened?

Cracking.

Shifting.

Screaming!

Oh God, the screaming . . .

Someone needed help.

She managed to lift her head to look up at the top of the cliff to the hotels.

There were no hotels.

There was no top of the cliff.

And she saw where those screams had come from. All of those people who had been milling around the gardens of the hotels had been swept away by that hideously strong blast. Rachel could see bodies lying everywhere on the slope that had been torn from the side of the cliff as the hotels had plunged into the sea below. Some people were clinging to debris from the ruin of the hotels or the scrawny trees that had been unearthed as the cliff tumbled into the ocean.

As she watched, a woman lost her desperate hold on a boulder and slid down the slope toward the sea.

And then she was screaming, too.

Rachel struggled to her knees. She had to get to them. She had to get to all of them.

"Rachel!" Brandon was suddenly beside her. He grabbed her shoulders. "Are you okay?"

"No." Didn't he understand? No one was okay. They were screaming. She had to get to them. "I didn't want to be right. But he did it, he did this. I have to get to them."

"The hell you do." He was feeling her arms, legs, looking at her shoulder. "Can't you see that every rescue crew on the island is streaming up that path? What there is left of it . . . I'll be down there myself as soon as I get you down off this cliff. The rest of it could collapse at any moment. That blast must have undermined this half of the island."

"Then he won," she said dully. "He changed the coastline. All those people didn't matter, did they?"

"No." He was helping her to her feet. "Not to him. But they do to us. Come on, let me take you where you can get some first aid. I want to get down there."

"So do I." The *screaming*. "That sounded like a child." She started to go toward the cliff edge, which was now only a scant twenty feet away. "I don't need first aid. I need to help." She shook her head to clear it. "Catherine. I couldn't reach her. She could be down there, too." Panic was growing as she spoke, and she tried to pull away from Brandon's restraining hand. "I have to—"

His hand tightened. "You have to leave here before the rest of this cliff falls into the sea," he said grimly. "Come willingly, or I'll lift you in a fireman's hold and carry you down."

"Screw you." She jerked away from him. "Can't you hear them? I have to get to where I can—"

"Catherine." He was looking beyond her down the slope. "You wanted Catherine. There she is. She's skidding down the slope, trying to get close enough to the rescue area."

Relief. "I'll go and see if I can—"

"No." He was at the edge of the cliff and calling down to Catherine. "Get up here, Catherine. I need you! Just give me two minutes."

Catherine stopped, looked up at his face, then was climbing back to the top. Rachel saw that she had a length of rope over her shoulder, but she didn't use it for the climb. "Two minutes," she said grimly. "I have to—" Then she saw Rachel. "You were here? Are you hurt?"

"I don't think so. Not badly." Brandon answered for her. "But I can't keep her from going down that slope without knocking her out. You do it."

"They're screaming, Catherine," Rachel said. "They need help. They need me."

Catherine stared at her for an instant, then strode over to her. "Yes, they are screaming, and they do need help." She took her by the shoulders. "And you do need to do it." She looked her in the eyes. "You're the only one who can do it now. But not down there with us, pulling them out of that hellhole. You need to go down there on the beach and set up a triage center for us to send those injured people we manage to rescue. It might be too late for some of them by the time they scramble and get medical teams here from San Francisco. You need to treat them now and try to save them. That's your job now, Rachel." She gave her a quick kiss on the forehead. "Now go down and do it. I hope we're going to need you very soon." She turned back to Brandon. "And you come with me. I think you're right, she's not badly hurt though she might have a minor concussion. But she's not going to let anyone hold her hand through this nightmare. No one knows better how to cope than Rachel." She was already skidding down the steep, jagged slope. "So cope, Rachel. I'll see you later. I think I heard a child . . ."

"You did," Rachel called after her. "I think he was near those rocks by the—" She stopped. Not her job. Not right now. She wasn't thinking too clearly herself, but Catherine had been able to point her in the right direction as she had so many times before. She turned to Brandon. "You heard her, help her find that kid." She turned and had to steady herself before she started down the path to the beach. "And I want him alive when you bring him to me, Brandon. See to it."

"Yes, ma'am." He was going down the slope. "And I'll call Monty and pull him off the rescue team to give you a hand. You might be able to cope, but Monty has certain talents that might come in handy . . ."

CHAPTER

11

8:40 P.M.

Rotors overhead.

More helicopters, Rachel thought wearily. She was used to the sound now. They had been operating nonstop since the disaster. Bringing in supplies, social workers, medical help, and equipment, families of victims, military . . . Thank God, they'd managed to keep out the politicians and the media. Though she'd seen news helicopters buzzing around since noon. She didn't think she would have been able to stand having them tour any of the tent facilities she'd managed to set up. It had been bad enough fighting all the military brass to get her way when she'd started setting up this makeshift hospital next to the disaster zone.

"That helicopter was for the amputee." Monty came

into the tent to stand beside her. "It has room for another patient. Do we have one?"

"No, but that pregnant woman died on the operating table. I wasn't able to save her. We couldn't find any ID on her. Send her to the medical examiner in San Francisco."

"I'll tell them." Monty started to turn away, then stopped. "You don't have to stay here, Rachel. There are only five patients left in that tent. They've got more than enough doctors and nurses here now. And there are more volunteers landing on every other helicopter. They're standing in line at the Red Cross and all the hospitals from here to the Oregon border. You've done your part, now let them do theirs."

She shook her head. "The rescue workers are still on the slope. They've not located all the survivors yet." All day long, she had seen the dogs and the rescue teams fight their way to that mangled wreckage of a cliff, looking for miracles. But miracles were few and far between. She'd had to order a morgue tent set up an hour after she'd begun receiving victims from that horror of a slope. The young pregnant woman had made the dead a total of sixty-four, and she'd lost count of the injuries she'd treated and sent out to hospitals in San Francisco, way over 150. She didn't want to remember right now. "I was told that there might be air pockets under that hotel debris that trapped those people under the water. I have to stay."

"No you don't," he said gently. "Brandon just called me from the slope. The divers say no possible survivors in the water. They've changed the mission from search and rescue to retrieval."

She flinched. "They could be wrong." She desperately wanted them to be wrong. But she had worked these disasters before, and she knew how hard it was for rescue workers to make that call. They'd still do their very best, but rescues would be rare. "What did Brandon think?"

"He thinks that you should let the volunteers you have in those tents do their job while you take a break." He paused. "And come to terms with the truth. He said if you didn't, he'd send Catherine after you. And they both need to be up there for the wrap-up before they come down."

They were coming down. Neither of them would ever abandon those victims if they thought there was a chance. She whispered, "It's over?"

"All you can do right now," he said quietly. "Go over to the mess tent and get a cup of tea. You haven't stopped since you came down from that cliff and hit the ground running. You're so tired, you're more a hindrance than an asset right now. I'll take care of delegating duties and responsibilities."

She didn't want to let go. She opened her lips to argue with him. Then she closed them and turned away. He was right, those few remaining patients deserved someone fresher and clearer-headed than she was right now. "Yes, do that. Tell them to call me if anything changes." It was hard to move one foot in front of the other as she left the tent. She hadn't felt the exhaustion while she was working, but that was always how it worked after the adrenaline began to fade. She went past the mess tent and turned to walk toward the pier. She kept her eyes averted from the steep, rutted slope and the hotels that were mere twisted piles of concrete in the surf. It hurt too much. So much destruction. So many deaths. She just wanted to find someplace to curl up and look at the sunlight on the water instead of that horror that had been her life for the last hours.

And pray for the souls of all those innocents who had died today.

"I've been looking for you," Brandon said as he came toward the piling that she was leaning against beneath the pier. "You didn't answer your phone. I didn't need that, Rachel."

"No, you didn't," she said wearily. "I didn't do it on purpose. My battery was down. I've been using it all day. I didn't realize it until I checked to see if Monty had called me when I got here." She gazed up at him. He looked powerful and tough but stretched to the limit. Who wouldn't be after the day he'd had on that damned slope? He was dirty, his jeans and shirt torn. There was a long scratch on his forearm. "You came straight from the slope? You didn't need to do that. You have to take care of yourself. Didn't Monty tell you that I'm fine?"

"As fine as you could be. I had to see for myself." He dropped down on the sand beside her, his gaze raking her face. "Exhausted, numb, heartsick."

"Not numb." She looked out at the sun, which was

almost down. "Every one of those people you sent me from the slope is still with me. How can I let them go? You can't, can you?"

"No." He reached out and covered her hand on the sand. "But that's me, I don't like to see you hurting. How can I help?"

"You're doing it." She looked down at his hand on hers. It was also dirty and cut, but it was warm and strong, and both the dirt and lacerations had been earned in the same battle she had fought. "You're making me feel that I'm not alone. That's good right now." She was silent, staring out at the water. "Huber wanted me to see it, didn't he? That's what that photo was about. Do you suppose he managed to use Nemesis to draw me here? He wanted me to come and see it and not be able to do anything about it."

"It's possible," he said. "But you did do something about it. It would have been even more of a catastrophe if all those guests had still been inside the hotels. At least fifty percent survived who were registered in those cliff hotels. And all the hotels on the beach strand were left untouched."

"You're wrong. No one was left untouched today."

He nodded. "I guess you're right."

"Do you think it was enough for him?" she whispered. "It was such a horror. Do you believe he's still planning another disaster for the twenty-fifth?"

"Catherine thinks this is only the preview Nemesis told you it was." He paused. "I tend to agree with her."

She was silent. "It can't happen again," she said unsteadily. "It's not that I haven't been caught in the middle of monstrous ugliness before. But this coldness is a wickedness beyond . . ." She drew a deep breath. "Catherine sent me to set up those tents to take care of survivors, and I went along with it because I knew I'd be more help there. But my father said there were times when you had to go after the bad guys and stop them." She forced herself to look away from the sea to the jagged, rutted slope at the far end of the island. Was it only imagination that she thought she saw blood in those ruts? "I won't let anyone send me away again, Brandon."

"I could see that coming." He stood up. "It's not the time for me to deal with it right now. I'm getting you off this island while it's still overrun with military and CIA. Once it settles down, Claire and her cohorts will be asking questions and proposing solutions that I might not be pleased with." He pulled her to her feet and frowned when she flinched. "What hurts?"

"My shoulder. Just a bad bruise. I was still able to work with it."

"Good for you," he said dryly. "We'll still stop at the hospital tent and have it wrapped before we get on the helicopter."

"Helicopter? What about the speedboat we rented?"

"All boats in the marina are being searched by the Coast Guard. It will be quicker to take Catherine up on her offer to fly us back to the mainland. Nate and Monty will bring the boat back. She told me to have you on the beach by the hospital tents in two hours. She had to make her report to Claire and Homeland about the rescue operation." He looked at his watch.

"You have forty-five minutes since it took me longer than I thought to find you."

"That will be long enough." She frowned as she glanced at the wicked scratch on his forearm. "I'll have to treat that first. We don't want it infected."

"No, we don't. Huber would get entirely too much pleasure out of it." He looked straight ahead as he drew her from beneath the pier. "We'll both get through this with a minimum of wounds to carry forward. Count on it, Rachel."

Catherine ran out of the darkness toward the heli-copter just seconds before it was due to take off. "Sorry. They wouldn't stop asking questions." She jumped on board and signaled the pilot to take off before she settled beside Rachel in the rear seat. "And I wasn't about to tell them I was whisking you off the island, Rachel." She nodded at Brandon, who was occupying the copilot's seat and talking to the pilot. "Brandon was so determined to get you away from here that I didn't want to risk his getting thrown in the brig. The island is under military jurisdiction until further notice."

"It doesn't surprise me," Rachel said. "They haven't found any hint of anyone belonging to Red Star on the island?"

Catherine shook her head. "But Huber has all kinds of technical capabilities. It wouldn't be difficult for him to have a minisub waiting off the island for a quick exit." She added soberly, "It amazed me when Brandon told me about the photo. If it was Huber, it had to be a direct taunt aimed only at you. But I doubt if he was actually here since it wasn't necessary for the blast. The charges that toppled those three hotels on the cliff were planted in the foundation of the buildings on a timer. Probably at least a week ago. It had all kinds of safety and firewall features and would have been almost impossible for a bomb squad to detect."

"Then he could have had someone else here ready to plant that photo."

"Or had it planted weeks ago as part of his master plan." Catherine shook her head. "I don't know, we'll figure it out." She leaned her head wearily against the backrest. "My brain doesn't seem to be too sharp at the moment."

For the first time, Rachel noticed the circles beneath Catherine's eyes and the tension in her every muscle. Catherine always generated so much crackling energy and sleek power that Rachel often took it for granted. Yet Catherine had been out on the slope most of the day with the rescue teams, and she must be totally exhausted, both physically and emotionally. And then she'd had to confront Claire and Homeland to give her report. "You're doing fine," she said quietly. "You always do fine." She smiled faintly. "And you saw to it that I pulled myself together so that I did fine, too." She leaned back and squeezed Catherine's hand, which was lying on the armrest. "And we'll both be better once we get a little rest." She had a sudden thought. "Did you call Hu Chang? He must have seen the news stories."

She nodded. "I called him when I left the slope. He

wasn't pleased. I told him that neither were we." She shrugged. "I can't blame him. I promised I'd take care of you. But I didn't have time to discuss it. He may call you."

"I'll be ready for him. If we managed to get through San Kabara Island, we can survive Hu Chang." She thought about it. Then she settled back and closed her eyes. "Or maybe not . . ."

Huber was eagerly looking at his tape of the CNN footage when Kraus called him. "It was magnificent!" He added immediately, "But all I could see were the aerial shots. I wanted close-ups. Why couldn't you get me close-ups?"

"Because Homeland and the CIA are afraid of us," Kraus said. "You wanted that cliff to fall into the sea, and I took care of it. But they weren't going to let news crews run around the island after it happened. You'll have to be happy with the aerial shots until they permit anyone but military on the grounds."

"They're afraid of me?" Huber's voice was excited. "More than usual, right? I knew they would be."

"Much more than usual," Kraus said. "There's talk that they think this was the main event that we were planning. It was that good." He paused. "So should we skip that one? You'd only lose a little prestige if we did."

"Don't be a fool," Huber said. "You've told me everything was going well with Fasrain. Why would I give it up?"

"No reason." He paused. "Except that I received a report today that Venable's daughter was on San Kabara Island today. She somehow found out that something was going on and caused the CIA to come in early. Unfortunate, the event might have gone even better if that hadn't happened."

"That bitch!" Huber was cursing low and vehemently. "How? It shouldn't have happened. She was supposed to get the photo later."

"I'm exploring how she could have known. Perhaps her father knew more than we thought. I just wanted to tell you that she might be a problem if we go forward."

"She won't be a problem. Because you're going to keep her from being a problem. I told you what she said to me when I called her. I won't stand for that, Kraus. You said that you had a plan to get your hands on her. Was that the truth?"

"I always tell you the truth."

"Then make that your main priority. I *want* Rachel Venable, Kraus."

"Then, of course, you'll get her at once. I didn't realize you were in such a hurry. There seemed to be so many more important things on the agenda."

"Get her!"

Kraus smiled as Huber hung up. Then he started to dial again. It was all going well, and soon it would be going even better after he made this call. He should have made this decision a long time ago. Red Star needed a strong man, and no one was stronger than him now that Conrad was gone.

Now it was only a matter of positioning Rachel
Venable.

And he knew just how he could do it.

BEACH HAVEN

It was Hu Chang.

No sound.

No movement.

But even before opening her eyes, Rachel knew he
was there in the darkness waiting for her to wake as
he had so many times before in Sazkar Prison. "What
are you doing here?" She saw that he was only a shad-
owy figure sitting in a chair a few yards from her bed.
"You shouldn't have come, Hu Chang. It was bad there,
but I was able to handle it."

"Of course you were. Are you not my student? I
would have cast you out years ago if I hadn't realized
that you were worthy of my attention. And the fact that
you were restless and crying out in your sleep was entirely natural under the circumstances. I forgive you
that small weakness." He leaned forward and turned
on the bedside lamp. "But I do not forgive you for being so inhospitable when I decided to pay you a visit.
Courtesy is always important. Did I not risk facing
Brandon to make him let me come in here to wait until you woke?"

"I don't regard that as a major challenge. And you
must have decided to pay me a visit right after you

talked to Catherine at the slope if you managed to get here this soon," she said dryly. But her gaze was focused eagerly on his face. Always the same. Serene. Wise. Knowing secrets. Creating secrets. Sharing secrets. Hu Chang. How she had missed him. "And four in the morning isn't exactly the proper time to come visiting."

He smiled. "There is no proper time between good friends. You know that, Rachel."

"Yes, I do." She sat up in bed. "But how can I be the best I can be if you come rushing to hold my hand when you think I won't meet the test?"

"Am I holding your hand?"

"Figuratively."

"I would never make that mistake. But you did meet the test, as I knew you would. I'm here because I wished to indulge myself when I know I should have more discipline. Occasionally, I do allow myself to fall from grace in that fashion."

"I've never seen you in the least undisciplined." She made a face. "And this is indulgence? Why?"

"Because Catherine, who appears to be wiser than I in this matter, convinced me that I should not be here with you at this time. That you need the opportunity to search your entire heart and mind regarding Venable with no interference from me during this period of mourning."

She shook her head. "I can't believe she'd say that to you."

"Why not? Catherine is very clever, and she was right to question me. She knows your history, and she knows me. There is a possibility I might have cheated you of years with Venable if I hadn't made myself available to you."

"No, you didn't. Any conflict was between my father and me. You were only being kind and generous."

"And a trifle selfish? I can't deny I enjoyed our years together. I instinctively reach out when I run across someone who reminds me of myself and the struggles I encountered during my very challenging earlier days. And when Catherine said that I should let you work this out for yourself, it struck a true note." He grimaced. "But only after she promised to take care of you in my place. I should have known that would mean standing beside you through the fray and not keeping you out of danger. San Kabara did not please me."

"So she told me." She looked him in the eye. "But standing beside me is what I needed from her. It was terrible there, Hu Chang. She was wonderful. She's been wonderful ever since I've known her. You're responsible for that in many ways. Just as you're responsible for making me a stronger person. So don't tell me about selfishness. That's bullshit."

He chuckled. "I only threw that in to arouse your protectiveness and instant rejection. We all realize that I'm very nearly perfect."

"Except for an occasional self-indulgence? Would you care to elaborate how this qualifies?"

"You've become so strong over the years." He tilted his head, and his smile ebbed away. "Disasters, disease, and pain, and overcoming so much. Sometimes

I can help, sometimes I can't. When one cares about someone, to be needed is a special gift. When Catherine told me about San Kabara, I thought that it might be the time you'd choose to indulge me with that gift."

"I'm handling it, Hu Chang. As you said, it's not my first disaster."

"Every disaster is the first if you care enough about it." He leaned forward, his dark, glowing eyes intent on her face. "And this one is different because it's connected to you and Venable. Huber wished you to feel that when he left that photo. You probably feel that you should have been able to do more. We both know you could not, but the feeling remains. So you will let every emotion, every sorrow, stay within and fester. That's why you toss and turn and cannot sleep. You know the solution. We've worked through it before at Sazkar." He said softly, "Talk to me. Indulge me and let me know I'm needed. Start at the beginning when you got off the speedboat. I want to know every single moment. Every sadness, every death, every triumph, every joy. Let me share this with you. Give it all to me so that you won't be alone with it. Then I'll be able to leave you and stay in the background unless I decide you need me again. When you wake, I won't even be here. That seems to be both intelligent and fair, doesn't it?"

"Hu Chang."

He reached over and turned off the light, and there was only darkness. "Let me share it," he repeated gently. "It's your gift to me."

She could feel her eyes stinging with tears. "Some

gift. You're completely crazy, Hu Chang. And don't you dare leave before I wake up."

"We'll see. Because Catherine is also right, I'm stealing this time from Venable. It's part of your period of release and adjustment. But I don't believe he would mind it tonight, do you?"

"No, he was always grateful to you. Almost as grateful as I was." She swallowed. "That's not true. No one could be more grateful. You don't have to do this. I'll be fine."

"Yes, fine and free and ready to live again. Are you trying to cheat me of my gift?"

"No way," she said unsteadily. "Just trying to give you an out."

"I don't want an out. Talk to me. Start when you got off the speedboat at the marina at San Kabara."

She was silent. No matter what she said, he would stay until he had his way. He would sit there in the darkness until he had his "gift," which would perform its usual miracle of healing as it had all those years ago.

Forget pride. Forget independence. Accept the miracle on this day, where there had been so few miracles to embrace. She began to speak, "It was all crazy. I didn't know what to expect, Hu Chang." She could once more see it all before her. "People were streaming out of the hotels. Everything was starting to happen. I jumped off the boat and took off running down the beach . . ."

* * *

It was late afternoon when Rachel opened her eyes again. She could see the slanted rays of the sun coming in the French doors across the room and making patterns on the rug beside the easy chair.

And Hu Chang was not sitting in the chair beside her.

"Awake?" The French doors opened, and Brandon came into the room from the veranda. "Good. It's almost five. Forgive the intrusion, but I was beginning to worry. You've been sleeping like the dead."

Like the dead of San Kabara? The comparison immediately occurred to her, and she tried to push it away. She knew from experience how dangerous it was to dwell on lives she had not been able to save.

"Was I?" She sat up in bed and brushed her hair out of her eyes. "Where's Hu Chang? I told him not to leave." She flinched as she felt a twinge in her shoulder. "But he didn't promise. You didn't say anything to him, did you?"

"I doubt if I would have been able to throw him out when he has you and Catherine defending him," he said. "Not to mention a certain aura of power he exudes on his own. No, I gave him a cup of tea about one this afternoon, and he bid me good-bye with instructions to take care of you if you'll permit it. He said to tell you that he'll be in touch if the occasion demands. I was flattered he thought me good enough to be a stand-in. It was iffy, considering our last conversation."

"He's an excellent judge of character. He wouldn't let that influence him. I think he trusts you." She added,

"He said he persuaded you to let him come into my room to wait for me to wake."

"Persuaded? He came sweeping into the house and said that he would require the time to make certain that you slept well and deeply after your experience on the Island. I would please not interfere or cause his task to be more difficult. That's persuasion?"

She smiled. "Well, you didn't try to stop him."

"I thought I might have both of you to fight. And I believe that he has a proven success ratio with you. Right?"

"Oh, yes." And last night had been no exception, she thought. She had regained balance and stability and the knowledge of her own character and worth. She just wished he was still here with her. "His success ratio is astonishing."

"You're disappointed. I'm definitely detecting wistfulness." His gaze was on her face. "Do you want me to go bring him back to you? I'd be willing to risk it. After seeing the way you looked when you crawled into bed last night and how different you look now, it would be worth it. Color in your cheeks, rested, even the mood appears mellow. Does he always have that effect on you?"

"Yes." She smiled. "But I wouldn't let you risk antagonizing Hu Chang. You'd probably pay for it. Why are you really here? Did something happen?"

"Not as far as I know. Catherine's been calling me all afternoon because she didn't want to bother you. She said you needed to sleep." He smiled. "She might think you're tough enough to cope with anything, but she's still incredibly protective. She asked you to call her back when you woke. No hurry."

"No hurry," Rachel repeated. "It seems as if everything has been urgent and high-speed for the last couple days. I don't know if I'll be able to handle a slower pace."

"I have faith in you." He was heading for the bedroom door. "Take a shower, get dressed, and come to the kitchen for a sandwich and bowl of soup. After yesterday, you need to take a deep breath and try to relax."

Everything seemed smooth and quiet and blessedly calm. For some reason, it was making her uneasy. "You're sure nothing is wrong with Catherine?"

"Absolutely sure." He smiled. "After what you went through yesterday, I know it seems strange that life could ever be even seminormal again. I always feel the same way after a rough patch. But we have to take what we can get and hold on to it as long as possible."

She couldn't look away from him. His light eyes were glittering in that lean, taut face, and she was as aware of his strength and intensity as she had been when he'd come to her at the marina yesterday. He was so alive and vibrant and she suddenly wanted to reach out and touch him, to let that vibrance flow into her, renew her.

His eyes suddenly narrowed, and he went still. Then he slowly shook his head. "I don't think so. I'll see you in the kitchen, Rachel."

The door closed behind him.

She wanted him back. She didn't know what had happened in that moment when she had wanted to reach out to him. But the impulse was foolish, she was better off staying in her little nest of safety.

But there was no real safety as long as a jagged cliff sheltering men, women, and children could be brought tumbling into the ocean. Monsters were hiding everywhere.

So get on your feet and get back to living, she told herself. *Remember that every moment is precious and every battle important.*

She threw back the cover, jumped out of bed, and headed for the bathroom.

Thirty minutes later she was ready to leave her bedroom, but she dialed Catherine as she was crossing the living room en route to the kitchen. She had kept her waiting long enough. Reluctant as she was to return to the memories of San Kabara, she knew Catherine was still immersed in the battle. She wouldn't leave her to fight it alone.

"You should have told Brandon to wake me," she said, as soon as Catherine answered. "Or called me yourself. I didn't need to sleep that long. It was totally—"

"Yes, you did," Catherine interrupted. "You needed to take time to heal yourself. Not only were you hurt and in shock, but you went through hell in that hospital tent yesterday."

"Everyone went through hell yesterday. I bet you didn't pamper yourself by lolling in bed."

"You'd be wrong. And I don't believe that lolling is

quite the word that applies when Brandon said you looked like you were in a coma." She paused. "And he said that Hu Chang paid you an early-morning visit. I didn't expect that to happen. Everything okay?"

"He was just concerned. Like you, he wanted to make certain I was handling my father's death with a minimum of angst. He said you'd given him a suggestion to stay away if possible."

"Busted. I thought you might be able to think more clearly and come to terms with your relationship. Should I have kept my nose out of it?"

"No, Hu Chang wouldn't do anything he didn't want to do anyway." She paused. "But I was glad to see him today. He was able to make me feel alive again."

"And that's a gift above price after San Kabara," Catherine said. "So hold on to him and forget anything I said about clear thinking and coming to terms. What do I know?"

"He'll probably call you and tell you that you were right. Or he might pay you a visit at the hotel."

"I doubt it. He doesn't like to deal with the CIA though he liked your father. Most of the time, I agree with him. After I got back to the hotel last night, I showered and called my son. I didn't care how late it was in Atlanta. I wanted to hear his voice. I wanted to remind myself how lucky I was that he was still in my life. How's that for pampering?"

She could see how Catherine would have been driven to reach out to Luke, who was the center of her universe. It was the same impulse she'd felt when she'd opened her eyes an hour ago. "Maybe not as self-indulgent as mine, but very human. But since you've called Brandon several times today, you've been up and working, haven't you? I guess I win."

"I slept a little longer than usual this morning, but Claire rousted me out of bed for a team meeting in her suite. The woman may be a pain in the ass, but no one can say she doesn't have energy. And at the moment, she's being very proactive."

"Amazing," Rachel murmured.

"She can be amazing when it suits her, that's why Venable respected her. Anyway, I thought I'd call and fill you in on what's happening. Late last night Red Star issued a statement bragging that they were responsible for the attack and warning of another one to come in the days ahead. Naturally, that caused a media meltdown and general panic. We've not been able to find any clues or apprehend any perpetrators yet. We've just been treading water. The reason Claire called the meeting was to tell everyone on the team that after San Kabara, the president had sent down orders that every organization in the government was to make catching Max Huber their top focus. No expense spared and everyone on the same page. On no account was there to be another attack or heads would roll. You can imagine how that threat would motivate Claire. She wants to survive and come out on top."

"Good, it might mean she'll cooperate."

"Maybe." She paused. "Or it might mean that she'll try to go that extra step that would impress her superiors. You can't tell which way Claire will jump."

"But it's making you uneasy."

"Oh, yes. She held me back after she dismissed the rest of the team. The head of the bomb squad had told her about that photo of you that Brandon had taken from underneath the explosive device at the Neptune. He described it to her, and it didn't take long for her to put two and two together. She was asking questions and demanding answers."

"Which you couldn't give her. We only have guesses."

"She wanted the photo itself. Brandon told her to go to hell when I told him. Then she wanted to bring you in for questioning. She said it was positively necessary considering the present emergency. I told her that you'd done more than your duty to help out in the emergency, and you'd consider it an insult to be brought in for interrogation. I also added that since those patients at the hospital were talking about you as if you were Mother Teresa, it would be very bad press." Her voice was grimly satisfied. "That stopped her cold."

"Mother Teresa? Really, Catherine."

"Well, Florence Nightingale was dated. It worked." She added soberly, "But she was intensely interested that Huber had reached out to you in that situation. I just wanted you to know that it's wise to be very careful right now."

"I'm tired of being careful of Claire when she's supposed to be on our side. Let her be careful of me."

Silence. "Whatever. Then I'll be careful of her for you."

Of course she would, Rachel thought. "No, you won't. Not your responsibility. I'm just a bit on edge right now. I'll be calmer and much more Mother Teresa tomorrow."

Catherine laughed. "See that you are." Then she said gently, "But not tonight, promise me that you'll give yourself the time to recharge and realize that life can be good. You've worked so hard not to let Huber take anything from you. Yesterday, he did his damnedest, and you can't let him have any victory. Tomorrow is soon enough to face the Claires and the Hubers of the world."

"I promise." She cleared her throat. "Why not? Because along with the bad guys, I have Catherine Ling here to balance the scales. As long as you slow down and do the same."

"Of course. I'm only going to stay in the hotel and try to reach out to a few contacts I made the last time I was in San Francisco. That's after I call Luke and say good night at a decent hour instead of waking him up in the middle of the night. I plan a very peaceful evening."

Catherine was seldom peaceful, always operating at high speed and intensity. Rachel could only hope this would be an exception. "Yeah, sure. I'll call you tomorrow, Catherine."

She pressed the disconnect and slipped the phone into the pocket of her slacks before continuing down the hall to the kitchen.

Brandon glanced up as she came into the room. "That's better, you look alive and ready to face the world." He looked her over from head to toe. "Very nice, indeed. Are you hungry?"

She thought about it and realized she was famished. "Yes. I don't remember when I ate last." She went over to the pot on the stove. "This smells wonderful. Another one of your shipboard recipes?"

"No, this was one Nate taught me. His sister is a chef at a restaurant in El Paso. Lots of spices." He grinned as he took down bowls from the cabinet. "Thought I'd warn you if you have a problem with them."

"I don't. I've spent a lot of time in Central America." She was tasting the stew. "It's wonderful. Where is Nate?"

"He and Monty are back in that makeshift lab in the library again, working. They both grabbed a sandwich earlier."

"Still looking for Nemesis's IP address?"

"No, Monty turned that over entirely to Sam Zackoff." He poured her a glass of red wine and handed it to her. "Now go out on the veranda and drink that while I set the table. I have my orders from Catherine. I'm supposed to make you relax and not think of anything but food and wine."

She shook her head ruefully. "She's impossible."

"No, she's got it right. It's the delegating that's impossible. Not everyone is as capable of diverting your attention from what you consider essential." He sighed. "So I'll give you the overview and nothing more. I checked your computer several times today, and there's no message from Nemesis unless it came in after you woke."

"No, I glanced at it before I left my bedroom. But

he told me he might give me extra time. He said I might be busy at San Kabara." Her lips twisted bitterly. "I wonder if he knew just how busy. He could be in Huber's pocket."

"Then we'll find a way to play him. As soon as Sam Zackoff locates him."

"Yet you're not considering him important enough to have Monty try to find him."

"He's important enough, he's just not on the urgent list any longer." He paused. "That ended at San Kabara Island. Red Star announced there would be a bigger, more deadly attack to take place in the near future."

"I know. Catherine told me."

"So we have to find out where that's going to happen. We'll use Nemesis if we can, but I'm not sure that's going to be possible. Any hint of trust in him is rapidly fading away. I'm wondering how he managed to earn Venable's trust."

"My father was smart, not infallible. He's made mistakes before." She tilted her head. "You put Monty to work on trying to hijack that South African satellite?"

"It's not a question of trying. He'll be able to do it since he already installed that back door. The only question is how soon. He said the South Africans had installed a few more bells and whistles in the last six months that might take several hours to even get to the door. It's going to take longer than he thought."

"Then we can count on getting through dinner before you have to run to Monty to give inspiration and intellect?" she asked solemnly.

He looked at her quizzically. "You're joking?"

"I guess I am. Strange, isn't it?" She took a sip of wine and moved toward the door leading to the veranda. "Satellites and bombs and Red Star seem very far away tonight. I think I might be glad I don't know how to hijack a satellite. Is there anything else you need to tell me?"

"I can't think of anything," he said slowly. "Is there anything you need to tell me?"

She stood there, staring at him, and felt once again that impulse to reach out, to touch, to bring him to her body. It was much stronger than when she had felt it before.

But she knew it was only the beginning.

As she'd told Catherine, those hours she'd spent with Hu Chang had cleansed and made her come alive again.

No fear. No hesitation.

Excitement. Anticipation. Curiosity.

"I'm not certain." She smiled. "If there is, I'll be sure and share it with you."

She went out on the veranda and gazed out at the ocean. Magnificent, eternal, shot with all the colors of the setting sun. After San Kabara, she had wondered if she'd ever be able to look at the sea again in the same way. Here was the answer. Not the same way, but not as an enemy either. It was Huber who had been the only enemy at San Kabara Island.

"You were right, Catherine," she whispered. "Life can be good and beautiful. And that's so easy to forget. I won't let myself forget tonight." She lifted her glass in a half toast. "I'm thinking about you. I hope you'll find something to remind you of that, too."

HYATT HOTEL

"You're becoming a real pain in the ass, Catherine Ling," Claire Warren said coldly when she answered Catherine's call. "I just talked to you two hours ago. You'd better have a good reason for bothering me again."

"Same reason. I'm just obeying your orders *and* the president's and giving this my entire focus. Have you heard anything more from your contacts about any current threats?"

"If I had, I would have activated the team had I thought it was valid."

Catherine stiffened. It was not a flat no, but one of Claire's self-protective dances. "Then let me investigate and see if I can determine if it's valid."

"I didn't say that I'd received any information." She paused. "You do know I won't continue to tolerate this constant disobedience and disrespect, don't you? Your entire involvement with Rachel Venable and Jude Brandon is an insult to me and the Company. I'm in charge, and your allegiance should be solely to me. If you didn't have a connection with Rachel, you'd have been gone after you arranged that meeting at the restaurant."

"I was surprised you hadn't authorized I be checked out of my room when I got back. But I know you'll put up with my 'disrespect' as long as I perceive a threat that you choose not to see. After what happened yesterday, it's your duty, isn't it? Who did you get this 'invalid' piece of information from? One of your assets?"

She was silent. "FBI. Special Agent Herb Jackson. It's part of this interagency cooperation thing the president is cracking the whip about. Jackson has a paid informant who's a prostitute who called and told him one of her customers was talking wildly about going to paradise to the angels and taking half of San Francisco with him. Jackson's going to go to see her, and he thought I might be interested in going with him." She shrugged. "I told him to report back after he verified."

"Playing it safe?"

"The woman might be a whore who only wants to con Jackson. I can't spend my time running around on wild-goose chases. It's very likely it doesn't have anything to do with this Nemesis or Huber."

"And it might have everything to do with them. Give me Jackson's number, and I'll follow through for you. The Company will be so happy to know how conscientious you are."

Silence. "That's true. No, I'll call Jackson and tell him I'm sending you. He offered to meet me on Third and Market if I changed my mind. Naturally, you won't mention anything about our disagreement. If you find any information I can use, tell me, and I'll decide what to do about it."

"Just call him so that I can get going."

"Delighted," she said sarcastically. "It may keep you from calling me again before morning. I'd much rather you spend the night interrogating some drug-whacked prostitute."

"So would I." Catherine pressed the disconnect and drew a deep breath. It wasn't a great tip, but it was all she had to go on. Huber often used members of the Taliban to do his dirty work when he didn't want to involve his precious Aryan militia. That remark about paradise and the angels could be significant. She'd already called all her own informants and gotten nowhere. But now she could call Rachel back and tell her that she might have a lead.

Might.

And why call Rachel when she'd told her to relax and try to forget everything that had to do with Huber and San Kabara for just one night? It could come to nothing, raise her hopes, then dash them.

She got to her feet and headed for the door. She'd handle it herself as she always did. Tell Rachel when she had good news instead of bad.

All she had to do was just talk to the informant.

And then try to find out the name of the John who was planning on taking half the city of San Francisco to the angels.

BEACH HAVEN

"You're very quiet." Brandon leaned back in his chair, his gaze raking Rachel's face. "Almost . . . serene. Not what I expected."

"Not what I expected either." She didn't feel serene

right now, she thought ruefully. All through the meal, she had been calm and collected, but that was disappearing rapidly. It was all very well to make up your mind and tell yourself that it was the right thing to do. It was another thing to broach an experience she had never encountered and try to make it happen. And Brandon was looking at her as warily as if he thought that composure on which he'd commented was going to fall apart at any minute. Exactly what she didn't want him to feel. So dive in and just be honest with him. She took a deep breath, then leaned forward and stared him in the eye. "And it's not working out for me. I've never done this before, and I'm getting nervous. And, heaven knows, you don't need that kind of response after all that stuff Hu Chang told you. And then there was what we both went through yesterday, and that probably makes me more fragile in your eyes. You're too damn protective, and that would be your first instinct. You wouldn't consider that it was a trauma that was shared. I can't have that, Brandon."

He stiffened. "You can't have what?"

She drew a deep breath and then said it. "I can't have you not wanting to go to bed with me. I'm trying to seduce you, dammit."

"Oh, shit."

She rushed on, "And I know I'm not good at it. I mean the seducing, not the sex. I think I'm pretty good at that. I've had sex before, but it kind of came out of the blue and I didn't think about it ahead of time. I wondered later if that was why it was so easy for me and I did it so well. Catherine thought it might be that."

She was talking too much. And she couldn't read his expression. It didn't matter, it all had to come out. "But what I feel for you isn't like that. I don't want it to be easy. I want it to be hard and real and honest like everything else between us. That's important to me. So I have to make sure you're not feeling sorry for me. It's not as if I want more than sex from you. I'd never obligate you in that way. I think you want to have sex with me, but I won't have you—"

"Shut up." He was around the table and jerking her to her feet. His eyes were blazing, his voice hoarse. "Just shut up, Rachel." Then his mouth was on hers, his tongue playing. His hands clenched on her buttocks, pulling her to him. "I can't listen to any more. I don't want to hear about your other lovers or what Catherine has to say about them." He was opening her blouse and pushing down her bra. "I particularly don't want to hear about how sorry I should feel for you because of what Hu Chang told me you went through. I've been fighting that battle since I hung up the damn phone with him." His fingers were plucking at her nipples as his lips covered her mouth again. "And losing it . . ."

She was burning, her breasts swelling. She instinctively moved closer, rubbing against him. "Then it's going to be okay," she gasped. "Maybe I didn't do such a bad job seducing you after all. I was afraid that all that stuff would get in the way and you would—"

He was pushing her away.

"You're lousy at seduction," he said hoarsely. "All you would have had to do was touch me to make me go up in flames. But you kept on talking. And you were bound to stumble on the wrong thing eventually."

She was staring at him in bewilderment. Something was going wrong. "But you said that those things I said didn't—"

"Until you mentioned what I felt about what you'd gone through yesterday." He said grimly, "I don't give a damn about what happened in your past. I know you're strong enough to overcome anything. But this was yesterday, this was on my watch, and I'm supposed to take advantage of a temporary euphoria because we managed to live through it together? I can't do that when I know how vulnerable you are." He took a deep breath and stepped back. "Hell, you almost had me. It *can't* happen. Not now, Rachel."

She was staring at him, stunned. Then the anger erupted. "You arrogant son of a bitch. What makes you think that you know how vulnerable I am? What makes you think I'm less strong now than I was at Sazkar Prison?" She took a step closer to him and her forefinger punched his chest. "If I wanted to have sex with you, it was because I wanted the sex and not a lecture on how fragile I am. I wanted to forget all about Huber and Nemesis for just a little while, and if that's euphoria, then I'm guilty." She whirled on her heel. "But don't worry, you'd have to beg me on your hands and knees to have sex with you now. You're stupid and egotistical, and you have no idea who I am. I promise you that you're not going to have to worry about either my euphoria or my vulnerability."

She left him standing there as she strode across the

veranda to the door to her bedroom. She slammed the French doors behind her.

Damn. Damn. Damn.

She didn't know if she was more angry or frustrated. For an intelligent man, Brandon was stupid, stupid, stupid. She knew how much he had wanted her, and he had completely blown it. She could still feel his hands on her breasts, the heat of—

And he had insulted her.

Yes, she was far more angry than frustrated. She strode over to the bathroom, undressing as she went. And where had those idiotic tears come from? She wiped them away, and she automatically glanced at the computer on the table. No red light. No message from Nemesis. She was almost sorry. She wanted something at which to strike out . . . *hard*.

She finished undressing, washed her face, and slipped into bed. She turned off the light and tried to relax and forget those last moments that had both angered and hurt her. Okay, admit it. Not only frustration, but hurt that Brandon had not given her the respect she deserved.

I'm not having such a good evening, Catherine. I hope you're having a better one.

Go to sleep. Sometime tonight or tomorrow they'd hear from Nemesis or Huber and it would all begin again. She had to be ready . . . and not *vulnerable*, dammit. That word was really sticking in her—

The French doors were opening.

"May I come in?"

She could see Brandon's tall shadow framed against the darkness. "No, you're not invited. I thought I'd made that clear."

"You did. But I thought you might have left an opening or two in that stinging condemnation." He was gliding toward her. "I decided if I made amends on your terms, there was a chance of being forgiven."

There was something different about him . . .

"My terms?"

"I was clumsy . . ." He chuckled. "And stupid. Let's start with that. You hated that I said you were vulnerable."

"And you're going to make that right?"

"I'm going to try. You wouldn't believe me if I just took it back. So I decided to show you that I'm vulnerable, too." He took her hand and put it on his thigh. "There's nothing more vulnerable than a naked man."

She inhaled sharply. Naked. She could feel the tiny hairs, the muscles, the warmth. And now that he was closer, she could see the dim outline of the rest of his naked body. "Go away, Brandon."

"I can't do that. But I assure you that I'm not going to do anything you don't want me to do. I'm feeling quite humble."

"You're never humble."

"That was before you pointed out how stupid and arrogant I am." He was slowly rubbing her palm up and down his thigh. "How could I help but be chastened?"

"You'd manage." She pulled her hand away from him, but she still felt the tingle on her palm. And though he was no longer touching her, she could still feel the heat emanating from his body reaching out, touching her. "And you *were* arrogant."

"But I think stupidity was the main sin. I told myself that Hu Chang's little nightmare stories weren't permanently affecting me, but some of the scar tissue evidently lingered. I couldn't stand the thought of your being hurt." He fell to his knees beside the bed. "So then I found my own way of doing it."

"Stop talking about it. No one can hurt me but myself."

"But I think I managed tonight." His fingers were moving gently on the hollow of her throat with a whisper touch. "Maybe just a little bit?"

She didn't answer. She was having trouble breathing.

"Okay, then I hurt myself more," he said. "You said hands and knees. In case you haven't noticed, you have me on my knees, and my hands are very much at your disposal. Will you please have sex with me, Rachel?"

His fingers had moved down to the hollow between her breasts, brushing against her nipples. She was burning, clenching. "What about my vulnerability and my euphoria?"

"Neither one exists. They were figments of my imagination."

"Yes, they were." She barely knew what she was saying. She was only aware of the darkness, his heat, his touch. "And there's no . . . reason for me to reward you for indulging them."

"There's one reason." He was lifting her nightshirt and tossing it aside. "It's part of my penance for being an arrogant son of a bitch. You said you wanted to forget all about Huber and Nemesis for just a little while." His lips were on her nipple, pulling, gently biting. She inhaled sharply as she felt the swelling, the tightening as he moved his cheek back and forth against her breasts. "I regard it as my duty to make that happen. I promise that you won't think of either one of them for the rest of the night." He moved up and over her, his hand widening her legs. "With your permission, Rachel . . . See how humble . . ." His fingers were suddenly entering, sinking deep!

She arched and cried out.

"You like that? How about this?"

His fingers were moving fast, deep, erotically stroking, while his other hand pressed down on her belly. "Tell me . . ."

She couldn't tell him anything. She was gasping through gritted teeth, her heart pounding, as sensation after sensation seared through her. She couldn't breathe at all now. Her entire body was on fire, melting. All she could do was shift desperately, lunge, try to give more, take more, while he held her maddeningly still.

"I think that might be a yes." He lifted her leg and went still deeper.

She couldn't hold back the cry that was almost a groan.

"Definitely a yes." His voice was hoarse, his breathing hard. "But it's not enough. I need permission." His hand had left her as he moved closer. "But that permission had better come very, very soon."

"Stop *talking*." Her fingers dug into his shoulders,

and she lunged upward, taking him deep inside her. She bit her lower lip to keep from screaming. "Can't you do anything right tonight?"

"Oh, yes." He was half laughing as he lifted her and plunged hard and deep. "Didn't I promise you? Watch me. Hold on. I'll do everything right . . ."

CHAPTER

12

You were very good." **Rachel tried to catch her** breath as she turned over and cuddled closer to Brandon. "As I told you, I'm no expert, but I think you might be extraordinary." She giggled. "It's no wonder Claire was pissed off when you dropped her."

"Has no one told you it's bad form to talk about another woman when you're making love to a man?"

"But we aren't making love, we're making sex. I promised you I wouldn't expect anything like that from you. So it doesn't count. Right?"

"There may be subtle differences. There were times tonight that I couldn't determine them. We'll have to keep on exploring."

There were times when Rachel hadn't been able to tell the difference, either. The passion had been too intense in the last few hours. Passion . . . and joy. She hadn't expected that feeling of companionship and joy. She was still shaking, but her body was beginning to ready again. "I believe that may be a good idea. But it could be very distracting." She laughed again. "And Catherine made me promise to relax and recharge tonight. She said nothing about future explorations."

"And we all know how much influence Catherine has on you," he said dryly. "Tell me you didn't discuss having sex with me?"

"No, I wouldn't do that. Though since she called Hu Chang to have him talk to you, she must have realized it might come up."

He chuckled. "Oh, yes. At least as far as I was concerned it was constantly coming 'up.' And why wouldn't you talk to her about me? Evidently, your other lovers weren't off-limits."

"They were . . . different. Catherine would never intrude if she could help it. But she went through a lot with me . . . while I was healing. It . . . helped me to talk to her. It still helps me." She stopped, trying to find the words. "Not because I still need healing but because she's always there, and I know that she always will be. I can always trust her to respect who I am but to still be there for me."

"Then thank God for Catherine Ling," he said thickly as he drew her closer.

"That's what I say." She amended, "Most of the time. I was upset about her calling Hu Chang. But it's hard to condemn anything that's done out of love."

"And does she ever condemn anything you say about her relationships? Turnabout is fair play."

"I never got the chance. Catherine is very private. She's never said anything to me about anyone she's slept with after her husband was killed years ago. He was also CIA and her two-year-old son was kidnapped by some scum of a Mafia dealer at the same time. It took her years to get him back. I think Luke and Hu Chang have been pretty much her whole life."

"Along with Rachel Venable," he murmured. "But Catherine's a gorgeous, intelligent woman, I find it hard to believe she's been living like a nun."

"I didn't say that. I said that if there's a man, she doesn't talk about him. And I don't ask. What she gives me is more than enough. I know how lucky I am to have a friend like Catherine." She rubbed her cheek against his shoulder. "You worked side by side with her on that slope. You have to know her now."

"She was magnificent. But I like her best in the role of your friend." He suddenly rolled back on top of her. "And I like her least when talking about her interferes with serious activity." His lips were moving down her body to her belly. "So I believe we'll have to delay laying any more accolades at her shrine to another time."

His tongue . . .

Her stomach was clenching as her fingers moved to tangle in his hair. "And this is serious?"

"What could be more serious than keeping my promise? You were getting entirely too philosophic and contemplative." His tongue was moving delicately, teasingly, erotically. "I think Catherine would agree, don't you?"

Her heart was beating so hard that she could barely

get the words out as she pulled him to her. "Yes . . . Catherine always believes in keeping promises . . ."

APARTMENT 2B
HOLMES APARTMENTS
SAN FRANCISCO

"You don't know his name?" Catherine shook her head as she gazed at Cindy Naris, who was sitting at the kitchen table of her studio apartment with one leg tucked beneath her. The woman didn't look like a hooker. She was dressed in a short black skirt and white tee shirt, two blue hair bows held her blond hair before it curled in tight ringlets over her shoulders, no lipstick, but rouge on her plump cheeks. She looked to be more thirteen or fourteen than a grown woman. But then Special Agent Herb Jackson had told Catherine that pretending to be an adolescent was Cindy's specialty. "Don't be afraid to tell us," she said gently. "You can be protected. We'll take care of you."

"I'm not afraid." Cindy Naris shrugged. "Herb's a good guy. I've been giving him information for over a year, and he's real careful that nobody knows that I'm a snitch." She smiled at Jackson. "And he never asks for anything on the side. Someday, Herb. I know you think the kid thing is kind of creepy, but I can go another way. Any way."

"The status quo works fine for me." The young FBI agent smiled back at her. "Now tell us about this John you had tonight. Have you ever serviced him before?"

"Once. Last week. But he didn't say nothin' then. I picked him up on Market. He was driving a gray van, and he wanted me to do it in the back of the van. I told him I knew better than that. Too many things can happen once you turn the trick over to the customer. I wanted my own turf." She shrugged. "He gave in and came here with me. He complained about it being a pigsty but stayed with me for most of the night. He hurt me a little, but not much." She moistened her lips. "But this time he was real rough. He said I should be proud to do anything he asked me. He was a hero, and everyone would know it. Then he said all that crap about angels and paradise and stuff." She looked at Jackson. "That's the kind of thing you told me to look out for, right? Not just about drugs."

"That's exactly the kind of thing I need from you," Jackson said. "It's that kind of thing those hijackers said on 9/11. You did good, Cindy."

"Sure." She grinned. "But I wouldn't know what those bastards said on 9/11. I wasn't even born then."

Cindy was almost as young as she looked, Catherine thought. Catherine had grown up on the streets of Hong Kong, with whores and thieves and the worst slime in the Far East, but she never became used to seeing how life could twist and hurt children. "I was older, it's strange how everyone remembers their circumstances on that day."

"That's what they tell me. It's nothing to me," Cindy said. "But Herb says those guys are terrible people. So I listen real close when they start talking like that."

"But no name?"

"Lots of guys don't give me names. He said to call him Larry."

"No address?"

She gave her a disgusted look. "Come on. Be for real." She turned to Herb Jackson. "But I did take a picture of him."

Catherine stiffened. "What?"

"After he was through with me and I went to the bathroom, I grabbed my phone and got a shot of him as I was coming back into the room."

"He didn't see you?" Jackson asked.

She shook her head. "Nah, he was in such a hurry to get in the bathroom himself that he almost knocked me against the doorjamb. I thought it was worth the risk. Do you want it?"

"You bet I do."

"Is it worth more money?" She brought her phone to him. "Maybe another five hundred?"

"It wouldn't surprise me." He took the phone and scrolled down to the photo. He studied it and handed the phone to Catherine. "Dark hair, dark eyes, looks Middle Eastern. Not your typical blond Aryan pedigree the Red Star prefers, but they do use Middle Eastern operatives on occasion."

"Particularly when they want to use them on suicide missions," Catherine said grimly. "They call Al-Qaeda and Taliban their brothers, but I've never heard of Huber sacrificing his men to Allah. Have you ever seen this man before?"

Jackson shook his head. "You?"

"No." Catherine turned back to Cindy. "Did he mention coming back here?"

"No, he paid me, then walked out the door." She made a face. "I should be honored? Rude bastard. I ran after him and got a shot of the van and license plate before he drove off. It's the photo after his picture."

"You shouldn't have done that," Jackson said soberly. "If he'd caught sight of you, it could have been—"

"But he didn't," Cindy said. "And I thought the van might help. Right?"

"Right," Jackson said. "Maybe more than his photo."

"See? Pretty smart, huh?"

"Extremely smart," Catherine said. "Do you know if he spent any time with any of the other girls on Market Street?"

"You want to find out if they know anything more about him? I don't think so. He likes the little girls, and I'm the only one who's willing to risk it. The pay's better, but the guys are sometimes into power trips."

"Why?" Catherine asked quietly. "Why risk it, Cindy. We've agreed you're pretty smart. You don't have to do this. I'm sure Herb could find an organization in the city that could help you go down another path."

"Maybe someday." Her lips twisted. She gazed at Catherine from her head to her toes. "I'm not like you. None of us girls are like you. Hell, you look like Angelina Jolie or some other movie star. You stand on any corner, and all the Johns would zero in on you. We'd be left out in the cold. And Herb wouldn't have brought you along if you weren't kind of special. I'm not special. I always have to have a gimmick." She shrugged. "But I do okay for myself."

"You could do better. You just have to decide you want to do it. I grew up in Hong Kong, where there weren't any charitable organizations ready to hold out a hand to help. My mother was a whore, and so were most of my friends. I could have been out on that street corner if I hadn't made another choice." She reached in her bag, drew out her card, and handed it to her. "If you change your mind, call me. Jackson and I will work it out."

Cindy stared at the card. She looked intrigued. "Why?"

"Because I don't like men who think it's okay to hurt little girls." She smiled. "And I believe the best way to 'honor' this 'Larry' is to climb so far above him that you can wipe your feet on him."

Cindy giggled. "I like that."

"Good. Think about it." She turned back to Jackson. "Did you transfer those photos? I can run facial recognition when we get back to the car."

"I transferred them. You appeared to be a little busy with my informant. And I'll run the recognition program, thank you." He turned back to Cindy. "I'll put in for your fee as soon as I get back to the office. And I'll let you know when we find him."

"You do that," she said absently, looking at Catherine's card again. "I may need it if I decide to take a break for a little while."

"No problem." He took Catherine's elbow and guided her toward the door. "A break is always good. A change can be even better." He smiled back at her. "Thanks, again. Let me know if he comes back. Good night, Cindy."

"Night . . ." She was still looking at Catherine's card as the door closed behind them.

"What was that about?" Jackson asked Catherine as he hurried her down the steep flight of stairs. "Get a little distracted? You told me you were in a hurry."

"I am." She opened the door and went out on the sidewalk. "It only took a couple minutes. Some things are worth taking the time. She's young and has her whole life ahead of her. You should have done it yourself. As you said, she's *your* informant."

"Maybe I should." He opened the passenger door for her. "I was always so busy . . . and she was a damn good informant. I didn't want to lose her. I would have gotten around to it."

"That's why you take the time to do it while you're thinking about it." She glanced at him as she bent to get in the car. "Hu Chang used to tell me that if—"

The apartment building behind them blew up!

Catherine fell forward, striking her face against the car.

Pain!

She was collapsing, falling to the sidewalk.

She couldn't hear . . .

She could see Jackson's face above her. His mouth was moving but she couldn't make out his words.

"Can't . . . hear . . ." Behind him she could see the small apartment building engulfed in flames.

Screams? There were no screams, she realized. It wasn't only that she couldn't hear. In an explosion that huge, there would be no one left alive to scream.

"Cindy . . ." she said hoarsely.

He nodded, his eyes glittering as his gaze went back to the inferno that had been a building. "Cindy."

"Lie still." Jackson was trying to hold Catherine down as she tried to get up. "I'll call an ambulance. You need to be checked out. You said you couldn't hear. You must have taken some of the blast."

"I'm okay. Better now . . ." She had heard half of what he'd said and her ears were now popping, clearing. The street was suddenly filled with people running toward the fire. She could also hear them, the sobs, the cries of horror. She looked up at the window that must have been Cindy's. Now it was barely recognizable in the raging fire. "She has to be dead," she said shakily. "No one could survive that—"

"She's dead," he said grimly. "No question. I'll call 911 and get someone out here to—" He started to curse as she sat up, then tried to stand. "Give yourself a minute to find out if you're hurt or not. Is that too long?"

"Yes." She grabbed his arm and used it to support her. "Help me up. Get me in the car. We have to get out of here."

"Okay. Okay." He steadied her, then settled her in

the passenger seat. "But I have to call in and report this. So do you, Catherine. Neither one of our agencies is going to want interference with the local police or fire department. It has to be handled."

She had a sudden memory of that fragile girl with her blue hair bows sitting at the kitchen table with one leg tucked beneath her and swinging one foot. All her life, Cindy had been handled. Now it seemed, even in death, it was going to continue. She found that thought incredibly sad. "Not just yet." She buckled her seat belt. "But someone has to have called 911 already. Not that it will do any good for Cindy. Drive to that park we passed on the way here and let me sit and pull my-self together. Don't hassle me right now."

"Your mouth is bleeding." His gaze was raking her face. "And you've got bruises. You could have a concussion. I should take you to the hospital."

"Bullshit. I hear the fire trucks. Get me out of here."

Jackson muttered something beneath his breath and pulled away from the curb. After complicated maneuvering through the crowds of spectators on the street, he made a left turn and a few minutes later was heading away from the burning building.

Five minutes later, he entered the park and pulled up to the curb underneath a gaslight. He turned off his headlights and leaned back in his seat. "So pull yourself together so we can get the hell out of here," he said gruffly.

She shook her head. "Take your phone out of your jacket. Let's start to work on getting that ID."

"I can do it later."

"You can do it now." She took a deep breath. "He killed her, Jackson. I can almost tell you when he planted that explosive. It would have been too obvious to leave it anywhere in that bedroom. Remember when Cindy said that he almost knocked her down when he pushed her aside to go in the bathroom? He probably put the explosive in one of the vanity drawers and set it to detonate when she opened it. It's a wonder she wasn't blown up before we got there. He was definitely tying up loose ends."

"We still don't know if he's our man."

"And we won't know if you sit there doing nothing with those photos."

He was silent. "Dan Taylor, my Special Agent in Charge, isn't going to like sharing authority with the CIA. Cooperation is one thing, but we could stumble all over each other if we—"

"Don't tell me that. Cindy's death should mean something besides a fight between the FBI and CIA." She looked into his eyes. "Let's find out who the bastard is and if we can locate his vehicle. Then I'll turn the results over to Claire Warren, and you turn it over to Taylor and let them do what they want with it." She added, "And then we go our separate ways unless we choose to share again. Okay?"

He hesitated, staring at her. "Then will you let me take you to the hospital?"

"I told you, I'm fine. And if we're lucky, we'll be too busy."

He slowly pulled his phone out of his pocket. "It may take awhile."

"Not that long. Do you think I don't know that your director authorized every agent on this case to be issued the new special phone equipment directly linked to facial recognition and the Interpol database? Your boss, Taylor, knows that his ass is on the line if Huber goes through with his threat. He's going to do anything he has to do to catch him. On the other hand, the CIA can claim that their hands are tied because you have the jurisdiction. Just what the president warned everyone against." She looked him in the eye. "So stop stalling, Jackson. I'd do it myself if your equipment wasn't better and more versatile in this case. We both know that Cindy was your informant, and you can't just write her off. I don't think you really want to do that. Let's get the son of a bitch."

He was silent. "On one condition. The hospital. After we're through, you go and get checked out. You look like hell. I don't want Taylor to blame me for causing bad feelings between—"

"Oh, for heaven's sake," she said impatiently. "Okay. I'll do it. Now check that ID."

He shrugged. "I would have done it anyway. You're right, Cindy was my responsibility. I kind of liked the kid. And I took you to that apartment, so you're my responsibility, too." His fingers were rapidly pressing buttons and bringing up screens. "Nothing I can do about Cindy now, but I can make sure that you're not collateral damage . . ."

4:50 A.M.

"His name is Lawrence Fasrain," Catherine told Rachel when she phoned her two hours later. "Sorry to wake you. But I think that we might have something. The explosion had to be a cover-up after Fasrain thought it over and decided he'd been careless. Maybe he'd planned to get rid of Cindy anyway. Huber doesn't tolerate that kind of self-indulgence in his operatives. Anyway, I think we've got to dive in and find him."

"Sorry to wake me?" Rachel repeated. "Catherine. You almost get yourself blown up, then consider whether you should let me sleep? Slow down and give me all the details."

"Well, obviously I decided to hell with not waking you and decided to put you to work." She went over all the events of the night quickly and concisely. "I'm sending you the Interpol and State Department reports right now. Huber evidently picked someone with a background clean enough to pass muster this time. American mother, Pakistani father. He spent a good deal of his time in Pakistan during his early years, but lived with his mother in Sacramento from the time he was twelve. He attended Berkeley and his politics didn't send up any red flags. He was never in trouble with gangs, and he worked part-time from the time he was sixteen. His mother died when he was nineteen. After that time, he spent summers with his father in Pakistan until his father was killed in a train wreck near the Afghanistan border."

"What kind of work?" Rachel asked.

"Office. He was working toward an accounting degree. After graduating from Berkeley, he was employed in Marin County, preparing tax returns with a very respectable accounting firm. He didn't show up for work one day two months ago and virtually disappeared off the face of the earth."

"Address?"

"No forwarding address at his apartment."

"So presumably he was radicalized by his father during those vacations and was turned over to Huber when he was needed. He must have been ordered to go underground for the last two months in preparation for Huber's big blowout."

"That would be my guess. And now he's prepared to surface for his glorious entry to paradise." She paused. "You do know he might not be Huber's puppet."

"He blew up that damn apartment house and that poor woman you told me about. It's too coincidental not to believe there's a connection to the event Nemesis was talking about."

"That was my call on it," Catherine said. "I just had to make certain that I wasn't giving you any false information."

"I'm happy to have any concrete information at all. No word from Nemesis, and Monty's been struggling. We'll start seeing what we can do about finding any info about this Lawrence Fasrain." She paused. "You're sure you weren't hurt, Catherine? You skimmed by that explosion a little too quickly when you were telling me about it."

"I'm not hurt. I told you, I was outside the building." She quickly changed the subject. "Jackson's team has started looking for the van. But it's the proverbial needle in a haystack. I called Claire and gave her the license number. She said of course she'd be glad to have our people search for it."

"Of course," Rachel said sarcastically. "We've always found her to be so cooperative. Anything else, Catherine?"

"There had to be a reason why Huber would recruit an accountant for one of his disaster scenarios. A tax preparer isn't exactly a likely or valuable choice in a situation like this. I can't figure it out. No useful contacts. Not like an airline pilot or a scientist. I'm trying to dig deeper, and I'll get back to you. Oh well, as soon as I take care of a stop I promised Jackson I'd make, I'll go back to the hotel and see if I can stir Claire to get some of her experts on it."

"What stop?" Rachel asked.

"Not important." All she needed was Rachel getting upset about that promised visit to the ER. "It won't take too long. I'll be in touch, Rachel." She hung up and turned impatiently to Jackson. "Come on, let's get this over. We've both got work to do."

BEACH HAVEN

Rachel pressed the disconnect and jumped out of bed. "Fasrain. How the hell do we find him, Brandon? Evidently, Catherine is frustrated about the chances if she's going to Claire." She was heading for the bathroom. "And I didn't like the way Catherine was acting when she was talking about that explosion, did you? It might have been worse than she told us."

"I don't have as much experience with all of Catherine's nuances as you do. I'll have to take your word for it." He got out of bed, and added grimly, "But as far as finding Fasrain, we have to get to work on him right away. She's right, it fits together. I'll go and see what progress Monty and Nate made on the satellite last night and bring them up to date on Lawrence Fasrain." He was heading naked for the French doors, where he'd dropped his clothes when he'd come in last night. He looked back over his shoulder. "And we will find him, Rachel. No question about it." His lips twisted. "If for no other reason than I'm mad as hell at him for making me break my promise to you. It truly was a rude awakening on several levels. He's got to be punished for it."

Rude awakening, Rachel thought as she closed the door of the bathroom behind her. After the erotic pleasure that had gone before, that was truly an understatement. They had been jerked back into Huber's ugly world again in the space of one phone call. Another horrible threat that hovered like a hungry predator in the darkness, a young woman killed, and Rachel still wasn't certain that Catherine was entirely okay.

But she should stop whining and worrying about what had possibly occurred and start working to see how she could repair the situation and keep any other damage from happening. She was acting as sickeningly vulnerable as Brandon had accused her of being last night.

She couldn't allow that to come to pass. So while she was showering, she'd work out some kind of plan of action about how to find Fasrain. And try to blank out that nagging suspicion that Catherine had not told her the complete truth . . .

CALIFORNIA PACIFIC MEDICAL CENTER
SAN FRANCISCO

"Okay, here I am, Jackson," Catherine said impatiently. "Though it's a total waste of time." She jumped out of the car at the emergency room door. "Now get moving and see if you can track down that van. One of us should be doing something that makes sense."

"You are," Jackson said sourly. "I'll call you if I hear anything about Fasrain."

"Right away?"

"Yeah, right away." He smiled. "Take care of yourself, Catherine. And don't you duck out of that emergency room the minute I pull out of here."

She smiled back at him. He wasn't a bad guy, and she felt as if she had known him for years, not hours. "I won't. I made you a promise. I'll give the ER a little time to bandage me up. And now you've made *me* a promise about Fasrain. See that you keep yours, Jackson." She turned on her heel and went through the sliding glass doors.

She could see a bustling nurse in scrubs bearing

down on her, and she quickly turned to the nurse checking in people at the desk. Three people were ahead of her, and she was glad she hadn't specified to Jackson the precise time she'd allow for this visit to the ER. Fifteen minutes tops and she was out of here. Maybe less . . .

"Stop looking at the door, Catherine. It's not going to do you any good."

She froze.

Cameron!

She whirled to see Richard Cameron crossing the lobby toward her. He was the same, always the same. The way he moved, those brilliant blue eyes. The sight of him took her breath. Don't let him see it. "What are you doing here?"

"Saving you time and energy." He was standing there before her, his eyes scanning her bruised, cut, face. His lips tightened. "And trying to keep my temper. I told you to let me know if you were going to run into anything I'd consider unacceptable." His finger touched her cut lip. "I definitely consider this unacceptable."

Her lip was throbbing, burning beneath that touch, and it had nothing to do with pain. She jerked her head back and away from him. "I don't take orders from you. I don't care if you're angry. And I certainly don't have time to talk to you right now."

"I can take care of the time factor. I'll deal with the rest later. You're evidently here for some first aid, and I've already arranged for it to happen in the quickest possible time." He took her elbow and nudged her toward a door down the hall. "The ER will take too long. I've arranged for a doctor to examine you and get you out of here."

"One of your avid followers?"

"Dr. Harry Nilsen. A very respected physician who also respects me. Isn't that convenient?" He opened the door. "I'll come in and make sure he doesn't do any procedure against your will, if you like. But I think you trust me enough to know I'd never let that happen."

"Sometimes." She met his eyes. "But other times I think you've gotten your way so often that you accept it as your due. That scares the hell out of me."

"I know," he said quietly. "One of the few things on this planet that does. But as I told you once, since we're meant to be together, we just have to accept it. I'll always come after you, or you'll hunt me down."

The intimacy of those words was disturbing her, and she instinctively pushed them away. "Well you came after me this time, but you still haven't told me how you knew I'd be here."

"I don't like your being here in this city at this time." His lips tightened. "I knew you had to be at San Kabara Island, and I liked that even less. I was in Buenos Aires when I heard about what was happening, and I knew I couldn't get back here in time to help you. I was very annoyed, Catherine."

"I didn't need your help. I never asked for it."

"That didn't change anything. Even if the need was entirely on my part. But, as it happened, you managed to come out of San Kabara alive without my assistance."

"I always do, Cameron."

"But not always without damage. And you no sooner escaped that death trap on San Kabara than you came back here and tried to get yourself incinerated in the blast at that apartment house. I was not pleased when Macklin told me about that."

"Macklin? Who is—" Then it hit home. She stared at him in disbelief. "You had me followed tonight?"

He shrugged. "I was considering doing it myself. I'd already arrived at the airport after zooming here to either rescue you or bury you during your sojourn on San Kabara Island. But I decided that it smacked too much of harassment and stalking and you'd consider it an insult to your independence."

"Absolutely."

"At the least it would have made you even angrier and you were annoyed enough. So I had Macklin, one of my operatives, keep an eye on you and tell me if he thought you were getting into trouble." His lips thinned. "Needless to say, almost getting yourself shattered into a million pieces tonight fell into that category."

"I imagine it would," she said dryly. "But I'd still consider it harassment since it was not your business. I can take care of myself."

"That doesn't seem to matter. I find I need you, Catherine. That means I can't run the risk of your getting yourself killed." They had reached the door, and he opened it for her. "I'll wait for you out here. Please don't crawl out a window or convince my old friend, Nilsen, to let you slip out another door. It would upset me."

"Heaven forbid," she murmured. "He probably thinks you're the crown prince of Never-Never Land like all your other loyal subjects and would be devastated. We mustn't have that."

"Never-Never Land has never been closer," he said soberly. "Huber is doing his damnedest to make it reality."

"Then help us *stop* it."

"I will. I've no desire to see the kind of holocaust Huber is weaving in his web. It would be just that much harder for me to pick up the pieces later." He added soberly, "But you have to realize that someday it *will* happen. My main agenda is to make certain we create a world that would keep it from ever happening again." He gave her a push into the room. "This is Catherine, Harry," he called to a white-coated man. "Check her over and don't let her con you. Fifteen minutes."

He shut the door.

"Hello, Catherine." Harry Nilsen shook his head ruefully. "Cameron insists on people performing miracles. Perhaps because he has no problem performing them himself." His smile was warm. "But I'll do my best. Come over here and let me get a good look at you."

It was thirty minutes later that Catherine opened the door to see Cameron leaning against the wall across from the exam room.

He straightened as she came out. "Okay?"

She shrugged. "Salves and creams, no stitches."

His gaze was narrowed on her face. "You wouldn't tell me if there was anything else. Never mind, after I walk you to the parking lot, I'll come back and talk to Nilsen."

"And, of course, he'll tell you everything you want to know. Doesn't everyone? I'd think you'd get bored with all that mind-control stuff."

"Not bored. Weary, sometimes. That's why I try to avoid it."

And in that moment he looked weary, she thought. What would it be like to have the responsibilities and mental gifts of Richard Cameron? The question was causing an ache somewhere deep inside her, and she had to banish it. She rushed on, "I told Jackson I wasn't hurt much. For an FBI agent, he got pretty queasy at the sight of blood."

"So did I. Because it was *your* blood. I'm hoping Jackson didn't have the same reason. I'd hate to have to remove one of the stalwart protectors that you need to save civilization as we know it."

"I barely know him. But I do like him because he *will* fight to save civilization. We have a common goal." She looked at him. "He's not a Guardian or a crown prince, but I never wanted either one of those."

"Yes you did." He opened the door leading to the parking lot. "And you will again. Because you want *me*, Catherine. And I want you and that won't change." He pulled a key chain out of his pocket and handed it to her. "It's the gray Mercedes rental car in the next row. I assumed you wouldn't want me to drive you to join Rachel and Jude Brandon." He smiled. "Because I'll wager you didn't tell either one of them about me."

"I'm not going to see them. I'm going back to the hotel." Her brows rose. "But no, why should I discuss you with them? You might be important in your world but not in mine. We can handle our problems ourselves."

"No, you're a little in shock at the moment, and that gets in way of thinking straight. But you'll come to the realization that I can be of help. And I can't let anything happen to you, so I'll have to help you save all and sundry." He turned and started to walk back toward the hospital doors. "Macklin tapped your devices while you were in that car with Jackson. He said you were looking for someone, and there was urgency. I have many contacts here in San Francisco, and you know they won't try to lie to me. If you decide that you want me to facilitate the search, let me know."

"I don't want your—" she stopped. "Wait." She might have doubts about the wisdom of letting Cameron back in her life but he was right, there was urgency. She couldn't afford to let personal considerations matter. She knew what a powerful network Cameron controlled. "I have to find Fasrain fast. If this Macklin tapped our phones, he has all the information we have." She added curtly, "Use it."

"I will." He continued walking back toward the hospital. "I was going to do it anyway. I was very displeased that this Fasrain had made the mistake of almost blowing you up. But it's nice to have your blessing. Dead or alive?"

"I'll need to question him."

"I can do that before I turn him over to you."

"Cameron, just *find* him," she said through set teeth. "After that, it's my game. I won't let you take control."

"But that's what I do," he said simply. He looked back over his shoulder, and his smile deepened. His brilliant blue eyes were glittering, and he was exuding all the charisma and power that she had come to know and recognize. "I'll try to restrain myself since you're permitting me to play your game. I wouldn't want to be cast out when I know how much we'll both enjoy it." He opened the door and disappeared inside.

She stood there, staring after him for an instant. The Guardian. Control. The most tremendous sexual appeal she had ever encountered. The power of mind and will combined in one entity. Dangerous. So very dangerous for her.

And so very exciting.

She could feel her pulse pounding in her wrists. The beginning of her body readying as it always did when he was near. Because it wasn't only the sex, it was the struggle, the battle, the conflict that was an integral part of their relationship.

"I've missed you, too."

She stiffened. "Get out of my head, Cameron. You swore you'd never do that to me again."

"Only when necessary." He was laughing. *"This is necessary. It's been too long. I had to check that you hadn't talked yourself out of what we are together. But I did let you know I was peeking, didn't I?"*

Then he was gone.

Maybe.

How the hell could she know when she had to take his word for everything?

Don't think about it. The only thing that was important was that she knew she could trust him to keep his word about finding Fasrain. Any battle between them dwarfed in comparison to that truth.

She turned and headed for that gray Mercedes in the second row.

BEACH HAVEN

Brandon, Monty, and Nate were all in Monty's makeshift lab when Rachel opened the door of the library forty minutes later. "Brandon told you?" she asked Nate and Monty. "We're going to have to find this Lawrence Fasrain. Do you have any ideas?"

Monty shook his head. "Not yet. I've been a little preoccupied. I was just telling Brandon that I'd managed to complete the satellite hijack and showing him how we could scan the coast for any signs of Red Star activity. Want to take a look?"

"Not right now." She knew it was tech wizardry at its finest but she was more concerned with the human element of the man who'd threatened blow up the city. "Would it be okay if we start with Fasrain?"

"Sure." Brandon's gaze was on her face. "Let's see if we can find out how an accountant came into the picture. He was swearing he was going to destroy half of San Francisco. Even if Huber supplied him with a nuke, he'd still have to have the technology to arm it. He's not a likely candidate for the job. We have to find out why he was chosen and if he has accomplices." He paused. "But Huber wanted to change the coastline of California, and we have to use that satellite to take a look and see what he might have had in mind. We just have to look at all sides, Rachel."

Rachel let her breath out as some of the tension left her. Brandon's attitude was the correct one. She was just feeling so pressured, she wasn't thinking straight. And hearing that violence had again come so terribly close to Catherine had shaken her. "You're right, Catherine might have given us the key we need. Now we've just got to find a way to use it and combine it with all that tech stuff of Monty's."

"Tech stuff?" Monty flinched. "Have a little respect, Rachel. You're talking about conquering the new frontier."

"Sorry, but I have a hunch Catherine might have had to do a little conquering herself to get this name. I want to be able to show her that whatever she went through was worth it." She turned back to her computer. "So let's pull up all the information she got for us. I'll take his background at Berkeley. Catherine said it was clean enough to pass scrutiny but there might be something . . ."

"We'll get there," Brandon said gently. "It's going to happen, Rachel."

"I know that." But she didn't want him to see how much those few encouraging words of trust and companionship meant to her. In the past, he and Catherine had expressed doubts about her ability to handle their violent world, and she'd had a few herself. But it was warming to have him here with her at this moment. "Let's just make sure it happens soon."

But it didn't happen soon.

Rachel went over all Fasrain's college records with a fine-tooth comb while Nate checked the scant records that Interpol could provide about Fasrain's time in Pakistan. They even went back into his mother's background to see if there was some clue of a connection with Huber there.

Nothing.

He was a loner. He'd had a few summer jobs, but they'd all been in the finance and accounting fields. He'd belonged to a Methodist Church in the area but had only attended infrequently. No suspicious associations.

After researching for the greater part of the day, Rachel gave it up and turned to Brandon in frustration. "Unless Claire or one of her sources comes up with more info about him, I'm coming up blank. Catherine said Claire told her she'd try." She turned to Monty. "So it's over to you, Monty. Dazzle me with all your new-frontier wizardry. Maybe that will work."

"Go take a break while I set up the screens with Monty," Brandon said. "We need to make adjustments and do a little testing before you need to jump in. Nate, go make some sandwiches and coffee. It may be a long night. Monty may be performing wizardry, but you and I will be doing hard labor."

"I don't need a break. Let me help."

"Go help Nate." He smiled. "I don't need to be distracted."

The smile was deep and warm, and the first sign of the intimacy that existed between them since she'd come into the room this morning. It surprised her and made a little of the frustration ebb away. She smiled back at him. "I need to call Catherine anyway and tell her what a failure we were and that we've gone high-tech." She headed for the door. "I'll come back in an hour bearing sandwiches and coffee, and you can tell me what kind of hard labor you have planned for me."

CHAPTER

13

"No word from Claire yet," Catherine said. "But I have another source in the city who might be of more help. I didn't want to involve him very deeply, but it might be the way to go."

"Who is it? That Jackson with the FBI?"

"No, someone else. Richard Cameron. I've had dealings with him here in San Francisco and other places around the world."

"I don't remember your mentioning him. Does he have better contacts than Jackson?"

"Oh yes, Cameron has better contacts than anyone else I've ever known," she said dryly. "Impeccable. And he knows exactly how to use them. By all means, go and work with Monty and Brandon if you believe that's an option. I'll turn Cameron loose on Fasrain.

He's probably already on the hunt. He didn't like it that Fasrain blew up that apartment. I'll let you know when he finds him." The next moment she had hung up.

When, not if, Rachel noticed Catherine had said. And she knew Richard Cameron very well indeed. In what capacity?

Not her business. But it had aroused her curiosity that Catherine had that much trust in Cameron. She just hoped that she was right. In the meantime, they had to go down the only other path left open to them.

Nate had already taken the tray of sandwiches so she picked up the carafe of coffee and followed him back to the lab. Brandon looked up as she came into the room. "Catherine okay?"

She made a face. "She didn't say she wasn't. She told me to go ahead with doing the coastal search, and she'd have one of her contacts locate Fasrain." She glanced at Monty. "Are you ready for me now? I gave you more than an hour, and that green screen looks intriguing. Are you finding anything?"

"Just the usual things that should exist on the coastline." Monty grimaced. "And loads of weird stuff that we're not at all sure is that unusual. It's California after all. I've been throwing that stuff to Brandon to check out."

"Then you can also throw it to me." She sat down in front of her computer. "Tell me what I'm supposed to do, Brandon."

"Just check any anomalies or anything we don't understand with Google or whatever authority is appropriate for the subject matter. It's not rocket science, it's just hard work." He was gazing again at Monty's satellite screen. "Monty, go back to those docks you just passed and take another look at the loading area. Rachel, you check and see if there's usually a crew that large at this time of night."

"You think you've found something?" she asked as she accessed the dock schedules and phone number for the union pages.

"No, but we can't pass up anything. Nemesis said that Huber wanted to change the California coastline. That could have meant anything. When Huber issued that threat of a possible attack, everyone automatically thought about 9/11. There are all kinds of other disasters." He shrugged. "I don't think he'd plan another explosion like the one he staged on the cliff at San Kabara Island. He'd know that we'd be on the watch for it. But destroying docks that receive shipments that keep the entire economy flourishing is something Huber would like."

Rachel's hands were shaking as she typed. Scenario after scenario was suddenly occurring to her. "Or setting off a nuclear explosion in the city itself that would make it radioactive on the scale of Hiroshima."

"Or it could be just poisoning the fields and killing the crops." Brandon was scanning the central valley and the water reservoirs. "That could have an effect that would cause the—"

"Please, be quiet, Brandon," Rachel said. "If you see a potential problem, tell me what to check. I don't want to have to think about nightmares until we're sure we have a target."

He nodded. "But you'll automatically put together the scenario even if I don't voice it. You're too bright to do anything else."

"Then I'd rather just keep so busy that I won't be able to think." She found a twenty-four-hour union telephone number on the Internet and began to dial it. "And checking on employee schedules for those dock-workers may keep me that busy." She looked at him while she waited for an answer. "Along with worrying about why I haven't heard from Nemesis by now. If he was so eager to make a deal, what's keeping him from contacting me? He must have known what shock value San Kabara gave us."

"I'm more interested that you haven't heard from Max Huber," Brandon murmured. "He doesn't hesitate to gloat when he believes he's struck a telling blow."

And San Kabara Island had been a hideous, crip-pling blow. "Maybe he thought sending that photo was gloating enough." Then she shook her head. "No, he'd want more than that. I'll hear from him when he thinks that he's able to hurt me again." She smiled sardonically. "So I'm not eager for him to contact me until we find a way to keep that from happening. I'd rather spend my time calling these damn dockworker schedulers who are *not* answering me." She started to dial the number again. "Go on to the next possible anomaly you and Monty are finding. I'll get back to you . . ."

6:40 A.M.

"Time for a break, Rachel."

She looked up to see Brandon standing before her. "No, it's not," she said impatiently. "We haven't gone over that area in Santa Barbara that would have a direct effect on northern California if anything happened to—"

"We'll do it later." He pulled her to her feet. "Four hours. You're so exhausted and strained, you can barely function. You haven't slept in over thirty hours, your eyes are red, and I bet they're stinging. Take a nap, and I'll let you work for the rest of the day. You'll be much more efficient working with a clear head. You've been a little slow for the last hour."

"That was patronizing."

"That was the truth." He turned her toward the door. "Come on, I'll tuck you in. Which is the only way I can be sure you'll go to bed. It's not as if these next few hours are going to make a big difference. It's two days until the twenty-fifth. We have a little time."

"Maybe." She reluctantly let him lead her from the room. "We're not making much progress. Every time we think there may be a clue that might lead us to Red Star, we draw a blank. *I* draw a blank." She ran her hand through her hair. "You're right, I'm blurry when I should be sharp. Do you know all the facts and figures and possibilities you and Monty threw at me tonight? Nothing is meaning anything. I'm not stupid. Why can't I fight through this haze and have it all come together? Hu Chang said the rule is always to be the best you can be, and I'm not doing that."

"May I suggest that you stop beating yourself up?" He opened the door to her bedroom and nudged her inside. "I'm not Hu Chang, but I know if you weren't doing the best you could, you wouldn't be suffering all this angst." He pushed her down on the bed and lay down beside her. "And it will all come together for you." He was holding her close. "Did it occur to you that I have a small amount of responsibility myself?"

"Yes, but that doesn't change mine." She looked at him. "You're here in bed with me. Does that mean you want to have sex?"

"No, that's not what it means." He closed his eyes. "What am I saying? Of course I do." His eyes flicked open. "But that's not the purpose at the moment. I wanted to comfort you and try to make you relax and feel better about yourself." He got up on one elbow and looked down at her. "Because there's no one who could have done better or worked harder." He brushed his lips across the tip of her nose. "You're an extraordinary woman, and after four hours rest, I'm going to demand extraordinary results from you." Then he was on his feet and pulling up the throw at the bottom of the bed and tucking it around her. "I'll see you in a little while. Then if I seem a little blurred, you can send me off for a nap. That's only fair."

She nodded. "Yes, that's only fair." Her eyes were closing and she didn't see him leave. Everything he'd done had been fair and smart and, in spite of her accusation, not patronizing. He had made her feel valued, treasured, and yet respected.

And if he was going to ask extraordinary things from her, she should let the whirling thoughts in her mind settle and function so that she could respond . . .

She didn't sleep the full four hours. It was only a little over three hours and twenty minutes when she came wide-awake. Her eyes flew open, and she stared unseeingly at the French doors across the room.

Stepfather!

It could be. She couldn't quite remember . . . it was before they had shifted to studying Monty's satellite. But she thought it might be . . .

She tossed the throw aside and was on her feet heading for the bathroom. After washing her face and running a brush through her hair, she was out of the bedroom and running toward the library.

"You're early," Brandon said as he turned to her. "I should have expected—"

"Hush. I think I might have found it." She sat down at her computer and pulled up the records they had on Fasrain. She flipped through two other related pages and found what she had been searching for. "Yes!" Rachel turned to Brandon, her eyes shining with excitement. "The docks. You thought that might be a possibility when you were checking earlier. Remember when you thought there were too many workers scheduled for the time of night at Port of San Francisco docks?"

Brandon nodded. "But you checked it and said that the schedulers had verified that it was all in order because of a shift in the arrival time of a Guatemalan ship due to a hurricane threatening the Panama Canal."

"They did, but I think we should go back and check again. We're looking for a reason Huber would choose an accountant for his grand mission? Boring. Maybe less suspicious? But definitely no interesting or valuable contacts that would be helpful." She gestured to her computer screen where she'd pulled up the State Department report on Fasrain. "But when he was in college, his mind wasn't always on numbers. His roommate during his junior and senior year was Michael Talcek. I didn't check his background in depth because I was focused on Fasrain. But Michael Talcek's application listed his legal guardians as mother, Nora, clerk, and stepfather, William Brady, salesman." She repeated, "Stepfather. And I realized I hadn't investigated anything about his roommate's real father. Michael's father was Allan Talcek, whom his mother divorced when he was eleven. Michael Talcek's father worked the docks from the time he graduated from high school. Over thirty years. Michael was at the university on a scholarship, but his records show he moved back in with his father during his senior year. So he must have stayed close to him during those years."

"Any sign of a relationship between the father and Fasrain?"

She shook her head. "No, not as far as I could tell. But Michael and Fasrain were roommates for two years. Their lives must have merged during that time. I'd bet that Fasrain made a lot of contacts on those docks while he was visiting the local bars with Talcek or his father."

"Guesswork," Monty said.

"Maybe. But two college kids sowing wild oats? They wouldn't do it on Fasrain's turf, too boring. No, they'd go down to the docks to raise hell."

"You seem to know a lot about raising hell." Brandon grinned. "You must tell me about your experiences sometime."

"I didn't spend all my time in the chemistry labs while I was at college," she said, her gaze on the screen. "I know my life must seem dry as dust to someone who played Huck Finn over most of the oceans in the world, but I'd appreciate it if you'd keep the mockery to a minimum."

His smile faded. "No mockery. I was joking. No one could call your life dry as dust. But I can't see you as a hell-raiser either."

And thanks to his talk with Hu Chang, he was probably still having moments when he looked at her as some kind of victim, she thought wryly. "You haven't known me very long." She reached for her phone. "I found a phone number for Michael Talcek. I'm going to give him a call and see what I can find out about his old friend, Fasrain."

"And verify if you're on the right track," he added.

She nodded while she listened to the phone ring. She said to Monty, "Check all the docks that are anywhere near San Francisco again, will you?" The phone was answered, and she said quickly, "Mr. Talcek? I'm sorry to disturb you so early, but it's something of an emergency. I understand you roomed with Lawrence Fasrain while at the university. I wonder if you could answer a few questions. It's very—"

"What's wrong with you?" The voice on the other end was rough and angry. "Who the hell are you? More detectives? Can't you leave me in peace?" His voice was hoarse with pain. "I told you that I don't know anything. And now you're bringing up my son's friends? Are you going to tell me they were selling drugs, too?"

She froze. Something was very wrong. "Your son? This isn't Michael Talcek?"

"You know it's not, you ghoul. This is Allan Talcek." His voice broke. "You know my son is dead."

After fifteen minutes Rachel hung up the phone and drew a deep breath. Staying on that call and forcing that poor man to talk to her had been incredibly difficult. She felt drained and like the ghoul Allan Talcek had called her as she turned to Brandon. "Michael Talcek was shot in the head the night before last in his car, which was parked behind a bar in Oakland. There was drug residue in the glove compartment which led to a search, and a kilo of heroin was found in the rim of his tire. The police are thinking he was dealing and was murdered by one of his suppliers."

"How convenient that the police were able to find the heroin, and yet the supplier who murdered him couldn't," Monty said dryly. "Was he a user?"

"No needle marks that would be a sign of frequent use, but there was heroin in his blood. But they don't have the complete autopsy report yet," Rachel said. "His father wasn't aware that his son was an addict, and he denies that he'd ever deal. As far as Michael's relationship with Fasrain, he said he didn't believe they saw much of each other anymore. He probably might know because his son moved in with him before he graduated and they were very close. But when they were roommates, he said Fasrain did hang out with Michael on the docks."

"Bingo," Brandon murmured.

"But Michael told his father that Fasrain was into some weird shit with the women he picked up at the bars, and he couldn't take it. He started to distance himself."

"Little girls?"

"Michael wouldn't say, just that it made him feel weird. After he graduated, he met a girl and didn't see much of Fasrain. They traveled in different worlds from each other. Michael got a job on the docks, but because of his university background he became an inspector for the union. He was making decent money, and he'd just given his girlfriend an engagement ring. His father said that there was no way he'd give all that up to become a drug dealer."

"Sometimes parents don't know their own children," Monty said. "Mine didn't."

"But you operate on a different planet," Brandon said. "Not many of us understand you." He was frowning thoughtfully. "And I'm leaning toward believing that the heroin was planted to give a motive why Talcek was killed. Rachel's reasoning about the docks being the target is looking good to me. It wouldn't be strange for Fasrain to give his old friend a call and ask him to have a drink to celebrate the coming nuptials."

Rachel nodded. "But why? What's the motive? And why kill him?" She was trying to figure it out. "Maybe the same reason he killed Cindy Naris? Tie up loose ends? He must have realized he should never have revealed what he did to her. Maybe he felt safe boasting because she was a hooker, and he knew he was going to kill her later."

"But if what Michael Talcek's father said was true about their estrangement, Fasrain wouldn't have been confiding his plans to Michael," Brandon said. "So he must have wanted something from him." He was silent a moment, thinking. He suddenly snapped his fingers. "He was a union inspector, right? What does a union inspector have that Fasrain could want?"

"ID." Rachel could see where he was going. "Entry passes for him to go wherever he wanted to go on the docks." She reached for the phone again. "I didn't ask his father if he had missing ID. I assumed that the police would have to have found ID when they discovered the body." She was dialing the number again. She hated to do this to Allan Talcek, but she had no alternative. She just hoped he'd pick up the call.

"No more," Allan Talchek said wearily when he answered. "I can't take any more, Dr. Venable. I believed you when you told me that you didn't think my son was a criminal, but I won't let you—"

"Just a couple questions and I'll hang up. I promise I won't bother you again. Did the police return your son's personal effects?"

"Yes, last night."

"Was there ID with them?"

"Of course, his driver's license, his phone . . . I was making a list of his friends to phone and tell about his death when you called tonight."

"What else?"

"Car insurance and his union documents."

Then maybe they were wrong, Rachel thought. Don't give up. Go another step. "You said he was a union inspector. Were his inspections limited to only one dock?"

"No, he was qualified to inspect any dock in the area. He wasn't a rookie. He had to work his way up. That's why he'd never—"

"And how did he gain entrance to those docks? Did he just have one ID and badge to access all of them?"

"No, he had to have an ID and pass for every area. It was a security measure Homeland Security demanded after 9/11."

"And all of his union passes were returned to you with his personal ID?"

Silence. "There were so many. The police didn't say they'd noticed any missing. I didn't go through them."

"Would you do that for me now." She paused. "Please. I realize it's an imposition."

"Yes, it is." Silence. "But it means something to you, doesn't it?"

"Yes, it does." She didn't try to hide the desperation

she was feeling. "And I believe it might mean something to you, too, later. Your son deserves to have the truth known."

"Stay on the line. I'll go get them." The phone went dead.

Rachel looked at Brandon. "It may all be for nothing."

"It's not nothing to Allan Talcek any longer," he said quietly. "You've made it important."

"It was already important," she said. "Not only to prevent a disaster but to keep Fasrain from making that father have to live with the ugliness of the nasty stain he painted on Michael."

"I have them all on the desk in front of me." Allan Talcek came back on the line. "Driver's license . . . Gym membership. Insurance card. There's so damn many of the union docs."

"Would you know if any of them were missing? Do you remember all the—"

"I worked on the docks for thirty-two years," he said sarcastically. "I'll remember every one of them." Another silence. "They all seem to be here . . . No, wait. Oakland is missing."

"Oakland?"

"The Port of Oakland Dock. Michael had to go there twice a month, and he was always complaining about the drive over the bridge. He said he always hit it at rush hour."

"You're sure it's not there?"

"I said it, didn't I?" he growled. "No Oakland entry pass. Is that all?"

"That's all, thank you. I really appreciate it. I'm sorry for your loss, sir." She pressed the disconnect. "Oakland. But wouldn't it be unsafe for Fasrain to use Michael's documents? Everything has photo ID these days."

"Photos and info can be changed on documents. It's the material of the ID itself that can't be easily duplicated. In some areas they have to be read by machines so they're specially coded. It's almost like a counterfeit dollar bill, there are all kinds of ways to trip up. With that many passes, it was fairly safe to accept that one of them wouldn't be missed. Particularly since the death was staged to be drug-related and have nothing to do with Michael's profession. All Fasrain had to do was turn the document over to one of Huber's experts, and within a few hours, he'd have a valid document for entry."

"Oakland . . ." Monty was adjusting the satellite to view the area. "Not small at all. I'm sure it would be as well protected as the other docks in the San Francisco area." He was enlarging the viewing scope. "At present there are three ships unloading there . . ."

"But how many will there be on the twenty-fifth? And what kinds of ships? An attack would be planned for maximum impact." Rachel was typing in a request for scheduling information on the twenty-fifth. "Nothing until 7:30 A.M. in the morning. The *Katrina Notalo* . . ." She froze. "*Shit.*" Her gaze flew to Brandon. "It's a supertanker."

He went still. "How big?"

"Does it matter? No matter how big it is, it could

be a nightmare." Of course it mattered. She was just so horrified that it had stunned her. "Big. Huge." She was reading the cargo manifest. "Over two million barrels of crude oil loaded in Saudi Arabia. The captain is Peter Van Deek who was hired eleven years ago by LetroFan Oil in Amsterdam." She shuddered. "That could definitely change the California coastline. It could change everything for everyone living here, not to mention the wildlife. Blowing up an oil tanker would poison the wildlife and destroy the fishing industry for decades to come." She moistened her lips. "We've got to stop it."

Brandon nodded. "But the question is how?"

"Keep that supertanker away from shore. Don't let it near the docks where Fasrain could blow himself and that supertanker into the stratosphere."

"And proof? Supertankers don't cancel unless there's proof of intent of sabotage. There's an oil glut going on, and tankers are lined up to unload their crude these days. Giving up their place in the schedule would put them at the end of the line again. It would cost a hell of a lot of money to their stockholders."

"I don't know how we get proof." She jumped to her feet. She couldn't just sit there. She wanted to run out and *do* something. "We just have to stop it. It all fits, Brandon. Fasrain and his ravings about angels and paradise. Michael Talcek's death. His missing credentials for Oakland. The supertanker due to arrive at 7:30 A.M. on the twenty-fifth."

"I'm not arguing. But I'm just saying we'll get an argument when we try to stop that supertanker. Our best bet is to go after Fasrain, and we can probably get help to apprehend him. But if we don't capture him, or he doesn't show himself as a threat, then no one is going to want to keep that supertanker away from those docks. Big money will be involved. You saw how Claire Warren reacted about Nemesis. She's going to want to see proof."

She didn't want to be reminded. Her panic was growing, and she could only think of that supertanker heading for the coast like some dark bird of prey. "We've got to stop it," she repeated. "Do something. You pulled a damn satellite out of your bag of tricks, didn't you? Do something like that."

"Sorry, Rachel," Monty said. "A satellite wouldn't help this time. We know where this threat's coming from." He turned to Brandon. "Drones? I'm very good with drones."

"Not unless we want to blow the supertanker up ourselves," Brandon said. "But drones aren't a bad idea. Supertankers aren't the only targets that can be blown up. If we can't stop the tanker, we might be able to stop Fasrain." He reached for his phone. "I'll call Catherine and see where she is right now. She might be able to trace Fasrain's location through his dock pass and see where he might turn up on that dock in Oakland. The only problem might be if he thinks the pass is too risky and finds another way to get on the docks."

Rachel couldn't believe it. He might be doing what Nate said he always did, take care of the problem. But he was calmly talking about taking out Fasrain on the dock itself? "And we'll still risk his blowing up those docks himself, or us doing it for him with a damn drone." She added in exasperation, "We have to *be* there. We have to find him."

"And we will," Brandon said. "I was only playing with options, Rachel. It's what we always do before we make decisions."

"I'm having trouble with the concept of playing," she said. "I have a tendency to be very serious about that much potential destruction. Can we please forget about drones and concentrate on capturing Fasrain?"

"By all means though I have trouble with the concept of capture instead of killing," Brandon said. "But I'll yield to your wishes in the matter." He smiled. "Since you might have delivered Fasrain and Huber's attack plan into our hands tonight." He added softly, "Extraordinary, Rachel."

She felt a rush of warmth as she looked at him, and suddenly her impatience was gone. She smiled back at him. "That's what you said I had to do. Extraordinary results." She turned away, "And now I'm going to let you call Catherine and fill her in on what's happening while I take a shower. I only splashed water in my face before because I was in such a hurry to check on Michael Talcek. I'll call her later and see if this Cameron she said she trusted so much has any leads about Fasrain. The twenty-fifth is the day after tomorrow." She felt another spurt of panic that she quickly squashed. A lot could be accomplished in two days. Now at least they weren't moving in the dark. Now there was hope. "Please don't decide to do anything radical while I'm in the shower." She headed for the door. "You owe me, Brandon. Like you said, I was truly extraordinary."

EAGLES REST

CANADA

"Something's happening," Lawrence Fasrain said as soon as Kraus picked up his call. "I got a call from that man you bribed at Interpol. He's been receiving some inquiries about me. There might be a problem."

"Oh, really?" Kraus said sarcastically. "And it didn't have anything to do with the fact that you blew up that whore's apartment building? Actions like that tend to generate 'problems.'"

Silence. "You know about that?"

Kraus couldn't believe the sheer idiocy of the man. "Did you actually think I wouldn't have you watched when you're a key piece to this grand plan of Huber's? I didn't mind the whore, I was planning on getting rid of her myself. But you have managed to make a major blunder. I had reports there was an FBI agent on the scene."

"I didn't make any blunders," Fasrain said quickly. "I did everything right. I took care of anything I thought might be a problem. It must have come from your people."

"It did *not* come from Red Star," Kraus said angrily. "I don't make that kind of mistake. So we're going to have to cancel?"

"I didn't say that. Find a way to get me on that dock, and I'll still be able to do my duty. That hasn't changed."

So eager to blow himself up and go to paradise, Kraus thought cynically. Well, that was exactly how he'd programmed Fasrain at Huber's command. In this case, that fanaticism might be a way of saving this operation. He just had to take control of the situation and turn it to his advantage. Don't show the idiot any more anger and bitterness. Now that he'd decided to continue using him, he had to handle him just right. Anyone as fanatical as Fasrain could ruin everything if they decided the setup didn't suit their mind-set. "Well the damage appears to be in the initial stages. No slipups about the tanker?"

"I told you, no slipups at all," Fasrain said. "How would anyone know about the tanker? Just find me a way to get on that dock and everything will be as before."

"I'll be working on it. Though I'll have to be very careful and handle all the details myself. We wouldn't want your task to be compromised. I'll fly out immediately and contact you when I arrive." He paused. "You're a brave man, Fasrain. I'm glad I'll have the opportunity to shake your hand before you leave us." He pressed the disconnect. He sat there and cursed long and vehemently before he phoned Huber. Everything had been going so well on this job that he'd managed to save from Huber's stupidity and inadequacy. And now he was going to have to rescue it once again because of that fanatic Huber had insisted on using.

And Huber would blame him, as usual. He was not

looking forward to it. But if he'd handled that asshole, Fasrain, he could deal with Max Huber. "You're not going to like this," he said when Max answered. "I don't know exactly what has happened yet, but we might not get all we wanted or expected from Fasrain." He cut Huber's angry expletive short. "I'm taking care that it won't be a complete fiasco regardless of what occurs. You won't be disappointed. But if Fasrain didn't screw up completely, then someone stepped up to the plate and spoiled our play." He couldn't keep either the malice or the rage from his voice. "As I warned you could happen if you insisted on not using our own men."

"It's your job to see that mistakes don't happen," Huber said. "And now you're telling me that you might have ruined my celebration?"

"No, I'm telling you that I'll keep it from being ruined at all costs." He paused. "And reminding you if I hadn't been busy recently giving you that little gift you demanded from me, I might have been able to concentrate more fully on what slipshod work Fasrain might be doing. You can't have it all ways, Max."

"Yes, I can." He was sputtering. "I *am* Red Star. I can have it any way I want it."

"As long as I'm here to pick up the pieces." Time to back off before he went too far. He might have already reached that point. No, he was still safe. Max had been too pleased with that last gift to blow up completely. "Which I'm about to do. I'll call you from San Francisco." He headed for the door. "Don't worry about anything. Enjoy yourself."

* * *

Rachel had time to take a leisurely shower and shampoo her hair before she received a call from Catherine.

"I was going to call you. Brandon said he'd fill you in," Rachel said quickly when she answered. "Do you think you can find out anything more about how to locate Fasrain? Or if we can definitely verify that Fasrain's van is actually in Oakland?"

"Rachel, I've only had an hour and thirty minutes since Brandon called me," Catherine said dryly. "Since then I've phoned Claire, called Brandon back, alerted Homeland Security about a possible threat, and tried to persuade Oakland Dock Security to start searching for Fasrain. Give me a break."

"Sorry. Where are you now?"

"I'm still at the Hyatt. Claire said she'd take care of everything, but I want to be here to make sure she's doing it the way Venable would."

As her father would. Everything kept coming back to him, Rachel thought. The difference between honor and duty and self-interest and ruthlessness. Yet he would be the last one to claim he was perfect, and heaven knows she knew he was not. But he was still the standard by which she judged others. "All she really has to do is keep that supertanker from entering the harbor. That would minimize tremendously any harm that could be done. Did she say that was going to be her first move?"

"She said she'd take care of it." She hesitated. "She

was balking a bit. But the minute she heard the name of the captain of the *Katrina Notalo* she started to backpedal. It seems Peter Van Deek is something of a superhero in both Europe and the Middle East. His credentials are awesome, war hero during the NATO engagement in Afghanistan, worked his way up to full captain in thirteen years. Popular with his men and his employers. He saved them a bundle when he repelled two attacks on his ship by Sudanese pirates in a matter of months. He has contacts all over the Middle East and was awarded a Royal Dutch medal by the Netherlands. No way would she want anything to happen to him. She's very conscious of bad press."

"Then there shouldn't be a problem. She'll be careful, all we have to do is find Fasrain, the man who wants to blow him into a million pieces."

"And himself along with our awesome Dutch hero. It may not be all that easy. But I have a few balls I can toss in the air."

"Richard Cameron? Have you heard anything from him yet?"

"No, but I'm sure by now he knows more about Fasrain's background and associates than Interpol and the FBI combined. I'll tell him to check Oakland for Fasrain's van. And I'll see if he has a contact he can tap in the Oakland dock area."

"You think he would?" Rachel asked doubtfully. "That would be rather too coincidental."

"Cameron's life is built on unlikely coincidences," Catherine said. "And they usually work out for him.

I'll give him the information, and I'll bet he'll be able to find Fasrain whether or not he's in Oakland."

"You have a great deal of faith in him. Did he work with my father?"

"No." Silence. "They weren't on the same wavelength."

"But he's on *your* wavelength?"

"Sometimes. Look, this isn't the time to explain Cameron to you. It may never be the time. Just accept that he can help if he wants to do it. This time he said that we have similar goals. We've just got to hope we can reach them in time."

"It will be in time if Claire calls in the big guns to stop that supertanker and goes after Fasrain," Rachel said. "Otherwise, nothing is going to be enough." She paused. "Maybe I should call and talk to her."

"No," Catherine said sharply. "Stay away from her. I can tell you're upset and vulnerable right now. She'll pick up on that right away and zero in on you."

"I'm not that vulnerable. Upset, yes. Who wouldn't be?"

"No one." She paused. "You've been going through hell lately. From San Kabara Island to Huber's using you for verbal target practice. I don't like the sheer venom Huber was showing you. And Brandon said your response was equally venomous. Huber isn't that stable. It might mean an escalation."

"And you're already worrying about it. Stop it. I'm feeling much less helpless and more hopeful than I did yesterday. We've just got to make tomorrow even better. If you want to worry about something, let it be about stopping Fasrain or that supertanker or both."

"I'm multitalented in the worry area. Okay, I'll drop it. Let me get off this phone so that I can call Cameron."

"Good luck."

"Cameron makes his own luck. The rest of us usually go along for the ride."

"Not you, Catherine."

She was silent. "No, not me. But sometimes it's difficult to not do whatever he wants. The Pied Piper is a novice compared to Cameron. I'll let you know when I know what he's up to. Bye, Rachel."

Rachel slowly ended the call. Just those few sentences Catherine had spoken about Cameron had been very revealing. No one was stronger than Catherine, but she was feeling uncertain about this man. And the picture Rachel was getting of him was both powerful and mysterious. She had no doubt Catherine would be able to handle anyone, but she had mentioned the word *difficult* . . .

Ping.

The red light had come on her computer across the room.

Rachel stiffened. Nemesis? It didn't have to be him. But the chances were that it was.

Dread.

Fear.

Stop being such a coward. Deal with him.

She crossed the room and sat down at the desk. She braced herself and looked at the message.

Have you missed me, Rachel? I hear you've been busy. So sorry you weren't able to stop Huber, but I gave you an opportunity. You just weren't clever enough to make it work. I find I regret that he managed to make such a fool of you. My actions might have taken another turn if you had shown me that you had any hope of matching him.

She quickly typed back.

The turn you did take let many people be slaughtered. We didn't have a chance. We did what we could. If you'd been there, you would have seen that. [She paused.] Were you there? How deep are you involved with Huber?

Hesitation.

As involved as I wish to be. I'd feel safer if I could just disappear into the sunset with your millions in my pocket. But there have been developments that make that less profitable and more dangerous. Huber and Kraus are making moves that require my services, and that means that our own deal may be null and void.

She sat there, shocked.

But the reason you told me about San Kabara was that you wanted a safety net. If you're going over to Red Star, that's down the drain. Think

about it. Or go all the way and not only tell us Huber's target but his location so that we'd know how to bring him down. That would give you both safety and cash.

It took a moment before the answer came.

But you failed on San Kabara. I'd find it difficult to trust you to bring him down. You're not your father, Rachel. No, I believe that I'd better go with Huber and Kraus, they have a record that's more impressive. However, I will keep your offer in mind. And I have no prejudice against double-dealing as long as it's safe for me. Just don't expect me to do anything that's not of greatest benefit for me.

She could hardly expect anything else, she thought in frustration. It had been the modus operandi of his behavior since day one.

Is that why you decided to email me back instead of just stopping all contact? You're leaving your options open?

Rachel, do I perceive bitterness? That's one reason, but I was also given a mission. I was told to break off negotiations with you and to demonstrate my loyalty to Red Star in a way that would be unmistakable in your eyes.

She went still. Not good. She felt a sudden chill.

Are you going to tell me about another attack?

No.

Relief.

Then what is it?

I'm getting to it. I'm sending you two photos. Kraus seemed to think they would be self-explanatory and would automatically show you where I was in the scheme of things. He told me that he might use me to communicate with you about them in the future. I believe his trust in Huber's professionalism isn't as strong as it might be. I'm sensing his disgust growing by leaps and bounds.

Another of those photos of her at Sazkar Prison? She thought wildly. That wouldn't make sense.

What photos, dammit?

Be patient. I've just pressed the button. You'll see they were taken quite recently, so I'll probably not be in contact with you until the status is more current. I'm sorry, Rachel, it's just business.

The computer screen went blank.

But she heard the signal on her phone for an incoming message.

She snatched up her phone and pressed the text access.

The first photo came up.

No! Dear God, no.

She felt as if she'd been kicked in the stomach. She had to close her eyes for a moment.

But when she opened them, the photo was still there.

Maria!

Two. There were supposed to be two photos.

She pulled up the second photo.

Blanca!

Shock. Horror. Nausea.

She ran to the bathroom and threw up.

Please. There were all kinds of ways to falsify photos. Let this be one of them.

But she couldn't think right now. She needed someone to tell her that it wasn't true. She couldn't find her phone. She'd dropped it somewhere . . .

It was on the floor by the computer desk. Her hand was shaking as she dialed Brandon. "Something has happened. Will you . . . come? I . . . need you."

She hung up and just sat there looking down at the phone. Brandon would come soon. Brandon would tell her it was a lie.

And then Brandon was throwing open the door and was there beside her. "What the hell's wrong?" He was pulling her up into his arms. "You're white as a tombstone. Are you hurt? You're scaring me."

"I'm not hurt," she said dully. "I just can't seem to think." She thrust her phone at him. "I need you to tell me it's a lie. Will you do that?"

Brandon took the phone and looked down at the photos. "Oh, *shit*."

"There are all kinds of ways to manipulate and falsify photos. They'd know them all," she said. Brandon wasn't saying anything, he was just looking down at the photo and it was frightening her. "Tell me he doesn't have her. She's just a little girl. Tell me he doesn't have Maria." She couldn't look at that photo again but it was engraved on her memory. Maria with eyes wide with fear, bruises on her face, lying on the ground.

"I wish I could," Brandon said gently. "Who sent it?"

"Nemesis." She was starting to shake. It was true. She couldn't escape it. "Only it was really Kraus or Huber. And there's another one. He sent me two. Blanca, Maria's mother . . . She might be dead. She's lying there on the ground in the mud . . . and there's blood. They wouldn't need her . . . except to do this to me."

He pulled up the other photo. "Rachel." He pulled her back into his arms and rocked her. "I'm so damn sorry."

"So am I. I didn't think of their being in danger after we left Georgetown. Maria was a patient, and there were so many patients. Why would he know she was special?"

"Morales' men must have told him you stayed

behind to go get her. Huber was searching for a weapon, and they found it."

"A weapon? She's eight years old."

"And this is Huber."

Yes, it was Huber and Kraus and Nemesis, and none of them would care that Maria was a child who had just received a fresh start after hovering so close to death. What had Rachel been thinking? And she had called Brandon to come running and tell her what she had known already? She was clinging to him now and had to stop. She had to rely only on herself as she always did. She took a step back and pushed him away. "Would you ask Monty if he can contact one of his tech buddies to verify that there's been no doctoring with the photos? I don't believe that there has been, but I have to be sure. Nemesis said that the photos had just been taken and it would be awhile before he contacted me. But someone will probably call me, and I'll have to know truth from lies." She nodded at the computer and said unsteadily, "You'll want to read Nemesis's message, it indicates a change in the scenario." She turned and headed for the doors to the veranda. "Don't come after me. I need some time alone so that I can see what has to be done. I'm not thinking very clearly."

"I don't *want* you to be alone," he said thickly. "You don't have to be strong all the time, Rachel."

"Yes I do," she said unevenly. "The best I can be. Though I wasn't very strong when I first looked at those photos." She opened the French doors. "I'm going for a walk; and then I'll come back and we'll talk. If you can think of anything to do that will help Maria . . . or Blanca, by all means put it into motion."

She closed the doors behind her and walked across the veranda and down to the beach.

The wind was blowing, picking up the sand and moving it from the dunes to swirl at her feet.

Look at the swirling sand. Look at the sea. Don't think of Maria for the next few minutes.

She would just look at the nature and the beauty surrounding her until she was able to forget those photos and remember Maria and Blanca the way she'd last seen them at the hospital. After that, she'd be able to work through the pain and think coherently, and then find a way to help them.

Just look at the swirling sand.

CHAPTER

14

Brandon was waiting when Rachel left the beach and came back to the veranda two hours later.

"All right?" he asked without expression. "As all right as you can be right now?"

She nodded. "I'm sorry I lost it," she said quietly. "It hit me hard. It took me a little time."

"Imagine that. And as usual, I couldn't help. All I could do was stand here and watch you down there on the beach." He smiled crookedly. "Well, maybe I helped a bit. Monty sent those photos to an expert at the Pixel Studio, and they verified that it was unlikely they had been doctored. Then we contacted the hospital in Georgetown and found out that Maria had been released from the hospital three days ago. She was in good health, but they placed her in a nursing home for observation at the CDC's request because they wanted to observe how fast she'd complete her recovery on the medication. As far as they know, she's still there."

"She's not there," Rachel said.

"I don't think so either. We're checking it out now. Your friend, Phillip, is still at the hospital, and he's going to the nursing home to see what he can find out. He said he'd call you as soon as he knew." He took her arm and pushed her gently toward the kitchen door. "Come in and have a cup of hot tea. You said we'd talk, we're going to talk." He gestured to a chair at the kitchen table. "Sit down. I'll have the tea ready in a minute. As I said, I've been waiting." He was getting cups and saucers down. "Nate and Monty wanted to come in to see you, but I told them that it would be better if they didn't. They wanted to let you know how sorry they are about Maria."

"I know they are. They're very kind."

"They like you, they want to help, dammit."

"They are helping. You told me that Monty—"

"Forget it." He put her tea down before her. "You still act as if you're walking around in a fog. I can't expect anything else, but I want to shake you and wake you up. Or break Huber into tiny pieces and cremate the bastard, so that he doesn't exist anywhere on the planet."

"I'm not in a fog any longer." She had to be clear because she knew she wasn't behaving normally. "This is . . . bad for me." She spoke slowly, trying to choose her words. "I learned a long time ago that when things became this bad, it's better if I draw into myself until I can get through it."

"Like you did at Sazkar Prison?" he asked jerkily.

"I suppose it started then. It's not that I don't appreciate that you and Monty and Nate want to help." She moistened her lips. "I'm just trying to hold on because I know there's more to come. You read that email. You know I'm right."

"Hell, yes." He dropped down in the chair opposite her. "Huber picked the perfect weapon, didn't he? He knows you're not going to let Maria be tortured or killed. He thinks he's got you in a corner."

"It feels like that to me as well." She lifted the cup to her lips. "I told Catherine that I thought we might be getting somewhere, that there might be reason for hope. That was right before I got the email. There doesn't seem as if there's much hope now." Her hand tightened on the cup. "But I can't think like that. If I do, I'll give up, and Maria will die. Because no matter what Huber says or does, no matter what bargain he strikes with me, he'll eventually kill her anyway. Unless I find a way to get her away from him."

"And you've just said that he'll lie," he said roughly. "So I'm sure that plan you've been hatching mentally for a trade won't do any good."

"Not unless I have someone to help get her out after the trade takes place."

"No," he said violently. "I'm supposed to snatch the kid and leave you with Huber? That's not going to happen, Rachel. We'll think of something else."

"We both knew that I might eventually have to be

the game piece that allows us to stop Huber." She met his eyes. "He just upped the stakes. The ideal situation is to destroy Red Star, kill Huber, and save Maria without sacrificing me. That's a big order. We may not be able to have it all. But I will have Maria. She *will* live, Brandon." She looked down into the amber depths of her tea. "And I'll promise you Huber if we can manage to get me anywhere close to him. You might have to take care of the rest yourself." Her lips twisted. "Such a small task, destroying a terrorist organization we haven't been able to touch for decades. Piece of cake, Brandon."

"Yeah, piece of cake," he said roughly. "Particularly since I'm not going to let you go get Maria by yourself. I might be a little busy."

She had been expecting this, but it wasn't time for arguments. "We'll see how things work out. I guess I'll have to wait for the next call from Huber or Nemesis." And that knowledge was causing every nerve to clench. "I don't think he'd reply to me this time if I tried to initiate. He's taking Red Star orders now."

"Unless he thought you had something better to offer."

She shook her head. "You know we can't trust him."

"We could if he has a knife to his throat," he said grimly. "It's amazing what that incentive does to a slimeball. One of the orders I gave Monty was to hop on Sam Zackoff to get me that IP, then the trace."

She remembered that Monty had said that Sam was close to finding the IP, but she was afraid to count on anything. "For a hacker as brilliant as Monty claims this Zackoff to be, it's taking a long time to—"

Her cell phone rang.

Phillip Sanford.

Her finger punched the access on the speaker. "Phillip, what did you find out?"

"Nothing good, Rachel," Phillip said gently. "Maria and her mother disappeared from their rooms at the nursing home sometime last night. There was a note on the nightstand this morning, supposedly from Blanca, saying that they were homesick and were going back to their village."

"Not true. Blanca wouldn't do that if Maria was still being treated."

"I know, I saw her before she left the hospital for the nursing home. When I got there today, I asked them to search the property." He paused. "They found Blanca in the woods behind the home."

Her heart lurched. "Dead?"

"No. But she'd been pistol-whipped, and she's still unconscious. It looked as if she'd tried to crawl out of the woods back toward the nursing home but couldn't make it."

Not dead. That was better than she'd feared. "Is she going to live?"

"She has a chance. Exposure. Severe concussion. She's lucky we found her when we did."

"But no Maria?"

"No Maria. I gather you weren't expecting us to find her."

"It would have been a miracle."

"But we talked about miracles. Sometimes they happen. Particularly with you, Rachel."

"This one would have been difficult to do. I'd appreciate it if you'd do your best to pull one off with Blanca. Will you do that, Phillip?"

"You know I will." He hesitated. "Would you like to tell me what you've gotten yourself into? I'd like to help."

"You'll help by letting me tell Maria that she has a mother to come back to. That's pretty big stuff. I'll check on her later. Thanks, Phillip." She pressed the disconnect and looked at Brandon. "He's the best. If anyone can save Blanca, he can." She drew a deep breath. "Severe concussion. She was probably fighting for her Maria. Her daughter was the most important thing in her—"

Her phone was ringing.

It was Phillip again. "It might not mean anything. There was something scrawled in the mud where we found Blanca. They might not even be letters, she might have just been digging her fingers in the mud to keep herself going."

"What are you talking about?"

"I don't know what I'm talking about. But they looked a little like letters, and Blanca might have been trying to tell us something. She would have been in pretty bad pain at the time, and I didn't just want to dismiss them."

"What letters?"

"It looked like a U and an A, and maybe an N and a C. As I said, it might be nothing."

"We'll look at it and see if we can make anything out of it. Thanks, Phillip."

As she hung up she saw that Brandon had taken out a pen and his pad and had written down the four letters . . . if they were letters. "He's right, it could be nothing," she said. "She could have been disoriented as well as in pain. Or struggling to crawl through the mud."

"Or telling us something she'd overheard from the men who'd taken them," he said. "You've just been saying how much she loved Maria. Wouldn't she do anything to let us know something that might help us to find her?"

"Yes." She took his pad and copied the letters on a sheet and tore it out of the pad. "Long shot, Brandon. A name?"

"Or a destination. A name wouldn't be nearly as important to Blanca as where they were taking her little girl."

"They'd be taking her to Max Huber."

"But where is Huber located right now? He operates all over the world. Presumably he's in Canada because that's where he was when Venable was supposed to meet with Nemesis. But he changes his compounds all the time, and we don't even know where all of them are located." He was staring down at his notepad. "Not much to go on."

"Long shot," Rachel repeated. "But sometimes long shots pay off and we have to try everything." She put her cup back in the saucer and pushed her chair back.

"I think I'll go back to my room and look at maps and see if it sparks anything."

"And then sit and wait for Huber or Nemesis to attack you again?" Brandon said savagely. His eyes were blazing in his taut face. "How long do you think it will be this time?"

"I have no idea. It depends how long it will take Maria to be delivered to Huber. Why are you so angry?"

"Because I want to kill someone, and I can't do it. Because if I take you somewhere and lock you away until this is all over, you'll hate my guts." He got to his feet and headed for the door. "It might be worth it." He stopped and looked over his shoulder. "Are you going to call Catherine?"

"No, she'd only worry, and what could she do? She's busy trying to find a way to locate Fasrain and keep him from blowing up that supertanker."

"What could she do? You're hurting. She's your best friend, and she might give you the comfort you won't take from me." His lips twisted. "Or you could call Hu Chang. He who dispenses all knowledge and wisdom."

"You're mocking him, but he does, you know. Or close to it."

"I'm not really mocking him." The savagery was suddenly replaced with weariness. "I'm just jealous as hell of him. But not too jealous not to ask you to call him and let him help you."

She could see that her withdrawal was hurting him, but she couldn't let go of the control she'd managed to retrieve during those hours on the beach. "I'm not going to be just sitting waiting for Huber. I have a few things to do." She looked down at the page she'd torn from his notebook. "Besides this bewildering scrap of nothing. I'll be fine, Brandon."

"Sure." He shrugged as he opened the door. "I'll be working with Monty and Sam to get that damn IP address. I'm definitely motivated to get my hands on that son of a bitch. Let me know if you decide that you're *not* fine."

She stared helplessly after him as the door shut. She knew he wanted to help, but she couldn't let him come closer. She had to be strong, and when he was here, she wanted to lean.

She straightened and headed down the hall toward her bedroom. She had not lied when she'd told him she had things to do. She glanced at the computer when she entered the bedroom. No red light.

Then she went to her closet and pulled out the small plastic container that she'd stored there. She sat down on the bed and opened the container. She gazed down at the six vials glittering in the dimness of the bag.

Glittering . . . and deadly.

It was time to make the choice.

No answer again, Catherine realized with annoyance.

She had called Claire Warren three times in the last hour. Every call went directly to voice mail. It was clear Claire wasn't accepting her calls, she thought grimly. She had made her thoughts and opinions about Claire's reluctance to move forward with any speed a little too plain, and Claire obviously didn't want to deal with Catherine if she could avoid it.

Well, she could *not* avoid it. She might be able to ignore Catherine's calls, but that only meant she'd have to confront her in person as she'd intended anyway.

Her phone rang. No ID.

"I believe my friend, Harry, probably told you to get some rest when he examined you at the hospital," Cameron said when she answered. "Yet I'll wager you're doing no such thing and probably about to cause me infinite trouble."

"How could I do that when you're not even answering my calls?" she asked curtly. "I called you twice today. You're as bad as Claire Warren."

"Oh, you're having problems with her again? Please don't compare us. It would be totally unfair, you know. I'll answer whenever you call, swim the deepest ocean, jump over high buildings with—"

"Except when it's inconvenient for you."

"As it happens, it was a little inconvenient. But all in your service. I was getting the current address of Lawrence Fasrain from a contact. Then, of course, I had to verify it. I wouldn't allow myself to ever give you incorrect information."

Her heart jumped. "You have his address? What is it?"

"I'll take care of it. I just wished you to know it was in process."

"No, *I'll* take care of it. I told you all I wanted was

for you to find him. You're not supposed to do anything else. Why are you?"

"I suppose because I wanted to make you feel . . . treasured. I didn't like the idea that you were almost blown up last night." He went on immediately, "But speaking of explosives, I'll ignore your lack of understanding and tell you that I've also located the van that you're looking for."

"Oakland?"

"Yes."

"The docks?"

"Close. Six blocks from the main gate." He paused. "You were expecting this. You might have told me and saved us work."

"I'm sure your bloodhounds needed the practice. But I didn't expect it before I talked to Jude Brandon a couple hours ago. He and Rachel tracked down Fasrain's connection with a union inspector and a potential scenario." She briefly outlined what she'd been told. "I was going to let you know . . . if you'd answered your phone."

"That did sting, didn't it? I'll try to do penance in the near future. I'd hate to discourage you. I can't tell you how much your reaching out to me in any way pleases me."

"I'm not one of your fans, Cameron. I have no intention of trying to please you."

"But that's totally impractical and unacceptable. Please me, and I'll forgive you anything, do anything to you, for you . . . Don't you remember?"

She did remember, and it was causing the heat to

sear through her. Damn him. She changed the subject. "Is this address you have for Fasrain in Oakland?"

"Yes. And the location makes perfect sense now that I have the background." He was silent a moment. "This Jude Brandon is competent, and you trust him?"

"I think I do. Venable definitely trusted him."

"And you trusted Venable." Another silence. "You're at the hotel trying to manipulate your friend, Claire Warren?"

"Not my friend. But, yes, I have to make sure that she—"

"You don't want to have to herd her in the direction you want her to go. It's annoying you. You told me that Brandon said that he'd start working on stopping or diverting the *Katrina* and that you trust him. Between him and this CIA person with whom you're so annoyed surely that's handled. You've always been an over-achiever, but you can't do everything, Catherine. So let's cross her out of the equation and concentrate on Fasrain. He's obviously the current danger. Agreed?"

"Yes, fanatics are always a danger. Give me his address."

"I have to finish what I started. I have to think of my reputation, after all."

"Bullshit."

"It's not as if I'm closing you out. I'll happily take you to Fasrain. I'm just . . . treasuring you." He added softly, "Let's go get him, Catherine."

It was tempting. Meaningful action instead of arguing with Claire. Providing she could even get in to see the damn woman. Claire wouldn't even talk to her on the phone. "Stopping that supertanker is important, too."

"One battle at a time."

And doing battle beside Cameron was always challenging and exciting.

"Not as good as sex," he said softly, "but close."

"Cameron."

"I'm innocent." He chuckled. "Well, not true. But in this case, I didn't break my word. I just know you, Catherine."

Yes, he did. And she knew him, and she could hardly wait to feel the vitality that was always there when she interacted with him. To hell with it. Trust Brandon to take care of the supertanker as he'd said he would. Go for the threat that was within her reach. "We don't know when Fasrain will go to that dock. He might already be there. He might have planned to go early and find a place to go underground to hide."

"Then we'd better start right away. I'll come down and meet you in the lobby."

"You're staying at this hotel?"

"I wanted to look into a few things concerning your team, so I checked in after I left you at the hospital."

"What things?"

"I just wondered why you were the only one who was given an assignment that could get you blown up."

"Because I asked for it."

"That was my first and most likely answer. I was merely verifying. Now let me get off the phone. I have to call Oakland and make certain the man I have guarding Fasrain's motel realizes how displeased I'll be if he slips away since he's been elevated to fanatic status. Manuel's a new recruit. See you in ten minutes."

She experienced a tingle of excitement as she pressed the disconnect. She felt suddenly alive and ready to cope with anything. But then she always felt like that when she was with Cameron. It was one of the most dangerous things about him that he could spark her mind and spirit as well as her body. But in this case she didn't have to worry about anything personal. It was all going to be about Lawrence Fasrain and that detonator he no doubt had in his pocket.

Ten minutes later, she got off the elevator and saw Cameron waiting in the lobby. He was smiling as he came toward her and took her arm and guided her toward the front entrance. "Right on time. This should put us in Oakland within fifteen minutes."

"Really? In San Francisco? We're not driving?"

"No, I called a friend, and he's put his helicopter at our disposal. It's waiting on the rooftop of his building about a block and a half from here." He had his hand beneath her elbow and was propelling her down the street. "I thought it would be quicker. Bridge traffic is always rough."

"So you picked up your phone and made a call. Fifteen minutes? As I recall, the last time we were here in San Francisco, it was a little harder for you to manipulate and control the surroundings."

"But that was several months ago," he said quietly. "I've had time to dig in and initiate adjustments and contacts. I've made enormous strides here. San Francisco is liberal, freethinking, intelligent, ready to reach

out and accept ideas that might seem radical to some."
He smiled. "In short, my kind of town. San Francisco
likes me, Catherine."

And she was wondering what other strides Cameron
had made in other cities of the world during that time.
She had heard nothing of his shadow movements,
but that was because silence had power, and so did
Cameron.

"Stop worrying." He wasn't looking at her. "I'm trying to be as honest as I can with you. We don't agree
on philosophy, but I've never harmed you or yours.
And in your heart you can't object to freedom of
choice. That's all I offer."

She made a rude sound. "It's not free if you dangle
all kinds of alluring promises and prizes that dazzle
people."

He laughed. "But I don't cheat. The prize is always
there. If someone comes when I call, it's because I
show the beckoning potential."

Why had she been lured into this argument again?
It was that glimpse of power that he seldom let her see.
"It doesn't matter," she said impatiently. "I should be
glad that your billionaire friend is willing to lend you
his helicopter when you snap your fingers. It may keep
him from losing his fancy skyscraper if we can stop
Fasrain." She made a face at him. "Not that I'd get any
credit. It's all about you." She repeated his words
mockingly, "San Francisco likes you."

"I'd give you credit. I'd give you anything you want."
He opened the glass door of a gray-granite skyscraper.
"Because San Francisco might like me." He punched

the button for the elevator to the roof. "But I like everything about you, Catherine . . ."

The Sea Gull Motel was a gray-clapboard, one-story building located a block off the Oakland waterfront. In the center of the U-shaped building was a small swimming pool with a blue plastic inner tube floating on the surface.

"Room 15," Cameron said as he helped Catherine out of the rental car. "Manuel says that it's the door with the DO NOT DISTURB sign, so the maids won't bother him. Fasrain checked in late last night."

"And he's still there?"

"His van's in the parking lot. Manuel has been staking out his room since we located him at 1:40 A.M." He glanced at a huge, dark-skinned man hurrying toward him. "Hello, Manuel, no problems?"

"No, sir. I did everything you told me," he said eagerly. "You didn't have to come. I could have brought him to you."

"I'm sure you could," Cameron said quietly. "But it wasn't necessary. I can handle it myself."

"I know you can. I didn't mean that you weren't able to do it. It's just that I didn't want you to have to bother. That's my job."

"And I'm sure you did it well, Manuel." Catherine stepped in to save time and effort. She had seen this attitude before in the people surrounding Cameron. She joked about his being treated like a crown prince, but every now and then she ran across a hero worship like Manuel's, and it was no longer humorous. It got in the way. Cameron was the Guardian, and his word was law in their eyes. "I'm Catherine, and I'm very glad to meet you. But we're in a hurry and, as the Guardian said, he wants to handle it himself." She gestured to the door. "He brought me to help him. Is that the correct door?"

Manuel nodded doubtfully and looked at Cameron. "Sir?"

"She's very capable," he said solemnly. "Wonder Woman has nothing on her."

"If you say so. May I take care of the lock for you?"

"I'll do it," Catherine said as she moved toward the door. "Anything to serve the Guardian."

Cameron made a clucking sound. "Sarcasm? You'll upset Manuel."

"Off with my head." She was silently picking the lock. It took only two minutes. She carefully tested the door. She tensed. "I don't believe the chain is on," she whispered. "He may not be inside."

Manuel was frantically shaking his head. "The van . . . I watched the door. He has to be here."

Cameron went very still. "I tend to agree with both of you," Cameron murmured. "We'll just have to see. Move!"

He didn't wait for her to move. He pushed her aside, and his foot crashed against the door. The next instant he was inside, dodging to the left with his gun drawn.

"Dammit." Catherine dove forward into the room and rolled to the side. "Cameron this was my—"

"Stay down," Cameron said. "Manuel's right. He's

still in here. I have to make sure that he—" He flicked
the light on. "And he is."

Blood.

Catherine froze. She was staring at a man dressed
in a striped robe kneeling on a prayer rug. Or he had
been kneeling; he was now crumpled to one side.

And there was a large, bloody hole in the back of
his head

Catherine got slowly to her knees, struggling with
shock. "Dead? Are we sure it's Fasrain?"

"Not yet. Check ID, Manuel."

Manuel was searching frantically through the suit-
case on the bed. "I didn't fail you, sir. I swear no one
got past me. Believe me, I wouldn't be that careless."

"I know you wouldn't," Cameron said soothingly.
"Fasrain was probably killed before you showed up
here. It's not your fault. You checked to make certain
he was registered. It's natural you assumed that he was
still here when you saw his van in the parking lot. Just
get me the ID."

"Here it is." Manuel handed him a brown leather
wallet. "No one came here, sir. I never took my eyes
off the door."

"Well, someone obviously came even if it wasn't
on your watch." He flipped open the wallet. "Michael
Talcek. With full union credentials." He knelt beside
the body and checked the face of the corpse against the
photo on the ID. Then compared it to the photo he had
of Fasrain. "Unless there are two Talceks, this is his
buddy, Lawrence Fasrain." He examined the wound.
"He was at his prayers, and he trusted whoever was in

the room with him. This shot was fired at close range." He stood up and turned to Catherine. "It looks as if we're not going to have to worry about Lawrence Fasrain any longer."

"I'm not certain if that's bad or good." She looked away from the body. "What about the explosives? Are they still here in the room? Detonators?"

"Manuel will check." He turned and gestured to the door. "I know you'd like to tear this room apart on your own, but it's better done by experts."

"And Manuel is an expert?"

"At many things." He smiled at Manuel. "That's why he has my trust. Nothing will get past him. You'll call me later and report?"

Manuel nodded, his face flushing. "Thank you for your forgiveness. I promise I won't make another mistake."

"I know you won't. But do it quickly please. Catherine will wish to turn the crime scene over to her people." He gave Catherine a gentle push out the door. "We wouldn't want to keep her waiting."

"Heaven forbid," Catherine murmured as she walked toward their rental car in the parking lot. "As if he'd care as long as he was able to please you. One of your more enthusiastic followers, Cameron. You were very patient with him."

He shrugged. "He's a good man . . . just young. He'll be better the next time."

"And be even more devoted because you were understanding." Her heart was pounding, and she glanced back at the motel. Manuel had shut the door, but there were still signs of Cameron's break-in on the splintered wood. She suddenly remembered something he'd said before he'd broken into the room. "You said that you thought Manuel and I were both right about Fasrain being the room. But I thought he might be gone and Manuel was sure he was still there." Her gaze flew to his face. "You knew he was in the room but he was dead, didn't you?"

"Now how could I know that?"

"I have no idea. I don't know what you can do or can't do. I just know you have more psychic abilities than anyone I've ever met. Certainly more than I'm comfortable with. I don't believe you want anyone to know."

His brows rose. "If it would make you uncomfortable, why would you want to know?" His gaze searched her face. "But you do." He shrugged. "I wasn't sure . . . sometimes I get a sense. Enough?"

"Enough." She looked away from him. "Someone will notice that door fairly soon. I should call Claire and get a cleanup crew out here right away. The Company won't want media attention until we know with what we have to contend."

"After Manuel gets through. The CIA sometimes tends to blur the truth if it suits them." He opened the car door for her. "Not you, of course, I'm sure your sterling character is an inspiration to everyone around you."

"Sarcasm? I don't give a damn about inspiring anyone. I just do my job with as much honesty as I'm able. That's all I can do."

"I wasn't being sarcastic," he said quietly. "I know you very well, Catherine." He started the car. "I believe it's sad that a unique person like yourself doesn't inspire as you should. That's why you should come to me."

"Don't." She held out her hand and was glad to see it wasn't shaking. "No recruitment effort, please. All I want you to tell me is if you arranged for Fasrain to be killed."

"I did not. I offered, you refused. That was the end of it. I set about doing you a service." He glanced at her. "Though I regret I didn't find him in time. You hoped to get information?"

"I don't know what I hoped. But information might have helped." She stared out the window. "I'm betting that Huber and Kraus decided that Fasrain was unstable after they heard about his blowing up that apartment building. Which one do you think paid him a visit?"

He shrugged. "Kraus. Though it's only a guess. The reports I've had today say that Huber saves himself for more spectacular acts of terrorism."

"Like Rachel," she said grimly. "I'm certain he has something special in mind for her."

"Then send her to me. I'll protect her." He held up his hand as she opened her lips. "And I'm not recruiting. I just don't want you to be unhappy. No strings. You can have her back later."

"How generous." She shook her head. "But no thank you, you're entirely too dangerous. Not many people decide to come back after they've accepted your protection."

"There are reasons," he said. "But I'll do what I can without full involvement. It's just more difficult for me to—"

His phone rang and he glanced at the ID. "Manuel."

He answered and listened. Then he said, "No, that was the only important item. Just finish and report later." He pressed the disconnect. "Manuel found the explosives. Several canisters with C4 and two suicide vests. Hidden, but easy enough to find. Anyone searching might assume that there was a falling-out among the terrorists and the other conspirator panicked and fled. Particularly since they left the explosives."

"Maybe," Catherine said. "Leaving the explosives might indicate a failed mission. But it's too . . . pat."

He was frowning thoughtfully. "Yet it's unlikely that Red Star would be able to find a substitute for Fasrain at this late date. When they decided it was too risky to go forward with him, they'd either have to cancel or go in another direction."

"But an oil spill of that magnitude would be exactly what Huber would have in mind for changing the coastline." Catherine was thinking, mentally trying out different scenarios. "It would piss him off royally to have to cancel. He wouldn't do it. He'd look for another way to make it happen. Yet now he no longer has a man on that dock to set off the explosion as the *Katrina Notalo* sails into the harbor. So what's the alternative?" She was working her way to an answer, "It's to have another method of setting it off. With Fasrain dead, everyone is going to assume that the principal threat is over. Oh, they'll be careful about examining all ID, and naturally the docks will all be thoroughly searched, but the DEFCON alertness will go down, and so will expectation."

He was smiling. "And what are *you* expecting, Catherine?"

Her eyes flew to his face. His expression was intent, yet alive with humor and curiosity. "You know very well. It just amuses you to watch me figure it out for myself."

"It's a wonderful process. You never cease to amaze and intrigue me. Tell me."

"Kraus could have arranged for a backup plan," she said bluntly. "There could also be explosives on the ship that can be set off when the *Katrina Notalo* gets anywhere close to shore. I'm guessing there's a possibility our heroic Captain Van Deek wasn't going to be a victim; he might be a coconspirator."

"Interesting. But I doubt if Van Deek would be willing to sacrifice his life as Fasrain was going to do. He might require additional incentive."

"Or a foolproof way of getting off that tanker before it exploded. I don't know how it would work. I was thinking that it might even be one of his crew, but Van Deek is too sharp, and he's supposed to be close to his crew. Wouldn't it be dangerous for Huber or Kraus to hire someone to try to fool him?" She shook her head. "No, having it be Van Deek makes more sense to me. Though it would be difficult to convince anyone that he's involved. A pristine record as a captain, and he even got a medal for heroism." Her lips twisted.

"Homeland would accept Van Deek as a victim, never as a perpetrator. They'd want proof."

"And your Claire Warren?"

"I'll make the attempt. She might be willing to act if she thinks it's to her advantage." She shook her head. "But if she doesn't, then I've got to find some other way. I can't let it happen." She looked out at the blue waters of the bay. So beautiful and clean, with the sun glittering on it. "Huber can't win this time. I've seen what an oil spill can do to the environment. It makes me sick to think of all the sludge and death that could be caused by that one explosion."

"Then we'll have to see that explosion doesn't take place," Cameron said quietly. "It's pure wanton destruction. I've been trained to accept it, but I dislike the idea intensely." He added thoughtfully, "But first I'll verify that Van Deek might be as crooked as you think he is. Then we'll take a look at how to bring him down."

She shook her head. "It's not your fight, Cameron." She paused. "You're always very careful not to attract the attention of the CIA or any other group that might become curious about who you are and what you do. This could arouse just that kind of attention."

"My dear Catherine, are you actually trying to protect me?" His eyes were twinkling. "It's almost worthwhile going after Huber to watch you do that. It shows me that you're coming very close to believing that I'm on the right side after all."

"Bullshit."

He chuckled. "Well, maybe not *very* close. So I'll accept that it might not be philosophy but something infinitely more personal. You're worried that I'll be thrown into some black hole for interrogation. Then you'd have to break me out, and that would cause you a great deal of trouble."

"What makes you think I wouldn't leave you to rot?"

"Catherine."

"Okay, but I wouldn't need to break you out. Your men would be causing a minor revolution if they thought they were going to lose you."

"Yes, and I've made sure that they're very efficient. Which should let you know how valuable I'm going to be to you." His smile disappeared. "So stop arguing with me, Catherine. I know exactly what this entails and the degree of threat to me. I also know that you're going to go forward no matter what I do. I find I can't tolerate the idea of letting you go alone. You might say I was extremely upset when I couldn't get to San Kabara Island in time to help you. So upset that I'm not going to let it happen again. Is that clear?"

"Crystal. But that doesn't mean that I have to—"

"Shh. Yes, it does. Better to keep me close where you can watch me." He was smiling again as he reached for his phone. "You can try to toss me out of your life later. Right now, I guarantee you're going to want me around." Then he was quickly dialing a number. "But it would be wise not to voice any theories you might have to your friends in the CIA or FBI until I can gather concrete information about Van Deek." The call was answered and he said, "Information about a Captain Peter Van Deek, Willis. Everything. Dig deep, and fast. Start off with the assumption that he's dirty and go from there . . ."

"Fasrain is dead?" Brandon repeated. "Weird. It had to be Huber or one of his men, Catherine. But it might mean Huber's plan is falling apart."

"Or that he wants it to seem that it is," Catherine said. "Anyway, we've got a few theories about what might happen down the road now that Fasrain been erased. I'm bringing Cameron out to Beach Haven so that we can plan the next step. We should be there in about an hour."

"We?" he echoed. "Cameron? Who the hell is Cameron?"

"I wasn't certain Rachel would mention him. That's why I wanted to call and prepare you. Richard Cameron. I've worked with him before, and you'll find him very . . . useful. At any rate, whether you do or not, I've agreed to let him help straighten out this mess."

"Indeed? We'll see, Catherine."

"Yes, we will," she said wearily. "Don't give me problems, Brandon. I'm having enough trouble controlling Cameron. You'll be smart enough to realize that I'm not making a mistake when you meet him." She changed the subject. "How's Rachel? Will you tell her I'll explain everything when we get there?"

"Rachel has a few major problems of her own. She

doesn't need any new ones appearing on the horizon. I'll see you in an hour, Catherine." He cut the connection.

"You're not pleased with our gorgeous Mata Hari." Nate's gaze was on Brandon's face. "Did I hear that Fasrain's dead?"

"Yes, but who the hell knows what that means." He rubbed the back of his neck. He was tired and on edge and close to exploding. "Catherine seems to think she does. Or maybe it's her new 'friend' who she thinks can run the show."

Nate gave a low whistle. "Maybe you're just tired. You and Monty have been working for hours on that IP address. No closer?"

"I don't know. Monty's going over the last proxy we took out with Sam Zackoff. I'm waiting to see if there was any breakthrough."

"You could go check on Rachel," Nate suggested. "She might need—"

"She doesn't need me," Brandon interrupted. "She made that clear. I'm better off here until I can give her something that will make a difference."

"It will take a hell of a lot to do that," Nate said. "I can see why she's a basket case. That poor little kid."

"She's not a basket case. She's too damn controlled. She won't let go. We've both been there, Nate. She's afraid that if she does, she'll shatter and never find all the pieces again."

"Yeah, I was like that after Afghanistan, but I never—"

"Brandon." Monty was at the door. His expression

intent, his eyes glittering. "Come in here. Sam and I want to go over that last proxy again with you. He believes we've got something. He thinks it might have led us down the right road."

CHAPTER

15

She was ready.

Rachel looked down at her hands. Very nice. Soft, pink, nails that looked capable but ladylike.

Oh, yes, she'd made certain they'd be more than capable. And the special coating she'd put beneath those nails would definitely do what she demanded of it.

With absolutely no way to detect its presence.

It was probably too early, but if she was careful, it would do. And if she wasn't careful, then she wouldn't live to worry about it.

She replaced the empty vial in the case and set the case back in the closet.

Her phone rang as she came back into the room.

She tensed. It could be Catherine. It didn't have to be Huber.

But she had been expecting a contact from Huber

since she'd received the email from Nemesis. He wouldn't let a personal triumph on that scale get by without indulging in a fit of malicious gloating.

The phone rang again.

Pick up the call.

"Hello, Huber, I've been expecting you. You're so very predictable."

"Then you realize what that little girl has in store for her when she gets here. I wanted to make sure that I had her by the time I started my grand celebration." His voice was silky soft. "Because that would assure that I also had you, Rachel. Maria is so young, far younger than you were at Sazkar Prison."

Don't let him know Maria means anything to her. It would be a weapon. "I barely remember her. She was just a patient."

"I've had reports that tell me differently."

"People lie to you. They know you're not very bright."

Silence. "You're going to pay for every one of those insults. Or perhaps I'll allow little Maria to share. Yes, that seems only fair."

Her hand tightened on the phone. "I barely remember her," she repeated.

"You will. Suppose I send photos and videos to you at every stage of torture I put her through until you admit that you recall everything about her. I do prefer reality, but that can come later."

She couldn't help herself. "She's only a kid. Does it make you feel big and strong to do that to a child?"

"Yes, power is power. It doesn't matter as long as it

exists and I can see it. I'll be able to see it so clearly when I have you here with me. It's up to you if I'll see it when I have Maria."

"Are you saying you'll release her if I turn myself over to you?"

"I might be persuaded. I don't have a good deal of time to convince you to step into my parlor before day after tomorrow. You're the one I really want."

"You wouldn't sacrifice yourself. Why do you think I would?"

"Because Kraus believes you will. I'm reluctant to admit it, but he's very seldom wrong."

"He is this time."

"Then he'll suffer for it. I've told him that I don't allow incompetence. But I'll take the time and effort to make certain he has the chance to prove he's right to me. Do you remember the first night that you were raped?"

She tensed. "No, it didn't mean that much to me."

"But Maria is younger, the pain will be greater. I'm already planning that night."

Eight years old. She wanted to *kill* him. Only eight years old.

"You're not speaking." His voice was filled with malice. "It seems Kraus was right."

"You're boring me."

"That will end soon. I'll call you again when I have her standing before me. She's left Guyana now and is on her way to me. It shouldn't be that long before my men deliver her to me. I think that discussion will prove much more interesting."

He cut the connection.

Her chest was so tight, she could scarcely breathe. She was hot and shaking.

Anger . . . and fear.

Huber would do it. She knew he would do what he threatened to little Maria Perez. There wasn't any evil too great for him.

And she also knew she could never permit it to happen.

She went to the French doors and opened them to let in the cool night air.

That was a little better. She moved a few steps out onto the veranda. Now she was able to catch her breath, and she didn't feel as hot and feverish.

"Rachel!" Brandon was at the bedroom door. "Where are you? I need to—" Then he saw her standing on the veranda. He crossed the room in three strides. His voice was crisp, curt, but threaded with underlying excitement. "I have to talk to you. It's not status quo any longer. Things are breaking and changing. Something is—" He frowned, squinting to see her in the darkness. "What are you doing out here?"

She wasn't ready to go into that nightmare call with him yet. "It was cooler." She hadn't been mistaken. He *was* excited. Let it be about something good. She had to give herself time before she could face anything terrible after Huber. "What's breaking and changing?"

"We've identified the IP address."

She went still. "You're certain?"

"I wouldn't be here if I wasn't. We checked and double-checked, and Sam Zackoff confirmed it."

Hope. But she was afraid to hope for too much. "And can you find him now?"

"We're working on it." His hands grasped her shoulders. "But it's going to be a yes, Rachel. All we need is a little more time. And once we get hold of Nemesis, I guarantee that I'll find Huber for you. Now that he's in Red Star's camp, he'll have to know where Huber's compound is located." He stared down into her eyes. "And Nemesis will tell me anything I want to know. I swear it."

She believed him. But that didn't nearly solve all the problems. "I don't know how much time we have. I don't know how much time Huber will give me." She was trying to figure out what this might mean to Maria. "Maybe if I can manage to stall him. But he's going to have Maria very soon." She moistened her lips. "He told me so."

He stiffened. "What?"

"He was very pleased with himself." She was starting to shake again and took a moment to control herself. "And he would like to hurt me through Maria as well as the punishment he's already planned. I'm sure you can imagine what he has in mind."

"Yes." He cursed low and vehemently. "And I can imagine what you have in mind." Then he turned on his heel and strode toward the bedroom door. "Forget it. Because we're going to find Nemesis before Huber has a chance to touch either one of you." He stopped at the doorway to look back at her. "Oh, and Catherine called me and told me that she'd be here in an hour. Only now it's only thirty minutes. She's bringing company. Richard Cameron." His lips twisted. "She's sure we're going to bond with him. It seems that she thinks that it's necessary since they just found Fasrain shot to death in a motel in Oakland."

"What?" Her eyes widened. "Why didn't you tell me?"

"I was going to get around to it. First things first. It was more important that I let you know that we have a chance of getting our hands on Huber by way of Nemesis. At least that was more important to me." He met her eyes across the room. "What about you, Rachel? Are you bound and determined to be a sacrifice on Maria's altar?"

"Not if I can help it," she said quietly. "That would mean Huber would win anyway. He's so evil, he wouldn't be able to keep himself from torturing and killing her." Her lips curled faintly. "By all means, let's find a way to go get Huber. Nate tells me there's no one better than you at doing what's necessary. But make certain any plan calls for Maria to get away alive." She added deliberately, "And be sure that you use every weapon you have in your arsenal. If you don't, I'll do it myself. Do you understand, Brandon?"

"You couldn't be more clear." The door slammed behind him.

She flinched as she went back into the bedroom. The status quo had indeed changed on several fronts, she thought. That last volley Brandon had hurled had been a complete surprise. She didn't know whether Fasrain's death would offer anything but confusion. She would have to trust Catherine and this Richard

Cameron to decipher what it meant since they had just come from the scene.

How many times had her father had to face this kind of double-dealing and vicious mayhem in his long career? But had there ever been terrified little girls used as pawns?

I know this is a fight that I have to win, but it's very, very hard, Daddy.

Richard Cameron was . . . unusual, Rachel thought as she watched him enter the living room. He emitted charisma and something infinitely more potent. She found she couldn't take her eyes off him. Did he have that same effect on Catherine?

Not visibly. But Catherine was able to hide her feelings in most cases. She was turning to Rachel after introducing him to Brandon. "This is Cameron, Rachel. You'll find he's totally trustworthy if he wants to be. And he's clever enough to make you think black is white if he doesn't." She looked challengingly at Cameron. "But he's promised me he'll be on his best behavior."

"Absolutely." His smile lit his face as he shook Rachel's hand. "Why shouldn't I be? I've been waiting a long time to meet you. Catherine thinks you're remarkable. I believe I'd agree with her."

Rachel suddenly felt as if she was wrapped in the softest velvet. Two minutes before, she had been almost somber, but she found herself smiling back at him. "It's Catherine who is remarkable."

"I know," he said softly. "That's why she's capable of attracting such interesting friends." He glanced back at Catherine. "Stop frowning. I'm only being civil." He turned toward Brandon as he came down the hall. "Jude Brandon?" He shook his hand. "Catherine trusts you, so I must. You don't have to obey the same rule. But you'll find that it will save time."

"That's a priority at the moment," Brandon said noncommittally. "So we might try it and see how far we get. Rachel will tell you I have to get back to the lab." He met Rachel's eyes. "I have my orders."

"Yes, you do. He and Monty found the IP address, Catherine. He's working on the trace."

"Good," Catherine said. "He didn't mention it to me."

"Recent development," Brandon said. "And you were having your own developments. So sit down and tell me what you think Fasrain's assassination will mean. You said you had theories."

"And they're still that status," Catherine said. "It made sense to me that Huber and Kraus wouldn't kill Fasrain without a backup. I think that Captain Van Deek isn't the hero everyone thinks he is and might be that backup. Of course, it could be one of his officers who was supposed to take over Fasrain's job. It just seemed that the least likely candidate would be the one Kraus would choose." She glanced at Cameron. "Cameron agreed it was a possible scenario, so he turned his bloodhounds on Van Deek and his entire crew. He got the first initial report just before we pulled into the driveway. The *Katrina* crew is coming up pristine. Van

Deek's guilt or innocence is more difficult to access just because there are so many things on the plus side that are getting in the way. His medals and heroics are definitely authentic, and he's well liked by his men and the owners of his ship. There was something a trifle shady about a few of his real-estate transactions in Kuwait but nothing that could be pinned down. There was a possibility it could have been purchased with drug money. We should know fairly soon if they're able to unearth any other dirt. Cameron thinks if there is any, it will be ambiguous and hard to prove without extensive investigation."

"Which means it will be hard as hell to get anyone to take action since he's a bona fide hero," Brandon said. "Claire?"

"Maybe," Catherine said. "Doubtful. I'll have to see what evidence we end up with." She shrugged. "I just wanted to fill you both in on the possibility that this is still the nightmare scenario Huber was originally threatening. Fasrain's death might not have any effect on it." She looked at Rachel. "It makes me sick just thinking about it. I have to be sure. I can't let this go even if I can't convince anyone that Van Deek could be crooked. I'll have to do something."

Rachel nodded. "Of course you can't. We'll have to find a way to stop it." Though right now it seemed to be an impossible task. All she could think about was Maria and finding a way to get her away from Huber. But if it was true that Van Deek was a conspirator, then they had to keep him from doing this horrible thing.

She just had to pull herself together and think how to do it.

"That goes without saying, Rachel." Cameron was suddenly on his feet, his gaze on her face. "But we're not here to toss the problem in your laps. As Catherine said, she just wanted to fill you in. No demands. We'll let you know when we hear something definite, then we'll work something out." He shrugged. "You appear to be a bit busy at the moment. Though I'd like to observe what you're doing with that trace, Brandon. Perhaps I could go back with you and talk to this Monty I've been hearing about. I promise I won't be in the way. You might find me useful." He didn't wait for a reply but turned to Catherine. "I'm sure you wouldn't mind waiting, would you? I know you and Rachel have things to talk about."

"Oh, do we?" Catherine's eyes were narrowed on his face. "You're probably right." She turned to Rachel. "I could use a cup of tea. Let's go to the kitchen, and I'll make us one." She said over her shoulder to Brandon, "Be careful. I've probably told him too much about Monty. Don't let him steal him."

"Maria?" Catherine was gazing at Rachel in hor-ror. "Dammit, when were you going to let me know about it? Were you just going to let me drive away from here when you have that hanging over you?"

"Perhaps," Rachel admitted. "I wasn't ready to talk about it yet. If your friend, Cameron, hadn't decided to send me off with you, I'd have taken more time to try to get some kind of plan together."

"That might not include me," she said flatly. "Do you think I don't see Huber has you backed in a corner?"

"What could you do? I'm responsible for what's going to happen to Maria. I'm the key to whether she lives or dies. In the end, I'm the one who has to make the decision." She lifted her cup to her lips. "But I do have a chance. If we can force Nemesis to give us Huber's current location, we might have a chance of getting Maria out."

"And you surviving. We both know what your decision is going to be. That son of a bitch. It's no wonder Brandon is looking as if he's walking on IEDs." She reached over and took Rachel's hand. "Don't close me out. Do you *hear* me? Let me help."

Rachel just looked at her.

"Rachel."

"Should I pull you into trying to rescue Maria?" Her lips twisted. "Gee, maybe I could lose another person I care about. No, Catherine."

Catherine gazed at her in frustration, then pushed her chair back and got to her feet. "You can try to keep me out, and maybe you'll succeed. But I doubt it. I'll just deal with Brandon. He's going to be a lot easier to persuade to let everyone and anyone keep you alive." She headed for the door. "I could see that when he walked in tonight. I just didn't realize what the hell was wrong with him. Well now I do and it sucks. Good night, Rachel."

"Good night, my friend," Rachel said gently.

Catherine looked over her shoulder and Rachel could see the tears glittering in those wonderful dark eyes. "Oh, shit. Change your mind. Call me and tell me you've changed your mind." Then she was gone, and Rachel could feel the tears sting her own eyes.

She got to her feet, took the cups to the sink, and rinsed them. Then she turned off the light and headed for her bedroom.

She had refused Catherine's help, but she couldn't refuse Brandon's unless she wanted to give up all hope for Maria. Did she have the right to let him risk his life because she chose to risk her own? Yes, it had been his battle from the beginning but now everything seemed different. Everything was shifting, changing, glimpses of hope, then deepest despair.

She would go to bed and lie there waiting for Huber's call to tell her that he had Maria. Maybe some stroke of inspiration would let her know how she could save that little girl and take down Huber without Brandon.

Impossible?

It might be a very long night.

Cameron was leaning against the bumper of the Mercedes when Catherine came out of the house, slamming the front door behind her. He straightened and opened the passenger door for her. "Give me the keys. I'll drive."

"I'm fine." She gazed at his extended palm and

threw the key ring into it. "It doesn't matter. Have it your way." She got into the passenger seat. "You usually do anyway."

"You're not being fair," he said quietly as he got into the driver's seat. "You're upset and worried and you're taking it out on me. I'm willing to be your whipping boy, but you'll just feel guilty later. It's that's damn integrity you're plagued with."

"I'm fine," she repeated. But she leaned back and tried to relax the muscles in her neck and shoulders. She said jerkily, "I guess you knew Rachel was in trouble?"

He started the car. "She was broadcasting it loud and clear. I'm surprised you didn't pick up on it when we walked in the house." He smiled. "You were too on edge, making sure that I be accepted on your terms by Brandon and your Rachel. I was flattered that you thought it was so important."

"It wasn't that important, I just didn't want any problems."

"And that was why I thought you should talk to Rachel. It could have escalated."

"I don't know how. It was bad enough." She looked out at the sea. "Huber has a little girl that Rachel treated in Guyana, and you know how he's going to use her."

"Hostage."

"Yes, she's so afraid for Maria." Her hands clenched into fists. "And she thinks she's not going to let me help. It will only make it harder for me, Cameron."

"But you always overcome. You'll work it out." He

glanced at her. "The solution appears to be to simply find out where Huber is now and go get Maria. Do you agree?"

"Simply?"

"Maybe not quite simply. But you already have such phenomenal help. I was impressed by Jude Brandon. He's totally unique as a leader. And I'd be happy to have Monty come to me at some later date."

"Cameron."

He held up his hand. "Later. He won't become disillusioned enough to give up on this madness the world is whirling toward as long as he works for Brandon. I'm just saying that finding that IP address was remarkable. It was buried very deep. Linking it to the location should be easier than it was to find it. But I think I may have been able to help them with it. My hacking team ran into a similar problem two years ago in Rome, but we found the roadblock eventually. I suggested Brandon take the same direction."

"And you believe he'll do it?"

"I told you, he has excellent leadership skills. He wouldn't discount any valid suggestion without testing it." He smiled. "We came to an understanding. So let Brandon do his job and locate Huber's compound while we see if we can find out more about Van Deek. I have a contact in Kuwait who might have more info. We'll check back with Brandon later to see if my suggestion has paid off."

"Are you manipulating me, Cameron?"

"It would be my pleasure, but I know it's a hopeless task. But I also realize that you need to distract yourself while that exceptional mind of yours tries to sort out options." His smile lit his face. "No manipulation. Not even seduction. Though both are on the table. Anything you choose, Catherine." His smile ebbed, then disappeared. "Except to let me see how unhappy you were when you came out of that house tonight. We have to get rid of that option."

She couldn't look away from him. He might be expert at manipulation, but that wasn't what she was seeing. He had used that masterful ability he possessed to help in so many ways tonight. That tip he had given Brandon might even lead to finding the key to locating Huber. And on an entirely different level he had realized how important it was that she talk to Rachel tonight. She forced herself to tear her gaze away. "You're right, I wasn't being fair. You accomplished more than I did tonight. And I obviously can't do anything about Maria or Huber right now, so I'd better focus on something else." Lord, how could she focus on anything else when all she could think about was Rachel's face in the moment before she'd walked out of the house? Just *do* it. She took her computer out of her bag. "We need more proof to show Van Deek isn't Mr. Wonderful? I'll go into CIA records and see if there's anything that looks wonky about him in the last five years. Five years is a long time to stay pure as the driven snow. Kuwait, did you say? I might be able to dip into his bank records and any investments if I tap the right people. Do you want to give your contact a call and tell them to expect more information?"

"Rachel!"

Her eyes flew open to see Brandon silhouetted against the light of the doorway across the room. His legs were slightly parted, and she could see the tension in every muscle.

The sight of him jerked her wide-awake.

"What's wrong?" She sat bolt upright in bed, her heart pounding. "What happened? Catherine?"

"No." He was across the room and sitting beside her. "Catherine's fine as far as I know. Everything might be fine. It looks that way, but I can't be sure." He pulled her into his arms, and his voice was as low and as tense as the muscles beneath her cheek. "But we might have to work it just right to get what we need from it."

"You're not making sense." She lifted her head to look up at him. "What are you telling me?" Then it hit home to her. "The IP address. You traced it to an actual location?"

"Two hours ago. The rest of the time we were checking and double-checking. We had to be sure."

"And now you're certain?"

"Yes, we went back to the proxies that were used to throw us off base and studied them. Monty and Sam told me that the IP address was so cleverly constructed and convoluted that it could have been created by the Chinese. And after we got the IP address, the trace kept us going in circles. But Cameron said his group had a similar problem with a trace, and they found out how it was being blocked."

"Great." Her hands dug into his forearms. "Brandon, dammit, tell me later *how* you did it," she said impatiently. "Right now I want to know how we can get our hands on that bastard." Then she had another alarming thought. "Is there any way that he'd know that we've traced him?"

"Monty says it's doubtful."

"Doubtful? That's not good enough. What if he finds out and skips out on us?" She pushed away from him and was off the bed. "We've got to go get him *now*."

"Easy," Brandon said. "We're not taking anything for granted. That's why I woke you in the middle of the night." He grimaced. "But I would have done it anyway. I know how sick you were about Maria. It's about time we had a break."

"More than that," Rachel's voice was shaking with excitement. "Huber. Nemesis might lead us to Huber and Kraus." She whirled away. "We have to leave now. I'll get dressed."

"Wait."

"Wait?" She gazed at him impatiently over her shoulder. "You said doubtful and I won't—" She stopped as she saw his expression. "Why should we wait?"

"Because it's not going to be that easy, Rachel." He got to his feet and came toward her. "The situation could become complicated. You have to be prepared for it."

"Complicated?" She was gazing up at him in bewilderment. That first tense excitement was gone from his expression, replaced by wariness. "Of course I'm prepared for complications. All hell could break loose when we corner him."

"That's not what I mean."

"Then tell me what you mean." She was suddenly frightened. "Brandon?"

HYATT HOTEL
4:25 A.M.

"This better be worth you getting me up in the middle of the night, Rachel," Claire said as she threw open the door of her suite. "You said you had news that might lead to catching that son of a bitch, Huber. That's the only reason I let you come. I need a confirmation that the threat is over. Catherine must have told you that Fasrain was found dead last night."

"She told me." Rachel pushed her aside and slammed the door behind her. "Though she's not sure that's going to be the end of it. What do you think?"

"I believe we'll have to be extremely careful, but it could be that Huber's failed at last. I've yielded total control of the operation to Homeland Security to check it out." She tilted her head. "I'm surprised that Catherine or Brandon didn't come with you. They're both so protective. They appear to think that I'm a ruthless bitch out to use you when my only aim is to convince you to do your duty to your father and your country."

"I'm trying to do my duty to my father." She looked her in the eye. "But I didn't bring Catherine because she works under you and can get . . . combative."

Claire's lips twisted. "Tell me about it."

"And Brandon thought that we couldn't trust you with what he'd learned tonight. We had differing opinions, so I told him I needed to come alone." She shook her head. "He wasn't pleased."

"Brandon and I have never been totally in sync." She was studying Rachel's expression. The she smiled, and added, "I'm glad you realize that you have to make up your own mind. I know how persuasive he can be." She crossed to the bar across the room. "Would you like a glass of wine?"

"No thank you."

"I didn't think so." She poured herself a glass. "I imagine it's probably something like not dining in the house of the enemy." She took a sip of wine. "Because you do regard me as the enemy, don't you?" She turned to face her. "Out with it, Rachel. You'd never make an operative, you're far too transparent."

"I didn't think I'd be able to fool you. All I wanted to do was get inside the room." She took a step closer. "Because I needed to know what was true or false." She said coldly, "Yes, I know you're Nemesis. So don't think you can lie about it."

"I wasn't about to try," Claire said. "It was always a risk I ran in this world of high tech. Though I did believe I had a chance of getting away with it. I had a few wild cards buried in those programs. I always have wild cards, Rachel." She took another sip of wine. "It's something Venable never learned in his entire career. I always had to lead him down the right path."

"Until you killed him?"

"I *didn't* kill him. Look, he knew I was Nemesis and working undercover to tap Huber's man, Kraus, for information. But he was the only one at Langley who knew. Huber has bribes out everywhere. If there was a leak, I could have ended up dead."

"Was there a leak? Did you have to save yourself by staking him out for Huber?"

"Not that either."

"He was supposed to be meeting with Nemesis when he was shot," she said skeptically.

"I thought I'd found Huber's compound in Canada. It turned out to be a trap . . . for me. I had to get out fast, so my cover wouldn't be blown. It was too late to warn Venable."

"So he died."

"Yes, he died," she said steadily. "People die. He was willing to take the chance. All he cared about was taking down Huber. And he didn't try very hard to persuade me not to try that Nemesis gambit. He'd lost his wife and son. He'd lost you. Since he knew I was running the risk purely for monetary and political advantage, he thought that it was only fair that I put my neck on the line." She put her wineglass down on the bar. "Now I suggest you take out the gun that you're clutching in your right-hand pocket. I imagine that was Brandon's idea?"

"No, it was mine." Rachel pulled the .38 out of her pocket and aimed it at Claire. "Because I knew the only way Brandon was going to let me come in here alone was if I had a weapon. He fought me tooth and nail. But I *had* to see you so that I could know for myself who and what you are. We might need you." She gestured with the .38. "You're probably as good as Catherine at hand-to-hand, but anyone can point a gun."

"But not everyone can pull the trigger. You don't impress me as being very intimidating. Whipping up a little poison cocktail is different than blowing a hole in someone." She smiled. "You're soft, Rachel."

"Yes, unless it comes down to getting rid of garbage. I'll have no problem with that. *Look* at me." Her hand tightened on the gun. "The only reason I'm here is that I believe we can make use of you to save Maria Perez. You remember Maria. You're the one who sent me the photo of her."

"Yes, I did," she said coolly. "Pretty child. I was a little upset to be caught in the middle of that squeeze game. I was hoping you might manage to find a way to wriggle out of it."

"But not if it meant your stepping in and helping?"

"No, I've been hunting Red Star for too long to give them up when I'm this close. As I said, people die." She added, "A child's death is sad, but if it saves hundreds, maybe thousands of lives that Huber might take in the future, one gets a different perspective."

"Only someone like you. You admitted that your hunt for Red Star was motivated purely by ambition. Don't tell me that you believe sacrificing Maria is only for the greater good."

She shrugged. "Then think what you will. You'd be amazed to know how many of my superiors at Langley would agree with me. It's all about numbers and percentages."

"My father wouldn't agree."

"Maybe not. Venable was always soft when it came to children. But don't be too sure. We've spent months and months trying to find Huber's compound with no luck. If he knew this Maria was the key to zeroing in on Huber, then he might have been tempted. Just as I was." She shrugged. "But it was all for *nothing*, dammit."

Rachel felt a jolt of shock. "What are you talking about? You *have* to know where that compound is located. Maybe not before, but you're working directly with Red Star now."

"Sorry to disappoint you." She stared her directly in the eye. "Kraus has to be one of the most secretive bastards on the planet. Hell, he plays his own game even with Huber. He doesn't want me near him. And he only told me what he had to tell me. I don't *know*, Rachel."

She was telling the truth. Rachel's heart plunged as she realized that all her hopes had been for nothing. No location. No way to find Maria. Rachel wished desperately she could believe Claire was lying. Maria . . .

Claire could see it and she lifted one shoulder in a half shrug. "I thought by doing a switch that I'd finally gain Kraus's trust and be able to find out more. But he isn't about to give up any info he doesn't have to. He wants to maintain total control. I've been wondering lately if he's getting ready to launch a takeover of Red Star." She frowned. "Because it's not as if I haven't shown him how valuable I could be. He was grateful enough that he could impress Huber with how clever he was by telling him that little snippet I gave him."

Telling him that little snippet I gave him . . .

Another shock as Rachel realized what that "snippet" must have been. "You told him that it was my father and I who were responsible for killing Conrad Huber," she said slowly.

She nodded. "Kraus knew I worked for the CIA. I had to give him something substantial to make him believe I was on the take. It was essential."

"Essential," Rachel repeated. "Yes, I could see how that would make him believe that you'd turned your back on my father and Langley. It was a total betrayal." She moistened her lips. "But my father told me he didn't tell anyone about it. How did you know?"

"He had tests run at the lab at Langley to check the efficacy of the poison. I was curious, and I did a little snooping. There might have been something that would have been useful to me."

"But Conrad's death didn't prove to be the windfall Langley hoped it would," Rachel said. "So you didn't claim any connection with it. Though it did prove useful when you needed to prove your worth to Kraus years later."

"I was getting close to earning Kraus's trust. I thought it might seal the deal. And he might have found out about Venable anyway." She shook her head at Rachel's expression. "I did send an anonymous warning to Venable to tell him that there was a bounty on his head."

"How kind," Rachel said. "I'm certain he would have been grateful if he'd lived to know how generous you were."

"You're still acting as if I killed Venable," she said impatiently. "I told you that wasn't true. He knew how dangerous it was to slip that poison to Conrad Huber. He did it anyway." She added sharply, "And I risked my own life trying to locate Huber's compound near Calgary. That was one battle we fought together."

"But it was a battle you lost. You were wrong."

"I told you that bastard Kraus never gives up information. He's always been one step ahead of me."

But Rachel had desperately hoped that this time Claire could lead them to Huber. "You're certain that Kraus didn't tell you anything, not even a hint?"

"Do you think I'm lying? I always knew Huber was my ace in the hole. I've worked years trying to bring Red Star down." Her eyes were blazing in her pale face. "It would make capturing Bin Laden look like kindergarten play. I could write my own ticket as far as money and prestige is concerned. Someday, they'll be making movies about me."

"And will there be a subplot about San Kabara Island?" Rachel asked bitterly.

"Only that I saw that you got the information that could have stopped it from happening," Claire said through set teeth. "You can't deny that I let you persuade me into doing that. I knew it was important. If I hadn't, then everything I'd worked for would have gone down the drain. It would be the difference between being a hero someone might elect as president and a scumbag on everyone's hit list. I told you *all* I knew." She said slowly and precisely, "Everything. I told you Kraus didn't trust anyone."

Again, Rachel believed her. She was beginning to think that she could read Claire. She might be completely immoral and self-absorbed, but she was driven by an intense ambition that would not be satisfied until she reached the top of the ladder. That reference to the presidential office might not have been without significance. "Then you're going down the wrong path if you think the entire world is going to embrace anyone who kidnaps and eventually murders a child."

"I never said I'd do that. I was just trying to make you see that there are more ways than one to look at things." She smiled slightly. "Actually, I wasn't planning on using the kid if I could avoid it. That was entirely Kraus. There are far too many wishy-washy people like you around to condemn me."

"Yes, you do want to avoid people like me, Claire."

She nodded. "I always thought you were the way to go instead. Idealistic and aching to right wrongs done to Venable and yourself. Not to mention the possibility of saving the city and perhaps much more. All I needed was to persuade you to turn yourself over to Huber, then track him to his compound when he sends a plane for you. I'd have the drone ready. *And kaboom.*" She shrugged. "But you had Catherine and Brandon standing over you with bared swords. I was having a good deal of trouble getting close to you. Pity. Huber does want you so desperately."

"Yes, he does," she said. "And I want him."

Claire leaned toward her. "And you want that little girl." Her words were soft and coaxingly persuasive. "You know you're never going to get her unless you go after her. I can make it work, Rachel. Listen to me. I've already made arrangements with Andrews Air Force Base to zero in on the plane Huber sends for you. No one is more high-tech when it comes to aircraft tracking. Then I'll have a SEAL team ready to follow you and help once you're in the compound." Her eyes were glowing, and her voice was almost mesmerizing. "Take a chance on snatching your Maria away from him, and I promise he'll never live through the firepower I rain down on him. I have the power and authority and the weapons. I'll make it happen. No more Red Star."

"And maybe no more Maria Perez," Rachel said grimly. "How could I ever get her out in time? You might have had a chance of convincing me if you'd known where that compound was located."

"If I'd known that, there would no longer be a Red Star compound," Claire said. "And the mayor of San Francisco would be giving me the keys to this fine city." She glanced at the gun in Rachel's hand. "Now will you put that away? We've come to an understanding, haven't we? You know exactly how far I'll go to get what I want, and I have the power and influence to protect me every step of the way." She added coolly,

"Because what I want is what most reasonable people in this world want. Including the president of the United States. To get rid of Red Star. Unless I screw up in some wildly improbable fashion, taking what I want will make me a superstar. And I'll use you any way I can to make that happen. But it's not going to be by shooting you, that would be counterproductive." She nodded at the bar she was standing beside. "Though there is a Beretta tucked behind that ice bucket which would be easy enough to reach. I know the game's changed again, and I'll have to accommodate it. So I'll give you and Brandon a little time to work out a solution that I hope will give me what I want." She regretfully shook her head. "You're so very soft, Rachel. If you get desperate enough, you might still take my offer. A slim chance is better than none."

"Don't count on it." She slipped the gun back in her jacket pocket and turned toward the door. "And we'll be the ones who will use you, Claire. You know how much Brandon loves control. When we find that solution, you'll obey orders or sit it out and let someone else take the credit for bringing down Red Star."

She slammed the door behind her.

CHAPTER

16

Satisfied?" **Brandon straightened away from** the wall by the elevator where he'd been waiting. "I wasn't." His expression was grim as he held up his phone. "Particularly when she mentioned the Beretta behind the ice bucket."

"I thought she might have a weapon," she said jerkily as she punched the DOWN button. "I didn't think she'd use it."

"But you couldn't be sure," he said tightly. "We couldn't be sure of anything except we couldn't trust her. Just as you were sure you couldn't trust me to go in that room with you. I'm not going to forget that, Rachel."

"I know you won't." And she'd known he wouldn't understand. She still tried to explain. "You and Catherine stride into situations like this and make them your own. It's your world. You're clever and tough, and you'd instantly dominate and try to get your own way." She entered the elevator and pressed LOBBY. "And you might do it since you're so good. But it might not be my way, Brandon." She didn't look at him. "And it has to be my way. I'm the one who's responsible whether Maria lives or dies." She swallowed. "And whether I cause anyone else to live or die. So I had to be one-on-one with Claire, so I'd know what I had to face. I believe I know her now."

"But you'll do the same thing again."

"Yes." She looked him in the eyes. "I'll listen to your suggestions, I'll even let you risk your life, but the decision will be mine. I can't let you shelter me. If you can't deal with that, walk away from me, Brandon."

Anger. Frustration. Despair. "Son of a *bitch*." Then his smile was both reckless and bitter. "Claire called you soft. No way, Rachel." He took her arm as the elevator doors opened and he guided her out through the lobby. "Did you manage to plant the two bugs I gave you in her suite?"

"On the chest beside the door. When I whirled and made my dramatic exit. You said I only had to touch the wood."

"At least you took that suggestion."

"I told you I would. I know that we can't trust her." She hesitated. "But I think she'll do what she said about giving us a little time. She does believe I'm soft and might go along with her suicide mission. She probably wants to let me think about it . . . after I talk to Huber." They were outside the hotel, and the valet was running to get their car. "Otherwise, we might expect more aggressive action from her. She was practically salivating at the thought of those drones destroying Red Star's compound." She shivered. "She wants it, and she'll go after it. I have to make sure that Maria isn't anywhere near it if she manages to find out where it is. Because Claire isn't going to care who else she kills if she gets Huber."

"Maybe you did learn something about Claire tonight." Brandon's lips twisted. "And I'd welcome her passion for Huber's blood if we could find a way to channel it. But I noticed she said she'd relinquished all authority to Homeland to investigate what Fasrain's death meant in the scheme of things. She's devoting all her attention toward capturing Huber and doesn't want to be distracted by trivial matters like massive environmental destruction."

"It doesn't surprise me." The valet had opened the passenger door, and she slipped into the seat. "You heard her, she regards Red Star as the crowning achievement on the top of the tree. No matter what happens, she can either claim victory or revenge if she can get her hands . . . or her drone . . . on Huber."

Huber.

She watched the first violet streaks of dawn brightening the sky as Brandon drove out of the hotel driveway. Dawn. Tomorrow was the twenty-fifth. The next dawn would herald what Huber thought of as his grand day of reckoning.

And it was coming too soon, she thought in panic. Claire had crushed her hope that they'd be able to locate Red Star's compound before she'd have to go after Maria. If she had to go in blind, then it would be an identical scenario to the one Claire had described. She might have to prepare herself for it.

"The SEALs are terrific at extraction, aren't they?"

"Shut up, Rachel." Brandon didn't look at her. "I knew the minute Claire mentioned her little plan that you'd be applying it to Maria. Yes, the SEALs are great, and so are my guys, but you don't have to worry about extraction if you're not being held prisoner. The goal is to make sure you're not in that position."

"Brandon."

"Don't give me that speech again," he said roughly. "I heard you the first time." His hands clenched on the steering wheel. "When you went to your room last night, you said you were going to go over those letters that Phillip found in the mud beside Blanca's body. Did you do it?"

He was reaching out for miracles, she thought. He was afraid for her and trying to find some way to keep her away from Huber. She had nearly forgotten those letters in the excitement and eagerness generated by the discovery that Nemesis was Claire Warren.

"No, I found I got caught up in something else I had to do." *A vial of poison glittering in the dimness of the container.* "And I know you didn't have time to do anything but check on Nemesis."

He nodded. "But we have time now. We'll go back and see what we can do. Like your friend Phillip said, it doesn't seem right to ignore what might be a message. It's a hell of a lot better than worrying about how efficient the SEALs might be in a mythical situation."

Not mythical, but he was right to draw her away from that less-than-hopeful solution. "Absolutely." She was fumbling in her handbag for her notebook. "Sorry. I'll take a look at it again. I almost forgot about it. It got lost somewhere along the way." Because there had been other, more concrete, solutions that seemed to be more promising. Now those solutions had faded away. "And I guess I've just been waiting to hear from Huber that he has Maria. The bastard promised me he'd let me know, and I've been worrying he might decide to do something to—"

"You're *apologizing*? Look, I'm feeling homicidal enough." He shot her a glance that was pure blue lightning. "Don't apologize for anything. Just help me find a way to get to Huber and Kraus that you'll give your blessing."

So much fury and frustration and pain in those words. She looked away from him and down at her pad. "Anything that keeps Maria alive."

Think.

Concentrate.

Don't let this be the end.

Find some other way.

She wrote down the first letter that Phillip had given her over the phone.

U . . .

* * *

The call came from Max Huber as they were pull-ing up the driveway of the house.

Brandon could feel her go tense in the seat beside him as the phone rang. He didn't say anything but pulled to a stop and turned off the engine.

She took a deep breath and pressed the access. "Hello, Huber. It took you long enough. Did you lose Maria along the way?"

"No, I just had to sure that no immigration officials got into their heads to stop me. She's a very valuable cargo. Do you want to talk to her?"

"Do you want me to talk to her?"

"Oh, yes," he said softly. "I've been waiting for it. But you might not understand her, she keeps crying. Imagine that. And we've hardly started."

"Really?" She tried to keep her voice without expression. "What have you been doing to her?"

"Just a few slaps to keep her in line. I haven't broken anything yet. I'm saving that for when I have you as an audience. She's not nearly as tough as you were at Sazkar. I heard wonderful reports about that first month you were there."

"I was fifteen. She's only eight. It makes a difference."

"Maybe she'll get better with experience. She'll have the opportunity for a good deal of that soon. I believe she's prettier than you, but then, I never liked redheads. But my men won't care. There's something exciting about taking a child . . . Here she is. Now do give her words of comfort. Even if it's lies."

"He lied, Dr. Rachel. I'm not crying." Maria's voice

was throaty and shaking, but she was clearly trying to hold herself together. "But those men hit my mama, and they said they killed her. Did they tell the truth?"

"She's hurt badly, and she can't talk, but she's not dead. She'd want you to be strong. She always told me how strong you are, Maria."

"I don't feel strong." Her voice had dropped to a whisper. "I'm scared. They're bad men. They hurt me."

"Very bad." What could she say to her? What had she learned? "But you only have to be brave one minute at a time. Then you just go away to some place deep inside and don't come out until it's over. Can you do that? It's what your mama would want for you."

"I'll try, Dr. Rachel. Can you come and get me?"

She did not answer. "Just one minute at a time, Maria. That will help you. I'm thinking about you and your mama."

"But that last answer was unsatisfactory for both of us, Rachel." Huber was suddenly back on the line. "I didn't want you to make her stronger. I'll only have to break her down again. And aren't you going to fly to her rescue? That's what this is all about, you know."

"You're asking me to sacrifice my own life for Maria's. Would you do that? I don't think so."

"But you're a bleeding heart. And you know what she'll have to go through. I believe you'll come around to my way of thinking. Maybe I'll decide to make it quick for you this time."

"And pigs can fly. The mere reason that I do know would make me never go through that again. I'm not that much of a bleeding heart. I learned my lesson."

"Is that why you fly around with all those doctors and act like some kind of saint? I think I've got you, Rachel." His voice lowered to a guttural hiss. "Make a decision. It's your fault that you decided to kill my father. This little girl wouldn't have been involved if you hadn't done that. Are you going to let her pay for your crime against my father? I don't believe you could take that kind of guilt, Mother Teresa."

"First, I'm a murderer, then I'm a saint? Make up your mind."

"No, *you* make up your mind." His voice was suddenly harsh with anger. "This is bullshit. I'm tired of this game. I'm the one who gives the orders. I'll have you regardless of what you do, and it will be my way. I'll give you until nine tonight to meet my helicopter pilot and let him bring you here to me. I'd like to have you even sooner, but you'll still be with me for the grand celebration. But I've decided that I won't start on the little girl before I have you here with me. I want you to *see* what I'm going to do to her. I'll start with breaking fingers, then go on to more interesting parts of the body. You'll both die, Rachel, and it will be terrible because you also forced me to take her as well." He paused. "Are you listening? You killed a great man. Now you'll give your life in return."

"I killed a beast. And I would have killed you, too, if I'd had the opportunity."

"I'm sure you'll still try, you little viper. Nine, Rachel."

He pressed the disconnect.

She had to sit very still and do as she'd told Maria. Go deep inside and don't come out for a moment.

"Rachel."

She shook her head. "Not . . . yet."

He sat there quietly. Not moving.

Two minutes passed, then she was able to function again. "Thank you." She drew a deep breath. "It's very . . . difficult. He brings back too much. I can't let him see it, or he'd run right over me."

"I guarantee you didn't let him run over you today," he said quietly.

"But I didn't get what I needed from him. I was trying to make sure that he thought he had to give me time because I was afraid and reluctant. I've got to buy as much time as I can." She shrugged helplessly. "Because it's running out, isn't it? We've got to fight for every minute. Maybe I'll think of something else to do, but it's so hard, Brandon. He thinks he has the upper hand. He knows what they did to me. He'd know how afraid I'd be. But I hoped I'd be able to stall him longer than nine tonight." She opened the car door and jumped out. "But I didn't, so we'd better get busy. We've exhausted most of our options. Lord, I was hoping that Claire would be able to give us that Red Star location."

"I know you were." He took a step toward her. "Rachel, I can't let you—"

"Yes, you can. If it has to be done. But don't think about it. We still have some time." She had to get away from him, or she might break. She turned and headed for the kitchen. "Will you tell Monty that it might be a good idea for him to go back to monitor those bugs I put in Claire's room? I think she's biding her time, but there's no telling what she'll do."

"I was going to do that anyway."

"Of course you were." She tried to smile. "Your world, Brandon. What was I thinking?"

"Doing a damn good job of making it your world," he said roughly. "I just wish you'd let me offer a little more support." He turned and disappeared into the library.

She didn't feel as if she was doing a very good job, she thought wearily. She wasn't sure that Blanca would think so either. She couldn't even find her daughter, much less rescue her.

And so little time to do either.

Nine tonight.

Thirteen hours . . .

HYATT HOTEL

Catherine turned to Cameron when she pressed the disconnect after talking to Brandon. "All hell's breaking loose," she said shakily. "I'm tempted to let you whisk Rachel away until this is all over. There's a good chance she'll end up dead."

"Say it and it will be done," he said simply. "But I can't save the child without a definite location. Do you want to risk Rachel's hating you? It would be better if we could find another road. Do you believe Claire

Warren was telling the truth about not knowing where his compound is?"

"If Rachel thought it was the truth," she said. "She's very smart, Cameron. This is terribly important to her. She probably gauged Claire very well." She frowned. "And I can see Claire being totally absorbed with Max Huber. It's no wonder she wasn't really interested in a potential disaster if she could slip by it and keep her skirts clean. She'd already earned big points with her work at San Kabara. Now she's free to concentrate on getting Red Star." She glanced soberly at him. "Those last reports on Van Deek were pretty ambiguous, weren't they?"

"It's what we expected. He's very clever. But there were a few omissions and sidesteps in his recent schedule that I'm interested in exploring."

"How?"

"Why, I'll just ask him."

She gazed at him in surprise. She knew exactly what that kind of questioning entailed. It started off with mesmerizing persuasiveness and usually ended with complete domination. "But you've always told me that you prefer not to use that kind of interrogation."

He smiled. "I make exceptions when it comes to people who destroy oceans. They upset me."

"And can you ask those questions before the *Katrina* gets in the Port of Oakland harbor?"

"If we decide it should happen." He looked down at his notes. "We have time. Right now, the *Katrina* is delivering oil near Santa Barbara. Later today, it will move up to San Luis Obispo for another delivery before it sets out for Oakland for the final delivery."

"Final delivery," Catherine repeated. "It sounds so . . . ominous. There has to be a way to stop it."

"Anything is possible," Cameron said. "But I wouldn't give odds if we rely on your fine organization to do it. It's not that they're not efficient, they just don't go all the way."

"I beg to differ."

He smiled. "There would be a few operatives who would remember Van Deek's medals and his fine record. It would get in the way. They'd ask questions instead of taking action."

"So did we."

"But we're willing to let suspicion be our guide." He tilted his head. "You're not going to let me take Rachel, are you?"

"I don't know."

"I do." He reached over and touched her hand. "So if you won't let me take Rachel, why not let me take the *Katrina Notalo*."

"Just like that?"

"There will be a measure of difficulty. I'll not only have to secure the ship, but I'll have to make certain that Van Deek is in Huber's pay before I turn him over to Homeland Security. Or kill him if that's what you need. You're a stickler for details like that. And it will have to be done quietly and discreetly."

"Piece of cake."

"Easier than solving Rachel's problem. But if it robs Huber of a victory, then it might make you happier."

His brows rose. "So could I please take the *Katrina Notalo*? I promise to make it satisfactory for you." His smile was intimate and full of mischief. "Have I ever failed you in that regard? I do deliver, Catherine."

She stared at him helplessly. He meant it. And she knew enough about his background to know that he might be able to do it. "Piracy on the high seas, Cameron?"

"It does have a definite ring to it. However, an oil tanker lacks a certain romanticism. But it's all how it goes down."

"Stop joking."

His smile disappeared. "As you like, I prefer humor when watching you try to save the world from its own barbarism; otherwise, I find it hurts me. Because someday it will hurt you." He added succinctly, "The options are these, I can arrange to have your friend, Rachel, taken and I can guarantee she will live. The child will probably die after extreme torture. I probably would not have time to locate the compound and get a force inside in time to rescue her if there's no Rachel as a distraction. Or I can give you the supertanker, and if Van Deek is crooked, as we think, I can stop Huber from destroying the California coastline. It will stave off any destruction until Huber gets a new plan in place. Tell me what you want me to do."

She swallowed to ease the tightness of her throat. "Not great options."

"They never are," he said wearily. "It's the world you live in. If you like, I'll promise to go after Huber later when I can put full force behind it. But you'll still remember that child, and so will Rachel. It will haunt you."

And how many painful decisions haunted Cameron, who made them every day, she wondered. "It already does." She jumped to her feet. "And there has to be something that I can do." She headed for the door. "I'm going down to talk to Claire. Maybe Rachel didn't do as good a job as I would at questioning her. She doesn't have the experience and—"

"You said she was very smart," Cameron said quietly.

"Don't throw my words back at me."

"And you're just looking for a way out. Fine, do you want me to come with you?"

"No! You've been avoiding the CIA since I've known you, and Claire is the last person you should be around. She's brilliant, ambitious, and completely immoral. You don't want more trouble."

"Are you trying to protect me? I'm touched you consider my problems your trouble. But I might be helpful."

"I don't need all that mind-control crap. I'll know if she's telling me the truth." She shut the door and headed for the elevator. That instinctive urge to protect Cameron had come out of nowhere. No one needed less protection than Richard Cameron. It didn't matter. In this battle, they were on the same side, and she wouldn't let him be hurt or taken down. Claire was a cold and formidable opponent, and Catherine didn't choose to let him even be on her radar.

And that coldness was clearly visible when Claire

opened her door a few minutes later. Every silky dark
strand of hair was in place, and her eyes were cool and
amused. "You're a little late. I expected you to escort
your little friend when she found it necessary to confront me. She told me that since I was your superior,
she didn't want you to be combative with me." She
smiled faintly. "Are you here to express your indigna-
tion that I didn't tell you I was working undercover as
Nemesis? But you know how it works in the Company.
That particular revelation would have been way above
your pay grade."

"I know how it works." She entered the room and
turned to face her. "And it didn't really surprise me.
Nemesis had a lot of your double-dealing characteris-
tics. Perhaps also a few of your insecurities and weaknesses."

She stiffened. "I have no weaknesses."

"But you don't deny the double-dealing." She made
an impatient gesture. "And I'm not there to waste my
time telling you what I think about you. I only have a
few questions. You'll answer, and I'll be out of here."

"Perhaps."

"One, was it true that you don't have any idea where
Huber's compound is located?"

She frowned. "Don't be ridiculous. I don't waste
time, Catherine. I'd have destroyed Red Star if I knew.
I spent too much time studying everything about how
they operate, who they are, during those months I was
undercover."

"Two, do you have any knowledge that Van Deek
might be an accomplice of Huber?"

"No, I do not. As far as I know, he's the hero everyone thinks him. This is a little denigrating, Catherine."

"Unfortunate. You can live through it. What time is Huber's big celebration supposed to take place?"

"How do I know? I told Rachel the truth. Kraus seldom lets anything slip."

"Seldom. There was a faint flicker there."

She shrugged. "He just referred to it once as a new dawning when he was talking about it. Nothing else."

"But you're used to putting two and two together where he's concerned."

"It's Max Huber's daddy's giant celebration. It's a big deal to Huber. He'd want his glorious spectacle clearly visible to all and sundry. That would mean he'd probably schedule it during the day. Or maybe dawn? Kraus would like the idea of starting Conrad Huber's big day by giving a wake-up call to the entire West Coast. I'd say that it will be scheduled around dawn's early light. Just a guess, of course." She tilted her head. "Not that it will do you any good. When doesn't tell us where."

"No, it doesn't." But it was frustrating the hell out of her that Claire didn't know more. Claire was superintelligent and experienced. She should have picked up on something more. "Last question. Have you made your plans for turning Rachel over to Huber?"

"Why, I'm not going to have to do that." Claire smiled gently into Catherine's eyes. "We both know that Rachel is going to do that for me. I'm just waiting until she makes up her mind that it's the only thing to do."

Catherine wanted to strangle her. She turned on her heel before she did it. "What's the decision on whether to keep Van Deek out of the Port of Oakland harbor tomorrow?"

"I believe that Homeland Security has decided that's totally unnecessary. They've decided the threat is gone. Captain Deek even invited Homeland to come aboard and search his vessel to make sure that there's no problem. But you'll have to check with them."

"Because you've washed your hands of such an unimportant matter?"

"Exactly." She smiled. "I've moved on. You'll be glad that I can concentrate on coordinating any strike necessary once I locate Red Star. I've already set up a tentative drone strike with Langley. It will completely destroy Red Star's facility once we trace the location. All it will take is for me to make the call. And it might save Rachel and that poor child."

"Or blow them both to hell."

"That would be very sad. But Rachel is such a giving person, I'm certain she'd be ready for any sacrifice." She smiled. "But then, you know that already. Good day, Catherine."

Catherine slammed the door behind her.

Breathe deep and don't go back in and waste your time fighting with Claire, Catherine told herself. It was just anger and frustration, and she shouldn't let it matter this much. But it did matter, and she stood waiting for the elevator while she tried to clarify anything she'd learned from Claire.

It wasn't that much. She believed that Rachel had it

right and Claire was being as honest as possible for her. The only difference was that the time of the ship's explosion was to be early morning if Claire was right. Was there some way they could make it work for them? Grabbing at straws . . .

Well, wasn't that what she'd always done? Catherine had been born to nothing and made the world what she wanted. She wouldn't let that son of a bitch kill her friend or steal a precious heritage from her son or the children who came after him.

Think.

Plan.

Take it apart and find a way.

Grab at straws . . .

Straws . . .

She suddenly stiffened. Perhaps more than a straw.

She turned and strode back down the corridor. The next moment, she was once more knocking on Claire's door.

"Really, Catherine?" Claire said as she opened the door. "This is no longer amusing. It verges on harassment."

"I won't keep you long. It just occurred to me that you could know more than you said."

"I did not lie to you."

"I just want to know why you chose the Calgary location when you went after Huber the last time."

"Everything pointed to it. Satellites showed activity in the area."

"Is that all? But you just said that you'd studied Red Star in depth. Surely you wouldn't have risked your neck without something more than a single source."

She shrugged. "Call it a hunch. It was the kind of landscape Huber liked. He spent a lot of time in Germany with his father and Kraus when he was a child. That scenery around the Calgary compound might have come out of a tourist book about the Black Forest. Even the small towns around the main house and compound reminded me of Red Star."

"Why?"

She made a face. "Well, one of them was named Eagles Prey. What's Red Star's symbol? A black eagle carrying a bloody star in its talons. Very much like Hitler's eagle carrying the swastika. Huber and Kraus do like their symbols. I've seen them use them in other places and situations." She shrugged. "And I might have caught them, dammit. There were signs that they'd occupied that compound earlier in the year. I figure it was just bad luck I was wrong that time."

"I'm sure Venable would agree that it was bad luck for him." Catherine turned and walked away.

She was on the phone with Rachel by the time she reached the elevator. "Look for eagles," she said curtly. "Eagles and anything else reminiscent of Hitler's Germany. Claire said that Huber and Kraus love their symbols. That was the reason she thought that Calgary might be the place. It fit the image."

"And you think that she might be right? She evidently wasn't right about Calgary."

"I don't know if she's right. I only know she's brilliant, and she knows Kraus better than anyone else.

She has good instincts, and some of that might also have a part in it. We don't have much choice, do we?"

"No. I'll get back to you. Eagles . . ."

Catherine pressed the disconnect.

Blind alley? Maybe. But she didn't know if she could tolerate the other options that Cameron had given her. There had to be another way.

Another straw that she could try to turn into gold. But she couldn't leave Rachel to find it by herself. They had to try to help her. Cameron was probably fantastic at turning straw into gold, and he'd offered, hadn't he?

She punched the button for the sixth floor.

BEACH HAVEN

"Eagles?" Rachel stared blindly down at the atlases heaped on the kitchen table in front of her. "Do you know how many towns and places in Canada have *eagle* in their names or title?"

"I've been finding out in the last three hours," Brandon said dryly. "From the mountains to the coastline . . ."

"The list is enormous," Rachel was rubbing her temple. "We've got to find a way to pare it down."

He nodded. "I'll go talk to Monty and see how we can run it through the computer with cross-references to landscape features."

If they could do it, Rachel thought. No, she wouldn't

be negative. She couldn't afford it. "That's a good idea."

"And here's another one," he said quietly. "Go out on the veranda and get a cup of coffee while I talk to him. It might be a long day, and we're both already a little dizzy from staring at these atlases. You need to be fresh."

She started to open her lips to protest, then closed them again. He was right, she needed to be sharp, as good as she could be. She got to her feet. "Maybe a Coke. Call me as soon as you can."

He nodded. "I'm not pampering you. I know the stakes."

She watched him leave the kitchen, then headed for the veranda. She must not be discouraged. It was natural to be excited when Catherine had given her the possibility of finding that compound. It was also natural to feel disappointment at the difficulty of turning hope to reality.

She didn't bother to grab a Coke. She just wanted to sit and let the sunlight flow over her and look out at the sea.

And maybe say a prayer for Maria.

We're trying so hard to keep you safe. We'll keep trying, little girl. We'll find a way.

She just wished that way didn't involve all those zillions of eagles.

Her phone rang ten minutes later.

Phillip Sanford.

Not good. She didn't need to hear that Blanca might

have had a relapse when she'd just been praying for her daughter.

She punched the access. "Is she okay, Phillip?"

"Not okay, but a little better. She regained consciousness for a few minutes today. That was a plus, I thought you might like to know." He paused. "You sound frazzled. Did I call at the wrong time?"

"No, I'm glad you called. I meant to phone you anyway. I was afraid that she might have gone the other way."

"Like the way things are going where you are?" he asked gently. "Is there anything I can do?"

"We're doing everything we can. Just take care of Blanca."

"I'm doing that, and I believe she's going to be on her way back soon. But I think she'd rather have you. When she woke, she called your name."

"Not Maria's?"

"No, your name. Twice. And then she drifted off again."

"Strange."

"Is it? But then you and she have formed a bond, haven't you? My feelings aren't hurt that she prefers you. I'll let you go now. I'll keep in touch."

"Thank you, Phillip." She slowly pressed the disconnect. Twice. Blanca had called her name twice the moment she'd regained consciousness. Urgency? Panic? The desperate desire to communicate?

"Blanca . . ." she murmured.

Then she reached into her pocket and pulled out her notebook. Let those blasted eagles wait for a few minutes. She was doing exactly what she'd done when Phillip had first told her about Blanca's letters. Putting it aside to work on something she considered more promising. How did she know what was promising? What could be more promising than a mother reaching out for her child? She didn't know if those letters meant anything, and she'd tended to ignore them because they'd frustrated her. But she could not ignore Blanca any longer if there was even a chance . . .

U A N C

If it was a destination in Canada, it was a complete mystery. What word started with U? She pulled up her Google. Uranium City, Saskatchewan; Upton, Quebec; Uxbridge, Ontario. Unity, Saskatchewan . . .

What the hell were you trying to tell me, Blanca?

And then she knew!

"We got it *wrong*," Rachel said when she burst into the library ten minutes later. "Or Blanca got it wrong, but who could blame her after she was hit on the head and almost killed. No one could expect her to be clear after what she—"

"Easy," Brandon said. "I take it this is not about eagles."

"I hope it is. That's why I came running to Monty instead of wasting more time." She tossed her notebook down on the desk. "U A N C. I couldn't put it together. If Blanca was trying to tell us where her daughter had been taken, I couldn't understand it. The letter U isn't used that much and I couldn't combine the other letters with it and make any sense. So I decided to put myself in Blanca's place, hurt, crawling, trying to scrawl a message in the mud." She tapped the first letter. "It's *not* a U. It's supposed to be a V. It's much easier to form a U than a V. Try it yourself."

"I'll take your word for it," Brandon said. "And that made it work for you?"

"I think it does. I hope it does. You tell me." She tapped each letter in turn. "V A N C. Where is it taking you?"

"Vancouver." Monty gave a low whistle. "A port city with access to the world and yet offers the ability to disappear into a virtual wilderness."

"But a very sophisticated city," Brandon said. "And one that a man with money and power could manage to control if the proper bribe was put in place." He leaned back in his chair. "But there's no way that the main compound wouldn't be hidden away in that wilderness you were talking about, Monty. Even knowing it might be there, it would still be hard to find."

"Then start looking for it," Rachel said. "Why else have you got that damned pet satellite hanging around? Make it earn its keep."

Monty grinned. "I'll do the best I can."

She shook her head. "Do better than that. I don't have much time." She looked at Brandon. "Does it make sense to you? Tell me if this is wishful thinking."

"It makes sense," Brandon said. "That doesn't mean that it's true." He smiled. "But we'll give Monty a little time to do his magic, and he might even come up with an eagle or two."

"How long?" she asked bluntly.

Brandon looked at Monty.

"Two hours to locate and verify if it's a logical site knowing what we do about Huber," Monty said. "But at least two to three hours more to get a detailed grasp of the entire setup." He added, "Providing it's not underground. That would be troublesome."

"Two hours . . ." Rachel felt limp with relief. Only two hours, and she'd know if there was a chance of saving Maria. As long as she knew that could happen, everything else might work out. "Will wonders never cease?"

Monty grinned. "Not as long as I'm here to orchestrate."

"Will you let me help?"

"No, not during the initial search. I'll only need Brandon until I've zeroed in on what might be the compound. But you can do fact and geographic checks like you did when you were scanning the California coast. Good enough?"

"Good enough." She smiled. "I'll let Catherine know what's happening and I'll be back to sit humbly at the master's feet."

Monty nodded mischievously as he glanced at Brandon. "Yeah, you do that, Rachel."

HYATT HOTEL

Cameron looked up when Catherine entered the room after talking to Rachel. Then he straightened and smiled as he studied her face. "You're excited," he said softly. "We have a new element? How interesting. Am I going to like it?"

"I don't know. In two hours we'll know if we have an opportunity." She strode across the room to stand before him. "You're the Guardian. You like to run everything. You gave me options before." Her eyes we're blazing into his own. Her hands clenched into fists at her sides. So much to win. So much to lose. She had to make him see how important it was to her. "I can't take any of them."

"No? Why is that?"

"Because I have to have it *all*."

CHAPTER

17

BEACH HAVEN

Catherine just called. She and Cameron are five minutes from here." Brandon was standing in the doorway of the kitchen. "She was curt and obviously in a hurry. All she asked was an update on whether we knew anything more about Huber's compound than we told her about an hour ago." He shrugged. "She wasn't pleased with my response. But then, neither am I. Monty's found out a lot, but we need to know more. I can't let you go there unless I'm sure you'll have an edge."

"I have more of an edge than I dreamed I'd have," she said quietly. "And you know that's true, Brandon. I can't expect it to be easy."

"Easy?" His lips twisted. "No, it won't be—"

"You look entirely too studious." Catherine was standing in the veranda doorway, her gaze on both of them. "Are those the maps of that Eagles Rest place? Bring them with you. I need you to fill us in on it. Then you can study the details after we've got everything else settled." She gestured impatiently. "But come with me out to the veranda. Cameron's waiting, and it's hard to get Cameron to wait for anything. Not to mention that I'm going to owe him big-time anyway." She turned on her heel and disappeared.

"You're right, very curt." Rachel got to her feet. "But I can't say I give a damn about keeping Cameron waiting. And I need to get back to—"

"Give it up," Brandon said. "She's moving at the speed of light. She's not going to keep us long." He nudged her toward the door. "And I spent some time with Cameron. It might be interesting to know why she thinks she owes him. He's more than impressive. He could be a fantastic asset."

"That's what Catherine keeps telling me. I just don't like the idea of her letting him dictate what she—" She broke off as she saw Cameron lounging in a chair a few yards away. No one could look more leisurely and at ease. So much for Catherine's worrying about keeping him waiting. "Hello, Cameron," Rachel said. "You're not the only one who is in a bit of a hurry at the moment."

"I realize that," he said gently. "And it's really Catherine who is in a big hurry. She's all weighed down by worry and responsibility. I, on the other hand, have none of the above. I just do what I have to do according to our agreement." He smiled at Catherine. "And part of the responsibility is mine because she knows

I'll never ask her to repay. Can there be a heavier obligation for someone like Catherine?"

"No." And he must know her very well to realize that about her, Rachel thought. "What agreement?"

He waved a hand toward Catherine. "I yield to the lady. I'm merely the silent partner."

"I didn't notice the silent," Catherine said dryly. She turned to Brandon, and said curtly, "And I'm sure you haven't been silent either. But I'll wager you haven't been able to convince Rachel not to turn herself over to Huber and Kraus."

"Not yet. Not from lack of trying. It's still on the table," Brandon said bitterly. "But at least I'll be able to follow her to that compound and try to work out a plan to get her out alive. Is that why you're here? Go ahead. She listens to you. You might be able to do it."

"No. Because that would be a waste of time. She's made it clear I'm not going to be permitted to help her." She turned back to Rachel. "You don't change your mind. You're searching desperately for a way to get both you and Maria out, but you're not finding it. In the end, you'll go to her anyway." Her eyes were glittering with moisture. "Okay, that's what we've got to accept. Though Cameron did offer to kidnap you for me."

"Excellent suggestion," Brandon murmured.

"You know it wouldn't work," Catherine said fiercely. "It would break her." Her gaze never left Rachel's. "I have to accept it. So let me go through the scenario. You go after Maria, you stall, you position yourself for extraction, probably with the help of

Brandon and friends. You know that Claire is going to be able to track you once she knows what aircraft Huber sends for you. So you'll have to rely on a signal from Brandon to tell you to grab Maria and run like hell." Her lips twisted. "And hope you're running in the right direction. Because one way or the other, that place will blow sky-high within minutes once Claire aims her magic dart. Is that how it's going to work?"

"Approximately." Rachel smiled faintly. "Hopefully without all the doom and gloom."

"I hope that, too." Catherine didn't look at her. "With my whole heart. You still won't let me help you?"

"Catherine."

"Just a last check." She looked at the maps Rachel was carrying. "So tell me about this compound. Eagles Rest? How close is it to Vancouver?"

"Not close at all. It's in the mountains northeast of the city. Perfect cover, can't be seen from the air. Probably well protected and nearly impossible to penetrate." She opened the first satellite scan Monty had made. "It appears to be enclosed in a stone wall, indications of a large mansion to the west and some kind of large central open area here. We haven't been able to decide exactly what it is. Monty is trying to narrow the focus of the satellite."

Catherine pushed the scan toward Cameron. "Helpful."

"I told you he would be," Cameron said, his gaze raking over the scan. "Have him transmit these and anything else he's able to get to me, Rachel."

"Why?" Brandon asked.

"They'll be needed. I don't send my people any-where that they're not fully equipped and informed." He smiled at Brandon. "Nor would you. But at present you appear to be a trifle short-staffed, so I'm going to lend you Malcolm Dillard, who I use frequently for problems in western Canada. But he does need to know where he's going and what he's to expect. Improvisation can go only so far."

Brandon's eyes were narrowed on his face. "And what's he to expect, Cameron?"

Cameron smiled. "Why, victory. What I always expect."

"Stop talking in circles," Catherine said. "And you sound arrogant as hell, Cameron." She looked at Brandon. "I'm not going to tell you anything more about him because you don't need to know. All you need to know is that Cameron can do it. He might be able to save Rachel and Maria. I've seen him do incredible things before in Tibet and half a dozen other places around the world. He's got the men and the weapons, and they'd have the stupidity to die for him if he'd ask. Just let him help save Rachel."

He nodded slowly. "You knew I'd have no choice. Time's running out. Rachel?"

She nodded as she looked at Cameron. "You can really save Maria?"

"No promises. It's much more possible than it was before we knew their location and could get a sizeable force into the area. It will still be difficult." He pointed to Eagles Rest. "It's important that our people have time to get Dillard and his team in place before you arrive. Otherwise, there may be difficulties that he can't overcome. He has to be able to arrange to slip a messenger into that compound to signal the time he'll strike, so you'll be ready. He'll have a helicopter ready to land and extract, but he can't get any kind of armed force near you without getting you killed. Huber and Kraus are bound to be too close to you."

"Maybe they won't," she said slowly. For the first time since that last call from Huber, she was beginning to see possibilities, to hope again. "Maybe we won't have to worry about them." She moistened her lips. "If something happened to them, it would cause chaos, wouldn't it? They *are* Red Star."

Brandon was gazing at her with narrowed eyes. "Rachel."

"You knew it was going to happen anyway. You watched me make the recipe." She smiled crookedly. "Though not put on the icing. I did that later."

Brandon turned to Cameron. "Find a way to get me to her, and I'll get them both out."

Cameron nodded. "It would be easier if I knew the layout of Huber's place. Monty had better earn his money, or I might rethink my decision regarding him."

"What?"

He waved dismissively. "Never mind. They'll get it done."

"They? You're not going to be there?"

"Possibly." He smiled at Catherine. "But unfortunately, Catherine has decided that she wants it all.

She was quite touching about how she couldn't let her Luke face a future without a clean Pacific Ocean."

"Shut up, Cameron," Catherine said crossly. "You're the one who practically lives and breathes Shangri-La. You should wear the tee shirt. You said you were leaving it up to me, but you'd never let that kind of disaster happen." She turned to Rachel. "You won't let me go with you, but I have to do *something*. If I'm guessing right, Huber is going to blow that supertanker sometime after midnight or early morning if he's not stopped. Probably early in the morning since he'll want to coordinate it with his damn celebration. I can't let him do it. Maybe if we can interfere with this part of his plan, it will cause a distraction that will also help you. Cameron has a helicopter waiting down on the beach. We're heading down to Santa Barbara to see how we can manage to stop the *Katrina Notalo*. It's delivering oil to a refinery north of the city before it continues on to San Luis Obispo, then sets sail for San Francisco." Then she was beside Rachel, holding her close. "I'll be checking with Brandon about you, so you keep safe. I know you can do this," she whispered. "You can do anything you need to do. I just want like hell to do it for you. Don't you dare let those bastards hurt you." Then she released Rachel and whirled away from her. "I've done all I can. You do the rest." Then she was walking across the veranda. "Come on, Cameron, we wouldn't want to keep Van Deek waiting. It's just your kind of razzle-dazzle mayhem. You'll probably enjoy it enormously."

"Guilty." He watched her go down the driveway

toward the car. "And so would she if she weren't stretched to the limit at the moment." He handed Brandon a card. "Malcolm Dillard. I've given instructions. I sent him to Vancouver the moment we knew it was a target. They're estimating they'll be near the Red Star site at Eagles Rest shortly after midnight. Dillard is brilliant, and you'll find the team equally efficient. I'll try to finish up with the *Katrina* as soon as possible, but if I can't be there, they'll answer to you." He turned back to Rachel. "And I'll be most unhappy if you don't follow Catherine's orders about keeping alive. I have great plans for you." His face was suddenly alight with mischief. "But don't tell Catherine, I'm trying to make her forget I mentioned it."

Then he was gone.

And Rachel was staring after them, her mind alive and sparking with everything with which it had been bombarded in the last minutes.

A chance!

She could feel the heat flush her cheeks.

Not a great chance, but it was more than she'd had before. After all, it wasn't every day that a woman had a small army put at her disposal.

"It's Red Star," Brandon said roughly. "You're looking as if you're ready to conquer the world. Don't get your hopes up. You've got to be so careful. One false step and it's—"

"I know all that." She turned to face him. She realized he was afraid for her, but she couldn't keep from smiling. "But even you can see that things look up a bit when you might be able to count on a little help from your friends."

"Yeah." His eyes were on her glowing face. He cleared his throat. "I can see that, Rachel."

"So I'm not going to worry about what happens after Huber takes me." She turned and headed back into the kitchen. "That will be a dance all its own. Right now, I have to make preparations for how I want this to go down. It has to be timed right for Maria's safety. If the *Katrina* doesn't give Huber his big finale on schedule, he might get impatient." She grimaced. "And we don't know exactly what time that's supposed to take place. And we've got to pray that Catherine and Cameron will keep it from happening. No, we've got to coordinate it so that we'll be sure that Huber doesn't get *anything* he wants."

"May I remind you that by that time you'll be with Maria."

"You can remind me." She went past him into the house. "But as I said, it's a dance all its own. And I have things to do. Didn't you hear Catherine?" Her pace increased as she headed for the library to talk to Monty, then call Claire Warren. She'd hoped to keep Claire out of any action, but that might not be possible. A delay . . . Cameron had said a delay was important. She might be able to use Claire to initiate that delay. "Catherine did all she could. Now, it's up to me."

"A Shangri-La tee shirt?" Cameron repeated as he got into the car and started it. "I almost flinched. You have no idea of decorum, Catherine. You take a great and learned idea and philosophy and trivialize it."

"You'll recover when you get back among all your sycophants. A little ego stroking, and you'll be just fine." She was blinking hard and trying not to look back over her shoulder as the car roared down the road toward the beach. It had been harder than she'd thought. She wanted to turn around and go back and tell Rachel to forget everything she'd said and let her take over. "And it was the truth. How would your brave new world survive if you let Huber start ruining the oceans?"

"I didn't say it wasn't the truth," he said mildly. "But you might remember that I'm sending a number of my extremely talented sycophants to both Eagles Rest and the *Katrina* to help your Rachel tonight."

"I never said that they weren't brilliant and talented, just misguided." She was looking straight ahead. "You wouldn't promise her, but she has a chance, doesn't she?"

"She has Brandon and an amazingly efficient group of some of my best people. She has passion and dedication and intelligence. She might have a very good chance."

Might.

Don't question, just accept and go on to something that she *could* do. "You said it was important for your people to have time to get Dillard and his team in place. That means arranging delays to keep Rachel from being taken to Eagles Rest too soon." She didn't want to think of how dangerous and painful it would be for Rachel if Huber were to get his hands on her with time to spare for the kind of treatment he'd meted out in Sazkar Prison. "We have to think of some way to—"

"No," he said quietly. "You turned it over to Rachel and Brandon. Step back, Catherine. You can't do everything."

But she *wanted* to do everything. She drew a deep breath. "Okay, what about Van Deek? I know he has something to do with it. I *feel* it. But we haven't found any firm proof that he's guilty of anything. There are just those checks and bank records that couldn't be explained. And those sidesteps that you want to question him about. And now he's offered to let Homeland search his ship? We might be wrong. We still don't really know that much about him."

He shrugged. "Sure we do. We just have to see where it takes us. He was born in Amsterdam and grew up on the waterfront. His father was a sailor and his mother worked in a souvenir shop. He hardly ever saw his father, but he had a good enough life until his mother died of heart failure when he was eight. His father disappeared into the sunset, leaving him in an orphanage. He took off when he was twelve, and the next time he appeared on the radar was when he was eighteen and working on a ship out of Madrid, Spain. He liked ships, it was a passion with him." He shrugged. "And the rest is history. We'll find out anything else we need when we make direct contact."

"You mean you'll find out," she said dryly. "I don't believe you're going to invite me to sit in on one of your weird mind sessions. At least, I hope you're not."

"Whatever you choose. It might not involve anything of the sort. We'll have to see. He's obviously an interesting man and worth a second glance." He added, "And, if that second glance tells us it's also necessary to shut down the *Katrina Notalo* to make sure Rachel has the time she needs to survive, I don't believe you're going to object to doing anything we have to do."

She shook her head. "Anything," she said jerkily. "I'll do anything." She looked away from him. "And thank you, Cameron."

"Ah, at last, a word of gratitude. And now it's over and we don't speak of it again."

"It's not over, it's barely started. What you're doing is . . . damn wonderful."

"No, it's only what you wanted." He parked before the helicopter pad. He added quietly, "And I'll always try to give you what you want from me. Because there's so much I can't give you." He got out of the car and came around and opened her door. "And I know you're aching to go back and fight Rachel's battle, but she can't give that to you, either. Some battles have to be fought alone." He took her hand and helped her out of the car. "So we'll have a great time fighting the battles we can." He was whisking her toward the helicopter. "I promise to keep you entertained." He was laughing as he lifted her into the copilot's seat. A strand of hair had fallen down on his forehead, and those bright blue eyes were no longer serious. "Both before and after.

You'll have to keep yourself amused during the action itself. We might be busy. I have a few ideas . . ."

"I'm sure you do." She fastened her seat belt. She was suddenly feeling that heady sense of excitement and exhilaration she always felt with Cameron, that tingling knowledge of something waiting just beyond the next corner. "And I can keep myself entertained. What kind of ideas?"

"Do you remember the last time we were here in San Francisco and spent a memorable evening at that firecracker factory in Chinatown?"

"How could I forget? The damn factory blew up. What does that have to do with anything?"

"Nothing directly. Just something to build on and mull over."

"What ideas?" she repeated.

"But that would spoil the surprise. It might even disappoint you." He turned on the rotors. "And I'd never want to do that to you." The copter lifted off. "Have I ever?"

HYATT HOTEL

"I've got Rachel Venable, Kraus," Claire said as soon as he answered his cell. "Or I will have her if you give me a few more hours. I have her positioned, and all I need to do is get rid of Brandon."

"I don't need you any longer," Kraus said. "Huber is handling it himself. He's given her until nine to turn herself over to him."

"You mean *you're* handling it. And that means that if anything goes wrong, you'll get the blame. And it will go wrong, Kraus. He's counting on Rachel's being all soft and sentimental about the kid. He doesn't know her."

"And you do?"

"Much better than you. Why else did you turn me loose on her? You were willing to pay me a fat bonus for Rachel because you knew that I'd manage to lure her to you. But now that you've got the kid, you think you can shut me out. I'm not about to give up the money you promised me when the entire deal goes south."

"We're handling it," he repeated coldly. He hesitated, then asked, "Why do you think that she won't cave about the kid?"

"Self-preservation. We both know that's what's important to everyone. She *is* soft. But Huber did a number on her in that prison. She's scared to death of that happening again. I watched her break down and tremble like a baby after she hung up from Huber. And she still has nightmares. You blew it, Kraus. She's not going to come meekly when you snap your fingers. She's going to ignore that little girl, go to bed, and pull the covers over her head." She paused. "It has to be force and trickery. I can deliver her. Just give me an extra three hours."

"He wanted her by nine." Kraus was silent. "And I told him using the child would work."

"Then tell him you have this brilliant backup plan in case it doesn't. You know you can manipulate him to suit yourself. All he cares about is getting what he wants." She paused. "He wants Rachel Venable as the showpiece of his little celebration. What difference do a few hours make?"

"It matters to him. He wanted her here before four. That extra few hours would cut it close."

"Your decision, give me the extra time, and I'll give you Rachel. Or you can deal with Huber's tantrums when she backs out."

Silence as Kraus thought about it. "If she refuses Huber when he contacts her at nine, I'll expect you to deliver. I won't be in a forgiving mood if you don't."

"She'll refuse him. As I said, she's probably as terrified as that little girl you're holding over her head. Remember to transfer funds to my account by 10 P.M." She pressed the disconnect.

Then she smiled and turned to face Rachel, who was sitting in the chair across the room. "Brilliantly handled?"

Rachel nodded. "But then you know each other so well," she said dryly. "And you have such similar aims. In spite of your heady ambition to take out Red Star, I notice you didn't forget to hit Kraus for the bank transfer."

She smiled. "He would have found it suspicious if I hadn't. And a woman always needs cash, doesn't she?" Her smile faded. "But I'd be on the Red Star hit list if I don't produce you. I'm taking a chance that you're telling me the truth about agreeing to my plan to give yourself up to Huber. Though you don't have much choice now. I'm going to be there when Kraus's helicopter picks you up, and I'll initiate the GPS tracking with Andrews Air Force Base on the spot."

"I assumed you would."

"But you've put strings on my little deal." Her eyes were narrowed. "Why do you want that three-hour delay, Rachel?"

"Perhaps I'm still looking for a way to save Maria." She smiled mockingly. "Or perhaps I remembered that Catherine told me that you thought that Huber's grand spectacular might take place close to dawn. I'd really prefer not to go through a night of sheer hell before he kills me."

"Understandable." She added thoughtfully, "And you're probably not telling me everything. Brandon might have some plan or other in the wind. But as long as I get what I need from you, I can tolerate that." She met her eyes. "Because I'm the one who will be in control. I can allow you a small safety margin, but no more than an hour or so after I know you've arrived in Huber's loving arms. Kraus was most adamant about Huber's wanting you there before four. I won't risk waiting much longer than that." She suddenly smiled brilliantly. "But, of course, I'll arrange to have that SEAL team staged to rescue you just as soon as I track the aircraft Kraus sends for you. I wouldn't send you on a suicide mission, Rachel."

"Perish the thought." But that warning had been very explicit. She doubted if Claire would risk tipping off Kraus and Huber about a pending drone attack by sending any SEALs to the area. Rachel got to her feet. "And I'm not allowing you to send me anywhere,

Claire. I came to you, on my terms, because I wanted
that three-hour delay, and I knew you might get it from
Kraus. You met them, and tonight I'll meet your
terms." She headed for the door. "I'll be at the helipad
on the beach at 11:30 P.M. But you'll know by then that
I've already done it because Kraus will have transferred your money."

"Yes, I will." She smiled. "And I meant it, Rachel.
I'll try to keep you alive. I owe it to your father. I told
you the truth about Venable's saving my life when we
were working together."

"It didn't seem to make an impression during those
last months before he died."

"I believe in gratitude . . . when I can afford it.
There was . . . pressure." She shrugged. "Whether you
believe it or not, I do pay debts."

Claire seemed sincere, but who knew how she related to any emotion? "If you can afford it," Rachel repeated. "I'll see you later, Claire." She closed the door
behind her.

Those last few sentences had been bewildering and
bizarre, but so had the rest of this day. But she'd accomplished the first stage of what she'd set out to do
with Claire Warren.

Now to do the follow-up with Monty, who was waiting at the elevator.

"Okay?" Monty asked.

"Good as it can be. Use Catherine's room to set up
and monitor what Claire's doing." She smiled. "And
Brandon's already given you your other orders."

He nodded soberly. "Lousy orders. Brandon never

leaves me behind while he and Nate go hunting. I don't want to stay back here, Rachel."

"I know you don't," she said quietly. "Hey, but you might be the one to save the day." She reached out and squeezed his arm. "I'm counting on you. Maria's counting on you." She got on the elevator. "Just remember that Claire won't take any chances with failure in this. Move fast, Monty. And be careful."

"Yeah, sure." His eyes were on her as the elevator door started to close. "*You* be careful, Rachel. I'll watch your back, but don't let them—"

The elevator was beginning to descend, closing him out.

It was just as well, she thought. She was choking up, and she didn't need that right now. In these last weeks, she had grown to know Nate and Monty so well. They had become friends and companions, and now she'd had to ask them to also run the same risks she'd asked Brandon to. The responsibility was becoming overwhelming.

She drew a deep breath.

I don't know how you took it, Daddy. How did you make it all those years? If Maria weren't at stake, I don't know if I'd be able to do it.

But Maria was at stake, so there was no question. Maybe in the end, that had been her father's answer, too. There was always someone to save, someone who counted, some idea that was worth preserving.

I don't know about all that, Daddy. But if you have any influence where you are, Maria is worth saving. I could use a little help tonight . . .

BEACH HAVEN
8:05 P.M.

The sun was just starting to sink toward the horizon when Rachel pulled into the driveway and turned off the ignition. She could see Brandon sitting at a table on the veranda, waiting for her. His tense body language told her that this meeting was not going to be easy. She sat there gazing at him for a moment before she reached for her phone. But then she couldn't expect anything to be easy tonight.

And there was one other thing she had to do before she got out of the car and went to face him.

She quickly dialed Hu Chang. "I told you not to dare leave me while I was asleep that day, and you did it anyway," she said as soon as he answered. "That was not courteous either, Hu Chang."

He didn't speak for an instant. She could almost see his mind working, exploring the true reason for her call. "I left you a message with Brandon. I admit I've been having difficulty restraining myself from interceding again. I've been monitoring what's been going on from the outside, and I believe the behind-the-scenes activity might be even worse. Brandon might be formidable, but I do like to be hands-on."

"I know that you do. But you'll have to leave it up to us this time."

Silence. "This is not a call for help?"

"No, I just wanted to thank you for all the gifts you've given me over the years. You've always twisted everything around whenever I've tried to do it before."

"Because they were not gifts. You just failed to understand. You still have much to learn. And that is why I do not like the tone of this conversation. It sounds very much like good-bye. I won't tolerate good-byes being offered at this early stage in your development. Do you understand?"

"I understand." She drew a deep, shaky breath, "And I promise I'll be everything I can be. But I had to say the words."

"You've said them, and I accept them." Silence. "When?"

"Tonight."

Another silence. "You have a chance?"

"I have a chance. It might even be a good chance if we all manage to follow your creed."

"Then see that you make sure that happens. I didn't train you to make mistakes. Will it change anything if I call Catherine?"

"No, she might not answer. She's a little busy."

"That's promising. The only promising thing since I answered this call." She could hear the harsh breath he took before he said, "I don't believe I will allow myself to follow Catherine's advice the next time I'm having doubts about my own motives. It's far too traumatic not handling everything myself. I do not like it." He paused. "But we have to get through this event first. There's nothing I can do?"

"You've already done it. You've made Catherine and me who we are."

"No, just honed down the rough edges. All the beauty and the artistry were already there." His voice was low and hard. "And I will not let my work be damaged or destroyed by a careless savage. You *will* survive. You *will* make sure Catherine survives. You will both return to me safe and sound. Do you understand?"

"Absolutely."

"And the first thing you do when you know you're safe is to call me. You'll tell me that in spite of the fact I was foolish enough to let you do this without me, you managed to come out of it in splendid shape."

"The very first thing."

"Then get off this phone and go do it. You've said what you wanted to say, haven't you?"

"Exactly what I wanted to say. Good-bye, Hu Chang."

"No, I told you that you haven't earned that word yet. We'll discuss it in another forty or fifty years." He ended the call.

And she sat there, filled with aching regret, memories, love, and hope, and a dozen other emotions she couldn't separate or identify. Then she opened the car door and started to walk slowly toward the veranda, giving herself time to recover. She'd had to make that call, but now it was time to put it behind her. As usual, Hu Chang was right, and she needed to forget everything now but what had to be done.

Brandon watched her walk toward him. "You took a long time getting out of that car. Were you on the phone?"

"Yes." She didn't volunteer any other information. She was still a little too emotional.

He didn't ask her anything else about the call. His

gaze was narrowed on her face, and she was once again aware of that tension. "Ready?"

She nodded as she dropped into a chair. "I told you on the phone driving back here that everything went well enough with Claire. She suspects that we might have a plan to rescue Maria, but she doesn't care since she thinks that no matter what happens, she'll get what she wants. She's nothing if not confident."

"No, I mean are *you* ready?" His jaw was tight as he looked at her. "You've been holding on, fighting the good fight, stiff upper lip, and all of that crap. But you must be going through hell inside." He snapped his fingers. "Oh, that's right, you only let it come to the surface at given times. The rest of the time it's tucked safely away. Isn't that the way you have to handle it?"

"That's the way it works for me," she said quietly. "Would it make you feel better if I let it all flow out? I could try."

"No." He reached across the table and grasped her hand. "This is bad enough. I can feel what's behind those barriers that you never let down." He amended, "At least, never let down with me. It's *killing* me." He grimaced. "And listen to me, I'm talking bullshit. I didn't mean to do this. It just came out. I was sitting here and thinking about you and wondering how the hell I could help more."

"You're going to help." She frowned. "I feel guilty that I'm taking so much from you and Nate and Monty. It's been bothering me that—"

"No, not that," he said impatiently. "It's so dark around you right now. I want to *give* you something, anything that will make it—" He stopped. And then he said jerkily, "I just want you to know that I'll be there for you. Tonight, tomorrow, whenever you want me. There isn't anything that can happen to you that I won't be there to heal. I might not be Hu Chang or Catherine, but try me. I'll never fail you."

She could feel the tears sting her eyes as she looked at him. "No, I don't think you would." She swallowed hard. "That was quite beautiful. And unexpected. Thank you, Brandon." She sat up straighter in her chair. "And, yes, I'm ready. How could I not be with good thoughts and friends who can move mountains? Did you think I was brooding? Not my style. When I was in Sazkar Prison, I was alone, yet I survived. And I think something different is going on this time." She met his eyes and paused, trying to find a way to make him feel what she was feeling. "Am I afraid? Yes." She moistened her lips. "But think about what's been happening. I was completely depressed after I found out that Claire had no idea where we could find Huber. Yet, slowly, things began to come together. Catherine dug out that bit about Huber's obsession with eagles. Blanca seemed to be reaching out to me about those letters we'd been ignoring. Then, out of the blue, Cameron appears with a possibility where there had been no possibility." She smiled. "I've been wondering if perhaps somebody up there is becoming very tired of putting up with all that evil Huber is spreading around. Maybe this is our time, our opportunity. If we try very hard, maybe we can make a miracle happen. What do you think, Brandon?"

"Whatever you say." He cleared his throat. "Personally, I believe you might be the miracle." He gazed out at the setting sun. "You have a little over three hours. You still won't let me go down with you to the beach to meet Claire?"

"No, now that would disturb me. You've already told me that you're flying out to Eagles Rest to meet with Dillard right away. That's a much better idea. I'd rather you be there to greet me."

"I'll be there. I told you, I'll always be there."

And she was becoming emotional again. She had to hold on. "Yes, you did say that." She got to her feet. "In a few minutes, I'm going into the house and take Huber's call, so he'll believe he's failed, and I'm too terrified to meet his demands. I think showing a little hysteria might be in order. Then I'll start sobbing and hang up. He'll probably enjoy that, and be so satisfied, he'll forget about Maria. I hope." She made a face. "And that will make me feel so dirty and upset that I'll come back out to you and we'll go for a walk so that I can calm down again. Maybe we'll watch the sun go down. Distraction will be everything at that point." She smiled. "I'd be tempted to seduce you, but that would be dangerous for both of us."

He grinned. "Dangerous? I assure you I'd be more than willing to risk it."

"No, believe me, you wouldn't." She was heading toward the house. "A walk will be fine."

* * *

Claire was talking on the phone as Rachel walked toward the helipad. "Right on time," she said as she pressed the disconnect. "And so is Kraus. We'll see his landing lights soon."

Rachel looked up at the night sky. "And I trust you received your money?"

"Of course. I told you it was important." She shrugged. "But it's not as important as respect and being first. There's a certain glow when everyone realizes you're the best." She added, "But Venable never understood that. He just plugged along and never reached out. Even when Langley told him he was the best."

"A difference of opinion," Rachel said absently. She was bracing herself for what was to come. Soon it would start. She had to gather strength. "Maybe he already knew he was the best."

Silence.

"Are you afraid?" Claire suddenly asked, her gaze on Rachel's face. "You're very smart, Rachel. And this is very stupid. Why are you doing it?"

"Yes, I'm afraid. I'd truly be stupid if I wasn't. And if you don't know why, I can't tell you."

She shrugged. "It's probably because you're like Venable."

"Maybe." She stiffened. "I think I see the lights of the helicopter."

"Yes, I saw them a minute ago." Claire took a step closer to Rachel. "Kraus has to believe that this delivery is authentic. I have to protect myself." She drew a hypodermic from her bag. "I'm going to be giving you a shot that will put you out. Hold still."

The needle went smoothly into her arm. "It's very fast, you'll be unconscious before they start their descent." She took a step back and looked at her. "But that's not enough." Her fist lashed out and struck Rachel's jaw with full force. "You've got to look as if you resisted. Now, the mouth, I think. Once more . . ."

Pain.

Dizziness.

She was falling to the sand.

"I truly hope you make it, Rachel," Claire said as she stepped back and started to wave at the incoming helicopter. "But don't count on those SEALs. It would be too risky for me. Four thirty. I can give you until four thirty. But don't push your luck. I've been as generous as I can . . ."

Blue lights like swords streamed down on Rachel from the helicopter.

Darkness.

SAN LUIS OBISPO

11:50 P.M.

"Not a particularly graceful vessel," Catherine murmured as she lowered the binoculars after gazing at the *Katrina Notalo* to glance at Cameron. "But the crew seems deplorably alert. That speaks well for the discipline of the captain. Not good for us. Are we sure we can't do this some other way?"

"No time." He slipped over the side of the boat. Even in his scuba equipment, the water was cold. So much for sunny California. Get rid of it. He concentrated and in seconds the cold vanished. "We have to do it now or try to climb on board when that tanker gets under way again. Even with an experienced SEAL team, that could be close to suicide for a number of reasons. I'll signal you after I've contacted Van Deek and we've come to an agreement."

"The hell you will." She was leaning over the side of the boat, her eyes holding his own. "There's no reason I can't come with you. You handle Van Deek, and I go direct to the communication room, secure it, and make certain that no messages are transmitted. You know that's the intelligent way to do it."

"It's one way."

"But not the way you want to do it," she said with exasperation. "And it has to be exactly as the Guardian commands, right?" Her hands were clenching on the oar. "It's not as if Manuel couldn't shoot off those fireworks without me. You said he wanted to prove himself. Let him do it."

"I'd prefer to have him supervised for that particular task. It's a very delicate job. I trust you, Catherine." He struck out for the ship. "Besides, you'd get in my way. Give me fifteen minutes. Get back to shore and make sure Manuel doesn't get too enthusiastic with those fireworks. Just close enough to make Van Deek nervous."

"Oh, a firework explosion near an oil supertanker should do that," Catherine said dryly. "Particularly since you told me to increase the firepower. But you're not going to park me on the sidelines for long. And get in your way? You'll pay for that, Cameron."

"Expected." He could barely hear her as he propelled himself through the water. He knew she'd make him suffer, but it was worth it to keep Catherine away from the first interaction with Van Deek's crew. They were outnumbered, and he'd protect her where he could. She was smart and professional, and he'd trust her without question if she were one of his own people. But she was Catherine and therefore in a class by herself. He just didn't want to throw heavier odds than necessary at her. Twenty-two men was fairly normal for the crew of a supertanker but they were good men who knew the ship well. And he hadn't been able to get more than seven of his own men on site at this late date.

He plowed silently through the water.

Three minutes.

Six minutes.

Eight minutes.

Twelve minutes.

Fourteen.

He lifted his head. He was within five yards of the *Katrina Notalo*. He positioned himself and waited.

Earlier in the evening, they'd set up the fireworks

display to go off at the Rodriguez Hotel, which was a prime tourist spot on the beach above San Luis Obispo. The hotel had frequent fireworks displays for various reasons throughout the year. No reason for suspicion or alarm for Van Deek.

The sky suddenly lit with scarlet-and-silver explosions of color over the hotel.

He could see some of the crew run to the rail on the other side of the ship to watch the show.

Not enough. He needed all of them there.

Then he heard a cry as a huge M-80 rocket exploded above the water not fifty yards from where the crew was standing at the rail. Then another rocket exploded twenty yards closer.

That did it.

If the entire crew weren't at that rail, it was very close. The captain? If he was as disciplined as reported, he'd be there with his men and probably on the phone to the Rodriguez to get them to stop the threat those fireworks were posing his oil tanker. Either way, it would give Cameron the time he needed. He knew exactly where the captain's cabin was located, and it was nowhere near that rail where Manuel and Catherine were causing their distraction. He should have at least six minutes before the confusion was sorted out with the hotel while they searched for the guests who were causing the display. In the meantime, Manuel and Catherine would lob three more firecrackers near the *Katrina* to hold their attention.

He started to swim silently toward the ship.

CHAPTER

18

Van Deek was coming.

Cameron could hear his footsteps on the deck outside the cabin.

It had taken the captain longer than Cameron had thought it would to settle the furor with the hotel. Which might not be good if it was because he was asking questions and exploring reasons for those fireworks aimed a little too close to his ship.

Cameron moved to the side of the door. He'd left the lights on because that was the way the captain had left the cabin when he'd run out to the deck.

The door opened, and Van Deek came into the cabin.

Cameron leaped forward and his arm encircled the captain's neck.

And he found himself pitched over Van Deek's head and on the floor!

Shit.

Van Deek's hands were on his throat.

He broke the hold, rolled to the side, and was on his feet. The next moment, his hand came down in a karate chop.

Van Deek collapsed and fell to the floor.

That had been interesting. Cameron took a deep breath before picking Van Deek up and putting him in the chair at the desk. Then he sat down on the edge of the bed and waited for Van Deek to regain consciousness. He was seldom taken down these days, but Van Deek had managed to do it. The captain was a lean man in his forties with white hair and a close-cut gray beard. His tan skin was weathered, and he was obviously strong, very strong. He had been taken by surprise, but his response had been faultless. If he hadn't been a little unbalanced, Cameron might not have been able to break the hold on his throat. At that point, he would have been forced to either kill him or use a mental adjustment.

A dangerous man, good to know.

Van Deek was opening his eyes, and he was immediately alert and aware the instant he glimpsed Cameron. "I'm obviously not dead," he said quietly. "How do I remain that way? Have you been paid to kill me? I might be able to offer you a better deal."

"I'll be glad to listen," Cameron said. "But I haven't been paid to kill you. I don't want you dead. On the contrary, I need you alive."

"Really?" Van Deek's expression changed. "You probably shouldn't have told me that. It gives me a slight advantage. You don't impress me as the type of man who would allow that to happen." He looked Cameron over from head to toe. "Scuba. I assume you were responsible for that hullabaloo with those fireworks? You must have good people if you could rely on them not to blow you up with the *Katrina*." He tilted his head. "But not many or you wouldn't be facing me alone." He looked at the gun in Cameron's hand. "What do you want from me? I have a Grand Cayman account that's sizeable enough to make you happy. I have influence in a lot of quarters that could be helpful to you. Some of them are on the underbelly, completely without morals, and would be willing to do me any favor." He was still gazing at the gun. "But I'd judge you to be a man who would prefer to take care of any issue of revenge yourself. Am I not right?"

"Yes." He smiled faintly. "Much more satisfactory. I'm sure you've also found that to be true. Which is why you still have those associates in the underbelly still owing you those favors. It gives you a comfortable cushion. Actually, I can see you dancing through life and working to create that safety net."

"Can you? But dancing and working are at odds with each other. Make up your mind. Are you going to tell me your name?"

"Cameron."

"Never heard of you. Did I hurt someone you care about?"

"Not that I know about. But you might be about to hurt someone who matters to me. That's what I'm about to determine. I need you to answer a few questions."

"And you believe I'd tell you the truth?"

"If it suits you and I'm very good at detecting lies. If it doesn't suit you to answer, then the situation will get a good deal more dangerous for you and difficult for me."

"Who do you think I might hurt? We can negotiate."

"I never negotiate where Catherine is concerned. You might meet her soon, and you'll understand." He paused. "But she believes that you might be cheating her son out of something that she thinks might rightly belong to him. You know how mothers can be about their children."

"No, I have no children," he said warily. "What does she think I might be stealing from him?"

"What Huber ordered you to steal from him. She wants Luke never to have to look at the ugliness Huber has planned for this magnificent ocean." He smiled gently. "And she will have what she wants, Van Deek."

His expression didn't change. "I don't know what you're talking about."

"Then you'd better think about it. I'll wait." But this was taking too long, Cameron thought. The captain was tough, and he found he didn't want to break him entirely. He'd gauged Van Deek's character and, for the most part, he'd liked what he'd seen. But he had to have complete control to get this over fast. So now it was time to dig deep. Find out everything he was and knew and thought. "However, I won't wait long. I tend to get bored." *He relaxed, opening his mind, his gaze fixed intently on the captain's face, letting everything flow into him.*

Bitterness, desperation, anger, and frustration. Why? Then the answers were all there before Cameron.

Ah, even more interesting than he'd thought and possibly easier to solve.

"I'd hate to be responsible for inflicting a sin that drastic," Van Deek said dryly. "I suppose you might be referring to the rumor I heard there was some nonsense about a possible attack at Oakland. But evidently there's no proof." He shrugged. "But since I always err on the side of caution, I asked Homeland Security to board my ship and do a search." He met Cameron's eyes. "They found nothing."

"Yes, I'd heard you'd done that. Clever. Because you led them in the right directions." He added quietly, "And when the ship explodes sometime tonight, you'll be stunned and everyone will say that you did everything you could to protect it." He added, "And to protect your crew. You even took on additional lifeboats before you left Saudi because you couldn't stand the thought of their being blown up by Huber. You thought you might save them if you were prepared. You knew what you were probably heading toward when you left port."

"Really?" He'd become suddenly stiff. "I hate oceans, but I'm still a humanitarian?"

"No, you love the sea. Ever since you were a boy

growing up on the waterfronts of Amsterdam, it's been the one thing in your life that you could count on." He was staring him directly in the eye. "But Kraus found something else you love more. You lied to me, Van Deek. You do have a child. He's the son of a woman who ran a shop in Kuwait. She was murdered a week before you sailed, and the boy disappeared. His name is Fahad. Which means jaguar. You liked the idea of naming him after a beautiful, intelligent animal because the Arabs believe that doing that might give those same qualities to a person." He paused. "He's only three years old."

Silence. But a muscle jerked in Van Deek's left cheek. "How did you happen to find that out?"

"Not the same way as Huber. He probably noticed that there were odd frequent discrepancies in the checks written on your bank accounts, as I did. After all, you had to support the boy and his mother. But, in my case, let's just say you're easy to read."

"Bullshit. Do you work for Kraus or Huber?"

"Neither. Which one is holding your son? I'd guess Kraus because lately he's been showing interest in that kind of hostage situation. He even arranged the kidnapping of a little girl recently."

"I don't know what you're talking about."

"I'm talking about a free pass if you work it right. Where are those explosives hidden?"

Van Deek was silent.

"Don't fight me," he said gently. "You don't want to do this, Van Deek."

The captain's gray eyes were suddenly burning

fiercely. "The hell I don't. There are no free passes in this world. But a child should not have to pay the price. Fahad's the only person I've ever loved. What do I care what happens if I can keep him alive?"

"You do care. And he won't have to pay the price. I can send someone to give him that pass. But in order to protect him I'll have to make certain Huber and Kraus are destroyed. Do you have any objection?" He tilted his head. "No, I can see you don't. We're progressing." He glanced at the door. "But not fast enough. This chat has taken too long. Catherine is impatient, and she's probably in your communication room securing it right now. She said that was the second area to be taken down, and she won't wait."

"This is the Catherine who wants me to save this ocean for her Luke?"

"Exactly. And after she secures the communications, she'll come looking for us. So it's time for you to contact the rest of your crew and make sure that they don't try to stop her."

"And what if I don't?"

"They'll die," he said simply. "I told you I don't negotiate where Catherine's concerned."

"Just like that?"

"No, depending on how much they try to harm her, it could get much worse." He held his eyes. "Now do as I say. Tell your crew to go to the bridge, and you'll talk to them there. You'll say that there's no threat, but Homeland Security has requested additional personnel to come on board because they want to make sure the ship is secure. Then you'll take me to the area where you've hidden the explosives and give them to my men for safekeeping. After that, you'll continue to proceed toward Oakland as if you're obeying Huber's orders. Perhaps at a little slower pace than you were told to sail. The rest of your duty will consist of stalling and giving the correct answer when or if Kraus contacts you."

"You're crazy."

"On occasion, as we all are."

"Or some kind of freak."

"I'm probably past that point, but you'll be glad to know I keep it firmly under control. I'm glad that you no longer believe I'm a spy for Kraus."

His gaze was still on Cameron's face. "No, I don't believe that, which probably makes me as crazy as you."

"We don't have much time. I can only give you a few more minutes." And he didn't want to use any more mental force than he'd already done. There was a slight possibility of damage. "Decide."

He moistened his lips. "And my son?"

"I'll call my contact in Kuwait, and he'll find the boy. He's very efficient and quite lethal. Before the night is over, I guarantee your son will be safe. I keep my promises. You can tell that, can't you? That's why it's necessary that I destroy Red Star. So that no one will be around to countermand that order. Don't worry, that's already in the works."

Van Deek's gaze was narrowed, probing. "And I'm supposed to believe you?"

Cameron did a reinforcement to make certain he

did. Then followed with a quick mental scan to verify. "You do believe me. You're already feeling relieved. You were looking for a way out. You were torn about whether or not you could do it. You hated the idea of being the one to destroy this place you consider your true home. You wanted to kill Kraus when he used your son as a pawn. However, *I* won't be relieved until you call your crew. Come on. Do it right now." He headed for the door. "Because Catherine is definitely on the move."

THE KATRINA

2:40 A.M.

"Do you intend to do anything but stand there and watch me?" Catherine called to Cameron impatiently from the bridge. She went down the steps and crossed to where he was leaning on the rail. "Not that Manuel or any of your other men would expect you to do anything you don't want to do. But you've been letting me give all the orders since Van Deek handed over those explosives. I expected you to step in and take charge."

"Why should I? You've been totally faultless. The ship is secure, and the crew knows that they can come to you while Van Deek is temporarily out of commission." He smiled. "Besides, I like watching you. It always pleases me to see you in action."

"No other reason?" She looked out at the *Katrina*

cleaving swiftly through the water and shook her head. "You're trying to keep me busy. You're worried because you couldn't reach Brandon to tell him that we'd taken the *Katrina*."

"Not worried. There could be any number of reasons why communications have broken down. It might be dangerous for Brandon to answer. We don't know the situation. I'll try again later."

No, she didn't know the situation, Catherine thought. She didn't know what Brandon was going through, if he'd been captured or killed.

And she didn't know what was happening to Rachel.

And it was scaring her to death.

Even if Cameron wasn't breaking his word about using that damn gift, she knew he was reading her terror. And sharing it with him was easing that fear in some strange way.

"But you know all this," he said gently. "Because you're experienced and intelligent, and you realize it's just a waiting game now." He reached out and touched her cheek. "So what do we do, Catherine?"

She wanted to rub her cheek against his hand. She wanted to step closer and feel that magical comfort that was another part of who he was. She forced herself to step back instead. "Why, we sail along and pretend we're on our way to blow up a part of this beautiful world." She turned away and headed back to the bridge. "And I put up with the Guardian lazing around and treating me as if I was just another one of his subjects in front of all his devoted followers." She glanced over her shoulder at him. "Unless I decide to toss you over the side, Cameron."

He smiled and shook his head. "But then you'd have to jump in after me and pull me out. And I've already told you how dangerous that could be."

"Still, it might be worth it . . ."

EAGLES REST

CANADA

"Wake up, Dr. Rachel. Why won't you wake up?"

Maria, Rachel realized dazedly. She was frightened. Of course, she was frightened. Just a little girl, and she had gone through so much . . .

"Please, wake up. I don't want to be alone here. They . . . hurt me."

Huber. Kraus. She struggled to open her eyes. "Not alone." She finally managed to lift her lids. "I'm here . . . Maria."

Maria's face above her. They had hurt her. New bruises. A cut lip, livid marks on her throat. Rachel could only hope for nothing worse. "Hi." She held out her arms. "Come here."

Maria flew into her arms. "Mama. Did Mama come? They could hurt her again. They're bad people."

"No, she didn't come." Rachel stroked Maria's hair. "She's better, but she sent me instead." She was looking around her. Bars on the windows. Concrete floors. A jail or dungeon of some sort. An arched door that appeared to lead outside and reminded her of something . . .

Sazkar Prison. It was like that sadistic bastard to want to remind her that she had never really escaped him.

But that door was different. She could see that the ornate arched perforations in the wood showed that it seemed to look out on some kind of huge dirt yard or field.

Yes, that wasn't the same, and neither was the concrete floor that felt cold against her naked body.

Naked. She tensed, a preparation for rape? Perhaps. But she could see her boots and other clothes had been stacked neatly on the cot across the room. It was more likely that she had been searched thoroughly both for GPS and weapons. Huber would be wary of her since she'd told him that she'd been the one who had killed his father.

Or it could be either, but she would be more prepared for anything to come if she was dressed. She *needed* those boots. She kissed Maria's forehead. "You've been very brave. You're going to have to be even braver before we get you back to your mama. Now I have to get dressed." She pushed her gently away and got to her feet. "How long have I been here?"

"I don't know. It seemed a long time." She was watching Rachel pull on her clothes. "Maybe not so long. But I didn't know if you were dead. And all those guards came in and were taking off your clothes and looking at them and I didn't know why. They didn't do it to me."

Relief. Maria hadn't had to face that particular horror . . . yet.

And she wouldn't, Rachel thought fiercely. "It was just the guards? Not Huber, not that man who hurt you?"

Maria shook her head. "Just the guards, some I hadn't seen before." She frowned. "One of them grabbed your watch right off your wrist. I knew you wouldn't like that. Mama said you always needed your watch when you were doing stuff for people."

"Yes, I do." She stopped in the middle of pulling on her boots. And Cameron's messenger might also have been informed about that fact about her. If that messenger had been Brandon, then he would certainly know it.

New guards Maria hadn't seen before.

A turmoil of activity in the cell where a discreet action or a new guard might be overlooked.

A watch torn from her wrist. "Perhaps I'd better check to make certain it wasn't stolen." Because she hadn't seen it lying on the cot with the rest of her belongings as she'd been dressing.

But then she saw the gleam of gold and leather half under the bottom of the cot. She slowly reached down and picked it up. "Here it is."

"Not stolen?"

"No." The watch seemed to be working and read 3:40 A.M. But the alarm had been changed to 4:45 A.M. "And it's working just fine."

Wrong. She felt a bolt of sheer panic. Claire had told her that she would give her only until four thirty to get

Maria away before she'd unleash those drones. If any rescue attempt was to be staged at four forty-five, it would be too late.

And it was now 3:40 A.M. and Huber hadn't even made his appearance.

"That's good, isn't it?" Maria asked, troubled. "You're not happy?"

"It's very good." She was off the cot and kneeling beside the little girl. "I guess I'm still a little dizzy." She cradled Maria's face in her hands. "But there might still be some bad stuff coming up, and you've got to be ready for it. I need you to do exactly as I tell you," she whispered. "Will you do that, Maria?"

Maria nodded. "Mama said I always have to do what you say. You saved me."

"And I'll save you this time. But you might not like how I do it. I might get hurt a little." She shook her head as Maria opened her lips. "Not bad, but you won't like it. Just know that I won't really be there. I'll just go away for a few minutes, the way I told you to do. Your job will be harder. You'll have to sit there and watch and not do anything. It's a very important job."

Maria was starting to cry.

"And you mustn't do that either, bad people like to see tears, it makes them worse."

Maria was nodding. "I . . . know."

And it made Rachel furious that she had learned that lesson in this short time. "But it will get better. They *will* be punished, but you shouldn't look when that happens, either. Stay very close to me. When I run, you go where I go, do what I do. Okay?"

Maria's arms tightened around her. "Okay."

She could hear footsteps on tile coming toward the cell. So familiar. So much like Sazkar Prison. She hadn't the slightest doubt now that that had been Huber's intention. "I think they're coming." She kissed Maria's forehead. "Be strong." She released her and pushed her gently toward the far wall. "Be the best you can be."

"I see you've put your clothes back on." She whirled to see Max Huber standing in the open doorway. He smiled maliciously. "Such a waste of time. You'll be kneeling to me naked from now on until the time I choose to put you out of your misery." He turned to Kraus, who had followed him into the cell, accompanied by two uniformed militia guards. "But that won't be for a long time, thanks to Kraus. I wanted to have you go up in flames at the same time as the *Katrina Notalo*, but you've cheated me by being such a coward."

"What a pity," Rachel said. She'd never seen either Huber or Kraus before outside of those photos Brandon had shown her, but they'd been such a part of her thoughts and nightmares that they were horribly familiar. "By all means blame Kraus. Heaven forbid, you shoulder the blame for anything. Tell me, which one of you killed Fasrain? That was a terrible mistake."

"It was not a mistake." Kraus said. "Choosing him was the mistake. He was tainted. I knew we should rely on our own men, who are good Aryan stock."

"What do you say, Huber?" Rachel said. "How good

is your fine Aryan stock? Did it save your father? He died like any other man. Probably faster, who knows better than I how quickly that poison worked."

"Bitch!" Huber's hand shot out and struck her cheek full force.

Pain!

She tottered back and fell to the floor.

Maria screamed.

"Shut up!" Huber whirled on her and was across the cell. "You want it?" he asked savagely. His hands were on the child's throat, pressing, bruising. "I've been waiting for this, Rachel. Watch as I hurt her. See how her eyes bulge when I—"

Rachel was on her feet and running to Maria's side. "I see." She had to get him away from her. Draw his fire. The edge of her hand came down in a karate slice on his wrist, and she tore Maria out of his grasp. She bent back his fingers. "I see what your men see every day. A coward and a—" She broke off as one of the guards reached her and knocked her away from Huber.

"A coward?" Huber's face was flushed with rage. He punched her in the stomach. "Bitch." He punched her again as she fell to the floor. "Cunt." He took a step closer and kicked her viciously in the ribs. "Scream, whore." He kicked her again. "Let me hear you!"

Go away from it. He's forgotten Maria now. Don't scream. Don't let it touch you. She was vaguely aware of Maria sobbing across the room as he kicked her again.

"She won't last any time at all if you keep doing that," Kraus said without expression. "And then you'll blame me again."

"It *is* your fault." Huber was breathing hard, his cheeks flushed. He kicked Rachel one last time and stepped back. "I wanted time to play with her before he blew the *Katrina*. You promised me."

"I gave you more than anyone else could give you." He nodded at two of the guards, who came forward and lifted Rachel to her feet. She gasped with agony before she could stop herself. "Look at her. I thought you wanted her to see your father's triumph with the *Katrina*. She killed him, and you're *wasting* her. He deserves better."

Rachel was managing to stifle the pain. "I disagree," she said unevenly. "Your father got exactly what he deserved."

Kraus smiled thinly. "And after you witness the show we've put on in his honor, I believe I'll let his son kick you until you bleed out." He flicked on the TV set on the wall, and the picture of the long, sleek tanker suddenly appeared. "It's a little after four, Huber. It should be almost dawn soon. Do you want to continue toying with this woman, or are you ready to honor my old friend?"

"Are you trying to shame me?" But the question was abstracted as his gaze was drawn in fascination to the image of the supertanker on the screen. "I can wait . . . It's huge, isn't it? All that oil . . . It will smother everything it touches." He gestured to the guards. "Take her out in the yard. I want to see it blow on the big screen. I want *her* to see it and know that no matter what she did, she could never stop it."

Rachel could still feel the pain and homicidal fury of those few moments with Huber. Kraus had saved her, Rachel thought dazedly. Why? There had to be a reason why he was obviously manipulating Huber. Something to do with what Claire had said . . . ?

But then she forgot him as panic swept through her when she realized that they had left Maria locked in the cell. She watched as one of her guards turned the key in the lock and slipped it into his pocket. She hadn't counted on Huber's separating them. She smothered that icy stab of sheer fear. She had known that she had to play this as it was dealt. Survey the situation and look for a way out.

The yard was just as big as she'd thought, she realized as she was pushed through the arched doorway of the prison out into the dirt yard. No one was locking that outside door. She had only Maria's cell door to worry about.

Only? There were at least twenty or thirty men wearing gray-and-taupe militia uniforms and high black boots milling around the area. A boxing ring occupied the center of the yard. To one side of the ring was a huge TV screen that now lit up the darkness.

The supertanker again, black, sleek, sliding snake-like through the water.

"Impressed?" Kraus was smiling as he gazed at Rachel's face. "Huber regards this as his very own coliseum. I don't believe you'll want to know what he'll probably do to you in that ring once he becomes too impatient."

"No, you know what a coward I am." Was that the sound of a rotor in the distance? Helicopter? Drone? Too far away to be sure. "You've beaten me, Kraus."

"I'm not too sure." He was studying her face. "You look amazingly calm. A stall? It probably doesn't matter at this late date, but I'm wondering why—"

"Why isn't it happening?" Huber whirled away from the TV screen, his eyes blazing at Kraus. "It should have blown five minutes ago. You told Van Deek that he had to be on time. You promised me, Kraus."

"It's only five minutes. Perhaps there's something wrong with the charge. Van Deek will fix it. You can see the ship is proceeding as scheduled."

"Call Van Deek." Huber's voice was almost a screech. "Call him right now. Tell him he can't disobey my orders. I want that ship to blow *now*."

"Just give him another—"

"Call him!"

Chaos. Tension. Huber at his most vicious and irrational. Neither Kraus nor Huber were paying her any attention. The two guards who had been supporting Rachel were now more interested in what was going on with Huber and Kraus. She might not have a better chance than this. She had to get back to Maria. None of this mattered if she lost Maria. She couldn't wait to see if that had been the sound of a helicopter or a drone.

Fast.

Hard.

Unexpected.

She kicked the guard to her left in the kneecap, jerked her arm away when his grip loosened. Then she did a backflip and a roundhouse kick that connected to the other guard's larynx. He went down, gurgling and grasping his throat. She grabbed the key from his pocket and took off running. She heard Kraus cursing as she streaked back toward the prison. She glanced over her shoulder and saw Kraus and Huber dashing after her. The two guards were still on the ground, struggling to get to their feet. Kraus hadn't called any of his other men yet. No real alarm since they probably thought they'd be able to trap her again when she reached Maria's cell.

She threw open the arched door and was once more within the prison. She motioned quickly to Maria in the cell as she threw her the key. "Not yet. Stay where you are!"

She whirled as Huber burst through the doorway. "You decided catching me was worth more than honoring your scumbag of a father?" She glared at Kraus, who had just entered. "I found I couldn't bear to watch you or that ugliness you planned. So why shouldn't I let you kill me instead? Why don't you just pull that gun and get it over with?"

"That was never your choice," Huber said. "And I'm very angry that you interrupted Kraus when I'd given him an order." He was coming toward her. "So I think that I'll give you a few minutes of my time before I have him make that call to Van Deek." He took out a lighter from his jacket pocket. "A few painful burns in excruciatingly sensitive places . . ."

"Stay away from her, Max," Kraus warned. "You saw what she did out there."

"Let's see how good she is while you're holding a gun on her. She said she wanted you to shoot her." He flicked the lighter on. "Let's see how fast that eagerness erodes in the next couple minutes." He tore open Rachel's blouse. "No fatal wounds, Kraus. I want her to feel every—"

She kicked him in the groin and leaped on top of him. She rolled to the side to try to use his body as a barrier to block any shot from Kraus. "No fatal wounds," she said through her teeth as her fingernails tightened on Huber's throat. "Not for me. But how many fatal wounds have you ordered, Huber? My family, hundreds of other families."

"Get her off me, Kraus." Huber screeched. "Take the shot!"

"But you told me that you wanted to have your fun," Kraus said mockingly. "I don't know which order to obey. You know I only want to please you."

It was the reprieve for which she had hoped, Rachel thought. Kraus was making his move. She could only pray that she'd be able to use it.

"What are you doing to me, Kraus?" Huber was struggling to get to his gun. He made a sudden motion, and Rachel was abruptly beneath him. "There. I knew she was nothing." He glared down at her as his hands moved to her throat. "Just a woman. Nothing like Venable."

All the deaths. All the torture. All the destruction. Do it. It was time.

"Just a woman," she whispered. Her hands moved gently to his wrists as she pressed and released the tiny envelope imbued in the polish beneath her nails. "But maybe a little like Venable."

She dug her nails into Huber's wrists!

He had no time to scream.

He went rigid. He was staring at her in horror, gasping for breath, as the painful poison entered his bloodstream.

He knew he was dying. She could see it in his face. The fear, the horror.

She removed her nails from his flesh. "No, I've changed my mind. I think I might be a lot like my father."

Huber was collapsing on top of her. She quickly reached for his gun.

But Kraus was there kicking the gun out of her reach. "No, I think that we'll have to end this right now." He was pointing his own gun at her. "Though you handled his assassination beautifully. But I do have to be the one who takes revenge for his death. It's only fitting, considering I now have a duty to take over Red Star. You're not surprised?"

"You stopped him from kicking me to death. I was told you might be hungry to take Huber's place. This was a convenient time for you to make a move. I thought I'd be a perfect weapon if you chose to use me." Her lips twisted. "But let's face it, I didn't have much choice. I had to take a chance." Keep talking, distract him. He was only a few feet away. She could roll fast and dig her nails into his ankle. He'd be helpless. The poison was so efficient, it froze any response but the death she'd designed.

"Stop thinking," Kraus said. "Make a move, and I'll shoot the child. She might survive if you don't—"

"Drop the gun, Kraus." Brandon was at the door, dressed in the gray-and-taupe uniform of Huber's militia. He didn't wait for a response but was across the room and tackling Kraus with blinding speed. His hand came down in a karate chop to Kraus's neck. Then the butt of his pistol came down hard on Kraus's head. As he went limp, Brandon whirled to Rachel. "Grab Maria, Rachel. We've got to get out of here. Dillard's men are giving us cover fire, but we've got to be over that wall in the next four minutes."

"You grab her." Maria was already unlocking the cell and Rachel motioned for her to come with them. "I can't risk touching anyone right now." She was running out the door. Shots from the walls surrounding the compound. Return shots from Huber's militia.

And that huge TV was still showing the sleek, dark supertanker on its screen.

Still? She supposed it had only been moments since she'd made that run to go get Maria. Or maybe longer since Brandon had said that they were out of time.

"Out!" Brandon had climbed the wall and dropped Maria to Nate on the other side. Then he was down again and carefully lifting Rachel. As she reached the top of the wall, she saw Kraus staggering out the door of the prison, blood running down his temple. His face convulsed with fury as he saw Rachel, and he began to run toward her. Brandon was dropping Rachel on the other side of the wall, and Kraus vanished from her view. "Get them on the helicopter, Nate. I've got to take care of Kraus and tell Dillard it's okay to pull his men out and lock that gate."

Then he was gone.

And Nate was rushing them toward a helicopter several yards away. He threw Maria into the copter, then reached out to Rachel.

She pulled back. "Grab my wrists. Nothing else."

"What the hell," he muttered. "Dammit, we've only got a couple minutes." The next instant he'd pulled her on board and gone up to the pilot's seat.

Where was Brandon?

The shooting was still heavy.

Kraus . . . he had been going after Kraus.

Kraus's twisted, enraged, expression as he'd run toward them . . .

And Rachel wouldn't even know where to find Brandon if Kraus hurt or—

"Off!" Brandon dove into the helicopter headfirst. "Now, Nate!"

"Shit, yes," Nate murmured. He lifted off and banked immediately and sharply to the left after gaining only thirty feet. "Too close, Brandon."

"Close as it had to be." He was checking his watch. "Get us higher. It's going to blow any minute."

But it was high enough for Rachel to see Kraus running, screaming, giving orders to the militia to ignore the locked gate and climb the wall and go after them.

"*Higher.*" Brandon's voice was tense. "We're out of time. Get away from the blast. It will rock—"

The compound blew, turning the entire area into one huge firebomb.

The helicopter rocked, dipped, as the shockwave hit it.

No more Kraus. No more compound. No Red Star. Just fire and destruction.

It took her breath away. She could only ride out the shockwaves as Nate fought to put distance from the drone strike.

"Dr. Rachel," Maria's eyes were wide with terror. "We're going to die, aren't we?"

"No." She lifted her head and gazed at the little girl. She realized that it was the first time that she could say that with any truth. After all the danger and horror of the past hours, they were going to survive.

And Red Star had gone down in that brilliant ball of flame.

She smiled at Maria. "You're not going to die. And I promise soon you're going to go home and see your mama." She leaned back against the wall of the helicopter. The words of comfort weren't enough after what the child had gone through. Maria was smiling tentatively, but Rachel could see the fear was still there. She needed to be held and comforted.

She turned to Brandon. "Would you go over to her and just hold her? I can't do it for her right now. She's been very brave, but she's missing her mother, and this has all been too much for her."

His lips twisted. "So I'm to be Mama?"

Considering the fact that he might be the most sexual and masculine man she'd ever met, it did sound a
little ridiculous. Yet in another way it did not. She had
found that Brandon managed to fill any number of
niches when called upon. She smiled. "I believe you
can handle it."

"And who's going to hold and comfort you?" he
asked tightly. "Between that stomping Huber gave you
and what you went through later, Maria got off easy
in comparison. I need to get you to a hospital."

"No, you don't. I'm not a child. You need to get me
back to Beach Haven so that I can take care of myself."
She stiffened, her gaze on his face. "You saw it all?"

"Most of it," he said curtly. "After I adjusted your
watch, I was drifting around the area keeping an eye
on you and trying to make certain that Dillard's men
would have access when they needed it. I only got
the last part right. Keeping an eye on you was pure
hell."

"It's over now." She hoped it was over. "Catherine
managed to stop Van Deek?"

"With considerable help from Cameron. She contacted us an hour ago. We just had to make certain
there was no leak from the *Katrina*, that everything
was not as Huber would exactly wish. Your situation
was a bit dicey."

"More than a bit. And I don't know what happened.
Did Claire send those drones late? She told me right
before Kraus took me that she'd only give me until four
thirty."

"No, then she was right on time."

"But you weren't scheduled to be able to come for us for another quarter of an hour."

"Schedules change. We didn't know exactly what time Claire would act. We just wanted to get you away as soon as we could. But Monty was monitoring Claire's communications with Langley, and when she started the countdowns with them, he notified me that we'd better get you the hell out of there."

"Monty." She shook her head. "I told him he might save the day. He didn't like the idea of your leaving him there."

"He's not going to let me forget it." He looked down at the blood on her nails. "Which poison did you use?"

"Puffer combined with a rare Tibetan poison. Instant paralysis followed by painful death within one minute."

"I like painful."

"So did I."

"Why can't you touch anything?"

"The poison was contained until I released a special envelope that adhered underneath my nails in the polish. Any remainder of the poison will stay active and alive until I rinse it with a remover I created. I couldn't bring the remover with me. I was able to make the poison undetectable, but I couldn't take a chance with hiding another substance."

"I can see how that might be a problem." He shook his head. "My, what an interesting manicure you've put together for yourself, Rachel."

"Not for myself," she said soberly. "I killed a man

with that poison. I created it intentionally. I have to admit it to myself and take the burden of any guilt."

"Self-defense."

"But how can I separate self-defense from choosing to kill because Huber and Kraus were so evil?" She looked down at her hands. "You once told me that you liked my hands because they looked capable, that they were capable because I'm a doctor. I didn't act as a healer today, Brandon."

"No? There are all kinds of healing, Rachel. You healed that little girl for the second time today. And we might have healed a hell of a lot more when we blew up that compound." He smiled. "And if I weren't afraid that I'd curl up and be taken by the Grim Reaper, I'd run the risk of paying my deepest respect to that hand of yours."

He got to his feet. "But to avoid temptation, I'd better go over and sit with Maria and practice my maternal skills." His eyes were suddenly twinkling. "Frankly, I think I'd almost prefer she was still mistaking me for Saint Gabriel."

"Wait." She'd had a sudden thought. "I need you to do something else first."

He looked at her inquiringly.

"Call Hu Chang. I can't do it, and I promised him."

"It can't wait?"

"I promised him he'd be first. Would you want me to break a promise to Hu Chang?"

"Point taken." He took out his phone. "It might take a little while for explanations. I assume he'll demand them?"

"In detail. Maria won't care if you don't talk to her, just hold her and smile reassuringly."

"I'll do my best."

And it was going to be a very good best, she thought, as he reached Hu Chang and started talking.

She watched Maria smile up at him as he settled beside her and drew her close. Brandon was giving her comfort and security and everything else she needed from him. As he had given it to Rachel during this nightmare they had gone through together.

Had her father known on that last day that he was sending her someone who would somehow be able to meet her every need?

She leaned back and closed her eyes.

I don't know if Brandon was right in what he said, Daddy. It sounded right. You said there was a time I'd have to go after the bad guys. Well, I did it. I hope you think I did okay . . .

CHAPTER

19

BEACH HAVEN

Where is she?" Catherine threw open the front door and ran into the living room. "Brandon, where the hell is she? Why did you bring her here instead of taking her to a hospital? You said you thought Huber had broken her ribs."

"And he probably did," Brandon said. "At least a couple. But Rachel said that she had a lot better chance of not dying if I brought her here. So stop giving me grief, Catherine."

"What? Where is she? I'll talk sense into her."

"No, you won't. Did I forget to tell you that she's dripping some kind of weird death serum, and no one gets near her until she sterilizes herself? Rachel's orders. She'll come out of her room when she's ready."

Catherine stopped short. "You might have neglected to mention that small fact. All you told me was that you were coming here, and no one was actually dead or dying." She gazed at Rachel's closed door. "Huber? What did she use?"

"I forgot you were also so versed in poisons. Yes, it was Huber."

"Good. I hope it wasn't over too soon."

"It lasted long enough to be very painful. And she said something about puffer. You might know more than I do about the effects."

"She must have combined it with something else. It has a few drawbacks that—"

"Yes, I did." Rachel stood in the open doorway of her room. "An herb from Tibet."

"Makes sense." Catherine flew across the room to her. She stopped as she reached her. "You're okay? You got rid of the aftereffects?"

"I'm clean." She reached out and carefully embraced her. "Just a little sore. How are you?"

"Fine. Nobody was kicking me and blowing up everything around me. We were just stalling and keeping Huber from thinking he should lob a rocket at the *Katrina* to complete the job he started." She tightly grasped Rachel's two hands. "And Maria wasn't hurt?"

"Hurt, but not terribly. That doesn't mean she won't have nightmares. She's in the kitchen with Nate, and he's applying BLT therapy."

"You look like you could still use a little therapy yourself." Her gaze was raking Rachel's face. "Bruises and pale as a ghost." She whirled on Brandon. "And I bet those damn ribs are killing her. Why are you letting her stand here? You don't have that dripping poison excuse any longer. Get her to a hospital and have them make certain she doesn't have anything worse than broken ribs."

"I was only waiting for you to check her out yourself," Brandon said blandly. "It's always easier to convince her to do something if you've chimed in."

"If it's just ribs, they can't do anything for me anyway," Rachel said. "They'll let them heal on their own."

"But Catherine demands that you go in for a checkup." He nudged her toward the front door. "And you have to set a good example for Maria. Isn't that right?" He glanced at Catherine. "Where's Cameron?"

She shrugged. "He's dealing with the owners of the *Katrina Notalo* and trying to persuade them it was perfectly normal that we appropriated their vessel for a short while. It might actually take him longer to do that than the hijacking itself."

"He's trying to leave Van Deek out of it?"

"Van Deek was also a victim. He was looking for a way out. He caved immediately. Cameron wouldn't be so generous if Van Deek hadn't cooperated so readily." She grimaced. "And he might be planning on using Van Deek at some point. He said he was clever and innovative. You can never tell with Cameron."

"And that's fine with me," Brandon said. "He can write his own ticket with me after Eagles Rest. I'll be there for him."

"That's a very dangerous thing to say," Catherine said. "But I'll try not to let him take advantage of it." She gave Rachel a hug very gingerly. "I'll meet you at the hospital. And I'll have to call Hu Chang before I get there and tell him that we managed to do without him. Otherwise, he'll be on your phone checking on you."

Rachel nodded. "Don't bother to hurry. I had Brandon call him the minute Red Star blew. But you can tell him that he was right there with us all the way. We did it just the way he taught us." She smiled into her eyes. "The very best we could do, Catherine."

Catherine gently touched her cheek. "Maybe he wasn't the only one who was there with you, Rachel."

"I can't be sure about that," she said quietly. "But I know I asked for a little help for Maria if there was any available."

"Maria's alive," Catherine said softly. "That might be a pretty good answer." She glanced at Brandon. "Keep an eye on her at that hospital. Claire Warren is trying to establish herself as the premier heroine in the downfall of Red Star. She's calling all kinds of news conferences and drawing on political favors. Rachel knows too much that could make her look bad. There's no telling what Claire might do to silence her."

"Nothing," Brandon said curtly. "It's in my court now. Rachel tied my hands while Maria was being held prisoner. I won't let her do it with Claire."

"*Let* her?" Catherine said. "Good luck, Brandon." She gave Rachel a kiss on the cheek. "Take care. I'll be there to back you up as soon as I can. I guess we'll have to trust Brandon until then."

The next moment, she was out the door and heading for her car. When she reached it, she stood there watching as Brandon carefully situated Rachel in the passenger seat of his car and drove away. He couldn't have been more cautious, and Rachel was probably getting impatient. That was fine, let him take a little flak. She was hurt, and he should take care of her.

"Catherine."

She stopped as she was opening the Mercedes' driver's door and turned to see Cameron coming toward her from his own car parked near the terrace. "What are you doing here? I thought you were going to be busy this morning."

"I did what I had to do, then delegated." He smiled. "I had something more important to do. How is Rachel?"

"Okay. On her way to the emergency room to be checked out. Brandon didn't mention that she had to stop over here to do a little necessary cleansing."

"Really? What?"

"Puffer."

His brows rose. "A challenge. I take it, she met it. Huber?"

Catherine nodded. How unique and special to be able to talk to someone who didn't have to have all the dots and dashes filled in with a conversation like this. But then there was no one on earth like Cameron. "Huber. Do you know how difficult it must have been to be able to carry that out after being searched? She had to make it totally undetectable."

"Yes. I know."

"Of course, you do. What was I thinking?" She

made a face. "And I shouldn't have remarked on it. You're already too interested in her 'talents.' You're probably ready to sweep her away after what she did at Eagles Rest."

He shook his head. "It would be the worst possible time. It's not only her body that will need healing. You'll have to take good care of her for a while, Catherine." He smiled. "I can wait."

"How generous of you." She was only half mocking. He could be exceptionally generous, and his reading of Rachel's needs showed a sensitivity that was just as remarkable. "But you'll wait a long time. I'll be watching her."

"I won't mind the wait. Because while you're watching Rachel, I can be watching you. Win-win, Catherine."

"A waste of the Guardian's valuable time, Cameron."

"I never waste my time." He paused. "Being with you will always be of value. Every time we're together, I get a little closer to my goal. Look what happened this time."

"Piracy and murder?"

"And saving that beautiful azure ocean out there for your Luke." He smiled. "You can't beat memories like that. Soon they'll all blend together, and every time you think of me, I'll be golden."

He *was* golden. Everything about him, every word, every smile.

"You didn't mention Eagles Rest and Rachel," she

said. "Now that's definitely a coup you should have tossed at me."

He shook his head. "Never someone you love. That will always be a gift."

More generosity. And yet that very generosity was forming unbreakable bonds. "Cameron, you know I'll never believe what you believe. You know I'll always fight you."

"I know you'll always try to fight me. I know that beliefs can change." He smiled. "I spend my life changing how people perceive their lives and beliefs." He added softly, "And I delight in fighting with you because there's always the possibility of a reward at the end of it. You can't imagine how I look forward to that possibility."

She stiffened. She could sense a sort of finality in those words. There was something . . . different about him.

And she was remembering something he'd said. "Why did you come here today, Cameron? Why did you 'delegate'?"

"There were signs that I was becoming a little too visible," he said quietly. "That business with the *Katrina Notalo* is going to be difficult to hide. I'll be able to do it, but it will take time and effort." He shrugged. "And a strategic exit and my absence for a while."

"Who's asking questions?"

"Your people, Homeland Security, politicians. It will take a concerted effort to remove them from power or destroy any evidence that would be awkward for me."

"That's exactly what I didn't want to happen." Her hands clenched into fists. "Dammit, and I *asked* you to do it."

"Yes, you did. But it was my decision." He grinned. "Remember? You said I should wear the tee shirt. I wasn't going to let the *Katrina* cause any disasters."

"But I was on board that ship." She frowned, looking at options. "I'll think of a way to cover for you."

"No, it's already being done," he said sharply. "You do *nothing*. The last thing I want is for you to look dirty to the CIA. The problem will just go away, and in a few months, it will totally disappear." He tilted his head. "If you want to be helpful, you'll disappear for a time, too. You miss your son, go spend time with him. Take him on a cruise."

"Hide out?"

He chuckled. "I know it's distasteful, but you'll survive. If you wish to do me a service, don't try to defend me. It's the worst thing you could do."

"I *hate* this."

"I know. Do it anyway." He added, "And while you're doing it, think of why saving an ocean should cause all this trouble. It will bring you that much closer to me."

"Only because you always make yourself the center of the hurricane."

"True. It's all my fault again."

"No, it's not." She moistened her lips. "When do you have to leave?"

He nodded down at the beach. "I'm having my friend send his helicopter to the beach to pick me up. Probably about ten minutes. Would you like to drive me down?"

No. She didn't want him to go. Ten minutes, and he'd be gone? She felt a surge of panic. "I suppose it's that same buddy who supplied you with the copter before. Is he helping to take care of the 'delegating' too?"

"He's adding his bit." His gaze was on her face. "It's going to be fine, Catherine. I don't expect anything of you."

"But I expect something of myself, and you're tying my hands." Her eyes were stinging as she jumped into the car. "Get in. I'll take you down to meet your damn helicopter."

She barely waited until he got in the car before she flew down the driveway toward the beach. She pulled into the pad area in less than five minutes. She stared blindly out the windshield at the empty pad. "He should be here. Doesn't he know you don't keep the Guardian waiting?"

"Catherine." He reached out and gently touched her hair. "You're hurting, and that hurts *me*." He smiled. "Don't you know that you should never do that to the Guardian?"

"Damn you." She still didn't look at him. "It's all wrong, you know. It can never work out. Every time we're together, nothing happens the way it should. You should never have come here."

"But I'll always come to you. Get used to it." His

finger was rubbing her lower lip, and she could feel it swell beneath his touch. "I can't stay away. You might have a slight chance if you could keep from hovering at death's door. But that's not going to happen. So I have to be near you."

She closed her eyes. His *touch*. The *scent* of him. His *voice*. "It probably won't last. It's too strong."

"Wishful thinking?"

"And I can't change. I won't go with you."

"I never asked you to change."

"I think I hear your helicopter."

"What are you going to do about it?"

Her eyes opened, and she turned into his arms. She couldn't breathe. She could feel her pulse pounding in her wrists, the tightness of her breasts. She was on *fire*. "It's what you're going to do about it." She opened her mouth and took him, her hands tangled in his hair. "You're going to send him away, and you're going to take me to a hotel. We're going to stay there for the next twenty-four hours, and we're going to do everything we've done before and more. I'm going to take so much of you that I'm not going to miss you or ache for you all the time you're gone."

"What a challenge."

"And then I'm going to wave good-bye and live my life the way I want to live it."

"Another challenge." His lips were lowering, only a breath away, as he asked softly, "But what if you want to live it with me, my Catherine? What a conundrum . . ."

CALIFORNIA PACIFIC MEDICAL CENTER
SAN FRANCISCO, CALIFORNIA

"Not good," Brandon said critically as he watched Rachel walk out of the ER. "You still look as if you lost a battle with one of the Avengers. What did the doctors say?"

"No serious internal damage. One broken rib, one cracked. Bruising." She shrugged. "I was lucky."

"That's not the word I'd choose," he said grimly. "But at least you're alive."

"And Huber is not." She moved slowly toward the front entrance. "And neither is Kraus." She looked at Brandon. "And I didn't mention that you managed to survive all that hell at Eagles Rest and took Maria and me out of there. I'd say that qualifies as lucky."

"I'd prefer the terms *brilliant* and *original*." He made a face. "And I considered that action pure self-defense. I wasn't going to leave there if I couldn't take you with me. I told you that I was going to be there for you."

"Yes, you did." She tried to smile. "You were quite eloquent. I was impressed." She changed the subject. "And now we'd better get back to Maria at Beach Haven. I want to bring her here to be checked over. I thought she'd be better off with Nate until I was certain I wasn't going to have to stay for any surgery. But she'll want me with her."

"You need to go to bed and rest. I can stay with her. You trusted me on the helicopter."

"That was different, I couldn't do it. And I want to call Phillip and see if she can talk to Blanca yet. It's better if—"

"You're in charge," he finished for her. "And you say that I'm a control freak? There's a phrase about a pot calling—"

"Rachel, you don't look at all bad." Claire Warren was suddenly beside them. "I should have known that I couldn't trust Catherine to give me an unbiased opinion. She tends to be overprotective." Her smile was brilliant. "But you might be better off sitting in the waiting room. I won't keep you long, but I wouldn't want to cause you stress."

"We were about to leave," Brandon said coldly.

"But then I'd only have to find a way to talk to her again." She smiled brilliantly. "It's much better that we take care of these details now. Rachel and I understand each other. Rachel?"

"Details?" Rachel said dryly. "Do you mean details the media might be interested in exploring?"

"Exactly." Claire was pushing her gently to a chair in the waiting room. "We wouldn't want confusion. Langley wants a clear picture of what happened at Eagles Rest to be presented to the public."

"And what have you told them so far?" Rachel asked.

"The truth. The daughter of a courageous CIA operative was being held captive and about to be executed. I managed to discover the whereabouts of Red Star's compound and sent a drone to destroy Max Huber and all those terrible criminals."

"And how was Rachel able to escape that drone?" Brandon asked.

"Through her bravery and the connections she'd made with Venable's old friends in the area. Thank heavens I'd managed to keep them apprised of her situation. There's some confusion there because the SEAL team I sent to rescue her wasn't able to reach her."

"What a surprise," Rachel said.

"I warned you," Claire said. "I told you that I wasn't going to lose that drone strike. And it seems I was right about your having plans of your own. I'd be curious to know what happened there, but it would get in the way of my own agenda." She smiled serenely. "So the story remains as I've given it to both Langley and the president. Actually, they're very grateful to me. I handled everything beautifully. The moment Red Star was destroyed, I even called the Canadian prime minister and convinced him what a political gold mine it would be for him not to make a fuss about us lobbing that drone into his country. All he had to say was he was glad to offer his cooperation to eliminate Red Star. In my story, everyone wins."

"Unless I choose to change it," Rachel said.

"Why should you?" Claire said. "You're a heroine, your father is a hero. You can go back to saving humanity in the same boring way you've been doing all these years. Everyone's happy."

"Particularly you," Brandon said.

"Which is only right. Red Star is gone. I had a sizeable role in getting rid of it. After all, we don't want the same things, Rachel. Give me what I want, and I might be able to give you something you want."

"I don't believe I'm tempted to give you anything you want at the moment, Claire."

"No?" Her lips curved in a smile. "But you haven't asked what I could give you."

"Shades of Nemesis," Rachel said bitterly. "I can see your alter ego raising its head."

"Funny you should mention that. Nemesis was very useful in many ways. As an undercover operative I was able to set up any number of scenarios and safe houses around the world to protect my identity."

"And sizeable overseas bank accounts as well. You can't pay me off, Claire."

"Can't I? It depends what you consider a payoff." She tilted her head. "Did you discuss Venable's funeral arrangements yet with Catherine?"

Her eyes widened in confusion. "No, we haven't had a chance to talk about anything concerning— Why are you asking?"

"Because you'd have problems with them. Unfortunately, his body wasn't in the best of shape after we managed to retrieve him in the mountains. I had to make the decision to cremate him."

"What? You had no *right* to make that decision."

"Actually, I did. I have rather broad powers these days. I'll have even more after I reap the benefits of the destruction of Red Star." She met her eyes. "Now ask me why I did it."

"God only knows."

"I found it the only convenient way to handle the

situation." She paused. "Since the body we found wasn't Venable's. He was one of Huber's militia that I disposed of during the hunt. I needed a body, so I let Huber take care of it for me."

"And what happened to Venable's body?" Brandon asked softly. "I admit I'm fascinated."

"You mean you don't know where I'm going with this?" She looked at Rachel. "Let's play a game of 'what if'. What if your father didn't die in that cabin? What if I arrived before Huber's militia got there, and I managed to drag him into the woods before they found him."

"He was dying," Brandon said. "I *saw* the wound. He couldn't have lasted more than a couple minutes. He was dying when I left the cabin."

She shrugged. "I thought that as well. So I didn't see any reason why I shouldn't try to drag him out of there. It probably couldn't hurt him." She grimaced. "But he survived it. Venable was always tough."

"But why did you do it?" Rachel asked.

"I had to be certain he wouldn't talk to Huber's militia. That's why I followed him back from the Calgary compound. If they'd tortured him, he might have told them about me."

"I'm surprised you just didn't cut his throat," Brandon said. "Much more efficient."

"Did I think about it? Yes." She looked at Rachel. "But I told you Venable had saved my life a couple times. I owed him. So I took the chance." She wrinkled her nose. "Which caused me all kinds of trouble. I wasn't sure for days that he'd live. I'm still not sure."

Rachel's eyes widened. "He's *alive*?"

"Maybe. I don't know. If he's alive, he's still very, very ill. I had to get him away. So I sent him out of the country until I had time to deal with the problem." Her lips twisted. "Or Nemesis did."

"Wait." Brandon held up his hand. "Let me get this straight. You're saying that you'll return Rachel's long-lost father if she goes along with your story about Red Star? What a bunch of bullshit."

"Is it?" Claire asked. "What if it's not?"

"My father's *dead*," Rachel said. "You can't just pull a story out of the air and expect me to believe it."

"Yes, I can. I've always told you that you're soft. You want to believe it. But this time it's true, so you're obliged to at least check it out before you dismiss it," Claire said. "So stall, keep my story intact. It won't hurt you." She smiled. "And, who knows, it might help you. When you want to talk, call me."

She turned and strode across the lobby to the front entrance.

"She's lying," Rachel whispered. "She has to be lying. You said you saw him die."

"I thought I did."

Her gaze flew to his face. "What?"

"He was dying. Did I see the last breath? I thought I did. How do I know? I was on the run."

"It could be true?"

"I'd bet against it considering what we know of Claire. She was vague as hell. She could be playing us."

"But there's a chance . . ."

"There's a chance. Do you want to play her game? Okay, we'll do it. Any way you want it." His gaze was suddenly holding her own, glittering with recklessness. "In spite of Catherine's doubts, you can trust me." He paused. "Until the end of the road."

She couldn't look away from him. "Catherine knows I can trust you. She was joking."

"But she doesn't know how far. But you do, Rachel. I've made it very clear."

"You were upset. You thought I might die." She got to her feet. "You were probably feeling guilty because you were responsible for bringing me here to use against Huber."

"Bullshit."

She shook her head. "I know how guilt works. For years my father felt—"

"I'm not your father," he said roughly. "I have a lot of regrets, but that's sure not one of them. I don't know where we're going with this, but it's going to be together. And Venable's shadow isn't going to be standing over us. I'm not going to let it."

"There's no shadow. What are you talking about? My father is probably dead."

"But what you were together was never really resolved." He took a step closer to her. "And that would make the temptation almost irresistible for you to reach out and try again. Well, that's for you to work out, and I know you won't let me interfere. But just know that I'm going to be there, and I stand alone. Unless it's with you. Think about it."

"I . . . will." She wouldn't be able to help thinking

about it. He was everything that was vibrant and sexual and desirable, and yet she kept thinking of him sitting in that helicopter and smiling down at Maria. "But you should really consider that you might have been influenced by—"

His fingers were suddenly over her lips. "I'm too selfish to be influenced by anything but what I want. I want *you*, Rachel."

And she wanted him, she suddenly knew. She wanted to reach out and take, and she didn't care where it was going or how long it would last.

"It's not smart of you to do this," she whispered. "Particularly right now. I've no idea where I'm going or what I'm going to do. I've been changing and evolving since the day you met me. I don't even know if I'm going to let Claire do this to me. It would probably be foolish." She added, "But I might, Brandon."

"I don't care if it's foolish or not. Your choice. We'd make the best of it."

"Yes, we would." She reached out and took his hand. Warmth. Joy. Desire. Trust.

Love? Yes, that's where they were headed. She didn't know how long it would take them to reach it, but it would be worth the journey. But there was something she had to tell him, something he had to know before they started that journey. "And you're right, there are still things I need to resolve with my father. He's a very good man, but I don't want you to be like him. I promise I won't compare you again, Brandon. I only want you to be you."

"What a relief." His eyes were twinkling as he

pulled her closer. "I've no desire to be anything else. Your life with Venable was much too complicated." His kiss was slow, sensuous, infinitely erotic, before he whispered, "I promise I'm going to keep *our* relationship very, very basic."